P9-DMY-989

# KETURAH

The Sugar Baron's Daughters · ONE

# KETURAH

# LISA T. BERGREN

BETHANYHOUSE
a division of Baker Publishing Group
Minneapolis, Minnesota

© 2018 by Lisa T. Bergren

Published by Bethany House Publishers
11400 Hampshire Avenue South
Bloomington, Minnesota 55438
www.bethanyhouse.com

Bethany House Publishers is a division of
Baker Publishing Group, Grand Rapids, Michigan

Printed in the United States of America

Library of Congress Cataloging-in-Publication Data
Names: Bergren, Lisa Tawn, author.
Title: Keturah / Lisa T. Bergren.
Description: Minneapolis, Minnesota : Bethany House, a division of Baker
    Publishing Group, [2018] | Series: The sugar baron's daughters ; 1
Identifiers: LCCN 2017036493| ISBN 9780764230240 (softcover) | ISBN
    9780764231636 (hardcover)
Subjects: LCSH: Young women—Fiction. | Mate selection—Fiction. | GSAFD:
    Christian fiction. | Love stories.
Classification: LCC PS3552.E71938 K48 2018 | DDC 813/.54—dc23
LC record available at https://lccn.loc.gov/2017036493

Scripture quotations are from the King James Version of the Bible.

This is a work of historical reconstruction; the appearances of certain historical figures are therefore inevitable. All other characters, however, are products of the author's imagination, and any resemblance to actual persons, living or dead, is coincidental.

Cover design by Paul Higdon
Cover model photography by Olena Kucher

Author is represented by The Steve Laube Agency.

18  19  20  21  22  23  24       7  6  5  4  3  2  1

*For Olivia,*
*In celebration of God's healing work!*

*I love you.*
*—Mama*

# CHAPTER ONE

**10 JUNE, 1773**
**RIVENSHIRE, ENGLAND**

In the hopes that at least one would get through, their father had sent three copies of his last letter from the West Indies; as it happened, his daughters received them all. The first arrived nine weeks after it was posted. A servant delivered the second on a silver tray, a week after they heard their father had perished. By the time the final, rather ghoulish draft came, the girls were weeks into their grief, and it was buried in a stack of condolence letters.

"I'm only glad that Mother isn't here to endure this," Verity said, handing her older sister the letter in her father's careful script. Her eyes were bloodshot, making them an eerie gold-green. Ket knew she hadn't been sleeping; she heard the floorboards creaking as Ver tiptoed downstairs each night. Their youngest sister, Selah, never left her room after retiring, but judging from her wan complexion and the dark circles ringing her own eyes, Ket wagered she tossed and turned all night too.

"Here is another you ought to see," Verity said, handing her a second letter as she shifted through the stack of notes sent from well-meaning kin and acquaintances. Keturah met Ver's concerned gaze before accepting it and glancing down. From the scrawl, she knew it was from her father's attorney, Clement Abercrombie, the temporary manager of the entire Banning estate—both that of Hartwick Manor, here in Rivenshire, and Tabletop Plantation on Nevis.

Keturah sighed and closed her eyes. She didn't know if she could bear to read the same words from her father a third time, describing his failing health, imploring his daughters to always remember his fervent love for them. And yet had she not scoured the first and second, searching for variances, any scant detail that might help her connect to their father one last time? No, better to remain in the realm of the head rather than the heart. To read of business, to know of the outcome of this latest sugar harvest. Certainly it had to be better than the last. They desperately needed some glad tidings.

She slid a finger under the wax seal and popped open the heavy linen paper, unfolding it. She settled back into the worn but beautifully upholstered damask chair, what had once been her mother's favorite. But as she read, her heart sank lower and lower. *No, no, no . . .*

"Ket, what is it?" Verity asked, setting aside the rest of the letters and leaning forward. "You look positively aghast."

Keturah realized one hand had gone to her throat and dropped it back to her lap. Her sisters teased her about her hand gestures, instantly reading her many moods. But this . . . Her eyes scanned the letter again. *Crop blight . . . Terrible drought . . . Machinery failure . . . Another overseer lost to the ague . . . Returns far less than the last . . .*

*Far less than the last.*

And the last had been fully half of the one prior.

She hadn't met with the attorney in London more than once since Father's death, but she knew enough to recognize that this was perilous news indeed. Mr. Abercrombie had hinted that it might be time to find a new West Indies overseer to manage Tabletop, that there were indications of mismanagement in the last years as her father's health deteriorated. Now that man was dead and there was no longer a choice to be made. He had to be replaced.

But finding a new overseer was a challenge in the West Indies—particularly for absentee owners. She'd overheard enough from male conversations at various social gatherings to tell her that those who saw to a plantation's "management" were notoriously given to *mismanagement* . . . skimming funds, abuse of the slaves, and a rather unfortunate susceptibility to death from either drink or disease. And now Tabletop had lost their latest manager—such as he was—as well as Father. Who was looking after the slaves? Clearing the land to plant the next crop?

"Ket," Verity said, obviously for the second or third time, striding toward her. "What is it?"

Keturah brought her head up and thought about her sister's words. What was it? What was it *not*? This meant everything was about to change for her. Again. "It appears . . . well, it appears I must pack my things and be on the first ship bound for the West Indies." She handed the letter to Verity and rose, her heavy skirts swishing about her as she strode toward the window. She needed to see the sun peeking through the clouds, some remnant of hope. Or was this just the latest reminder that God had utterly abandoned her?

"The West Indies," Selah repeated slowly, as if she had misheard Ket. "But you cannot. Father forbade us to go there!"

"Father isn't here any longer," Keturah muttered, her mind racing. "Such matters now must be decided by us alone." She shook her head as if to clear it and glanced over her shoulder at her sisters. Neither of them knew how dire this word truly was . . . Ket didn't need another meeting with her father's attorney or accountant to tell her that this crop failure meant they were in danger of losing not just Tabletop, but their holdings here in Rivenshire too.

Taking a deep breath, she turned to fully face her sisters. "The harvest was . . . far less than we hoped for, and our latest overseer has died of the ague. The difficulty is this: Father borrowed heavily against Tabletop *and* Hartwick Manor in order to make some improvements in the Indies. We were counting on a good return from the harvest in order to make a recovery and keep our creditors at bay. Given this news," she said, gesturing to the letter, "I would expect we have only two, perhaps three years to turn things around. Our creditors shall undoubtedly grow impatient after that and demand satisfaction."

Verity's mouth dropped open, and Selah covered hers.

"Surely it cannot be as dire as all that," Selah said.

Keturah only soberly met her gaze. Verity's mouth clamped shut. Selah stepped forward and anxiously wrapped her hand through the crook of Ver's arm, her delicate brows knit in anxiety. But Ket's eyes returned to Verity.

"That leaves us with two options, Ver. Either one of us must immediately marry, and marry a very *clever* fellow, capable of managing our declining estates, or I must go and find a new manager for the plantation. Our future depends upon it."

Verity frowned. Selah blinked and stared at her. Not a one of them had a suitor they wished to encourage at the moment. Selah, after all, was only eighteen. Ver was notoriously picky. And Ket— well, Ket had decided to never risk her heart again. Not that the finest unions were built on love. No, in their circle, there were far more factors to consider. And those factors had led her to marry Lord Edward Tomlinson. Just the thought of it made her clench her hands.

Verity was the first to recover. "Perhaps there is another solution?" she said, glancing hopefully between the unread letter in her hands and her sister.

"I fear not," Keturah said, turning again to the window. She could not bear to stare upon the combined fear displayed in every line of her sisters' faces—it tripled her own. "These last days I've been poring over the ledgers. Last harvest's profits from Tabletop were but a portion of the previous one. We needed a strong crop to recover, and given sugar's long growth cycle, we now will not have a chance at it again for more than a year."

*And that was if I were there this very day, hiring a new man.*

*But I am here, months away from the Indies!* She swallowed hard, forcing her terror back, determined not to allow her sisters to see anything but decision and clarity—attributes they'd admired in their father, attributes they would look to her now to provide. She forced what she hoped was a determined, confident expression to her face and slid her shoulders back before glancing at them. "Due to those declining profits, Mr. Abercrombie suspected we needed to replace our overseer; now we must do so in all haste."

"Can that not be done from here?" Verity asked. "Or can we not hire a man to go in your stead? Cousin Cecil, perhaps?"

Keturah shook her head. "From what I've been able to ascertain, the best managers must be wooed away from other plantations or practically escorted from the docks before another secures their services. It is most competitive."

"Keturah!" Verity said, picking up her fan and sweeping it in front of her blushing face. "What a ghastly thought! The thought of *you* fraternizing with men on the docks? The thought of you on the islands at all! There are reasons Father forbade us to accompany him, and illness was but one."

Ket knew she was right. She looked back out the window, unsure of how to respond. *What am I to do? Is this madness? Or is it direction?*

Selah stepped up beside her and was silent a moment before weaving her slender fingers between Keturah's. Together, they looked out at the sprawling, pristine formal garden of the manse. The gardens Keturah had poured so much of her soul into since her return from the north. Gardens she'd freed of weeds and rot and had seen hints of new life in of late.

"Ket, you yourself know why Father didn't want us in the Indies," Selah said. "The stories . . ."

"I have grown weary of the stories," Keturah returned, still staring outward. "I want to see it for myself. And truly, Selah, I do not believe we have a choice in the matter. Our entire future rides on the success of that plantation. I have a head for financial matters as well as horticulture. Perhaps I am a better choice than any man."

"But no man shall give you the time of day, Ket," Verity said, stepping to her other side. "At least in regard to such matters."

"I shall find a way to gain their attention," Keturah said with a heavy sigh, her eyes tracing the hedges of lavender waving in the afternoon breeze. She would miss that deep purple, as well as her rows of prizewinning roses.

"You cannot be serious," Selah said. "Mother never wished to go. Father would turn in his grave if . . ." Choked by tears, she broke off.

Keturah wrapped her arm around Selah. Could she truly bear to leave her? And Verity too? What would the girls do without her? And yet what choice did she have? They couldn't lose Hartwick Manor, their childhood home and their last connection to their parents and grandparents before them. The thought of the Banning girls without Hartwick was . . . unfathomable.

Her sisters needed it. To know that home was always right here. A refuge. Sanctuary. A place of peace.

*She* needed it.

She bit her lip. Did God so loathe her that He wished to see every bit of her once-strong foundation destroyed? Well, she would show Him, as well as every man who stood in her way. A determined woman could find her way. Surely she could . . .

Ket took a deep breath and turned from the window. "It is our time, sisters, to make our own way forward. Our parents are gone now, but our lives must go on. And if you do not wish to live in utter squalor, or accept the suit of the very next young man who wanders through our front gates, we must press forward at once. The only way I can see to do that is to sail west."

"But the illnesses, Ket," Verity tried again, wringing her hands. "Some say that four out of five newcomers fail to survive the year."

"I am quite hale," Keturah returned, reaching for her hand, seeking to reassure her. "I haven't had a day abed in years."

"But what of the wretched way they treat slaves?" Selah said. "I do not think I could bear to see such suffering. 'Tis one thing to give our servants here in England a proper opportunity to live and learn of the Lord. To learn how to comport themselves and learn the value of hard work. 'Tis another to force them to work the cane fields."

Keturah's mouth became dry at the thought. She knew seeing that firsthand might be the worst aspect. She'd heard enough horror stories from other ladies, whispered behind fans. Worse, there were constant threats of slave uprisings, plantation families kidnapped. Wives raped. Children murdered. And she doubted it was all titillating rumor.

"What I envision is three years there, perhaps four, but no more," Keturah said, resolution gradually steeling each word. "Just enough time to hire a proper overseer, make some investments to improve the plantation, see in a couple of harvests to pay our debts and recover a bit of our fortune, then prepare the plantation for sale at a handsome profit."

"Four years?" Selah said, her voice cracking. "I cannot be without you that long, Ket," she said, lifting a knuckle beneath her nose as her pretty brown eyes welled with tears.

Keturah pulled her closer. "Come now, Sissy. I shall write constantly, and you to me."

Selah only shook her head as if refusing the thought.

"You shall not go alone, Ket," Verity said. "If you must go, I shall accompany you."

Keturah's heart leapt at the thought. It would be so much easier if she were not alone. And yet Verity had suffered from some illness in this past year, and they couldn't both sail away and leave young Selah alone here. "No, Ver. I cannot risk you."

"Why not? If you choose to risk it, so may I."

With one look into Verity's determined gaze, Ket knew she wouldn't dissuade her.

"No!" Selah said in horror, tears dripping down her cheeks as she looked back and forth between her sisters. "You *both* cannot leave me!"

"Then you must come with us," Verity said, reaching out a hand in invitation.

13

Keturah wanted to protest, and knew she should, but the thought of having both of her sisters with her made her feel almost as strong and capable as when her father lived. For the first time since they learned of his death, she felt a surge of hope in her breast. Moreover, for the first time in years, she knew the thrill of *anticipation* beating in her heart.

She and Ver eyed Selah, waiting on her.

The adorable girl wiped her eyes, sniffed, and squared her shoulders, making her blond curls bounce around the nape of her slender neck. "We shall do as our mother taught us and pray upon it." She took a firmer grip on each of their hands, practically daring Ket to disagree.

With a sigh, Keturah closed their small circle, taking Ver's hand too. Far be it from her to dull the shine of her sister's coppery faith. It had sustained Selah—Ver too—through these last years, even as it had utterly failed Ket.

Heads bowed, Selah said, "Lord, it is with great trepidation that we come to you. And yet I cannot deny a desire to remain with my sisters, and you have planted this plan in Keturah's fine mind. We beg you to confirm it to our hearts. Is this of you? Shall we be brave and follow where you appear to be leading us? If not, urge us away from what many would call madness. If so, make us courageous, Father. Courageous."

They stood there in silence, their heads inches from one another. Ket stiffened as she heard them both sniff, knowing tears likely rolled down their cheeks as they continued to pray in silent passion, as their mother had before them. But Ket? She remained silent, teeth clenched, as she waited for God to do what He would with her sisters. Would it not be like Him to keep them from her? To make her sojourn alone, perhaps never to see either of them again?

This, *this* thought made her eyes well up at last and her throat swell. She sniffed, and Selah squeezed her hand, obviously assuming she was praying too. "Thank you, Lord. Thank you," Selah whispered, as if she'd received word from the Almighty himself.

14

And Verity whispered, "We give you what is already your own, Lord. Our very lives. Go before us, beside us, and behind us. Amen."

Both looked up at Keturah then, and she scanned their beloved faces, her heart in her throat. Ver was decided, more firm now. But Selah? She couldn't tell. Her big brown eyes certainly held a measure of conflict in their depths.

"Our journey shall be undoubtedly rife with challenges," her little sister said, suddenly seeming more womanly in her countenance and demeanor as she decided. "But where my dearest ones go, so shall I."

Keturah huffed a laugh and then enfolded both girls in her arms. This felt good to her, so good. Hopeful. How long had it been since she felt such hope, since she felt so . . . alive?

Since before Edward, she was certain. Before her life with him had slowly deadened her heart, piece by piece.

*'Tis behind you now, Ket,* she told herself, hugging her sisters even tighter. She giggled and laughed with them, each one sharing glances that said, *Can we really be doing this? Is it true? Are we mad?*

Were they mad? Or brilliant?

Brilliant, she decided. Or at the very least, inspired. And inspiration, after so long feeling anything but, was exhilarating.

*Yes. The time of death is over. Ahead is life. Hope!*

She was certain of it.

# CHAPTER TWO

"You are utterly mad," Lord Cecil Blankenship, first cousin and self-designated guardian to the Banning women, said. "This blow—your father's death—has most assuredly led you to this." He squinted his eyes at Keturah and slowly waved his long oval head back and forth. "You must forget this plan. We shall find another way for you three. A far more suitable way for women of your station. After all," he sputtered, "as I understand it, the only females who sail alone for the Indies are women of ill repute."

Ket bristled, but did her best to conceal it. She'd had quite enough of men telling her what to do. Over the last week, the girls' decision had in turns both terrified and thrilled them. But overall, all three of them had determined that this course was right—her sisters certain the Lord himself encouraged them to do so. Their unity was all the confirmation Ket needed.

Folding her hands in her lap and forcing a genteel smile to her lips, she replied, "I believe we are in our right minds, Cecil, as mad as it might seem. Trust me, I well know it's a great deal to consider, and on such short notice. But—"

"Short notice!" he burst out, rising and beginning a pacing path about the parlor, clearly meaning to lecture her. "You sent word only yesterday that you intend to embark upon this mad journey, and then today I find out that you intend to do so in the *week to come?*" He drew up to his full height of six feet, lips trembling with further unspoken words, glowering at her.

Taking a deep breath, Keturah bent, took hold of her teacup, and lifted it to her lips. She sipped slowly, allowing him to recover his composure before answering. "Cecil, as I explained, time is of the essence and the *Restoration* was the first ship we could secure for the voyage. I found it is not every captain who is willing to accept three unescorted women as passengers, but also their cargo—"

"Cargo? What all do you intend to take? If you must go, can you not simply voyage there, hire this overseer, and return home where you belong?"

"No, Cecil. I do not believe that would help us at all. I believe we must go and be prepared to stay for several years. In that time, I hope to see two strong harvests brought in."

Her cousin came around the settee and sat next to her, pinching his nose as if to press back a gathering headache. "Keturah, you must think again about allowing me to attend you, or better yet, to go in your stead. Three women alone . . ." He shook his head, his bulbous eyes blinking rapidly. "I shudder to think what will become of you. Uncle Richard would never have sanctioned such a plan. If you will not listen to me, consider what your father would have advised."

She glanced to the open doorway, well aware that her sisters might be hovering near, attempting to eavesdrop. "Father left us here in the manor because his intention was to protect us all our lives. But it was all a ruse, dear cousin. The walls are soon to crumble about us. He sent Mr. Abercrombie enough funds each year to keep us in comfort here, but he gambled it all upon the return of this last harvest." It was her turn to shake her head in frustration. She sighed heavily and reached out a hand to him. He took her smaller hand in his long, bony fingers, hope blooming in his cheeks that she might be softening to his advice.

"You have had the opportunity to review the ledgers yourself, have you not?" she asked gently.

He frowned, giving her a reluctant nod.

Keturah glanced over her shoulder to make certain her sisters were not hovering about. They need not be reminded of their financial predicament. "By my calculations, if we remain here, and if little changes on Nevis, we have but three years' time. That would be enough to sustain us in coal and food and keep our creditors at bay. But, Cecil, in that same time, Tabletop Plantation has a chance to turn a profit—if I see to it myself. If I remain here, hoping that you or a potential overseer might make it work . . ."

She leveled a gaze at her cousin. "Forgive me, but I cannot trust our future to anyone's hands but my own. You may very well never understand that, Cecil, and if that is the case, I am truly sorry. You have been a fine cousin to me. A friend, really, more than kin. But you also know me well enough to know that when I decide to do such a thing, I cannot be dissuaded."

Cecil sank back on the settee, appearing worn. "There are other options, Ket. You could marry. Or Verity . . ." he added hurriedly, averting his eyes. It did not require kinship for those in their circle to know how grim her first union had been.

"Given the . . . *difficulties* of my first marriage," she said delicately, "I have no intention of . . ."

Her words trailed off as Cecil looked to the doorway behind her, his brows rising in recognition. The hair on the back of her neck rose, knowing that they were no longer alone, even as Cecil stood up. She glanced over her shoulder.

And there, leaning against the doorjamb, tricorn in his hands, was Gray Covington. All devilishly handsome, broad-shouldered, long length of him. He casually gestured back toward the front entry. "Primus allowed me in and then was called away. I'd beg your forgiveness for my intrusion, Keturah," he said, "Cecil," he added with a nod, stepping forward to shake his hand, "but it appears as if my timing was most fortuitous."

Cecil frowned, even as he gripped his hand. "How so, old friend?"

Gray glanced down at Keturah, clearly awaiting an invitation. She had an odd memory of him as a child, rudely taking a seat

18

between her and Cecil, shoving them apart, fully confident that they both wanted him near. Stifling a sigh, she motioned for him to sit in the chair beside her own. "Dish of tea?" she asked, forcing herself to be perfectly polite.

"Please," he said and leaned back in her father's wing chair, relaxed and yet firmly erect at the same time. If there was one thing her childhood friend had always been able to do, it was to cut a fine figure. Keturah forced herself to look to the teapot, pouring the steaming liquid into the cup and then lifting it toward him. How much had he heard? Inwardly, she congratulated herself for not letting the cup rattle on the saucer as she offered it.

Cecil shifted beside her as Gray took his first sip. "So you said your timing was fortuitous . . ."

"Indeed," Gray said, "indeed." He leaned forward and set the cup on the table between them and glanced from Keturah to Cecil and back again. "I was at the docks today, seeing to the details of my voyage, when I caught wind of the Ladies Banning and their own intent."

What was this? A voyage? He was off on his own?

"And then I arrived here to learn of this predicament that seems to be causing a most serious rift between two of my old friends." He grinned at Cecil and then Ket.

*Old friends,* she mused. But she hadn't seen Gray for more than a year. They hadn't had a conversation of any length in what, four, maybe five years? What was it he required?

"You, Keturah—"

"Lady Tomlinson," she gently corrected, feeling a rising need to distance herself in what he clearly deemed a closing gap.

He paused for the first time, his swaggering smile dimming a tad. "Forgive me. *Lady Tomlinson*, it seems you are in need. You intend to embark upon a ship that has never welcomed ladies of esteem, unaccompanied by proper escort." He lifted his hands in excitement. "As it happens, I myself am leaving on that very same ship, bent on the very same task." He grinned and nodded his head. "The very same!"

Keturah's eyes narrowed. She held her breath.

"Providentially, I have arranged to secure my inheritance in one lump sum rather than as a yearly allowance. My intention is to abide upon Nevis and turn my father's plantation into the profitable venture it once was for him. Just as you yourself intend to do with Tabletop, I gather."

Ket blinked slowly. Had he said what she thought he'd said? He, too, was going to . . . Nevis?

Gray's smile widened, flashing white teeth and dimples that made debutantes in their circle fairly faint, even as they lamented his poor financial affairs. For some time it was widely discussed how unfair it was that Gray's elder brother—not nearly as handsome—inherited nearly everything, while his younger brother was all looks and light of purse.

Gray leaned forward, elbows on knees, looking to Cecil. "Keturah and her sisters clearly cannot sail to Nevis alone. 'Tis simply not done."

Ket bristled and frowned, her heart beginning to thud in rage.

"And so I offer myself as a protector, a counselor, an escort for the Ladies Banning." He paused, ducked his head as if chagrined. "Doubtless you'll wonder about my suitability."

Suitability? Thoughts of his countless conquests over the last years swirled in Ket's mind. Missy Hedlund. Jacariah Stevenson . . . more than a score of her friends—or her younger sisters'—could probably admit to Gray stealing a kiss, if not more.

"But I have worked hard over the last year to prepare for this journey, to change my ways and dedicate myself to learning about the Indies, as well as horticulture and finance. Mark me, I intend to make Teller's Landing one of the grandest plantations on Nevis. Why not assist the Bannings as well?"

Keturah's breath was coming fast and shallow now. Her eyes narrowed. Teller's Landing alone? Or did he now have designs on her own Tabletop too? Think that he might woo her? Gain a handsome dowry in taking her hand, that he could invest in Teller's Landing? Of all the pompous, imperious, assuming . . .

He shrugged and cast a meaningful grin Ket's way. "You're in need of a man. A man to see to you and yours. We are old friends. Why not—?"

"Gray!" Keturah rose on trembling legs.

The men followed her to their feet, both clearly surprised by her tone.

"This is a . . . most unsuitable course of discussion," she stammered.

Gray frowned. "Ket . . ."

"Do not call me that! What gives you the right to assume such familiarity? After all this time? You have no say in my life! Not my present, nor my future. No say! I did not invite you into such intimacies, and I do not need an escort."

"Ket . . . Pardon, Lady Tomlinson—"

"No!" she said, lifting a palm in his direction. "No." Her hand snapped back to her other as she forced herself to take a long, deep breath. She was hyperventilating, and in her corsets liable to faint if she wasn't mindful. *This man has no jurisdiction over you*, she told herself. *You need not resort to fear.*

"Keturah—"

"*Lady Tomlinson*," she gritted out, opening her eyes and finding refuge in her old title. Distance. "You have overstepped, Mr. Covington. Severely overstepped, I fear. We were childhood friends, nothing more. And whilst the world sees that I should shelter in a man's protection, I have no intention of cowering so." She turned to Cecil. "No intention," she affirmed.

# Chapter Three

She looked back to Gray, golden eyes fairly glinting with resolve. Had he ever seen her this strong, this lovely? This forceful?

"Happenstance does not indicate *providence*, Mr. Covington. It appears we are to be neighbors on Nevis." She gave him a thin smile and lifted a brow. "'Twill be a blessing to see a familiar face on that far isle among so many strangers. But that is *all* we shall require of you," she said, her tone so hard that each word almost tumbled from her wide, beautiful lips like stones. "Now I must bid you both good day, gentlemen. Cecil, we may resume our conversation, if necessary, after we sup. But mind that I've said all I intend. I am firmly decided."

With a nod to each of them, she grabbed hold of her silk skirts and swept out of the room. Gray stared after her, seeing her exit again and again as if she did so as a circulating spirit. She was so thin, the muscles of her neck and collarbone protruding like he'd never seen before. And yet she was unaccountably stronger than he remembered her, as if something within had turned to iron.

He blinked slowly, rotated his tricorn in his hands, and then looked to Cecil, well aware that an uncommon blush burned at his jawline. "It appears as if I mishandled that in a most grave manner. Forgive me."

Cecil sighed heavily and shook his head, his shoulders drooping. "Truly, you might have handled it better, Gray." He lowered his voice, his eyes darting to the empty doorway and back. "But 'tis also true that I am most glad that you happen to have booked passage on the *Restoration*." He stepped closer. "May I ask you a favor, man-to-man?"

Gray nodded.

"Might you look after them?" he whispered. "The best you can. Obviously, Ket will not tolerate you meddling in her affairs. But you and I know that men can do much behind the scenes . . . enter into conversations and learn of matters that ladies of stature might never encounter themselves."

Gray nodded again, this time with more trepidation. "Indeed." It was his turn to glance at the empty doorway. "But, Cecil, even if I learn of things that might be in Ket's best interest, it's clear that she does not wish for me to interfere."

"But I do," Cecil said firmly. "Promise me, Gray, that you shall do your best. Look after Ket—and Verity and Selah too. And in return, I shall honor your efforts."

Gray lifted his chin and narrowed his eyes. So that was it. Cecil was offering to give him payment. He bit the corner of his cheek, practicing what had taken him so long to learn. A bit of restraint.

"There shall not be any need of *honoring* such a task, Cecil," he said, lifting his hat toward him. "Mark me, I shall do as you ask. But solely to honor our friendship, and that which I once shared with Ket. Nothing more. Despite what she thinks of me, I am a man reformed."

Cecil leaned slightly back, as if taking him in for the first time. Not as a boy, but as a man. "I would be most grateful," he said slowly.

"Consider it done," Gray said and reached forward to clasp his hand again. "Come see us in the Indies," he added with a smile. "Every man should glimpse the tropics for himself at least once in his life."

"From what I hear, such a view might well cost him his life. Are you quite certain of this course, Gray?"

"Quite."

"Then God be with you," he said, still soberly grasping his hand, as if saying farewell to a dead man. "God be with you."

Gray galloped down the manicured courtyard road of Hartwick Manor, through the towering stone and metal gates, then along the county road for some distance before he eased his gelding into a canter, then a trot, and finally a walk.

Pulling off the road and onto a wooded path, he urged the horse to the top of a knoll, where he slid from the saddle and let the gelding loose to graze. Gray walked to the edge; from this vantage point, he could see back to the Banning estate, and beyond it his own childhood home, the towering Teller Hall. He ran his hands through his hair, aggravated and confused.

What had driven him to such audacity? Such assumption? And yet, had he not meant well? He'd come to Hartwick to rekindle his friendship with Keturah, to share his good pleasure over the fact that God had seen them brought together again after so long apart. He'd been giddy at the thought. Amazed. And eager to discuss all that was ahead of them.

Then he'd somehow managed to so offend her that she might not speak to him before they reached Nevis.

He sat down on a stump and pulled one booted foot upward so he could rest his elbow on his knee. He bit his lip, staring down at the elegant stone building that dominated the region. Soon, Keturah and her sisters would be on their way to the Indies, leaving the manor to be run by the servants. There would be no parties or teas, no county gatherings or meetings. The hulking building would remain a ghost of what it once had been when the elder Bannings had been alive.

He remembered Keturah's longing glances well, when they were little more than children. How Verity and Selah followed him around like ducklings after a goose. But Ket had always held herself apart, too proud to admit she found him attractive. And he'd found some delight in making her jealous, cavorting with countless other beauties of the county. Not that he'd ever wanted her.

Until . . .

He'd always thought that making her jealous was a bit of sport, a young man's folly. But he was a grown man now. And the thought of her no longer looking his way . . . of him somehow repulsing her . . .

Gray ripped the head off a stalk of grain and idly peeled off the kernels. What was it about her? She certainly wasn't the prettiest. Too tall for certain—only an inch or two shorter than he. But why was it that her eyes burned into his soul? The color of amber. *Tiger eyes*, he thought wistfully, with that haunting hint of green.

"You've made a mess of things, Covington," he muttered, rubbing his neck. *"Cart before the horse,"* he could hear his father say. *"Counting your chickens before they hatch,"* chimed in his mother's voice. Both were dead and gone now, the estate in his brother's capable hands. All three of them had seen him for all he wasn't. All he had yet to be.

Well, he'd show them of what he was made. He'd prove them all wrong. He was not some penniless dandy, as he'd overheard more than one person call him. He laughed mirthlessly. *Well, for now, that might be a fair assessment.* But he had the deed to his father's Nevisian plantation and a plan. In three or four years he'd be a man of means, in a position to court a woman and make her his wife, if he so wished.

Even a woman like Keturah.

He stood up abruptly, brushing his hands together, sending the last of the weed's head to the wind. Not Keturah. Never her. She clearly was no longer even fond of him, as she once was. That much was certain. The years and their dividing paths had left them little more than strangers. Their paths . . . and her husband.

He swallowed the rising bile in his throat at the thought of her late husband, Lord Tomlinson. Her overheard words—*"the difficulties of my first marriage, I have no intention . . .*" Intention of what? Marrying again? Ever again? What had the lout done to her to make her so distant, so guarded? How terrible had her short marriage been? To make her *this* determined to fairly swear off all men, even the offer of her own cousin's care? Cecil's desperate plea for Gray to look after the Banning girls, given no other recourse, lingered in his mind.

As Cook would say, if you boiled a stew down, you were left with the most important ingredients, but all that dissipated could still be tasted. Boiling Keturah's stew down . . . Her mother was dead, her father too. And her family's estate was in jeopardy, if what he'd learned in the hallway were true. But more of her stew's flavoring resulted from the years that she supposedly sheltered under Lord Edward Tomlinson's wing. Those years between the day she took his hand as a bright-faced, hopeful bride and the day she returned to Hartwick as he'd seen her today.

Taut. Wary. Defensive.

Gray's hands clenched into fists. He longed to return to the evening he first spied the older man, Lord Tomlinson, observing Keturah across the room as she chatted with the other girls. Sizing her up as he might a prize heifer. Gray had felt a surge of protection in that moment. But it had confused him. It hadn't been his place to object. It had been her father's. But her father had wanted her to marry Tomlinson. Gray assumed he knew best, and he'd been too intrigued with the pretty girls about to give his old friend further thought.

Then.

He took a deep breath and ran his hands through his hair and closed his eyes, feeling the wind on his face. "I was a fool, Lord," he whispered. "So foolish. In so many ways. Thank you for not holding it against me." He smiled. "Please grant us favor in the Indies," he added, "both for Keturah and for me. Lead us forward into a happier future. Help us to find . . . friendship again. Somehow. Someway."

Gray opened his eyes and looked at the manor again. *Patience* was the word that rang in his mind. *Distance* was another. *Time to heal.*

Keturah would require patience and distance? In order to heal her heart? How was he to allow that? He let out a humorless laugh and turned back toward his gelding. "That shall be rather difficult, Lord," he muttered, "aboard a *ship* for six weeks, and then living next door on an *island.*"

But if there was one thing he'd learned in these last few years, he mused, it was that his Lord had a sense of humor.

They arrived at the wharf with little time to spare, followed by three wagons full of furniture and supplies. Keturah thought she might not ever wrest Verity away from the stables—she'd literally had to tug her weeping sister from her beloved stallion—and as soon as she managed to settle her in the enclosed coach, she had to retrieve a distraught Selah from the arms of their beloved cook.

In the years since their mother had died, the girl had formed a special attachment to the woman; for the hundredth time, Ket wished that for Selah, Cook was just ten years younger and able to make the journey with them. Unfortunately, though six servants accompanied them, both she and Cook knew from the start that the old woman wouldn't be among their number. Not that that had kept Selah from trying to convince her.

As one of two paid Hartwick servants—the rest were slaves—it had been Cook's choice. Ultimately, she chose to leave the manor and go to a daughter in Manchester rather than remain. The thought that she would not be at Hartwick, even upon their return, threatened to be Selah's undoing. Truly, it had been as much a hardship to watch the two part as it had been to tell Selah that their father was dead. Perhaps it was because Cook had been more mother figure than servant to Selah, Ket surmised. Indeed, Mother had died when Selah was but thirteen, and Cook had filled the gap.

It agitated Ket, these further forced partings for both her sisters. Their pain was borne as her own, leaving her heart burdened and her ears ringing as she listened for ways she could soften, deter, distract.

Meanwhile, two of the Negro gardeners had been acting quite oddly, as if they had half a mind to run rather than board the ship. Ket studied Edwin's wide eyes and Absalom's furtive gaze as they struggled to untie two crates, giving the sailors access, but as if in search of an escape route. Had they heard the terrible rumors of how slaves were treated in the Indies? Did they think she might transform into some ghoulish mistress once her feet were upon island sand rather than firm English soil?

She sighed in exasperation and brushed it aside, once she saw Baxter, her white butler, taking command—and clearly keeping an eye on the two young men. They had nothing to fear. They were under her protection; everyone knew that the Bannings treated their slaves like family. It'd be no different when they reached Nevis. But what would happen when Baxter was no longer with them to assuage their fears? He, too, had elected to remain behind. It was good, she told herself. She needed Baxter at Hartwick to keep an eye on things and manage the hulking house. To keep up with correspondence and act in her stead. But still, the thought of doing this without him . . .

The maid who was to attend them—a lithe, pretty Negress of sixteen named Grace—as well as Cuffee, a lighter-skinned stable-boy of twelve, brought to keep track of Verity's falcon and Table-top's livestock—had formed a tidy line with Gideon and Primus, carrying boxes along the gangplank and aboard the *Restoration*.

The ship was a huge schooner, armed with twenty-four guns. The sight of the cannon windows in the hull gave Keturah a start, thinking of the need for defense. *Thank the Lord that Britain is at peace*, she thought. No pirates. No privateers. No, this, this was the perfect time to set out for the Indies, even for a woman.

A sailor stopped beside Ket, catching her pensive stare toward the cannons. "Plenty of firepower to keep you safe, m'lady," he said with a wink and touch to the brim of his hat. "Not that a British vessel has needed to fear in recent years." He was ruddy and round-faced, about her height, but in a clean, faded blue shirt and breeches, and polished black shoes.

"Indeed," she murmured politely, aware that he was too far beneath her station to address her in so forthright a fashion. Apparently he was not equally informed.

"No, the storms are far more fearsome than any threat of pirates," he went on, propping a leg up on the edge of the gangplank and allowing his small brown eyes to droop to her tight bodice and back before seeming to remember himself. "Our navy does a right good job keeping the passage clear for us. 'Tis in her Majesty's best interest for you Indies planters to get to your land. After all, if we're to bring back sugar, we—"

"Selby!" shouted the first mate from the deck, his neck red with agitation, and slicing the air with his hand. Clearly he wanted this Selby to be doing something other than chatting with one of the passengers.

"Beggin' your pardon, Lady Tomlinson," the man said. "Duty calls and such. Sailor Urquhart Selby, at your service, ma'am." He removed his hat and bowed gallantly. Or at least as much as a commoner might assume the ways of a gentleman.

She was charmed, in spite of herself, sensing this as a bridge between her past and her future. Would she not soon have little recourse but to speak to any man necessary in order to get what she needed done? "Lady Keturah Tomlinson," she said in return. It was awkward, an introduction without the benefit of a mutal acquaintance. Perhaps this might be her common circumstance in the Indies? She blinked, trying that on for size as she might a new cloak, smiling as Selby scurried aboard. Selby adeptly circumvented her man Gideon—an ebony-skinned, square-jawed footman in his early thirties—jumping to the railing and on board as if he were more lemur than man.

At the top of the gangway, the first mate leaned in toward him, angrily gesturing to him and then to Keturah and back again, then pointing to the ropes. As she watched, the man leapt to the cross section of rigging and rope ladder and scrambled upward as easily as he had jumped to the rail and aboard. She shaded her eyes and watched, wondering what it would be like to climb that high. So impossibly high . . .

"It's much taller than the old oak on Crabapple Hill," said a low voice beside her.

She started and turned toward Gray. "What? Oh yes. Much." She paused, it taking a moment to remember climbing the giant oak with Gray when they were children. Part of her wished to seize this temporary cease-fire and reminisce, whilst another urged her to make her excuses and walk away. Ket was about to do so when he beat her to it, touching the brim of his smart-looking black tricorn hat and leaving her side with a curt, "I fear I still have much to do before we cast off. Good day, Lady Tomlinson."

"Good day," she murmured. She looked back to her cargo as if disinterested but allowed her eyes to slide back to him, watching as he lifted and carried his own trunk aboard the *Restoration*— following Philip, his longtime servant and friend, who was carrying another. Her eyes searched for others assisting him, but to no avail. So, she surmised, he intended to make his way to the Indies without the benefit of more than one manservant. Was it not impossible? Her eyes scanned the docks, certain she'd misunderstood. But there it was. His wagon, drawn by two horses and a slave she recognized from Teller Hall. Then a second wagon, containing nothing but a shining silver plough, so new it glinted in the sun.

*A plough?* The Bannings had arrived at the docks with three wagons full of goods for their new home, but he intended to embark with little more than a plough? Half of her admired his gumption; the other half wished for the simplicity of being a man. After all, was it not far more simple for a gentleman to dress himself than a lady? But what of laundering? Cooking? Tea? Making not only a home but a footprint in this new world before them? Surely it was shortsighted of him not to bring even one footman. His brother, Samuel, most assuredly offered.

Keturah frowned. Perhaps he hadn't. Selah had heard a rumor that Samuel was completely against Gray's scheme to make a fortune in the Indies. Samuel had said that fortunes were no longer made among the islands, that again and again he'd seen them siphoned away. According to him, the "glorious days" of the Indies were over. Keturah certainly hoped he was as wrong as she'd insisted with Selah, because she was betting their future on it. She glanced back at her sisters, who hovered on the edge of the dock, chatting with three children who had come to see Verity's falcon Brutus.

*Please, Lord, let me not be wrong in this.* She swallowed hard. She well knew that she prayed not as a believer, but out of some vestige of wanting to protect what was hers. She looked toward her sisters.

She'd lost her mother. Her father. Even Edward—as little as she cared for him. But she'd lost so many and dared not consider losing more.

She looked to the tarnished-silver waves, washing along the planks of the ship. When she returned here to this wharf, she wanted to disembark with the Banning fortune restored, both the plantation and the manor safe from creditors. Her sisters' future ensured. Verity and Selah needed to know Hartwick Manor would always be a haven for them, just as it had been for her after Edward died. Even before he'd died, she'd dreamed of returning to it. Of—

"Lady Tomlinson?"

She looked up to spy Lord Harrison Shantall, an old friend of her father and president of the West Indies Company. The man, perhaps in his sixties, smiled as he took her hand, bowed, and kissed it. He stooped a bit with age and yet was still taller than she. "So 'tis true," he said, clasping her fingers, eyes filled in wonder. "I thought it nothing more than society whisperings, the rumor that the Ladies Banning were to sail for Nevis."

"It is far more than rumor, Lord Shantall," she said, sliding her hand from his. "We're off on quite the adventure, it seems."

"Quite," he said and forced a smile. She could see the same

concern behind his eyes as she'd seen on nearly everyone's face since making her decision.

"But we do not travel alone," she added, hating the edge of defensiveness in her voice. "We have a number of servants to accompany us, so we shall enjoy every comfort of home, even in the tropics."

His doubtful eyes followed her gesture toward the line of servants still unloading the wagons. High above, the two massive crates containing furniture had been bound, and with the use of a winch, the first mate was shouting orders, seeing that they were carefully loaded into the hold. She saw Gray walking down the gangplank again. He looked to her and Shantall as if assessing them before turning to make his way to his wagon.

Gray's casual observation chafed. She faced her companion more squarely. "Lord Shantall, are you embarking upon the *Restoration*?"

"Alas, I am not. I am merely here to see you off. Have you met your captain?"

"Not as of yet," she said, his words running through her mind. Why was she so disappointed that he, too, would not be a passenger? Had she not insisted to Cecil that she needed no man to attend them? "If you would be so kind as to introduce us, Lord Shantall, I'd be grateful."

"But of course." He gestured forward whilst taking her arm. She looked to her sisters, and catching Verity's eye, they hurried to join them. At the gangway, Lord Shantall waited for Keturah to proceed, and then her sisters, before following behind. As she moved along the slanted walkway, feeling the water progressively farther beneath her feet, her heart began to beat faster and faster.

It was no longer merely a plan. They were truly doing this, *embarking upon a ship set to sail for the West Indies*. Over all these years, Keturah had imagined what it would be like to walk along the sugarcane, to see Nevis's towering dormant volcano rising above, to swim in the warm waters of the tropics. Now she would no longer have to imagine it; she would know what it was like firsthand. In a way, the best part would be to know what their father had experienced, perhaps understand him a bit better as a result of living in that corner of the world. *Somehow it would make him feel closer*, Keturah thought. Almost as it did to wrap herself in his morning coat or scarf.

They reached the deck, and Lord Shantall led them forward. Spying their approach, the captain—surprisingly young, only a few years Ket's senior—dismissed his men and turned toward them, greeting Lord Shantall as he might an old friend. The captain was brawny with sun-bleached brown hair and hazel eyes that seemed to glint in the sunlight, his face ruddy from years at sea.

He looked from Keturah to Selah and then settled on Verity, his keen eyes taking in her long leather glove and the fine falcon she carried, then back to her. Cocking a crooked smile, he gave Verity a courtly bow. "I take it ye are Lady Tomlinson?"

"No, Captain McKintrick. I am Miss Verity Banning." She gave him a brief curtsy as she blushed furiously under his gaze.

"I beg your pardon," he said with a grin, "but still, I am in your service, Miss Banning," he said, giving her a nod that spoke of breeding. His eyes lingered on her a moment longer before turning to Keturah. "Then ye are Lady Tomlinson . . . unless this wee sprite at your side is a grown lady in disguise."

"I am," Keturah said, curtsying, "and this is my youngest sister, Miss Selah Banning."

"I am in your service," he said, casting them each a gentlemanly but slightly roguish smile. Then he turned back to Verity. "And who is this?" he asked, taking in the golden feathers and crooked beak of Brutus as the bird's eyes darted back and forth. "I dinna recall offering passage for such a bird."

Verity's mossy-green eyes opened wide in fear, and Ket's heart sank. "This . . . this is Brutus," her sister managed to say. Might he truly object?

But Captain McKintrick was smiling as he reached up to stroke the bird's chest with the back of his finger. "Dinna fash yourselves, ladies. I only ask that he kill every rat he sees in exchange for his passage aboard my fine ship."

"That he shall gladly do," Verity said with a nod, and in that moment Ket could see how her eyes shone. How she now cast this man the tiniest coy gaze, looking to Brutus and then slowly back to him. She fancied him!

Well, her sisters had license to choose their own beaus, but Verity would do well to remember that Ket and Selah had to approve of said beau, and a sea captain would not be her first choice. If some thought moving to the islands was dangerous, it was nothing compared to the dangers a man who routinely spent his days on a schooner encountered. Storms. Disease. Mutiny even.

"This is my first mate, Mr. Gordon Burr," he said, turning to the tall silver-haired man who had been dressing down Urquhart Selby and shouting orders to the large crew ever since they had arrived at the wharf. "Burr, this is Lady Keturah Tomlinson, and her sisters, Misses Verity and Selah Banning."

"At your service, misses," said the man, nodding toward each but not offering to take their hands. Clearly he did not welcome them as their captain had. Crossing his arms, he leaned over to say something in McKintrick's ear. The captain turned back to them as the first mate bowed briefly and then departed, again yelling orders to a man up in the rigging.

"Burr has told me that your servants have been shown the way to your quarters, Lady Tomlinson," he said, his attention straying to Verity again. "I would advise ye and your sisters to become comfortable there now as we finish preparations to make way. I'll send a man to fetch ye when we're prepared to weigh anchor, but until then it'd be best if ye lasses not remain abovedecks. Three as fair as ye are a sore distraction when I need every man to be paying keen attention to their tasks."

"Indeed," she said, lifting her chin and yet striving not to take offense, even as she seemed to feel the lingering stares of crew-members now as she hadn't before. One man slowly untying a knot of rope. Another on a mizzenmast, methodically securing the sail. Apparently neither man was moving with the efficiency that their superiors demanded. "We do not wish to get in your way, Captain, nor your crew. We shall look forward to your kind instruction as to when we might comfortably return to the deck."

"Oh aye. I'll send a man to fetch ye so ye do not miss your last moments near English soil. Then I'd be most gratified if ye three would dine with me this night," he said with another curt bow. He cast a grin in Verity's direction. "The falcon, however, shall remain with the other animals. I dinna welcome birds in my quarters."

"No?" Ver asked, pretending to be surprised. She reached up and stroked Brutus's neck feathers. "Even if he slays a rat beforehand?"

"Aye, even if he manages it, he shall eat that rat in the stables rather than astride my table."

"Pity, that," she said, pretending to sulk, even as she gave him a sly smile.

Keturah frowned. This was no evening soiree. Her sister forgot herself. "And my servants, Captain?" she intervened. "Where shall they sup?"

The handsome man's eyes flicked past her to the line of men and women who still carried the Banning wares into the hold. "After they manage loading the rest of your considerable cargo, m'lady, I would imagine they'll be fair famished. Cook will see to them after the crew."

With that, he bowed and turned from her and walked with the first mate down the side of the ship toward the enormous wheel. She didn't miss Burr's glance over his shoulder at them as the two talked, the first mate waving his hand in agitation.

"I take it they disapprove of all we're taking with us," Keturah said. "We did pay a great deal for our share of the cargo space."

"Pay him no mind," Lord Shantall said soothingly. "These men are merely unaccustomed to women traveling to the Indies, and all they require. In time it will settle with them."

*I hope so*, Keturah thought. Otherwise it would make their six-week passage all the longer and more tedious. Or might it be a good thing? A wedge to discourage this bubbling interest between her sister and the captain?

"Well, I wish you a fine voyage and prosperous months ahead

in the Indies," Lord Shantall said. He slid a card out of his inner jacket pocket. "I took the liberty of writing down the names of a few friends your father and I had in common on-island. Seek them out for advice when in need. Anyone else might prove . . . unsatisfactory."

Keturah looked down to the fine linen card, and her eyes welled up. It was uncommonly kind of him to think of her in this way—something her father would have done. "Thank you, Lord Shantall. That is most thoughtful of you."

"My dear . . ." He paused, his eyes shifting back and forth, as if wanting to say more. She tensed, sensing warning and hesitation in his demeanor. "At Tabletop, you might encounter some . . . surprises."

She laughed under her breath, which she knew was entirely unladylike but could not resist. "I would imagine, Lord Shantall, there will be far more than *some*."

"Yes," he said, brows lifting in relief, "quite." He seemed to shake off whatever he had meant to say, finding quarter in her casual dismissal. "Be well, Keturah," he said, leaning down to kiss her hand. "We shall look forward to reports of how you fare across the Atlantic."

Ket gave him a wry smile. "Giving you more fodder for discussion at the summer soirees."

"But of course!" he said with a wink. "The sugar baron's daughters will do quite nicely in that capacity."

She curtsied as he bowed, and then he left the ship, walking straight and tall. Watching him from the rail, Keturah felt another pang of longing for her father. How many times had she seen him walking with Lord Shantall among their gardens? At parties? Entering the study in the manse?

She was then distracted by the sight of Gray, bringing another heavy chest up the gangway on his back. It was so unsuitable, a gentleman doing manual labor! She'd never seen anything like it. He'd given up his neckcloth, and his shirt was open and untucked from his breeches, exposing smooth flesh and muscles.

36

Sweat beaded on his brow and dampened the armpits of his shirt, but he appeared so strong, so capable, that it stirred something within her.

She hurriedly looked to the sea, washing against the planks of the ship below, knowing she did not want to be caught staring. But when she glanced up again to turn and make her way to her cabin, she saw that his steady gaze was upon her, a small smile tugging at the corner of his lips. He knew she'd been looking. And although she expected shame to be caught doing such a thing, there was nothing in him but . . . pride. *Of all things! Pride?* Flustered, she moved down the side of the ship, dodging sailors carrying crates, rolling barrels, and hauling rope.

Catching sight of Edwin and Absalom entering the hold with the last of their crates, she followed behind, assuming her sisters had already gone to their cabins as she bade farewell to Lord Shantall. She knew she'd promised Captain McKintrick they would hide away, but she wanted a chance to figure out the layout of this massive ship before they were fully underway. Once they left the wharf, her exploration might feel more intrusive when a third of the crew was likely to be belowdecks at a time, but for now she had the freedom to see all of the *Restoration*, from stem to stern. And if she was to sleep at night in the middle of the vast sea, she knew she'd want to run her hands across the strong beams, observe where the hundred men of the crew slept, count the casks of water and hogsheads of flour that would keep them all alive.

Because it had all seemed like a grand idea when she first thought of it, this adventure to the Indies. But now that she'd left her homeland's soil for the last time—not to touch ground again until her slippered feet were atop sand and volcanic earth—she found her heart raced and her hands trembled.

She swallowed hard, took a deep breath, and then turned toward a cabin to her right where she heard her sisters chattering and laughing. It was so good to hear them that way, and she felt the tug of a smile on her own lips. How long had it been since they had sounded so young and excited? *Since before we knew Father had died.*

Concentrating again on the joy rather than the sorrow, she rounded the corner and spied her sisters, merrily trying to settle their things in the tiny, cramped space. Selah spied her in the doorway and came to her, face flushed and grinning. "Have you seen anything like it, Keturah? Why, we're packed away like sardines in oil!"

"I like it," Verity declared, hands on her hips. "I think it cozy."

Keturah lifted one brow, looking over the narrow cots and the trunks, stacked one atop the other and anchored with ropes to the wall. Selah saw her looking and went over to them, placing her hand on a sturdy rope. "To keep them from sliding, they say," she said. "Can you imagine? Seas so rough that they could move these heavy things?"

Such a thought was not welcome, Keturah decided. And moving the trunks to get to those below for a change of clothes or other items her sisters needed would be a daily trial. But Selah took her arm and urged her to the doorway. "Come, your room is just across from ours. You are fortunate not to have to share with Ver," she said under her breath. "You know how she talks in her sleep. I'd much rather be with our Grace. Besides, she only has one small trunk. Ver insisted on three!"

Keturah smiled and in two steps stood at the threshold of her cabin. While her own trunks were also bound at the end of it, there was far more room because of Grace's sole small trunk. Each of the servants had been allowed the same trunk—Baxter had purchased six of them and saw to their packing, making certain each had three sets of clothes, a cloak or coat, and other pertinent items. "If she gets too loud, you can come and sleep with me," Keturah whispered to her sister. "Come, let us go explore the rest of the ship belowdecks and find where Brutus is to roost."

"Ooo, a grand idea!" Selah enthused. "Let me fetch Verity. Here is your key to your cabin." She slid a skeleton key on a chain from around her neck and placed it around Keturah's. "We were given firm instructions by a crewman to always keep our cabin doors locked. Apparently, they do not wish for any of our 'finery' to be tempting to the crew."

"Honestly?" Keturah said. "How would they hope to escape with it? There are only so many places a man could hide something aboard a ship."

"All I know is that the mate said the captain doesn't wish to be forced to deal with such repercussions and that he would hold us as accountable as he would the man who stole from us."

"Truly?" Keturah shook her head. "The thought!"

"This might be a long voyage," Selah whispered, leaning close, "if the captain proves to be unpleasant. But how can a man as handsome as he be unpleasant? And that Scottish brogue . . ." She sighed. "I could listen to that every evening with pleasure."

Ket lifted a brow. *Six weeks*, she told herself. She could endure anything—or anyone—for six weeks. But all she needed was not one, but two sisters to be endlessly flirting with the captain.

After collecting Verity, the three set about exploring the hold. In the back was a vast section stuffed full with exports. Hogsheads—rounded vessels holding sixty-five gallons each—of flour, salt, casks upon casks of wine, crates of bottles labeled MADEIRA, others labeled CHAMPAGNE, thick bolts of fabric, three harpsichords, and ten fine hutches. There were crates of stationery and India ink and gowns and hats and much more.

"'Tis quite fascinating, is it not?" Verity asked, looking up one side of the towering stacks that reached the ceiling. She turned back to her sisters. "In a way, it's a glimpse of what we might be clamoring for in a few months."

"Indeed," Keturah said, admiring how the crew had packed it all so tightly. Even in heavy seas, it would not likely shift. And she saw that the cargo had been evenly divided, with half the wine casks on the starboard side, the other half on the port side. *In order to distribute the weight*, she concluded.

Verity edged around a metal contraption, partially crated. It took Ket a moment to recognize it.

"What is that?" Selah asked.

"I heard Gray call it a field plough. He had it built," Verity said, stopping beside them to admire the contraption. "He said the

Romans once used something similar to it. He intends to plant his own sugar in tidy rows rather than the customary mounds. He's quite proud of his plan."

Keturah's eyes moved over the metalwork, the sturdy, elegantly curved wooden frame between the curved blades. The thought that Gray had the foresight to bring such a thing with him startled her. How on earth had he come to decide on such a course of action? Make such an investment? Why not do as their fathers had done on the island, as their fathers had before them? What had worked in England and the islands for centuries?

They moved on to a section containing the stables. Pigs and chickens and even a cow that would serve to feed all those aboard. "Poor dears," Verity said, already lamenting their living conditions and fate as future suppers. She walked past the stalls toward the back where Brutus's cage had been set inside one stall. *So this is where he will roost*, Keturah thought.

Verity went to the big cage and opened the door and stroked his neck feathers. "This is where you shall rest each night, my friend," she said. He moved along her glove, clearly agitated by the noise all around them—the pigs and chickens all seeming to be intent upon complaining. "I think I'll take him outside when we're allowed up again. Give him a bit of time to stretch his wings before we're at full sail and he has to be in his coop."

Keturah thought this a solid idea and followed behind, Selah still at her arm. For the hundredth time she observed that her sister and her falcon made a striking pair. Brutus had similar coloring to Ver's hair—golden brown with bits of light and dark—and was so big that he had to duck his head as they passed through doorways. Keturah had held him a couple of times and knew he was heavy on the arm, but Ver never seemed to mind. And she was grateful that it was possible to bring him on the voyage, because it helped Verity adjust to the idea of leaving her beloved stallion behind.

Keturah planned to purchase more horses as soon as they got to the island, or perhaps her father had left behind a few fine mounts. Four had been listed on the will that the lawyer had read to them all. But they could either be old nags, weary after years of work in the field, or handsome pairs fit to draw a carriage. There was so much they had yet to discover, so much she wished she knew already. Lord Shantall's vague warning came back to mind, and she wished that he had been more plainspoken. What had he wanted to say?

*Probably a thousand things.* There were thousands upon thousands of details about island life and running a sugar plantation that she had yet to even consider. The thought of it threatened to overwhelm her. *One step at a time*, came her father's voice to her mind. *One step at a time leads to a mile crossed, and then ten, and then a hundred.*

*Oh, Father. If only you were there to greet us . . .*

But then, of course, they would not be on this ship at all.

They passed through a smaller hold where the servants were to lodge, a sprawling room with nothing but beams and columns, hammocks hanging in lines, and a small crate bolted to the floor beneath each—presumably for the meager belongings of each person—and a similar, but much larger, space that was for the crew. On either side of the ship, she spied twelve large cannons, and between them lay stacks of supplies for the voyage.

Among the slaves, men and women were together, something that grated on Keturah's sensibilities. But she figured it could not be helped. The few white servants—none of them belonging to the Bannings—were separated by a canvas curtain on the far side.

As they walked through the crew's quarters, several men glanced their way. Keturah hurried her sisters along. It would not do to be caught in such an intimacy. She noticed they were in the crew's primary passageway leading to their quarters and resolved to tell Verity she'd have to use the other side to reach the stables and Brutus's roost so as to avoid most of the men. Better yet, she should send Cuffee, the stableboy, to fetch the bird while Verity awaited him abovedecks. With more than a hundred men aboard ship and presumably a portion of them down here at a time, resting, it would be wise to stay out of these passageways as much as they could.

"I want you two to stay together as much as possible," she said to Selah, knowing Verity would hear her too. "If the other is unavailable, then you must wait for a servant to accompany you. Do you understand?"

Both bobbed their heads. Selah's warm brown eyes widened, taking in the edge to Ket's voice. At first she wanted to soften the fear she felt shake her little sister, but then she decided to let it stand. Best for her to err on the side of caution.

They passed other cabins with several men and one young family getting settled. Having not yet been properly introduced, they merely nodded at one another and continued on, knowing that in time they'd all be practically kin, given the cramped spaces. There was already a feeling of camaraderie in the air that thrilled Keturah, as if the shared adventure of sailing across the Atlantic would forever bind them.

It was with that thought they approached Gray's cabin, and it was with some dismay she saw Verity pull to a stop and brazenly glance inside. "Gray!" she said with delight. "Is your work complete? We're about to take in our last bit of British breezes, as soon as Captain McKintrick sends for us. You should join us!"

Gray's cabin was a mirror image of Keturah's, and just six doors away. She swallowed hard as she saw him tuck his shirt into the waistband of his breeches and look her way. He gave Verity a small smile. "You are most gracious, Miss Verity. Allow me to see to a few more things and then I shall join you above."

"Very well," she said brightly and moved on.

Keturah didn't look back into his cabin but felt Selah's grip tighten on her elbow. "He truly is such a handsome man, do you not agree?" she cooed, leaning close.

"Do you think so?" Keturah asked, forcing a blank tone.

Selah giggled. "As if you weren't the first to notice, Ket! You always had eyes for him."

"Shh," Keturah said, scowling at her little sister. "That is patently false. Mr. Covington has many admirers, to be sure, but I assure you, I am not one of them."

Selah said nothing more, but Ket could feel her tremble with laughter. Verity, to her credit, never turned to join in her sister's jibes. They were about to return to their cabins when the sailor Selby came for them. "Cap'n says you might wish to return above-decks," he said, eagerly nodding. "We're about to set sail."

"Thank you, Mr. Selby," Keturah said. Together, the girls reached the steep stairwell where, lifting her skirts with one hand and carrying Brutus with the other, Verity adeptly led the way upward. Keturah didn't know how she managed without a hand on a rail, but Verity had always had impeccable balance. It was part of what made her such a fine horsewoman. Whereas Ket was reasonably secure in a sidesaddle, Ver acted as if she had been born to it.

They reached the deck again and moved to a space on the aft deck, away from masts and ropes and clamps, where there seemed to be no men in need of working for the moment. Untying the falcon's leather strap from her wrist, Verity said, "Away!" and lifted her arm. Immediately the falcon spread his wide wings, sank perilously close to the dock, caught the wind and rose with surprising speed. Time and again, Keturah thrilled to watch him fly, wishing she had the same ability. To climb into the sky, to sail higher than the crow's nest, so far above them? It made her heart pound to think of it.

"Will he know where to return?" Selah asked, eyes wide.

"Oh, he will know," Ver said confidently. "After he finds that nice, fat wharf rat to eat."

The bird was rather indifferent, and Keturah never understood how Ver could be so attached to it. But while Brutus seemed to care for no one but himself, she knew he was fiercely protective of Verity and obeyed her every command, proving that the two had some sort of mysterious bond.

The girls watched Verity's falcon continuing to fly in circles, ever widening but always keeping the *Restoration* in sight. Then he tightened his attention on a portion of isolated dock, tucked his wings, and dived straight downward. Keturah turned, not wishing to see or even think of the soon-to-be dead rat. Not that she cared for rats; she detested them. But the thought of . . .

A low whistle brought her head up. Gray was beside her, leaning over the rail, watching with them. "That certainly is a fine bird, Miss Verity," he said admiringly.

Ver looked past Keturah to him. "Why, thank you. I would wager that the gentlemen of the Falconer's Club are relieved to hear he's off to the West Indies. I half expected that some might appear here to wave farewell to their fiercest competitor."

Verity had shown up every one of the men in the Falconer's Club contest when Brutus brought back not one, not two, but three rabbits in the allotted time. Keturah would never forget the look on the men's faces when she'd arrived without invitation. In deference to her absent father, the doting men had allowed her to compete as a lark. After her victory, however, half were delighted and amazed, the other half red-faced and furious, desperate for Miss Banning to be on her way—never to set foot in the club again.

Gray laughed, a warm, low sound. Keturah chafed, frustrated by how even his laughter did something odd to her belly, and turned to Verity. "Verity, a lady never wagers or even mentions it," she groused under her breath.

"I was only jesting," Verity whispered, frowning at her. Her confused expression told her she wondered what was truly bothering Ket, and when her moss-colored eyes moved to Gray, they softened in understanding.

Which only agitated Keturah more, of course. Taking a deep breath and letting it out through her nose, she said, "I think I shall take a turn around the deck. Stretch my legs. Come along, sisters."

The two fell in step with her. They were nearly three steps away when Selah glanced back. "Are you not coming, Mr. Covington?"

"I think not," he said graciously. "Someone ought to stay here in case Miss Verity's falcon returns, should they not?"

Selah smiled and then shook her head, sending her blond curls bobbing. "Oh no. Verity could go miles from here and that falcon would find her."

"Truly?" he said, stepping after them.

"Truly! Isn't that right, Ver? You don't even seem to fear us setting sail while Brutus is out."

Verity turned back and tilted her head, considering, then nodded once. "'Tis true."

"Consider me even further impressed," Gray said with a slight nod to Verity. He offered the youngest Banning his arm, and she took it. It was all Ket could do to keep from rolling her eyes as she turned to lead the way around the ship. They'd been so nearly apart from him, but Selah—with her constant desire to include anyone within her reach—could not restrain herself from inviting him along. Honestly, her younger sisters might usher her to an early death.

They came to the stern and found four of their servants circled around, laughing and teasing one another. Catching sight of Keturah, Gideon straightened and nudged Edwin. The two others hurriedly fell into line behind them. "'Tis well," Keturah said, waving her hand. "A bit of liberty now is good for us all. We're soon to set sail. Pass the word to the others—we will not have need for any of you to attend us until shortly before supper. Until then you are free to do as you please."

"Thank you, Lady Tomlinson," said Primus, bowing his head with its short-cropped hair. "Will you wish for us to be in livery this evening, ma'am?"

"Only you, Primus. You can attend us. Make certain Grace returns to our cabin by five to help us dress." Keturah hadn't seen the girl since they embarked, but judging by Primus's calm expression, she was somewhere about.

"Yes, ma'am," he replied, nodding again deferentially.

The others followed suit.

They walked on by. It agitated Keturah that they had not found her and asked her permission before they took some time to themselves. Was that not what their mother had always demanded? And yet there wasn't anything they were to do beyond stow the Banning wares. In truth, there was naught for any of them to do before supper. How long had it been since an expanse of hours lay before her with so little to fill it?

A bell clanged. "Release the mooring ropes!" shouted the first mate. "Prepare to make way!"

His commands were immediately repeated across the decks. Men went scurrying up rigging to the halyards—crossbeams that held the sails. Shielding her eyes, Keturah could see others climb even higher, awaiting further commands. Her heart began to race. It was truly happening. They were about to leave England for . . . forever? *For quite some time*, she reassured herself.

Suddenly she feared that this was the worst decision she'd ever made, though something in her thrilled to the hope of what the new adventure would bring.

"Mooring ropes loose and secured, Captain!" cried a man.

"Mooring ropes secured!" Captain McKintrick yelled, taking his place behind the huge wheel as Burr stepped aside. His eyes scanned the horizon ahead of them, observing skiffs and rowboats hurriedly getting out of their way. "Let loose fore and aft staysails!"

Again it was repeated along the length of the *Restoration*.

The sails were unfurled, falling fast and heavily to their full lengths and filling with the morning breeze with a satisfying *whoomp*. Beneath Ket's feet, she felt the ship surge forward, the pier sliding slowly away. Men and women on the docks lifted hands and hats to them in farewell. The sailors waved back, and as Keturah and her sisters joined them at the rail, so did they. When they were a fair distance from the small boats that crowded the wharf and others could clearly see their path, Captain McKintrick called for the jibs and then topsails.

With a *whoosh* and a ruffling noise, one sail after another was unfurled. They caught the breeze and snapped outward, filling into wide arcs. The ship groaned, as if complaining at the combined strain upon her masts, and the *Restoration* rapidly picked up speed.

Verity took one arm and Selah the other. She knew Gray hovered nearby, but it was her sisters that she was most aware of in that moment. They were heading to the Indies. It wasn't a dream anymore, nor a madcap idea. It was reality.

In half an hour they were among ten other vessels. In an hour they were one of three within sight, and England looked impossibly small behind them. Within two hours they could not see land at all. The *Restoration* was at full sail, tilting at twenty degrees with the strength of the wind and slicing through the water at thrilling speed.

They'd stood there in silence through it all, as if in stunned reverence. It was Brutus that seemed to break them out of their reverie, with his sharp cry as he circled high overhead. With a smile, Verity strapped on her leather sleeve and lifted her arm, beckoning him to come. He circled again, his head darting left and right, assessing, and then on his third pass he flew down to alight on her arm.

Nearby, the sailors cheered as if she'd just performed a feat of magic, and Gray smiled so broadly that Keturah had to look away. He cut so fine a figure, and when he smiled . . . well, she didn't care at all for what her heart did when that occurred.

Gray accompanied the Ladies Banning to their door and then bade them a brief farewell, knowing they would see one another again at the captain's table. It had not escaped him, Keturah's careful methods of ignoring him, even when he was in her immediate proximity. Was she truly so angry over his offer to look after her and her sisters? Clearly he had overstepped his bounds, but would she punish him for the remainder of the trip?

He went to his cabin and grabbed a pail, heading to the hold where he knew the passengers were allowed to retrieve one bucket of fresh water every other day. He stood in line with servants, his face burning at the impropriety of it. After all, his brother had offered him one of his own slaves at a bargain price, aghast at the idea that he was to go on this voyage with neither footman nor valet to accompany him.

But Gray knew that he would need every pound and pence to his name to do what he intended on his new estate and could only afford to pay Philip, a man who had become more friend than servant. He'd read countless books and memoirs, spoken to a score of planters who had spent time on plantations in the Indies, consulted professors of agriculture. No, he had not the funds to hire more servants. His plantation would require every bit he had to man it. In the meantime, he could suffer the social embarrassment and bathe and dress himself. *I am no child.* No fool, desperate to prove himself with social niceties rather than seeing to his future. *Because my future is at Teller's Landing Plantation. I am the newest owner of a plantation, a planter*, he thought, practicing the words, trying them on for size. *And once I make that a success, respect shall come.*

He concentrated on that fact as he dipped his bucket in, well aware that a trio of black faces stared at him in silent consternation as he did so. But as he turned and walked past them, he thought, *This won't be the last time you see me.* In fact, once he got to the plantation, he expected he'd be unlike any planter the slaves had ever seen before. He wanted to be in the fields, digging in the dirt, hauling manure and settling it around each cane seedling. He wanted to know his land from a foot deep and upward, not be told of it as he lolled about.

Because his time as the idling younger son of James Randall Covington was over. And his time as the master of the soon-to-be-profitable Teller's Landing was just beginning.

# CHAPTER FOUR

In his cabin, Gray carefully poured out a portion of the water to reserve for use the next day. As he undressed, bathed, and shook out a clean shirt from his trunk, he considered Keturah Tomlinson again and why she might have taken such affront.

He knew that something dire had happened between her and Lord Tomlinson, and the thought of it made his head pound in fury. Partly his anger burned for the older man, who had clearly abused her in some way, making her wary of all men. Yet part of his anger was reserved for himself, because by the time he had become aware of her engagement, it was too late. In point of fact, he hadn't even realized he might wish to consider anything beyond friendship with Keturah until the day his mother had casually shared the fact that Ket was to be married a fortnight hence to Lord Tomlinson.

He could still see his pretty mother in the warm light of the parlor lamp, the words slipping from her lips in such an offhand way. But her eyes had been sharp upon him, penetrating, well aware of her effect.

There had been no recourse for him. He had not the means to court one such as Keturah Banning. He was years away from amassing the fortune necessary to approach her father, not even having a home of his own, which was vital if one was vying for a bride.

*A bride.* Seeing her in her lace and finery that day had left him unaccountably despondent. To pick up one of the fine dining room chairs and smash it against the wall. To laugh uncontrollably. To drink until he forgot his pain. All of which he did with some gusto, finally, after the wedding party had waned and he was alone at home again.

Nothing was the same after that. He had chalked it up to losing one too many of his childhood friends, those who abandoned the champagne and dances and furtive walks among the gardens that led to long kisses, and take their places among the boring, staid adults they'd mocked for years. Not that Keturah had ever been like that. She was far too serious to engage in the antics that had distracted him since they had come of age. But when she walked down that aisle . . . something seemed to come unhinged within Gray.

It was his brother Sam who had found him among the sharp remains of the chair, several deep gashes in his mother's wallpaper. A slave had hovered in the doorway, her eyes filled with fear. But Gray could only alternately weep and laugh.

Sam had crouched down before him, put a hand on his shoulder, and squeezed. They were silent for several long breaths together. It was the only moment of compassion he could remember from his brother since they were boys. Then he'd said, "You're a young fool, Gray. 'Tis time to end this before you become an old fool. But you must be the one to decide that."

Later, as Gray splashed his face and then watched as the water dripped back down to the bucket again, he considered his brother's words. At first he'd been enraged, but days later he'd decided it was truth. And the truth felt as bracing as this water in the bucket before him. Had not the Lord himself been telling him the same thing? His path was going to bring him nothing but pain and boredom; it was an endless cycle of seeking the next conquest, the next daring thrill, each of which became progressively harder to find. He needed challenge, hope, something *beyond* him. And he'd found it when his eyes scanned the map of the West Indies framed in his father's old study.

Now he had only to make his inheritance produce something grand. Perhaps then all might look his way anew. He shaved his cheeks smooth, splashed tonic on his face, straightened and tucked his shirt into his waistband, then tied his neckcloth in a smart knot and pushed the ends inside his collar. He reached for his jacket and tugged it across his shoulders, thinking of Keturah and her sisters. Briefly, he considered the adorable Selah, who was the prettiest of the three by far, and certainly warm in her attentions. Or Verity with her fascinating way with animals. She was rather attractive too.

He stood with arms outstretched, bracing himself against the doorframe, thinking. About Selah. About Verity. He might have some success in courting either of them. But no, if he were honest with himself, it was Keturah who drew him most. With her smoldering golden eyes and deep intensity, even with her apparent wounding and defensiveness. But it was her surprising gumption to do this—to head off to the West Indies—that seemed to awaken his old, belatedly discovered attraction to Keturah. What sort of woman did such a thing?

"The sort of woman, Covington," he muttered to himself, releasing the doorjamb and straightening his coat, "who can never be yours."

Promptly at six, Keturah and her sisters were led to the captain's quarters in the aft portion of the ship by their servant Primus. As requested, he'd donned his perfect black-and-white livery, and Keturah appreciated that he'd taken the time to shine his buckled shoes. The women had dressed in evening gowns, and as they made their way down the cramped hallway, Ket worried her sisters would not pay attention and step on her own gown's short train, a lovely burnished copper color. So far, they had not, even as they struggled to walk a straight line as the ship moved to and fro over the waves.

Perhaps they truly were becoming women of care and consequence, she thought. Mother would be proud. At twenty-three and a widow, Keturah thought of herself as far their senior. But

Verity was already twenty-one, and even Selah had recently cel-
ebrated her eighteenth birthday. She knew she ought not think of
them as children any longer—after all, they'd bravely taken on the
decision to accompany her to Nevis, something that made many
adults quake at the thought—yet she resigned herself to always
thinking of them as her chicks to be kept in line. Perhaps it was
an older sister's lot, whether one was twenty-three or eighty-three.

*Would that I might reach the ripe age of eighty-three!* She had
known a few women who had reached their eighties, but no men.
Most she'd known in society died in their fifties or sixties, when
fevers swept through and winnowed out many in their declining
years. It was as if Death went through the orchard of the living,
cutting down those trees no longer producing fruit, or those too
young to yet do so. The old and young, always dying, as well as
some in between. *Mother, Father, oh how I miss you . . .*

She blinked back tears, realizing they'd reached Captain Mc-
Kintrick's quarters. He and his first mate, Mr. Burr, greeted them.
She curtsied and hurriedly moved to the chair at the captain's right
when the first mate slid it out from the table for her. Once seated,
they were introduced to the other guests already at the table. A Mr.
Munroe Smith, a long-nosed tutor on his way to Nevis to school
the Grimshaw children. He stood beside the balding, round-faced
Mr. Odell, a merchant who hoped to build three stores in Jamaica,
St. Christopher, and Antigua, all specializing in fine linens.

There were four other gentlemen present: a pair of young society
men about Verity's age, whom Keturah soon gathered intended to
do little more than gamble in every port, and two shipwrights on
their way to the shipyard of St. Christopher, one of whom wore
spectacles. The two gamblers engaged in a hearty conversation
with the shipwrights. Ket hoped the more honest, earnest pair
would keep from falling into the more wily pair's hands. Because
from the start, she sensed that Mr. Wood and Mr. Callender, the
gamblers, were up to no good. There were far too many days ahead
on their voyage with little to distract them.

Gray Covington took a seat at the far end. He was in a clean shirt and coat but wore no powdered wig like the first mate and most of the men did. A pang of regret ran through her. As much as his presence irritated her, she'd rather it be him across from her or by her side than the abrupt first mate, or the captain who was already paying far too much attention to Verity, quizzing her about Brutus's "last English prize."

A steward poured wine into their crystal goblets that were fashioned with uncommonly wide bottoms, perhaps to keep them more stable. When all were served, Captain McKintrick lifted his goblet and surveyed each of his guests. "May the sea be kind to us and the winds favor our journey."

Keturah smiled benignly, even as the captain hurriedly turned to raise his glass to her, then to Verity on his other side.

"Is your cabin to your liking, Lady Tomlinson?" asked the first mate in an obvious attempt to be pleasant.

"It is quite sufficient," she answered. "But I wonder if my sisters might have access to additional storage. With all their trunks, their quarters are quite cramped."

"I fear that shall not be possible," the first mate grumbled, setting down his goblet as a steward brought the first course, a savory stew, before them. "Every spare inch of this ship is full of wares bound for the Indies. Half of them with the Banning name on the crates, I expect."

*Half?* It was an outrageous claim. Keturah sucked in her breath and held it, refusing to bite. There was something familiar about the first mate's ways, something that reminded her of her late husband, Edward. He'd never been one to mince words or choose the polite way to word a response to her—at least after he'd married her and had her safely at home at Clymore Castle. *After I had no escape.*

She inhaled slowly, willing herself to maintain her poise. "Now, Mr. Burr, you and I are both aware that we paid our fair share for every square inch that our cargo has taken in your hold. Did we not?"

He looked over at her with hooded eyes as he hunched over his

bowl of stew, then shifted his attention to the meal before him. He
didn't have the temerity to respond. Instead, he waved her away
as if she were a pesky fly.

"Do be good enough, Mr. Burr, to answer the lady," Captain
McKintrick said, his voice tinged with warning. All semblance of
merriment in his eyes was now gone as he stared at the older man.

Conversation ceased as everyone glanced from the captain to
the mate and back again.

Mr. Burr wiped his mouth with a napkin, took a swig of wine,
and stared dolefully toward his superior. "Very well, Captain. I
shall answer the lady." The way he said *lady* made Keturah feel as
if he thought her the very antithesis of it. He turned toward her.
"Yes, Lady Tomlinson, you paid for your cargo space. We have
been fairly compensated for your cargo, cabins, as well as passage
for your slaves. I only hope that you do not think of this vessel as
some parlor at sea. We are a working ship, intent on getting to the
Indies as fast as possible, and getting on to America. Anything
that gets in the way of that causes me . . . agitation."

"Mr. Burr," said the captain, his voice rising abruptly, "a word.
*Outside.*"

"No, Captain," Keturah quickly said. "I appreciate your coming
to my aid, but this ship, as grand as she is, is hardly big enough to
contain such animosity. Shall we not clear the air here and now?
Shall we not all enjoy a more peaceful voyage if we do?"

The captain appeared caught between his rage and his desire
to please her. But when she stubbornly held her seat, he took his
seat again and gestured to her to continue. "Please."

"Mr. Burr," Keturah began, "why is it that you seem to resent
our presence upon the *Restoration*?"

He tucked his chin and studied her a moment. "May I speak
frankly, Lady Tomlinson?" he asked.

"Of course." Under the table she twisted her napkin, fighting
not to cower in the face of his uncouth, frosty manner, or in the
heat of attention of every other guest at the table.

"I believe that women of station have no business sailing to the Indies, certainly not without the protection of a man. I think it rather foolhardy. And I believe that you are a temptation to my crew. A dangerous distraction. There is a reason that women are considered ill luck on the high seas."

The captain leaned forward, fingers steepled before his nose, rage radiating from him. But he held his tongue, allowing her to reply.

Keturah swallowed hard again, wishing she could take a gulp of wine. "I see," she said carefully. How she handled this, she knew, would color the rest of their voyage. "You have a right to your opinion, and I shall take your warning under consideration. Believe me when I say that my sisters' well-being is my utmost concern, and we do not wish to be a distraction to your crew."

"A ship has no quarter to coddle the fairer sex," Mr. Burr pressed, his eyes slowly drifting down her neck and up again. "Now I must not only see to our demanding schedule, but make certain you and yours are not . . . molested."

The vague threat behind his words proved too much to bear. She rose so abruptly that her thick skirts knocked over her chair. Thankfully, Primus caught it and set it to rights behind her. Every man around the table rose too, the last being a reluctant Mr. Burr. But she was not done.

"Rest assured that traveling to the Indies was not a mad, girlish lark, but rather our only possible decision, Mr. Burr. I would ask that you give us the respect that such a dire choice deserves, rather than treat us in such a demeaning, churlish manner. It is beneath you, is it not?"

"'Tis most certain, lass," the captain said gravely. "And mark me, should Mr. Burr share your table, he shall not speak to ye in such a manner again."

Slowly, Mr. Burr bent and reached for his goblet, lifted it in silent toast, and took a deep drink of it. "I shall not address you in such a forthright manner again because I think we have come to an understanding," he said, gesturing her back to her seat as if dealing with a trifling girl.

She paused beside the captain. "I refuse to dine with a man who threatens me and mine. Either you have control of your crew or you do not. Do you?" This she directed to the captain.

"Rest assured, Lady Tomlinson, I do. Regardless of what Mr. Burr intimated."

"That is heartening to hear. Nevertheless, this has quite taxed me. I think it best my sisters and I take our meal in our rooms this evening."

Regret passed over the captain's face. "That is most understandable. Good evening, Lady Tomlinson."

"Captain," she said with a brief bob. "Gentlemen." She nodded to the rest, carefully avoiding looking at either Gray or Mr. Burr.

As she swept from the room, her sisters right behind her, she heard the young gamblers trying to cover laughter beneath the pretense of coughing and felt her cheeks blaze at the spectacle she'd been a part of creating.

But there was nothing for it. She simply could not stand to be in the presence of the first mate—nor how he raised the spectre of her late husband—for one moment longer.

# CHAPTER FIVE

"What a fine piece of female countenance," whispered Mr. Wood as the captain set to grumbling with the first mate, gesturing a beefy hand toward the door and gritting out words they could not quite hear. "What a fine, fine woman."

"What do you think her story is?" whispered his friend Mr. Callender. "Her sisters are prettier, but did you see the lady's eyes? They're positively bewitching. Catlike."

"And she clearly has claws to match," Wood said. "I take it that she is a widow. I wonder if she has a chest full of gold to match those eyes. If so, I think I—"

"*Gentlemen*," Gray interrupted in a choked voice, leaning forward as he struggled to keep his temper in line. He'd barely kept his tongue—and his seat—throughout Keturah's exchange with Burr. "The Misses Banning and Lady Tomlinson are friends of mine. I would ask that when you speak of or to them, you speak with respect." He eyed Wood for a long moment, then Callender.

Begrudgingly, he hurriedly shoveled in a spoonful of stew. Whilst he wished he could follow after the women, he knew it was not his place. Besides, he had no stores of extra food in his cabin. He'd paid his fare for the passage, including meals, and he was bound and determined to collect every morsel owed him.

"You are friends of theirs?" Callender dared to ask with unconcealed glee. "What a boon for you! Three women ready to hang on your every word and look to you as the protector the mate demands." He gestured down the table to where the captain and mate had taken their seats again, but ate now in silence.

Gray scowled at him. "Clearly, you do not yet know the Misses Banning and Lady Tomlinson."

"Come now, man," Wood scoffed, leaning back in his chair, wine goblet in hand. "The only unattached women of consequence on board this ship appear to be more than acquaintances. Do not tell us you do not intend to press your advantage."

*If only that I could,* Gray lamented. But in turn, he knew that it might be best if these men thought the girls were attached to him and under his protection, even in so slight a measure. He shrugged.

Wood bumped his companion on his shoulder. "What of a wager?" he whispered. "I bet that Covington here succeeds in persuading one of those girls to fall for him during the course of this voyage. What could be more romantic than sunset strolls aboard ship?"

Callender offered his hand. "I'll take that wager. But make it solely Lady Tomlinson. She's the key, and judging from Mr. Covington's eager defense of her, she's the one he wants. If he ends this journey with the lady as his intended, you win. But if he does not—and judging from that feisty female's manners, I think he shall not—then I win. What are the stakes?"

"Gentlemen," Gray said, intent on intervening. *Of all the rude, audacious suggestions.* "This is hardly suitable fodder for a wager."

"A pound?" said Wood, ignoring Gray.

"A pound? Make it three, you coward!" said Callender with a taunting smile.

"Done," said Wood, shaking his friend's hand. Gray didn't miss his new perusal of him and how a shadow stole over his face—he doubted his chances with Ket. *Belated wisdom as he calculated his odds,* Gray thought. Every man at this table could see Keturah was not a woman to swoon before any man.

Gray sighed and shoved another spoonful of stew in his mouth, seeing how this would progress. He'd be saddled with them both, Mr. Wood trying to maneuver him into intimacies with Keturah, and Mr. Callender endeavoring to keep him from it. Both scenarios were intolerable. But the wager was set. The two had shaken hands.

He pointed the two tines of his fork at one and then the other. "I shall allow your silly wager to stand. But I warn you both, keep out of my way, as well as Lady Tomlinson's. What transpires between the lady and me during the course of this journey is none of your concern, only the outcome. Agreed?"

Callender lifted his hands and eyebrows, the picture of innocence, and Wood followed suit. Gray sighed again, heavily. And then as the two gamblers attempted to engage the cantankerous captain, he finished his stew, his mind back on Keturah and that beautiful copper gown. It had made her eyes practically glow, and the way the gown had clung to her curves . . . well, he knew he wasn't the only man on this ship who might continue to think of her this night.

It pleased him to consider that Wood might even have a chance to collect on the wager. But he sided with Callender. Keturah Tomlinson clearly needed time. Time to heal from whatever abuses Lord Tomlinson had meted out to her, time for her heart to heal, and time for her to explore what it meant to be a West Indies planter. Gray had spent a year in preparation; Keturah had had a matter of two weeks. His darker side thought he ought to bet the young gamblers on her odds.

Gray knew she had the intellect and tenacity to run a plantation. But could she truly manage the enormous challenges that would face them both on their respective lands? Rude men like Mr. Burr would be the least of her concerns. He sliced into the roast lamb that was served to them next and considered the two halves of the meat. Half of him was glad that he would be but a mile away from her, able to come to her assistance if she needed it. But half of him dreaded it. Because if she chose not to reach out, he'd be forced to watch her falter and not intervene. He knew that society mixed on-island on a frequent basis. What would it be like to see her and her sisters struggle but not be invited in to help resolve it?

He bit into the lamb and forced himself to chew, tasting bitterness. If only he had been born the eldest.

If only he had not been forced to seek his own fortune.

If only Keturah hadn't been betrothed to another.

If only it had not taken seeing her wed another to confront his feelings for her.

If only it had not taken him so long to see the folly of his ways. To find a way forward that might garner some respect.

*If only . . . if only . . .*

He forced himself to swallow the meat and take another bite, chew, and wash it down with wine. Well, he was weary of if-onlys. God had made a way for him in the Indies; he could see it. And who had the Almighty placed on his very own ship? Lady Tomlinson.

Perhaps . . . just perhaps, Mr. Wood wasn't the only one betting on his chances with Keturah. The thought of it set his pulse to racing—that God himself might have a hand in his circumstances. *You're a fool, Covington,* he told himself, unwilling to get carried away with such fanciful thoughts. *Keturah is not at all ready to risk her heart again. Look at how defensive she'd become with Mr. Burr.* No, the only thing on her mind and in her heart was her land, her sisters, and saving their plantation and Hartwick.

*But perhaps I can be by her side if I assist her with those things,* he thought. Her plantation. Her sisters. Saving the family's old manse. If he could find a way to assist her in making Tabletop successful, protecting her sisters and saving Hartwick—all while he made a fortune from his own plantation—would she see him differently, in time? Could something new grow between them, something beyond the vestiges of a onetime friendship?

No, Callender would most assuredly win this bet. By the time they reached Nevis, all Gray could hope for was a measure of civility, perhaps friendship again, between them. But after a year on Nevis, or two?

He took another swig of wine and watched as the steward refilled his glass. The conversation had turned to Mr. Smith, the tutor, and the family he was to serve. But Gray heard little of it. His mind was entirely on Keturah and how she might look in a gown the color of Madeira red.

Keturah was still trembling by the time they got back to her cabin—both enraged and shocked at the first mate's behavior. Deep down, she had to admit she was a bit surprised at her own fortitude and how she'd spoken to the man. She was torn between shame and pride.

Never had she dared to hold her ground or speak to Edward in such a manner, at least not after that first tepid attempt. To do so now made her feel both stronger and wrought with fear, an odd twining that fairly twisted her heart in two.

Verity said, "Well done, Ket. Well done! That man has not been in polite society for some time, it seems. He does a discredit to his station. First mate! How does the captain tolerate such a man?" Her eyes shifted back and forth, as if silently arguing both sides. "Perhaps he's a fine sailor."

Selah was pacing and wringing her hands. "I am not so certain, Ket. Do you truly believe that was the best way to handle such discomfort? Could you not have laughed his poor behavior away and preserved the evening?"

"It was the *only* way," Keturah said firmly, pacing in the opposite direction in the tiny room, nearly colliding with her sister. "With men like that . . ." She lifted her hands and then cut outward, letting her motion say the rest.

She knew her words were heavy with history, with meaning. Both of her sisters sat down on her cot and watched her pace a while.

"Was it truly that awful, Ket?" Ver asked carefully after a long moment of silence. "With Edward? Was he somewhat like Mr. Burr, then?"

Keturah looked down into her sister's eyes, surprised that she had so easily made the connection. At first, her instinct was to deny it, but Verity's expression was soft, caring, making her momentarily weak. They had not known Edward. After the wedding, he had squired her away to his castle in the far north and never allowed Keturah's family to visit, nor her to go to them. "It was . . . far worse," she said.

Verity's jaw clenched a moment. "I'm so sorry, dearest."

"But surely he wasn't *so* awful. Not *every* day," Selah tried, her innocent heart in her eyes.

But it was time that Selah knew how awful men could be, so that she might not be lured into a trap like Ket had found herself.

"Every day," Keturah corrected, pacing again, three steps forward, a turn, then three steps back.

"But he was merely unkind in speech," Selah tried again. "Like Mr. Burr. Rude?"

Keturah drew up and rubbed her forehead, feeling an ache building there. "Edward was unkind to me in a *myriad* of ways." She sighed heavily and placed both hands on her hips.

Both girls stared up at her. Selah's mouth gaped open slightly. Verity's remained a grim line.

"But . . . Mother and Father thought it was a fine match," Selah tried again, her voice high and tight, and Ket's heart melted a bit. "Aunt Elda crowed about your union until she lay in her deathbed."

She didn't want her sister to think poorly of their parents, or even Aunt Elda—Cecil's mother—who had thought she'd done Keturah the ultimate favor. "They did indeed. And on the surface, it was true. Marrying the Earl of Avaline made me the envy of every girl we knew. Truth be told, I *was* proud of the fact that I was to become *Lady* Tomlinson. Me. The least pretty of the Banning sisters."

Both girls murmured their feeble complaints against her self-recrimination, but she ignored them.

"The reality of our marriage . . ." Keturah sank to the cot between them, feeling unaccountably burdened, beyond her wide, heavy skirts. "The reality of our marriage was a horror." She took a hand of both of her sisters and drew them into her lap. "So I hereby pledge to never encourage, entice, or force either of you to take a man's hand in marriage. I want you each to choose for yourselves. To know, to truly know and love the man you wish to marry."

They were silent a moment. "But he shall have to be approved by the other two sisters," Verity said firmly.

"Of course!" Keturah laughed, eager for a bit of levity. "Always. Let us pledge to always look out for one another and guard one another from a man's mistreatment, regardless of that man's situation or how much said man promises his 'love.'"

"I pledge it," Verity said, squeezing her hand.

"I pledge it," Selah repeated, still looking a little dazed.

Girls in their circle had had dalliances with beaus, secret affairs of the heart, but few had managed to meet those same men at the altar. The best marriages were between two where love happened to grow, over time. Mother and Father had enjoyed just such a relationship, and Ket had hoped for the same with Edward. She had *so* hoped for it. But try as she might to please him, it was never enough. And then it became ugly . . .

A knock at their door was a welcome interruption to her dark memories. Startled, she rose and went to it. "Who is there?"

"It is Primus, Lady Ket," the servant said.

She unbolted the door and opened it. The man held a tray heavy with food and entered, setting it on a trunk beside the cot that Keturah had made her makeshift table.

"Mr. Burr, Lady Ket," Primus said, uncovering one dish and then another, "he's wanting you to accept his apologies over the way he purported himself." Behind him, Grace appeared, carrying a pitcher and three pewter mugs.

Keturah smiled. "Now, Primus, did he truly apologize, or are you simply trying to mend fences again?" The slim, middle-aged black man was known for trying to make certain everyone in his household got along. Now he appeared to have transferred that need to the ship.

"Not in so many words, Lady Ket," he said, giving her a rueful smile. "Not in so many words. But he felt it, I could tell. As soon as you and the misses bustled out of that cabin, he regretted his actions."

"Or Captain McKintrick began to make him regret it," Verity said confidently, spooning some stew onto a plate for each of her sisters. "Actions *after* a quarrel prove the heart's intent, Mother always said. We'll see how Mr. Burr conducts himself tomorrow and in the weeks to come."

"Good enough," he said with a contented nod. "Good enough."

"Would you like some supper too, Primus?" Verity asked, spoon poised over the tureen in invitation.

"Yes, please, Primus," Ket joined in.

"No, Lady Ket, don't you fret over me. Grace and I will go to the others now. They're eating in the hold. I'll come back for that tray in an hour or so, if that's all you shall be needing."

"Good, Primus. Thank you," Ket said. "Grace, you shall return with him and attend us in an hour or so?"

"Yes, Lady Ket," the girl said.

Primus left through the door after Grace. Selah rose to lock it behind him.

The three ate in silence for a time. Keturah had lost her appetite but made herself put one bite in her mouth after the other. She knew she'd be hungry in a few hours. And she had heard enough stories from her father to know that the first few meals aboard a ship were among the finest one would get for weeks. At some point they'd likely be eating hardtack and drinking grog—the sailors' preferred form of watered wine—day and night. Until that day she was determined to obtain every morsel of decent food that was fairly theirs.

She shoved another bite in her mouth, smiling as she chewed and thought of Mr. Burr. Despite what he intended, the sisters Banning were here to thrive. Thrive. Not wither or cower away.

*Thrive.*

The thought of it made every bland bite taste delectable.

Gray walked down to his cabin after supper, pausing briefly beside the Banning sisters' cabin. He could hear them inside, and their chatter—and even laughter—heartened him. He lifted a hand to knock, then dropped it, shaking his head. She had made no effort at all to bridge the divide between them. He doubted she would welcome him now. It was not his place to intervene or to check on them, even after what he had witnessed in the captain's dining room.

With a sigh, he turned and walked the rest of the way to his cabin, unlocking the door. Philip was inside and hurriedly rose at the sight of him. "Master Gray," he said with a nod. He moved to reach for Gray's coat, but Gray waved him back to his cot.

"Sit, sit, my friend," he said, shrugging out of his coat. "Please, if we are to be bunkmates, we cannot have you rising every time I enter the room. Put aside that formality for the duration of our voyage, at the very least. And rest assured, I can manage my own wardrobe."

"As you wish," said the older man hesitantly, slowly taking a seat.

Gray noticed his furrowed brow and confused eyes. After twenty years of service, old habits like this would be hard to break. But he suspected that even when they reached Nevis, he'd need Philip to be more partner than servant. The thought of it had even infiltrated his dreams. "Philip," he said, hanging his coat on a peg, "once we are on-island, I do not expect you to serve me as you did in England. There might be a time and place for you to resume your role as my valet. But the reason I invited you to attend me was that you, out of all my family's servants, have always been most dear to me."

He could feel the heat of a blush rising on his cheeks at such a frank declaration. But Philip needed to know this. "What I mean," he hurried on, untying his neckcloth and placing it over the peg too, "is that I needed a *friend* with me on this journey, Philip. A dependable man I could count on. A friend, a brother really, more than servant." He rubbed the back of his neck, aware that he probably wasn't being quite clear. "We shall encounter circumstances ahead when I shall need your frank opinion, not the deference of servant to master. I shall need a brother's counsel when I have none."

"I see," Philip said, stroking his chin thoughtfully between finger and thumb. "I am more honored than ever, then, to be invited along on your grand adventure."

"No, 'tis my honor that you accepted, old friend. I know that it would have been a far safer road to remain on my brother's estate."

"Safer," the older man soulfully acknowledged, dropping his hand, "and yet rather mundane. Truthfully, ever since your father died, I found myself rather anxious for a new challenge. All your talk over the past year of Nevis and sugar had me thinking that I would not mind a glimpse of the 'Queen of the Caribbees' myself. When you asked, I confess I was quite delighted."

Gray smiled and pulled his shirt off, then sat down to unlace his boots. "You never doubted? I thought I sensed a reasonable degree of hesitation."

Philip pulled his head toward one shoulder and then the other, in that old familiar gesture that meant he was relaxing and considering his response. Gray had seen him do it a hundred times in his father's chambers. "I was only a bit befuddled, at first," Philip said. "There you were, asking me to accompany you. Until that very moment, I had not realized how dearly I wished to do so. It surprised me. And after a good number of years in your father's company, I knew well what you proposed we *risk*, going to the West Indies."

"The stakes, you mean," Gray said, pulling at his boot. When it refused to budge, Philip motioned for him to let him assist. He relented and let the older man pry it from his foot, then the other one too.

"Yes," Philip said. "All my life, the only time my feet left English soil was when I accompanied your father. To France. And even then I was quite content to return home."

"And Nevis is much farther away than France."

Philip smiled and nodded. "'Tis a far piece from home, indeed. But I assure you, I am most delighted with this venture already. To be aboard a ship with no land in sight is—" he looked to the side of their tiny cabin, as if he could see through to the waves, and shook his head in wonder—"exhilarating," he finished. "If my father could see me now, he would be proud, just as I know Master Covington would have been proud of you."

"You believe so?" Gray asked, wincing inwardly at the weak need present in his voice. And yet he couldn't help it. All his life he'd hungered for his father's approval, but it seemed the old man had been blinded by the bright sun that was his brother. In every sector, Gray had been compared to Samuel and routinely deemed wanting.

"I do," Philip said gravely. "He appreciated men who were willing to do what it took to improve their station. I oft heard him speak of it."

"Is that what I'm doing?" Gray asked, turning to wearily lie down on his cot. Every muscle in his back and arms and thighs ached after loading the crates and trunks onto the *Restoration*.

"I would say so," Philip said. Now that Gray was settled, he began to undress himself.

"I hope that we can make my plantation a success," Gray said. "To be able to write to Samuel and tell him of it . . ." He closed his eyes in reverent hope and took a deep breath.

"That would be most satisfactory," Philip said. "Perhaps I might begin reading some of the horticulture books you brought along? When you are not in need of my service, of course."

"That is a grand idea," Gray said. "It would be most gratifying to be able to discuss my plans with another." He'd been hungering for the opportunity to do so with Keturah, to begin to subtly prepare her for what was ahead and ply her clever mind for her own ideas, given her talent with gardening. But she clearly wasn't interested in anything more than exchanging the briefest of pleasantries.

But the voyage would last six weeks or more. Perhaps, in time, he'd find a way to rekindle their friendship, to demonstrate how he'd changed. Then he'd be able to honor his promise to Cecil to look after them. He wanted her to succeed with Tabletop, to thumb her nose at Edward Tomlinson's memory, even if she could not do so in person. But would it be possible? For a woman on her own, even with the support of her loving sisters?

Gray knew that the Banning fortune had been in some decline for years. When word came to his brother that Richard Banning was selling a portion of his Rivenshire estate, a portion of land that he'd allowed to be sharecropped for years, they'd gathered it was grim indeed. There'd been a hurricane and some sort of blight in Nevis, creating several years of hardship for the island's planters. But Banning had been renowned for his prowess at managing the fickle sugar crops, for over a decade even succeeding in bringing in the best yield on the island.

"Some say he might be going mad," Samuel had told him, looking over the letter from Banning, asking about interest in outright purchase or to inquire among their contemporaries, if they had none. "Or that he dips his cup too often in the rum."

Gray had frowned at that. He'd never known Banning to be a drunkard or have a hint of madness about him.

"They say he's abandoned his crops for two years," Sam went on, casually setting the letter aside. "Intent on terracing the ground or whatnot." He waved his hand in dismissal, but Gray moved to the corner of the desk and picked it up, saw the staggering sum Banning requested for the rolling hills to their east. Clearly, the elder Banning still believed in what the soil of Nevis could produce more than what he could grow in England. That was when the idea had first struck.

"What if I were to claim my annual stipend for the next twenty years?" he'd muttered before the idea was fully formulated in his mind. "Take that sum and buy Teller's Landing, making it my own. Go and see if I can match old Banning's yield of sugar."

His brother was looking at another letter and slowly dragged his eyes to meet Gray's. "Hmm? What?"

By that time, Gray's excitement was starting to build. He rounded the desk and began pacing back and forth. "What if I took my annual stipend now, in one lump sum? And sail to Nevis to create my own fortune?"

Sam had scoffed, leaning back in his chair and looking at him as if he were mad. "Did you not hear what I said?" he asked, picking up Banning's letter. "The planters—even Banning—are struggling. Few men have made a fortune in Nevis in recent years. Perhaps in our grandfather's day, and his own grandfather's before him, but now? Everyone is quite aware that sugar plantations are faring better in Hispaniola or Saint Christopher than in Nevis." He shook his head. "No, the soil has been tapped out. Nevis's heyday is long over."

"And yet Richard Banning sticks to it." Gray gestured to the letter. "If he thought there was better opportunity there, would he not be selling Tabletop instead of his land here?"

"Banning is a stubborn fool. A dreamer. A gambler."

"As am I. But perhaps that's what it takes to be a successful planter."

Sam leaned forward again and tapped his steepled fingers against his chin. "You are serious."

"I am," Gray said.

His brother blinked slowly, contemplating. "And so you are saying that if I grant you this sum, you shall travel to Nevis to become a gentleman planter?"

Gray nodded slowly. He knew that Sam would find it a relief to see him engaged in anything remotely respectable, rather than simply enjoying society as he'd been doing for years. And it would take him far away. Given that the brothers' relationship was only civil . . . that would be a boon too. For them both.

Sam dropped his hands and began drumming his fingers on the desk, then stopped. "What is to keep you from coming back to me for additional sums when your funds run dry? When *you* face the hurricane? The blight?"

"No matter what happens, I shall not return to you for additional sums."

"Even if you encounter the worst?" Sam pressed.

"Even if I encounter the worst," Gray had pledged.

Now Gray lay on his cot listening to the waves wash by the ship in a soothing lullaby, even as his pledge to Sam rattled in his mind.

As Philip blew out the candle in the lampstand and wished him a pleasant night's sleep, Gray began to pray that he'd not made the biggest mistake of his life. That the worst would *not* happen.

For him . . . or Keturah.

# Chapter Six

Six days later, Keturah and her sisters were taking their afternoon walk around the perimeter of the ship while Brutus stretched his wings high above—when they came across Philip, Gray's longtime servant. He was sitting on a massive coil of rope, intently reading.

"Why, Philip," Selah said, "what has you so captivated?"

The older man looked up at them and quickly rose, giving them a slight bow. "I beg your pardon, ladies. I confess I *was* rather captivated." He lifted the cover so they could see the title: *Horticulture of the West Indies*.

Keturah cocked her head and extended a hand. "May I peruse it?"

"Indeed," the man said, handing it to her. "Master Gray recommended I read it so that I might be better prepared to assist him."

Keturah nodded and scanned the first page. She'd seen precious little of "Master Gray" in this first week of their voyage, and that was fine by her. Perhaps he was taking his own constitutional at other hours than they, not confined as they were by the captain's request that they be safely in their quarters by sunset. After only a few sentences, she was intrigued. "Might you ask Gray if I might borrow this volume when you are finished?"

"Take it now," the man said. "I shall complete my reading after you are done."

"Oh, I couldn't," she began.

"Please, I insist," he said, nodding earnestly.

With one look into his brown eyes, she knew it would be fruitless to protest further. "You are most kind, Philip."

He gave her a wry grin. "It is easy to be kind when I know Master Gray has ten other volumes in our cabin he would like me to read."

*Ten others?* Keturah frowned. She'd only been able to secure one relevant volume before they departed. In their haste to embark upon the *Restoration*, there'd been no more time. It was her hope that her father's daily journal—which she would presumably find at Tabletop—would be her best way to learn what had worked on the plantation, as well as what had not.

"Master Gray has become quite the scholar," Verity said, casting a curious glance in Keturah's direction. Ket ignored it.

"Why, yes, he's been studying the ways of planters for more than a year now. As soon as he'd learned he was to travel to Nevis, he became most dedicated to his preparations."

Keturah blinked. "More than a year, you say?"

"Yes," Philip said, tapping his chin as if counting backward. "'Twas about that time more than a year ago that he and his brother made arrangements for him to purchase the plantation."

Keturah swallowed hard. Taking such time to prepare made her feel foolish in comparison. "Why did Master Gray not set off for Nevis at once?" she asked.

"He knew this was a tremendous gamble," Philip said, puffing up like a proud father. "So for months he interviewed many absentee planters, gleaning what he could from them. Then he went to university to attend two classes in horticulture of the tropics. That is where he found his fine books that he is lending me . . . and now you, Lady Keturah." Again, he nodded in deference.

"Yes. Well . . ." *University.* She had heard he'd been at Oxford for a time. Two friends who lived in Rivenshire told her they'd met him at soirees and balls. She'd assumed he was there to find fresh female conquests rather than something more. Shame over her assumptions washed through her. "It is quite commendable, what he has done in preparation," she went on, eying the cover of the book again. "I confess, it makes me feel rather ill prepared myself."

"Ah, but you have the benefit of a lengthy voyage yet ahead," Philip said with a kind smile. "You and I shall both be able to read through the master's volumes in that time."

"That would be wonderful," Keturah said.

"Consider it done," Philip said. "As soon as I complete my reading, I shall pass the next to you. Now, ladies, I must look in on Master Gray. Enjoy your afternoon."

"You as well, Philip," Keturah said.

---

Philip opened the cabin door and stood there a moment, hands behind his back. Gray looked up at him, brows knitting in consternation. He'd been sketching atop a portable lap desk. "Philip? What is it?"

The man entered the cabin, closed the door and leaned against it, arms folded. "Is there a reason, Master Gray, that you sent me abovedecks with that book today? The one I'd nearly completed?"

Gray's eyes went to his empty hands, and a small smile tugged at the corners of his lips. "Did you slip? Did it fly into the sea?"

"I suspect you know exactly what became of the volume," Philip said, "which is why you shooed me out of this cabin promptly at two."

"Because?" Gray said, cocking one brow.

"Because the Misses Banning and Lady Tomlinson take their afternoon constitutional promptly at quarter past two."

"They do?" Gray attempted to be the picture of innocence, but let loose a sly smile even as he went on. "What a happy coincidence. Did you greet them for me?"

"In so many words," Philip said, sitting down on his cot, still assessing Gray. This far into their voyage, much of their long-standing formality was slowly eroding away into comfortable familiarity, and that was fine by Gray.

"May I ask why you did not give the book to Lady Tomlinson yourself?" the man asked.

"Because Lady Tomlinson wants nothing at all from me," he said with a sigh. "Or so she believes." He bent to dip his pen in the inkwell and quickly sketched three more lines on his plans for a new millwork.

"Not even the loan of a book?"

"Not from me," Gray said. He took a compass from a pile of drafting tools on the cot and made an arc to indicate where the edge of the kiln would be, even as it made him think of the circle of the train of Keturah's bronze gown dragging behind her.

"I see. But have you two not been friends since childhood? It seems to me that when I arrived at your father's estate, you were fairly inseparable."

Gray stopped and looked up at him. "We were. But once we came of age . . . that all faded. And her marriage to Lord Tomlinson was less than ideal, souring her to anything that feels like a man's attempt to guide her again."

"I see," Philip said soberly.

"I complicated matters when I went to call upon her at Hartwick, right before we departed. A servant allowed me in and then was called away, so I followed the sound of voices to the parlor. She and her cousin Cecil were in an argument."

"You eavesdropped?" Philip's graying brows lifted in surprise.

"Only for a moment. But long enough to know that Cecil desperately wanted her to allow him to go in her stead—or at the very least, allow a man to accompany her. I foolishly chose that moment to enter, volunteering to do as Cecil wished, to serve as guardian."

It was Philip's turn to sigh. "And the lady did not take it well."

"No, she did not." He set aside the lap desk and ran his fingers through his hair. "Now she sees me as yet another meddling man in her life. Someone who wishes to control her rather than merely come to her aid in any manner necessary. I do not believe one person, aside from her sisters, agreed with her plan to sail to Nevis. Truth be told, I doubt it myself. And there we shall be neighbors."

"Better you than a thousand other men," Philip grumbled, looking troubled.

"But there is much for her to learn. Do you think she might like to read other volumes from my library?" Gray asked.

"Oh yes, we already agreed to such an arrangement. As soon as I finish one book, I shall pass it along to her."

"Excellent, excellent," Gray said, his smile returning. His plan was coming along better than he'd hoped. If she indeed read the ten books he'd brought along with him, she'd have at least half the information he'd learned over the last year. "I'll warn you, she's an astute learner and a fast reader," he said to Philip.

"Then I best light a candle and resume my reading without delay," his friend said with a wink.

It was Selah and Verity who convinced Keturah to relent and return to the captain's dinner table, a week after their grim exchange with the first mate. Mr. Burr had made a brief attempt of apology the day after it happened—clearly only doing so to honor his captain's command. After that, he seemed intent on ignoring them. So when Captain McKintrick approached and invited them to supper that night, Keturah thought she was ready.

"You are most kind, Captain," she said, watching as the big man's eyes drifted to Verity behind her. "Might I ask another favor of you?"

"Anything, m'lady," he said.

"After supper, might you escort us about the deck? I know you wish for us to remain confined to our quarters come sundown, but with proper escort, might we not be allowed to watch the sunset? See the sea reflecting the stars?"

Keturah resolutely waited. She knew Captain McKintrick had felt their refusal to return to his table as a sort of chastisement. He was eager to make amends. And to be free of their cabins fairly any time they wished would be a relief. Their quarters were tiny, and a week into their voyage, all three of them were already suffering from taut nerves. She'd imagined watching the sun descend into the sea, leaving the sky stained with the remnants of its path, giving gradual sway to a tapestry of stars. She kept that image fixed in her mind as she awaited the captain's response. Apparently, it would require some bargaining.

What did he fear? Surely the crew would be as courteous to them at night as they were during the day.

"I do not wish to confine ye lasses," McKintrick finally said, his ruddy cheeks becoming a bit more red as Verity stepped up beside her sister. "'Tis only that the crew is allowed an extra mug of grog after supper, and they tend to be a tad more rowdy come sunset. I dinna wish for any of them to offend any of ye."

"What if we employ the aid of two of our male servants to accompany us? That is, if you are not available."

That seemed to ease his mind a bit, so Keturah pressed further. "Shortly before we embarked, I read in the *Times* that daily walks are most edifying for a woman's state of mind as well as for her physique. Would it not be a credit to you and your ship if we arrived in Nevis in finer health than when we departed?"

"Oh, we'd be ever so grateful, Captain," Verity put in.

"And we'd tell everyone we meet of your kindness," Selah added, joining them.

Blushing even more furiously than before, he said, "Very well. But your slaves will not be enough, I fear." He paused and shook his head. "Some of my crew dinna respect any but a white man as your protector. Enlist Mr. Covington and his man Philip, or the tutor Smith. Even Wood and Callender, if ye can stomach their company."

Keturah smiled at that, even as the inference made her angry. They were safer in the gamblers' company than on their own? But if this was what the captain required to remove the only measure of confinement they faced . . . "They are rather like rowdy boys more than gentlemen, are they not?"

"True," he said with a wink.

"We shall do as you say. After sundown, if we should wish for a stroll, we shall request the aid of our fellow passengers. Now, thank you kindly for the dinner invitation, Captain, and your attention to our needs," she added, pausing in the doorframe. "We must prepare to attend you and your other guests this evening. See you shortly?"

He stood there looking at her as if he already regretted the decision. Before he could change his mind, Keturah gave him a sweet smile, tucked her head, and quietly closed the door.

Turning to her sisters, the three of them shared excited glances, holding their collective breath until they heard the telltale squeak of a board outside the door, indicating the captain had departed.

"You did it!" Verity said, squeezing her hand and sinking gratefully onto the cot. "Tonight we can finally be out."

"We shall sleep so deeply after an evening stroll," Selah added dreamily, flopping down onto her bed and putting her wrist across her forehead.

"I think we three must take time to fix our hair and wear our finest tonight to celebrate," Keturah said, clapping her hands together. "Make the captain and his crew glad that we have left the confines of our cabins and welcome our company past sundown. Do you not agree?"

"Oh yes!" Verity said. Then she narrowed her eyes at her sister. "Or is it for Mr. Covington that you wish to dress in your finest?"

"Verity!" Keturah chastised with a frown. "You know better than that."

"Why ever not? Did not learning of his dedication to his studies earn him some respect in your mind?"

Keturah shook her head and moved toward the door again. "I do not wish to discuss it."

"You do not wish to discuss it because you think you might have judged him unfairly."

"Sissy . . ." Selah whined, not wishing for an argument to brew.

But Verity stared solemnly at Keturah when Ket glanced back at her. Keturah licked her lips and drew in a deep breath. "It seems I may have been judging Gray by his past rather than his present. Now, might you leave it at that?"

Verity gave her a barely concealed smug smile and single nod.

"Shall I call for Grace to attend us? Help with our hair and our dresses?"

Keturah pulled a pocket watch from her waistband. "No need to call for her. She should be by to check on us at any moment. I think I shall lie down for a bit before we begin our ministrations. See you soon, sisters." She didn't spare them another glance or opportunity to speak. It was enough—Ver's challenge, her admission.

As she unlocked her cabin door and slipped inside, then saw the borrowed book on her cot, she felt a pang of regret. And fear. Only partway through the volume, she was well aware of how much she had yet to learn.

She slumped to her cot and let her head sink into her hands, closing her eyes and thinking of handsome, quick-witted Gray Covington. One of her oldest friends. She knew Verity pressed because she knew that, as a girl, Ket had dreamed of something more with Gray. But once they were of age, he'd never had eyes for her. Always it was the other girls in the room, those prettier, more petite and coquettish. He'd made her feel more like an old fishing mate than a romantic interest. Until . . .

She lifted her head and stared at the dancing flame of the lamp hanging in the corner of her cabin. The gentle sway of it, rocked by the massive waves rolling beneath the ship, reminded her of the men and women dancing at that ball in London, when she was the secretly bruised bride of the Earl of Avaline and she'd come face-to-face with her old friend.

He'd been so frightfully handsome, setting her heart to pattering when she spotted him enter the room. And when he approached her, took both hands in his, and brought them to his lips? Eyes shining as if she were the best thing he'd seen in months? With question after question, earnestly wanting to know much of her new life?

It had been all she could do not to pull him away to the gardens, confess to him what a nightmare her marriage was, and beg him to secretly escort her back to Hartwick Manor under cover of darkness. In that moment, she had fancied him her rescuer, her longed-for prince, at last awakened from his slumber to discover he was truly in love with her, there to make all that had gone so wrong, right again.

But that had not been his intent, of course. He was a friend, nothing more. Merely interested in renewing their acquaintance, perhaps calling upon her at Clymore Castle, curious where her advantageous match had landed her. Something to chat about with others at future soirees. *Have you heard what has become of our dear Keturah?*

So she had lifted her chin, answered his queries with the briefest of responses, politely asking him some of her own. It was there that she learned he intended to go to Oxford. But in her rush to cover her embarrassment, she had not asked about his goals, only assumed it was to cavort among a new social sector. *How rash I was then . . .*

Keturah sighed heavily, remembering that he'd requested she join him on the dance floor. How she'd glanced Edward's way, saw he was talking and laughing with two other gentlemen, and agreed, knowing with a sick feeling in her gut that it was a mistake.

Then Gray had placed a hand on her back to lead her to the floor, and the gesture made her suck in a pained breath.

"Keturah, what is it?" he asked, those dark blue eyes searching hers in concern as he turned toward her. "Are you hurt?"

"'Tis nothing," she'd insisted, urging him with a press of her fingertips to lead her into the allemande dance that everyone else had begun. "I in my clumsiness managed to hit my back on a table corner yesterday," she said quietly, just over the strings of the musicians.

"I see," he said. And yet when she chanced another glance to his face, she felt as if he had seen far more than she intended.

They finished the dance in silence, each of them taking the steps of the dance—Keturah in rote fashion, too aware of his inquisitive gaze upon her, too aware of the intimacies of the allemande—the stroke of her hair, his hand brushing her lower back, searching for hers as they turned . . . intimacies that, if Edward were watching, would infuriate him. Even though every other couple on the floor was doing the same. At the end, Gray had bowed, she'd curtsied, then blanched at the sight of Edward hovering behind him, awaiting the next dance.

Gray had clearly seen her pale and followed her gaze to her husband. But he had no recourse—he could do nothing but nod in deference and leave them.

And when Edward placed his hand on her back for the next dance, she almost cried out. It was no accident that he dug his fingers into the area he well knew was bruised from hip to rib, because it was where he had kicked her, after he'd thrown her to the floor of their bedroom. Silently, he reminded her that it could well happen again, if she displeased him.

And that night after he'd found Keturah dancing with Gray—

A quick knock sounded at her door, startling Keturah out of her reverie. She shook her head, trying to drive away the foul memory. Grace unlaced her day dress and helped her into a royal blue gown, then did her hair, chattering on about how the "boys" had been allowed to climb all the way to the crow's nest today, more as a game of chance for the sailors and two gentlemen passengers who bet on three of them than as a favor to Cuffee, Edwin, and Absalom. All the while, Keturah fought to keep her mind and heart in the present rather than in the past.

*It is over*, she told herself.

*Edward is dead.*

*You are free.*

*You are healing. You have a vision of a different future now. Hope. Hold that in your heart. Drive away those old, bad memories.*

*It is over.*

*Over.*

*Over.*

*Edward and England are behind you.*

*And no man will ever hurt you again.*

# CHAPTER SEVEN

Grace unpinned her hair, ran an ivory comb through it, and then rapidly pinned it again in a bigger, more dramatic fashion. "Lady Ket," she said, placing dark hands on her shoulders, "are you feeling quite right?"

"Me?" Keturah stirred out of her reverie for the tenth time. "Oh yes. Only a mite weary, I suspect."

"You need a proper supper with the captain to revive you," said her kindly maid.

"Let us hope we fare better than last week."

"Ahh, you most surely will. The way I've heard tell of it, the captain was most sorry for the way the mate mistreated you."

Keturah smiled and rose, liking the swish of crinoline and silk, letting her skirt settle about her. Grace clasped her favorite pearl necklace about her neck, then stepped back. "Lady Ket, you get prettier and prettier. I think this voyage is doing you good, giving you that pink to your cheeks while the rest of us remain a fair shade of green." She giggled, knowing any such color would be hard to decipher on her dark skin. "Well, you know what I mean."

"I do," Ket said, reaching out to take her hand. "Forgive me, Grace. Have many of you been suffering?"

"Ah, well, me only once or twice a day. But Gideon? That man can't seem to get out of his hammock other than to turn and retch."

"How awful." Keturah realized she hadn't seen the man all week. She felt like a poor mistress indeed for not noticing his absence. And yet with their relative confinement and simple daily itinerary, there had been little use for anyone other than Grace and Primus to attend them. "Do you suppose he shall spend the entire voyage so ill?"

"Some of the sailors say that if a body doesn't adjust to the sea in the first few days, that body isn't likely to do so. But do not fret over him, Lady Ket. We'll see to him. There's little else for us to do aboard this ship. Once we get to the islands, Gideon will make a quick recovery. You shall see."

"If you're certain . . ." Keturah said, allowing her to open the door. "But you will fetch me if he takes a turn for the worse?"

"Of course, Lady Ket," said the maid, fairly shooing her along.

Her sisters' door opened then too, and the two of them joined Keturah in the passageway.

---

Gray had heard the second mate mention that the Ladies Banning were to join the gentlemen again at supper, and the first mate was sure to be on his best behavior. Pleased with the promise that feminine company would elevate the demeanor of their nightly affair, he allowed Philip to unpack a fresh set of clothes—breeches, shirt, neckcloth, and coat. They'd only packed six sets of clothing for him in the trunk that resided in their room, carefully allotting one change per week.

It was with some relief that he retired the sweat-stained set from the previous week, bathed as well as he could, and dressed. He felt like a new man. But as he studied his reflection in the tiny black-flecked mirror that hung on the cabin wall and tied his neckcloth, he knew his stomach clenched with anticipation for one reason: to be near Keturah.

All week he'd studiously avoided her. When he spotted the sisters abovedecks, he sequestered himself below. When they were in their shared passageway, he hid around the corner or in his cabin until he could walk the same route alone. Now, as he entered the captain's dining room, he was intensely curious if Keturah had even noticed his absence.

Mr. Wood and Mr. Callender greeted him, eagerly pumping his hand as if they hadn't seen him just that morn. It did not escape him that just as the ladies entered, Wood edged over to his right, pushing him toward the empty seat on his left, opposite the two empty chairs across the table—the three seats the women would inevitably take. The man seemed to be seizing the opportunity to try to bring Gray and Keturah together.

While it grated on Gray—he'd much rather have the chair between them—it was too late to do anything about it. And he didn't object to the opportunity so much that he would allow Callender to slide between them.

Mr. Burr ended the shenanigans. The first mate pulled out a chair in the center of the table and looked expectantly to Ket. Then he gestured to the two others across from hers for her sisters. Callender and Wood were there to help them bring their chairs forward, and then all the rest took their seats.

Keturah said little more than his name in greeting, nor throughout the dinner, which overall came off far more splendidly than the first. The first mate was rather subdued, as if keeping himself in check, and the captain enthralled the women with tales of travel along the coast of Spain and the Barbary Coast, more than once with a privateer on the chase. The food was bland, but there was plenty of it. As usual, Gray ate heartily, trying to ignore how Keturah picked at her own plate. Was she ill? Suffering from the motion of the waves, perhaps?

But he could not ask her. He would not. No, it was up to her to reach out to him. He did not want her to see him as pressing at all. Even as he burned with questions . . . Had she begun reading *Horticulture of the West Indies*? What did she think about the author's assertion that there was a way to treat sugar blight with lime? Had she not had her own garden successes at Hartwick, even when her neighbors had struggled? How was it that she drove back the algae that one wet summer that swallowed every one of her neighbors' gardens?

Callender was talking to Verity about Brutus, her falcon, and gently inquired if the bird cared to fly at night.

"Brutus adores flying at every opportunity," Verity said. "If he was half as good at fishing as he is at ratting, I'd never get him back aboard—other than to eat."

"Well, if your bonny bird continues to kill the rats, I might reward him with sardines," the captain said. "Others swear by cats or terriers aboard ship for the task, but Mr. Burr tells me your bird has captured three already."

"Four," Verity said proudly, cocking a brow.

The captain smiled and lifted his hands in pleasure.

"Shall I bring him out this evening on our stroll so you can observe?" Verity asked.

"Aye, lass. I'd enjoy that." The man's eyes lingered on Verity, and Keturah shifted in her seat as if in agitation.

*Well, this was something.* The captain himself intended to escort them this very night?

"Perhaps Mr. Covington would care to join us," the captain said. "He's as good at pointing out constellations as Burr here. And Mr. Smith? Perhaps some astronomy would be good for ye as well, as a future tutor."

Gray and Keturah stiffened together. Gray recovered himself first. "It would be my sincere pleasure," he said, "if Lady Tomlinson finds the prospect agreeable."

"I thank you, Mr. Covington, for the offer," she said, wiping her pretty lips with a napkin in the most distracting manner, "but I think I shall retire early this evening."

Gray's eyes jerked up to meet hers—realizing he was staring at her mouth in the most ungentlemanly way—even as Selah let out a pouty breath. "Ket!" she whispered furiously. "Did we not just agree to a turn around the deck? Under the stars? You said—"

"*Selah,*" Keturah hissed, giving her little sister an icy glare. A blush of anger rose at her neck. "Remember your *place.*"

"Please," Gray said quietly to her so only she could hear. "Do not let the prospect of my company keep you away or exclude your sisters from their evening stroll. I'm certain any of these other fine gentlemen would be happy to take my place."

"No, Gray. 'Tis not that," she protested, but her heart clearly wasn't in it. He knew her well enough to know that the prospect of walking the decks at any given hour would be her heart's desire. Only one thing could be keeping her back when the opportunity had finally presented itself.

"Is it not?" he asked, daring to stare back into her golden eyes a moment too long. "No matter." He lifted his chin and looked down the table. "Might there be another who could escort Lady Tomlinson this evening? I fear I must see to my studies."

A chorus of offers arose, and arrangements were made for the middle-aged merchant Odell and also Smith to join as escorts. Gray hastily said his good-nights, well aware that Callender was giving Wood a victorious smile.

He left the dining room, after forcing himself to give his thanks to the captain for supper with the utmost civility, wondering if it was his imagination or if Keturah's catlike eyes truly followed him all the way to the door. No, surely not. Clearly, the woman still wished to steer clear of him. He would go to the deck as he did each eve, to play. It was the thing he'd come to anticipate most each long day aboard the ship. But 'twould be *after* the sisters were safely returned to their quarters.

---

Keturah took a long, deep breath as Gray exited the cramped dining room, studiously avoiding her sisters' curious gazes. She knew she'd offended her old friend for perhaps the hundredth time. And whilst she dearly wished to cease doing such harm, she found it a relief—his exit. His presence . . . agitated her. She had been far too aware of his leg, just inches from her own below the table. Of his hand settling his napkin across his lap, his fingers perilously close to her hip. Even his elbow, for pity's sake, so close to her own as he cut his dry roast beef when she brought her fork to her mouth.

*What on earth has me in such a state?* she wondered. She was entirely too aware of everything about Gray. Ever since he'd come to see her at Hartwick Manor. And while she wanted to mend fences, that was all she wanted. Because the last thing she needed was a man captivating her thoughts. All through dinner she could barely keep track of the conversation because she'd been distracted by the smell of his fresh linen shirt, even the leather of his belt. It was all far too . . . intimate.

She'd been aware of Edward like that. But it had been different. She had been alert to every nuance of his movements—a stiffening shoulder, a clenched jaw, the rising of that vein at his temple—but as warning. Like a rabbit in her garden, lying low with its ears tucked, waiting, waiting, waiting for an attacker to either pass or give chase. She forced a smile and accepted Mr. Odell's round hand, assisting her to her feet. She asked him how he enjoyed his meal even as her thoughts inevitably returned to Gray.

They made their way down a passage and out onto the deck, where Keturah took a deep breath of the crisp damp air, relishing how the cool washed over her hot skin. She asked another question of Mr. Odell—about what he intended to do when he reached Nevis—and they began their stroll around the deck, following the captain and Verity, with Selah and Mr. Smith behind them. As Mr. Odell prattled on about his intention to make Nevis but a stop on his way to other islands, and how he wished to open a linen shop in each, Keturah returned to her thoughts about Gray and how she reacted—no, *responded*—to him.

That was it. It was more a response than a reaction. It wasn't at all like how it had been with Edward. He'd give her a hint of what was to come, and she would flee or brace. What she felt around Gray was more like some sort of curious, visceral pull and push. Not so immediate—deeper. She looked to the dark sea, spreading for so many miles, and so many fathoms below. Yes, it was akin to something more like the tides. Something welling from within, responding to the moon's silent call.

As a small girl she had fancied herself in love with Gray Covington. But when they came of age and he looked at every girl but her, she had convinced herself it was nothing but a childish fancy, not love. And now . . . was she truly battling that old attraction? Could a handsome man so easily unravel her carefully knit blanket of protection with but a bit of kindness and attention and grace?

*Gray shall not be the next man to reign over you, Keturah Banning Tomlinson. You are free. And you shall remain that way forever. Remember?*

She took a deep breath and forced herself to concentrate on Mr. Odell and how he was prattling on about his connections in Spain and the fine Madeira he was importing to the Carolinas—once he sold half of it to the planters in Nevis. It would assist him in funding his linen shops.

"So I suppose, with your connections," she said, "that you hope England remains at peace with Spain for some time."

"Ahh, yes, France will forever be a potential enemy. But whilst Spain is our occasional friend, I wish to capitalize on that peace." He gave her an appreciative glance. Politics was seldom a subject that women willingly entertained.

Verity, hearing the topic, urged the captain to a stop and turned to them. "Do you not think that with our superior naval power, France will forever be cowed into compliance and peace?"

Mr. Odell's grizzled brows rose even higher. *Two* women interested in such a topic? he plainly wondered.

"France, perhaps," the captain said. "But the colonies find Britain's reign taxing. There are some who whisper of revolution. Separation. And I canna say I blame them."

"Why, Captain!" Verity said, turning to him in dismay, "what a traitorous thing to say!"

"'Tis truth more than treachery, lass," he said, unperturbed by her anger. "It would be traitorous to throw my hat in with the colonials." But the way he said it made Keturah think that he'd given it some thought. There was more than one Scotsman who chafed under the heavy hand of British politics. Whilst every one of them had to swear fealty to England after the Battle of Culloden, many did so only to save their necks.

"Are you intimating that you have Jacobean sympathies?" Verity asked, a hand drifting to her neck as she stared hard at the captain.

"The Jacobite cause is dead," the captain returned soberly. "I'd be a fool to admit to such a thing, especially given the fact that I captain a British vessel." But again, he did not deny such leanings.

"Indeed," Verity said, and Keturah was relieved to see that the captain's surprising political stance had cooled some of her ardor. As the great-granddaughters of a British general, the girls had always taken pride in their nation, Verity most of all.

"You ladies are soon to be planters. You'll find that fellow planters have their own complaints against the Crown."

"Then we shall remind them of how they owe a great deal to England," Verity fairly huffed.

The captain gave her a gentle smile. "Let us not speak of it further now, lass. In a year or two I shall come to call and see if the warm winds of the tropics have thawed your icy ideals."

Verity blinked quickly and shifted in agitation. She turned to Grace. "Please go to Cuffee and ask him to bring me Brutus. I think he would be a welcome distraction."

The girl curtsied and hurried off to do her mistress's bidding.

"I dinna mean to upset ye, lass," the captain said, leading them to the rail. "But 'tis best if ye are prepared for what is ahead. You've lived all your life in the shelter of the aristocratic fold, I take it. The world is vast. And full of many who are against our beloved Britain."

"And those who are for her too," Keturah said soothingly, turning toward the rail and looking down to the wash of the waves thirty feet below. "As gentlewomen planters, what affects England—and those for or against her—will come to bear upon us."

"To be sure," he said and cast Ket a grateful glance.

He was right, though. Politics were another thing to which she would need to apply herself. Once on Nevis, she could subscribe to the paper published on St. Croix. And at parties she was sure to overhear much talk among the men—once they were deep in their cups. Her servants could listen for relevant information to pass along to her. In time she would find a few trusted sources, so she could plan on how to capitalize on the wars and alliances that endlessly arose. When and to whom she should sell her sugar. When and with whom she should trade. What she needed to succeed.

As she read Gray's book, she regretted that she had not thought to bring thirty new machetes—they'd be ten times as expensive on-island. Inwardly, she chastised herself for thinking so much about the clothing and furniture they might need, but precious little about the crops that would sustain them. She'd been so intent on setting sail, thinking that once they arrived, they'd find their new overseer and he would see to all that pertained to the crops. But as she became increasingly aware of Gray's meticulous preparations, she became all the more aware of her own shortcomings.

Over the captain's shoulder she spotted Philip, reading on what was becoming his customary perch atop the coil of rope. She noticed now that it was near a posted lamp, allowing him to see the page, even at this hour. "Pardon my intrusion, Philip."

He looked up as she neared, smiled, and rose. "Not at all, Lady Tomlinson. How do you fare this evening?"

"I am well. Your master is not out and about too?" she asked quietly, feigning ignorance as to where he might be as she looked around the deck.

"No, m'lady. He is hard at work on his plans for the new mill. He has become quite the adept draftsman, it seems." He shook his head and shot her a rueful grin. "I fear I shall long for my days of leisure aboard this ship once we reach the island. Master Gray's plans surely mean we will be at work from sunup to sundown."

She gestured to another spot on the rope. "May I?"

"But of course," he said. And with her, he sat down again.

"What are you reading now?"

He turned the book's spine to show her.

*Tropical Storms and Hurricanes*, she read. "It will not be much like our gentle, steady English rains, I hear."

"No," he said. "But 'twill be something to behold, will it not? A strong bracing storm always reminds me of the power of our good Lord."

Nodding, she said, "I only hope the coming storms shall not tear down all that Gray and I hope to build and accomplish on our plantations."

"Lady Tomlinson," said Mr. Odell as he approached, looking with some bewilderment at her sitting with Philip. Perhaps he felt as though he was shirking his escort duties by allowing her to chat with a mere servant. "Shall we resume our stroll?"

"Yes, Mr. Odell," she said, rising to take his arm again. "Good night, Philip."

"Good night, Lady Tomlinson," he said, tipping his head.

Keturah and Mr. Odell went on to follow her sisters and Mr. Callender and Mr. Wood around the perimeter of the ship. When they reached the bow, there were four sailors tuning fiddles while others gathered around. Their escorts hastened them past as the bawdy men turned to bow extravagantly in their direction. A few made comments under their breath. Keturah looked over her shoulder as they passed, listening to the first plaintive notes of one of the men's fiddles.

"Oh, I do wish I could sit and listen to them. Between the wind and the waves and the music . . . beneath the stars, there's something poetic about it all."

"Ach, but 'tis no place for a woman, Lady Tomlinson," the captain said. "The sailors get to playing rather uncouth songs."

She could well imagine, she thought with a hidden smile. Tavern songs with bawdy lyrics, she supposed. Songs of lost women and lost dreams.

"That doesn't keep Mr. Covington from joining them on occasion," Mr. Odell said, reproach evident in his tone.

"Gray? Mr. Covington plays with them?" She had a dim memory of him struggling to practice on his violin as a child, but she hadn't thought that he had kept up with it.

"Regretfully, yes," was all Mr. Odell said.

Keturah looked out to the waves and wondered what it would take to sneak up here some night and listen. There was something in her that would love to see Gray playing, when he had no idea she was watching. She'd like to see him interacting with the sailors too. Would he play only his own music, or would he join them in theirs?

Yes, she thought, smiling to herself. This evening's stroll was but her first excursion abovedecks after sunset. She'd allow a week or two to go by before she dared, gathering the information she needed to do it, and she would not come without escort. That would simply be begging for trouble from the captain. But Mr. Callender certainly seemed eager to bend the rules here and there. Perhaps he would be a willing accomplice.

# CHAPTER EIGHT

Halfway across the Atlantic, Gray was as accustomed to the deep groans and creaks of the *Restoration*'s timbers as any seasoned sailor. And like those seasoned sailors, when he awoke in the deep of night, he knew that the ship was under strain like never before on this voyage.

Philip was already up, by the sound of it, fumbling with a flint at the lamp's wick—which had sputtered out—while sliding back and forth in his stocking feet across the floor. The waves were huge, the cabin feeling as if it rocked at frightfully steep inclines. It wasn't a surprise, really. The whole crew had been talking about a storm on the horizon yesterday. Still, Gray was not ready for the sheer terror of it.

He'd certainly spent hours contemplating their relative size against the width and breadth of the sea, feeling small and yet mighty, courageous even. The *Restoration* was a fine ship, only two years old, and Captain McKintrick, for all his youth, was widely respected by the crew. But facing a storm like this one, weeks away from any land, made Gray's stomach twist in fear.

*Lord, give me peace and strength,* he prayed silently, taking embarrassing cheer as Philip finally succeeded in getting the lamp alight again. He laughed softly as the man slid in his nightshirt, back and forth, stubbornly holding on to the lamp chain to keep from falling onto Gray's cot. "Well done, friend," Gray said. "A bit of light is what we need."

And yet, as he watched the cabin tilt, he wondered if it was indeed better. Now he could *see* that they were climbing waves that set them at a full forty-five-degree angle, then cascading down the far side. With the wash of waves outside—as well as atop—he knew they were actually plunging prow-first into the next wave. What was it like on deck?

His thoughts moved to the Bannings. How were they faring? Hurriedly, he reached for his jacket, pulling it on without a shirt. Unlike Philip, he ran hot and preferred to sleep without a nightshirt. Then, nearly falling over, he reached for his breeches that hung on a peg and sat down to pull them on.

"As soon as you're dressed, open the door," he said to Philip as they plummeted down another wave, and this time water ran across the ceiling above and dripped down into their cabin in several places.

Cocking a questioning brow but saying nothing, Philip yanked on his own breeches and hastily tucked the tails of his nightshirt into the waistband. He pulled off his nightcap and opened the door, looking left and right.

"Are any of the other passengers opening their doors?" Gray asked, watching the ceiling as another wave rushed across. Thunder boomed, startling them both.

"Now they shall," Philip said.

Gray moved to the doorframe and braced himself against it, watching Keturah's door. But as lightning cracked and thunder rumbled, as if registering its complaint of their presence, it was the younger girls' door that opened first. Selah was there, in a dressing gown hastily thrown over a shift, her blond curls loose around her shoulders. Spotting him, her bowlike lips opened in relief, and she rushed to him as she might a brother. "Oh, Gray! Is it not awful?"

He took her hand. "Now, now, 'tis only one of the Atlantic's famous storms," he said, patting her hand awkwardly. "Come, let us get you back to your cabin. You may keep your door open, though." He led her back, taking slow steps and bracing so that they did not careen all the way down to the far stairs.

Verity appeared in the doorway just as they neared, in a similar state of dress. It was fine, even fashionable for ladies to be in their dressing gowns at home . . . but only in the relative sanctity of their closets. Men were even invited into those private places on occasion, to drink tea as the women prepared for balls or parties, but they were *invited*. And there were not sailors liable to be passing by.

He had just deposited Selah back in her room, under her sister's capable arm—even if her skin was a bit wan—when Keturah's door flew open. He glanced over at her and took a step back, holding on to the girls' doorframe, so she could see her sisters were well. But more to give him precious seconds to look upon her.

Never had he seen her more beautiful, with her long brown hair sliding around her shoulders in rumpled waves. Her dressing gown—painted with flowers all down the trim and across the train—opened to expose a thin sheath of a night shift. He swallowed hard and hastily looked to her bare feet, remembering with a smile the two of them running through mud puddles as children and returning to their homes to face the switch. There they were . . . the same exact toes, only now a woman's.

"Gray?" she asked, and abruptly he realized she'd caught him staring at her toes, even as they disappeared beneath the trim of her shift. She wrapped her dressing gown tighter around her and nodded into her cabin. "Might you do me an enormous favor and assist Grace with our lamp? 'Tis gone out."

"Ours did too," he said, moving at once, relieved to have a task. Philip met him in the passageway, silently fishing out the flint and handing it to him. "Keep the door propped open, would you?" he asked Keturah, hoping to glean a bit of light from across the passageway.

Grace, her servant, moved aside as he neared. "I think the wick is too short," she said. They heard either Selah or Verity retching, across the hall. Grace, stumbling and bracing herself, reached for their chamber bucket. "I shall attend her, Lady Ket."

Keturah obviously agreed, for the servant disappeared. Gray pulled a knife from his jacket pocket, flipped it open, and set to pulling out a bit more wick and then trimming it—all of which was far more complicated this night than on calm seas.

It was then that he heard distant shouts of sailors above. Alarmed shouts, right before a rogue wave hit. This time not from the front but from the front *port* side of the ship. The *Restoration* made horrendous noises of complaint, sounding like she might be cracking apart, and with a cry Keturah came tumbling toward him from the door.

He heard the girls' cabin door slam shut and had just barely turned to brace himself and catch her when she rammed against his chest. Her left hand was inside his jacket, against bare skin, the other against his upper right chest.

"Oh, Gray, forgive me," she said in the dark, clearly horrified. She tried to pull away, but another wave shoved her further against him. *And did she ever feel good in his arms . . .*

"'Tis all right," he said, huffing a laugh. "I hardly think you would throw yourself at me if you had a choice in the matter."

"Yes, well," she said, finally finding the footing to lean away from him when gravity allowed, leaving him a tad breathless. Stubbornly he turned back toward the lamp, cursing himself for wishing for another rogue wave. He fished in his pocket for the flint, sparked it twice, three times, and on the fourth it caught, glowed, and slowly rose in flame.

"You did it!" Keturah said gratefully. "Thank you. Such fearsome storms are ever so much more negotiable with a bit of light, do you not agree?"

"Indeed," he said, staggering toward her, obviously aware that he must not be caught alone in her cabin with her—regardless of circumstance—if he was to preserve her reputation. "'Tis like life itself," he said, pausing near her, broad hands clutching the doorframe above her head. "One can face much darkness with the aid of light, whether it be the Lord's or a flickering flame in a dancing lamp." He grinned at her and hooked a thumb over his shoulder.

It was then that Callender and Wood opened their door and spied them together. Wood's face lit up in surprise and delight at the sight of them so close while Callender scowled.

Keturah shifted uneasily in the face of their misguided assumptions. She pulled her dressing gown tighter around her, but as she did so, another wave sent her grasping for the doorframe.

"Selah!" she called. "Verity! Grace! How do you fare?"

Grace managed to open their door again between waves. "We are well, Lady Ket. And you?" Her dark eyes surveyed her mistress from top to bottom like a worried hen over her chick, then shifted to Gray. Keturah could see her eyes rest on the broad expanse of his muscular chest. Hurriedly, she said, "We're well. And Mr. Covington was able to get my lamp lit again," she added loudly, hoping Mr. Callender had heard her over the wash of the waves.

"That's one way to phrase it," Mr. Wood said, lightly punching his companion in the gut. At least, that was what she *thought* he said. Surely he wouldn't have the audacity to insinuate . . .

They heard the shouts of sailors above once more, and Keturah had just had a moment to think *not again*, when another rogue wave struck the ship, sending Keturah careening toward Grace. Grace herself toppled back, landing hard on the cot and bumping her head on the wall. Just as Ket was about to follow suit, she felt Gray's hand close around her wrist and pull her to a stop.

"I have you," he said, holding the doorframe with one hand and her with the other. His legs were spread-eagled to give him better stability, and his jacket yawned wide, giving her a glimpse of even more of his chest and belly—muscles far bigger and more defined than when they last swam together at the swimming hole. A man's now. So much more defined than Edward's had been. His dark hair flopped partially over his eyes in a way that she knew would make most women swoon. "Come, Ket. Grab hold here."

He pulled her closer and placed her hand firmly on the doorframe and swung out to the passageway with the momentum of the next wave. There, he grasped one of the many bars that ran across the ceiling for just such an occasion as this. "Is Grace all right?"

Ket glanced back. "Grace? Are you injured?"

"No, mum. Just hit my head," she said, rubbing the back of it.

"Stay seated, Grace," Gray said. "'Tis far safer."

Keturah noticed water sloshing past his bare feet, and any temporary relief over her firm hold fled. "Gray, are we . . . going to sink?"

He shook his head. "No. Though the waves are fierce, the *Restoration* is a stout vessel."

Verity appeared in the far doorway again. Gray turned and began to ask Ver about Selah—who was vomiting again. He looked down the passageway at Mr. Callender, who held fast to a bar as he did. "She cannot withstand many more of those rogue waves," Mr. Callender told him.

"Yes, she can," Gray gritted out, not glancing Keturah's way. But she knew he said it for her and Ver. "She was built to withstand this storm and worse."

"Better for us to encounter a privateer than such wrath from the sea," grunted the man.

"There's still time for that!" quipped Mr. Wood from their cabin doorway. "I wager a gold florin that we shall outrun at least one privateer before we reach Nevis," he said to his companion.

Gray let out a sound of disgust. "Gentlemen! There are ladies present! I must ask you to confine your idle musings to your cabin rather than unnecessarily alarm them." Carefully, he began to make his way down toward them as if he intended to lock them inside.

Verity's eyes met Keturah's. *Privateer?* they seemed to silently ask her. *Truly?* They'd read the horror stories in the papers of entire families held for ransom. Others were killed, people whispered, their belongings spirited away.

Keturah forced a smile. "England is at peace. And the British

Navy shall make sure the *Restoration* reaches Nevis unmolested,"
she said. "'Tis only this storm and any others that we need to
manage. And we are weathering this one with pluck, are we not?
If those waves did not capsize us, nothing will."

Verity nodded slowly, her brows still knit with concern. "I wonder how Brutus fares."

"He's probably slumbering through the entire ordeal," Keturah
said. "Birds know when storms are life-threatening and when they
are not. If he thought it was truly a danger, do you not think we
would hear his screech, even from here?"

That seemed to bolster her sister, and her pretty moss-colored
eyes shifted toward Gray—who was leaning toward Mr. Callender in a threatening manner—then back to her sister. "So?" she
whispered, cocking one brow and glancing to the empty cabin
behind her. "Tell me something to distract me from this storm."

Keturah stiffened. "There is nothing to tell."

"No?"

"*No.*"

"Pity, that," she said, her eyes wandering to Gray and back
again. "He is frightfully handsome, is he not?"

"*Verity.*"

"What?"

"Ladies do not speak of such things."

Verity laughed. "Ladies do not," she said under her breath, "but
sisters *do*. Come now, Ket. Admit it. He's handsome."

Ket's cheeks burned. She knew her sister only whispered, but the
idea that he might hear . . . Still, she knew how Verity was when
she got in this sort of mood. If she did not give her something,
she was liable to keep after it. "Of course he is handsome," she
whispered back, hating that she sounded defensive. "He has always
been one of the most handsome in our circle."

"And the one who," Ver said, leaning closer to cast a glance
down the passageway to make sure he was staying put, "has a
new eye for you."

"No. That is not so," Ket said.

"Say what you will," she said smugly.

"No. Perhaps our childhood friendship has been rekindled. Nothing more."

"Has your widowhood made you blind, Sissy?" Verity asked. "Or perhaps you do not wish to see it. He is rather careful around you. But I've seen him," she whispered. "When he thinks you unaware, he steals glances in your direction."

"No," Keturah said stubbornly. "If he was to have eyes for anyone, 'twould be for you or Selah. You two are far prettier. And . . ." *Undamaged*, came to mind, but she held her tongue.

Verity stared at her, rocking with each wave, her muscles tightening to keep her grip, but her eyes remained steady. "After all this time, Ket," she said, her whisper full of sorrow, "you still believe such lies?"

"'Tisn't a lie. Merely fact. 'Tis good to acknowledge such truths and accept them," she said, feeling as sensible as her words. "Father always said that one does best when one faces facts."

"Then you, dear sister," Verity said softly, "must face the fact that not all is in the order you desire. Ket, you fail to see that you have become quite lovely in womanhood, with attributes that draw many a man's eye, beyond even our dear Gray."

Her words struck Ket. Pierced her. She cursed the tiny bit of hope that lit within her, like an aching girl's heart, desperate for attention and approval, rather than a woman grown.

"They do not know what to do with you," Ver added with a laugh as Gray began to make his way back toward them, "but that does not keep them from being curious. Especially this one," she hissed, just as Gray came within earshot.

Ket stared back at her sister furiously, refusing to look his way. Had he heard that? Known they were talking about him? After all that had transpired this night, that would be the worst. Because the last thing she needed—no matter how attentive, how charming, how handsome Gray might be—was another man sidling into her life.

No. Her path ahead was complicated enough.

Gray looked from Ket to Verity and back again. "Are you well? Has Selah's stomach settled?"

"Well enough, thank you," Keturah said, her tone crisp. "I do believe you're right, Mr. Covington."

He leaned back, as if the return of her formal address was a slap, but she pressed on.

"This storm will surely pass and the *Restoration* shall see another dawn, with all of us aboard her. We might as well try to get some sleep, shall we not?"

"Indeed," he said, a hundred questions in those dark blue eyes. More water rushed past his feet, and she recalled his staring at her bare toes, as if remembering that day they had splashed through one mudhole after another.

"Good night, Verity," she said to her sister. "Send Grace to me if Selah doesn't soon settle, will you?"

"Yes, Ket," she said obediently, momentarily slipping back into line.

With a formal, close-lipped smile and tip of the head to Gray, she eased back, got a firm footing, and grabbed hold of the door. "Good night, Mr. Covington. Thank you for coming to our aid."

"You are most welcome, Lady Tomlinson," he said, his own tone now clipped.

Keturah closed her door but did not move away from it. Instead, she leaned against it, letting out a breath and sucking in the next, as if she had forgotten how. She put her palms and forehead against the wood, as though reaching out to him, feeling him just outside, hovering there.

Then, when the next wave passed, she hurried to her cot and sat down before she went tumbling. Remembering him, so close she could smell him—all sea salt and sweat. His eyes covering her, staring at her in such a way—for just a moment—that she might've believed Verity's words were true. The feel of his touch, holding her firm, safe. Not at all like Edward's had been—all claim and demand and force.

She put her head in her hands and closed her eyes.

*Cease this, Keturah. Cease.*
*Gray is not yours. Nor shall he ever be.*
*Think of Tabletop. Your sisters' future. Saving Hartwick Manor.*
*And nothing more . . .*

# CHAPTER NINE

She did well, sticking to that train of thought. For weeks she and Gray exchanged only the most formal of conversation. Mr. Callender seemed glad that there was a division between them but made no effort of his own to woo her. Meanwhile, Mr. Wood acted rather put out by their separation. It was he who caught her pacing one night in the passageway outside her cabin, unable to sleep. She was shaking, she was so nervous, sick unto death of the confined space of her cabin as well as the whole ship. The *Restoration* reeked from stem to stern. There was not a body aboard her who didn't need a hot bath and a change of clothes. And now, just a week or two from reaching Nevis, all Keturah could think about was finally arriving, finally having her feet on solid ground again, finally being off this cursed, wretched ship. . . .

"Lady Tomlinson!" Mr. Wood said, coming up short outside his cabin after obviously enjoying a cup of grog or two with the sailors abovedecks. "Whatever is the matter?" he asked, turning toward her.

"Oh, 'tis nothing. I simply could not sleep. Nerves, I suppose," she added ruefully, in a whisper, hoping he would quiet down. She didn't want her sisters to awaken and find her pacing like an unsettled house cat.

"I hear tell it happens to all of us at this time in a voyage," he said kindly while edging closer. "Would you like to take a turn around the deck?"

The thought of it brought her instant relief. A bit of exercise, clean air . . . and perhaps even a chance to hear Gray play. She glanced toward her cabin door. "Perhaps I ought to rouse Grace to accompany us."

"Ah, no need to awaken the poor girl," Mr. Wood said, lifting his hands. "I promise to be nothing but the most courteous escort. Have we not already taken a hundred turns together around those decks?" He looked up to the ceiling.

It was true. They had. But in the company of her sisters and others. And yet he was right; it was horribly late and the last thing the weary Grace needed was for Keturah to cut into her slumber simply because she felt the need to stretch her legs. Was Keturah not as much a target here in the passageway, so near the crew's quarters, as she was abovedecks?

"Come along, Lady Tomlinson." Mr. Wood offered her his arm. "A bit of fresh air will do you wonders."

She wondered how he knew that. Again, she could not figure what he intended with her. He seemed drawn to her, though in a purely platonic manner. There was nothing predatory about him, and yet she kept getting the sense that something else lurked below the surface.

*You really are beginning to imagine far too much, Keturah,* she told herself as she climbed the steep stairway after Mr. Wood. He waited above for her, took her hand, and tucked it into the crook of his elbow. But Keturah's eyes were on the masses of stars above— far more than she had ever seen in England or even on the voyage so far. They had always returned to their cabins just as twilight began to fade. This late, millions of stars appeared. "They're so beautiful!" she gasped.

"Indeed," he said with a chuckle, leading her to the rail. "With no moon, they're the prettiest tonight. Perhaps that's why," he added, "they are still at their music at this hour."

Keturah noticed it then, the barest hint of music above the

noisy waves. She glanced at Mr. Wood, merely a silhouette beside her. "Do you think . . . we might edge somewhere closer to hear them?"

He hesitated. "Well, now. Perhaps. But not too close. And I warn you, not many of what these sailors sing are songs a lady would choose to hear."

"That is all right. I am not your average lady."

He chuckled again and set off with her, offering his arm. "That you are not. A gentlewoman planter? I'll wager the Nevisians will be rather surprised when you join them."

"As you wager on everything," she chided.

She felt, rather than saw, his shrug. "My winnings are funding this passage for me. Is it my fault that I'm rather good at gambling?"

"Is it what your father wished for you?"

"Never," he said easily, unoffended. "Is becoming a planter what your father wished for you, Lady Tomlinson?"

She stopped, and he turned to face her and removed his tricorn hat. "Forgive me," he said. "That was horribly cavalier."

She sighed. "No more than I was. Please, forgive me as well." Once again they set off, Keturah's mind on her father and how terribly dismayed he'd be were he to see her and her sisters aboard this ship. When they finally turned the forecastle corner, the music and laughter grew louder, thankfully distracting her from her dark thoughts.

They hovered just on the edge of the circle of light, and Keturah leaned against the wall, watching.

There Gray was, his shirt open halfway down his chest, sleeves rolled up. His hat was not to be seen, his jacket lying across a crate to his right. Around him were four fiddlers, each racing him to the crescendo of their raucous song. Each of the five at their instruments was sweating profusely, so fast were they moving. Keturah grinned as the men sang of a tavern wench who stole the heart of every passing sailor but stubbornly refused to give her favors to but one. Sadly the one had died, and the prettiest girl in all the isles was forever alone, even while forever surrounded by men. The sailors lifted mugs of grog to the sky at the end as if saluting the tragic idea of that girl, and their voices came to an abrupt halt just as the musicians finished. Except for one, of course. Inebriated, he went on, thinking there was another verse. His mate shoved him backward off his perch and he fell, making all the rest laugh uproariously.

Keturah gasped. Mr. Wood leaned closer and said, "Ah, that lad is surely all right, m'lady. Do not fear on his account. The grog will keep him loose."

But Keturah was once again hungrily watching Gray as he laughed and chatted with the men all about him, his face in captivating lamplight and deep shadow. How did he do that? Manage to befriend both nobles and sailors alike? Ever since they were children, he was always the charmer, befriending the milkmaid as easily as the county judge. Was that part of what made her distrust him? And was that fair when it was clearly an honest gift rather than a ruse? For Gray looked as alive and content here in his shirtsleeves as he did in his finery at a ball. Perhaps even happier.

It had never been her own gifting to enjoy such a wide array of people. She liked to have her intimate circle of friends—she considered the rest something to be endured. Much like Gray, Selah reveled in parties and calling upon people. Verity found herself somewhere between her sisters in what they'd come to call "people tolerance."

Once again she wondered if Gray might like to court Selah, in a few years. *After he makes a success of himself,* she caught herself thinking, and yet the thought made her mouth go dry. She didn't care for the idea. It made her feel . . . jealous.

The men were needling Gray, asking him to do something when he clearly was preparing to turn in for the night.

"Just one more, gov'nor!" cried one man.

"The sad one, about your lost love!" called another.

"Yes, that one!"

"Please, your lordship!"

The men gave him titles that were not his own, poking fun at his separateness as a passenger of the upper class, but in their teasing treating him as one of their own too.

"Well, all right," Gray said reluctantly. "Just one more." He held up his index finger, shooting a warning glance about the circle. He raised his violin to his shoulder and nestled his cheek against it when someone said, "Tell us who she was."

"What was her name?" called a man from the far side of the circle.

"Yes! Tell us her name, gov'nor!"

"Her name?" Gray smiled in that way that made his eyes twinkle. He pretended to be about to tell them, but then seemed to remember himself and shook his head. "'Twould be ungentlemanly."

"But you're no gentleman!" protested another. "You're here with us!"

"Sailors kiss and tell after every port!" guffawed another.

Gray shook his head again, then tucked his cheek against the mahogany instrument and began to play.

The notes were high and plaintive, spare and yet serene. Keturah found she was holding her breath. It was unlike anything she had ever heard. Something . . . Gray had written himself? It unfolded from his instrument, building and building with lower, more complex notes and speed, in a way that made Ket wonder if it was somehow pulling her in, whispering to her of the story behind it.

Because it truly sounded like longing . . . desperation, hope, and sorrow. As the last note hovered in the air, the crowd around him utterly silent and somber, Keturah blinked as though trying to rouse herself from a dream. Had that beautiful song truly emerged from Gray Covington's violin?

Two of the sailors called good night and walked past Keturah and Mr. Wood just as Gray lifted his head and smiled at the group. His eyes caught hers as the passing lamp illuminated her presence and stayed on her even after she was once again enveloped by darkness. At first his eyes showed pleasure and surprise, but then they quickly narrowed. He wasn't pleased she was here. Because he feared for her safety or reputation? Or because she had witnessed him perform such an intimate song?

"We should retire," she said to Mr. Wood.

"Yes, of course," he agreed, but he moved terribly slowly when she was feeling the utmost urgency. She practically tugged him along.

"Lady Tomlinson!" said Gray, catching up to them when they were but partway down the ship's starboard side.

Keturah stiffened and turned to face him. "Mr. Covington. I had no idea you had become so accomplished a musician. You should grace the captain and the rest of us with your talent on the morrow."

Gray shook his head. She noticed the violin and bow occupied both hands. "No. I never play for such gatherings. Only for pleasure, not to present myself as a spectacle."

Mr. Wood was making some excuse, slipping away now that Ket was "in other capable hands," but she couldn't keep herself from looking at Gray. She knew of what he spoke. In their set, playing an instrument became a duty, a manner in which to show off. Rarely was it played for a pure love of music. "I see," she said at last as he offered her his arm and they began strolling back to the passenger quarters. "'Tis a pity. That last song was truly beautiful."

"You think so?" he said softly. "Thank you. That means a great deal to me."

"Did you write it?"

He hesitated. "Yes."

"I only wish you would share it with a larger audience. You saw how the men responded. Everyone thought it a wonder."

He laughed under his breath. "With that much grog in them, there would be little I could play that they would not deem a 'wonder.'"

They reached the stairwell. Gray descended first and then reached up a hand to help her down. She had time to wonder how Mr. Wood had made it back to his quarters so quickly when they themselves had not lingered. Had the man run for his cabin?

Gray paused outside her cabin door while she patted her skirts for the key, tied with a ribbon at her waist.

"Would you tell me the name of it?" she asked lightly, wondering if she knew the girl who had elicited such emotion from him. Then she silently cursed herself for being so nosey.

He smiled at her and waited, staring until she met his gaze. Then he took her hand. "Do you not know, *Keturah*?" he whispered, lifting her knuckles slowly to his lips, never dropping his gaze.

Her heart stopped a moment, then surged.

No. Surely not.

She pulled her hand away. "You jest. 'Tis a song you've played for others. A ploy to steal the heart of every lady you meet with a simple change of title."

"Is that all you think of me?" he asked, hurt making his eyes droop.

"I . . . I do not know what to think of you, Mr. Covington."

"Clearly. I am partially to blame for that. I have been inconsistent. Pigheaded. I ignored you when you needed my friendship. I assumed you needed my help when you did not. I was a fool. But can we not begin again, Keturah? Can you not call me Gray as you once did? Can we not at least be friends again?" He stepped closer.

She swallowed hard, wanting to ease the hurt she had caused and yet also wanting to end this intimacy. Because there was something in his eyes that did not speak solely of friendship. "All right. We shall try that, Gray. Thank you for seeing me to my cabin. Good night."

With shaking hands she turned and fumbled with the key, finally managing to slip it into the lock as he hovered near . . . so near.

She gave him a tentative smile and quietly closed the door, hoping not to wake Grace. She settled atop her blanket, not bothering to undress, and turned on her side, hands beneath her cheek, thinking of Gray playing that song. His intimation that the song was for her. He'd seemed so intent, so truthful, and so hurt when she doubted him. But was it a game he played with all women?

The reason why so many had allowed him to kiss them? The man knew how to wheedle his way into a woman's heart. "You're such a fool, Keturah," she muttered to herself, sighing heavily. *And now you've agreed to friendship . . .*

Now, more than ever, Nevis could not come fast enough.

# Chapter Ten

After the endless days at sea, it felt like a strange dream as they were finally approaching Nevis. The sailors cheered when someone in the crow's nest that morning shouted, "Land ho!" So did the passengers, all rushing to the deck to peer out at the horizon as the West Indies came into view—as one welcome, glorious green dot after another amid the blue sea. Within hours they'd drawn closer, and Captain McKintrick didn't miss the opportunity to direct everyone's attention to Nevis's towering peak. Moving close behind Verity, the captain pointed over her shoulder when she couldn't make it out for herself.

"And is that her sister isle, Saint Christopher, just to her north?" Keturah asked, silently reminding the man that she was watching and he ought to resume a proper distance from her sister.

"'Tis," he said and cast her a bashful grin as he stepped away from Verity.

It was but one more reason she would be glad to be off this ship. Whilst the captain's political leanings had put off Verity for a while, over the last week his consistent charms seemed to be drawing her in again. She'd gone on and on about his "delightful brogue" last night, imitating one phrase after another and dissolving into giggles with Selah.

She looked around for Gray, certain he couldn't be far since everyone had turned out, all of them staring off toward land. She spotted him shaking the hands of various sailors as if in congratulations for getting them all safely to their new home. When he caught her eye, he hesitated before making his way to her, joining her at the rail.

"Are you ready for this, Keturah?"

"I do not know," she said truthfully. "I have not yet finished your ninth and tenth books."

"Ah, well, you've read the most important volumes, at least. And I won't be far. You can borrow the others anytime you wish."

"Thank you," she said, looking again to the islands as they loomed closer. Her heart was racing. Because of Nevis? Or because Gray was so near? Since that night in the passageway, he'd seemed to begin avoiding her again, which she thought was for the best. She concentrated on the island, her thoughts turning to the fears she harbored about her new life on the shores ahead. How was she to manage it? Truly? Even with Selah and Ver to help her . . .

"Remember the giant oak tree we climbed," Gray asked quietly, "when we were but children?"

She blinked, then nodded.

"Do you remember how I hated heights—and what you told me when you were coaxing me upward?"

Ket smiled. "One limb at a time, Gray. Just look to the next limb, not all the way to the top."

He smiled with her, his dimples deepening. "Those words have helped me through many a trial, Keturah. Perhaps they'll help you, too, with what lies before us."

The captain shouted to the few dozen passengers to return to their cabins, stow their belongings, and prepare to disembark. To the crew he began shouting orders, bringing the *Restoration* about, beginning to tack toward Nevis. Everyone moved at once, and in the crowd, Ket became separated from Gray. Was it odd that she lamented the fact that she had probably spent her last intimate moments with him? She'd spent all six weeks of their voyage alternately drawn to him and, when they were together, scurrying away. With two busy plantations to run, how often might they see each other?

*'Twill be what 'twill be,* she thought with a sigh.

They anchored in Charlestown's harbor, and a group of men set off from shore in long rowboats to assist the crew in unloading the cargo and passengers. Ket and her sisters were helped into a boat with the small family who had remained in their cabin for the majority of the trip, all four of them seasick. They looked thin and wan, and Keturah hoped time on land would quickly set them to rights.

She saw that Gray and Philip were in another boat, along with the gamblers, tutor, and Mr. Odell. It was reassuring, somehow, to know he was nearby.

When their boat struck sand, hands onshore hauled them several feet inward. Keturah and her sisters shared an excited glance. "Here we go," she whispered, then took the hand of a sailor and rose to her feet.

"Easy, mum. First steps ashore are challenging for most," he said. And he was right. Weeks at sea made her first steps on land feel as though her legs were unaccountably heavy.

She giggled as Verity stumbled toward her. "Now I know what 'sea legs' feel like!" Ver said.

"Indeed."

"What is that horrible odor?" Selah asked, looking around and bringing a handkerchief to her nose.

"I have no idea," Keturah said. "I thought the *Restoration* smelled poorly."

"Slaver," said a sailor beside them who had overheard their conversation. "The *Champion* just anchored this morning." He nodded grimly toward the wide-bottomed ship.

Keturah blanched, because now she knew what that smell was. Rotting flesh and excrement and decay. Death.

"Oh no," Selah said, her brows arching in horror.

"Get used to it, mum," said the sailor. "'Tis common here in Nevis. Many captains stop here to reprovision as well as to sell off their stock. Slaves that the planters do not purchase here are taken on to other islands or the Carolinas. But the Indies are their best market."

The next boats brought the rest of the white passengers, and then their servants arrived, as wide-eyed and frightened as Ket supposed she and her sisters appeared. Swiftly, she set each of them to a task. She did not want any of them asking about the odor. There would be time enough to face that question later. She pulled out her purse and began distributing coins. "Gideon and Primus, see about securing several wagons to get our cargo to Tabletop. Grace and Cuffee, go and buy some fruit and cheese and bread so we can all eat. Edwin and Absalom, you await the boats that will bring our cargo and see that it is brought right there by the road," she said, pausing to point, "where we can load it."

Nodding, the servants set off to do as they were told.

She thought Gray had actually disappeared into the crowd without a farewell when she turned and saw him standing before her, Philip to his right. He had his tricorn in hand. "It seems you have things well in hand, Keturah," he said. "But I would be remiss in not offering to escort you to Tabletop—given, of course, that Teller's Landing is just to her south."

She smiled. "That is most kind of you, Gray, but I think we can manage on our own." Now that she was finally here, she wanted to make her own way up this tree. She had to do so. "One limb at a time."

"One limb at a time," he repeated with a thoughtful nod. Was that respect in his eyes? "Good day, then. Send for me at Teller's Landing if you find yourself in any need of assistance."

"Thank you. I shall. Good luck!"

Along the beach and the quay, gentlemen and a few ladies under parasols began to gather and approach, one after another greeting them, welcoming them to the island, barely concealing their surprise that the three women had journeyed here alone, then inviting them to visit their own estates, sharing that they had known Father.

Ket did her best to smile and politely receive all the inquiries and greetings, but between the heat radiating off the sand and the reek of the slaver ship, she was having a hard time breathing. She noted that the women not only carried parasols here in town but also nosegays of bright tropical flowers, which they held beneath their chins. Without something similar, Selah was soon gagging, making it all the worse for Keturah, whose own stomach twisted at the sound. Seeing their plight, several gentlemen swiftly offered them handkerchiefs to cover their noses, yet just moments later, Keturah knew she was losing the battle.

Hurriedly, she excused herself and dragged her sisters to the side of a fishmonger's stall, not wanting to lose sight of them. Once there, she discreetly threw up every bit of the hardtack she'd had at breakfast. And when she was done, it was Selah's turn.

"Honestly," Verity fussed, looking back out the alley, "the Nevisians shall think us weak!"

She was right, of course. But there was nothing for it. Together they returned to the market, Selah trailing behind. Keturah found herself hoping for another glimpse of Gray, missing his steady, strong presence, and then silently chastising herself for such foolery. The man had set off on his own as she had instructed—which was only right. He was as excited as she was to be here, his attention on his own future, his own needs. *You cannot look to Gray, Ket. This has to be on your shoulders now, only yours.*

And when she looked around again, she saw that Selah was no longer behind her. Nowhere about in the crowd . . .

With alarm, she looked from Verity and around in a slow circle, telling herself not to panic. All about her, people spoke in Spanish, French, Dutch, and German, as well as English. There were women selling candy and cakes, fishmongers selling fat red snapper from trays strapped around burly necks. Another vendor was selling casks of wine, still another trading Spanish doubloons and pieces of eight for the island's currency, stamped with the letter *N*.

*Where is she? How could she pick this moment to wander off?* Ket wondered in indignant agitation.

Ket's heart sank when she finally glimpsed Selah's blond curls.

She was standing next to a slaver's platform. Primus, dear Primus, was standing beside her, looking back to Ket with terror in his eyes, even as he did his best to keep watch over his youngest mistress.

Above them, a man paraded a black female slave about, and the young woman was entirely nude. Heat washed up Keturah's cheeks, and she thought about confronting the irreverent man atop the platform when she spied two other platforms nearby that were identical to the first. Men and women and children, each of them chained at the ankles, with only a few wearing the scantest of fabrics to cover themselves. The rest were naked and clearly miserable, half of them barely able to stand.

Most haunting of all were the babies in their mothers' arms. Not a one of them cried, though they had more than enough cause. They were eerily silent, stoically watching for whatever was to come next, as if nothing could further shock tears from their tender souls.

The crack of a whip startled her, and she forced herself to move again, toward her sister. She'd just settled a hand on Selah's shoulder when the slaver roughly lifted the slave woman's jaw, wrenching her mouth open to show the buyers she still had a full set of teeth.

The woman bit down on the slaver's finger. He let out a shriek, trying to free himself, but the woman stubbornly held on. In that moment, Keturah thought she could feel the woman's desperation as her own, somewhat like what she'd felt when she decided she was coming to Nevis regardless of what anyone said. Her action said, *That is enough. 'Tis here I take my stand.*

The slaver rammed his fist into the woman's nose, and blood spattered in an arc, showering Keturah, Selah, and Primus. The woman collapsed to the platform, sprawled out, arms stretched directly toward them. The slaver unfurled his whip and it arced in the air as if it had a life of its own—a snake about to attack—then came down across the naked woman's back. Her mouth opened wide as her skin flayed open, but she only let loose a small gasp, then another as the whip struck again. Tears welled in her dark eyes, yet she remained quiet, staring at Ket. A Negro man surged from the lines, trying to get to her, but another slaver savagely clubbed him across the back. "Stay where you are!" he shouted.

Keturah heard him, but her gaze remained locked with the young woman's bloodshot eyes, taking in her hair, shorn tight, and hollow cheeks. The girl stared at her unseeingly. How many weeks had they been at sea sailing from Africa? How many of her kin and friends had been lost to disease or starvation, their bodies part of what made the harbor reek of death? How strange and dreadful would this place seem to her? What hope had she?

The whip cracked in the air again. Keturah looked up and saw, with fresh horror, that Selah had climbed onto the platform.

"Stop this!" Selah shouted, lifting her hands.

The whip came down toward them both. "Stop!" Ket screamed, and the slaver lifted his whip at the last possible second, sparing Selah's tender flesh.

Her sister threw herself atop the woman, shielding her.

"Selah!" Ket cried. "Selah, what are you doing?"

Two men who had been bidding on the slave from the other side looked at each other in agitation and then climbed the steps too. One burly gentleman rushed over to Selah and looked down at her. "Get up, miss," he said in a thick Creole accent, gesturing for her to stand. "This is no way for a lady to act. It is not how we conduct ourselves in the Indies."

"Not until I know she shall suffer no further harm!" Selah said, tears welling in her eyes.

"Who are you? What is your name?" asked the man, and Ket saw the whip at his belt. He crossed his arms. "Where is your father?" He scanned the crowd behind them.

Keturah froze. She couldn't believe this was happening. There had been slavers in the ports of London and Liverpool, of course. This certainly wasn't the first time she'd witnessed an auction. But her father had carefully shielded the girls from more than a glimpse and, judging from what she saw here, for good reason.

"We shall take them!" Keturah called to the auctioneer, seeing only one way out of the situation. She well knew that if it got out that Selah was a slave lover, it would not bode well for them among the other planters. She was green to this particular saddle, but not so green that she couldn't keep her seat. Or at least pretend to do so.

"And you are . . . ?" said the slaver.

She took a deep breath and climbed onto the platform and went to Selah. She looked up at the square-jawed man with the whip and then the auctioneer. "I am Lady Tomlinson of Tabletop Plantation."

"Tabletop!" said the man, incredulous. "Why, there—"

Ket turned to the auctioneer. "I wish to purchase this girl," she rushed on, with a quick nod to the woman still on the platform. She hissed to Selah, "Get up, Selah. *Get up*. Remember yourself." Then to the slaver, "And we'll take that man too."

The slaver considered her, chewing his lip as he rolled the whip up and settled it at his hip again. He followed her gaze to the man who had strained at his bonds when the girl was whipped. "That will cost you a pretty penny, Lady Tomlinson. This girl here is worth ninety pounds, and her man is a hundred and ten."

Keturah glared at him. "I'll give you eighty for each of them."

"Ninety, and not a penny less."

"Done."

He began to reach for her hand and then thought better of it, clearly used to dealing with men.

"Release them both from their shackles," Selah said, wiping furious tears from her eyes.

"Come now, miss. This here is Nevis," said the man with the square jaw, turning to spit. "Take it from me," he drawled, "a man born and raised here. I'm Angus Shubert, the overseer of Red Rock, which is at Tabletop's northern border. Now, I recognize you're new here, but I will tell you—if you let loose your slaves from their shackles before they've been *acclimated* to the island, they're liable to run." He swore, then turned to spit again. "Some have been known to fling themselves into the sea. If that happens to you, you'll be the proud owner of two drowned slaves, and out your one hundred eighty pounds sterling. That will do no one any good. And ma'am," he added, dropping his voice, "knowing what I do of Tabletop, buying slaves who turn around and drown themselves is the *last* thing you need."

Selah edged between the slave—now rising to her hands and knees—and Mr. Shubert. "We believe that human beings respond to kindness and respect."

Her words made Angus Shubert's bushy brows rise. He barked a laugh, as did his companion and slaver too, though he had the good sense to try to hide his own laughter by turning partially away.

Selah, her face burning in embarrassment, looked back to her sister.

"Release them from their shackles," Keturah said.

The slaver turned back to her. "Don't come crying to me when you find they've run off," he said with a shrug, silently beckoning to another man and then catching a ring of keys that sailed through the air.

He bent to unlock the woman's shackles, and as they fell away, Ket grimaced. The metal bands had worn her skin raw, and the wounds were swollen with infection. Her man's were no better, she soon saw.

She turned to Primus at her side. "Find them some clothes," she said and drew a shilling from her small purse. "A simple gown for the girl, breeches for the man."

"I'll need payment before you take them," said the slaver, tucking his thumbs in his belt and looking Keturah up and down, eying her purse that had just dropped back to her waist. The little purse didn't carry the amount she needed in sterling.

"We have only just arrived," she said, lifting her chin as if she had not a care in the world. "Come to Tabletop in three days and I shall have your money."

He gave her a rueful smile and shook his head slowly. "Why, you *are* just off the boat, aren't you, girl?"

"*Lady*," she corrected, recognizing she needed every edge she could find. "Lady Tomlinson."

"Pardon *me*, m'lady," he drawled with no semblance of respect in his tone. "You see, if I continue on with my task, I will sell these two slaves to any of the fine gentlemen on the far side of the platform within minutes. Mr. Shubert, for one. Slaves are needed by the hundreds here on Nevis. You only caught my eye, given your companion's—"

"My sister's," Ket corrected.

"Your *sister's* misguided actions." He let out a scoffing laugh. "'Tis common enough. Proper English ladies, paling in the face of what they see here. But you'll grow accustomed to it in time. They all do."

Ket's eyes ran across the line of miserable humans, torn from family and friends and all that was familiar. All her life she'd grown up with slaves. But they had been servants, an integral part of her family life—not merely a tool. Never had she known a slave fresh from the docks. Most of their servants had been born in England, the second or third generation, or purchased from others. They had proper British accents and sounded much like any white servant.

These . . . these people, there was a wildness in them. Desperation. Anger. Fear. Confusion. It jarred her as nothing had before. And with one look at Selah, she knew she felt the same. But what were they to do? They had not even their cargo from the *Restoration* with which to barter. Keturah knew not in what state they'd find Tabletop. And her own funds? It might take months to secure a transfer from Britain.

"Here, take this as security," Selah said, wriggling off the emerald ring she inherited from their mother.

"Selah," gasped Verity, finally coming to their aid, still looking so green she might retch again.

"I wish for it to be returned to me when we have your coin," the girl said to the slaver. "It is worth more than two hundred pounds. If we do not have your funds in three days, then you may keep it."

The slaver grasped the ring between thumb and forefinger and lifted it to the light, then bit the gold. He pursed his lips, nodding, and slipped it into his vest pocket. "Very well, Miss Banning. I shall see you in three days' time at Tabletop. Good luck with your two new runaways." He moved past her then, taking hold of a young man of about fourteen, obviously ill, and wrenching him to his feet.

Keturah set a hand on Primus's forearm as he returned with the clothes. "You found wagons?"

"Yes, ma'am. Gideon should be with them, up there by the road."

"Good. I shall send him to help you get the man and woman to our carriages."

"Yes, Lady Ket," he replied with a nod. Sweat dripped down his head and neck, and she knew it wasn't entirely from the heat of the midafternoon.

No, there was a shadow in his eyes that she never remembered seeing before. A shadow of memory? How old had he been when he came to work for the Bannings? All her life, for certain. But he'd been a part of Father's family before that. Had he not?

The thought of it shamed her, that she did not know. How could she not know the history of every servant in her care? She felt foolish. How could she not have anticipated how being here, seeing slavery at its most vile, would not affect her own servants? And what were they to do with these two new arrivals, who most likely did not speak a word of English? How was she to figure out how to ease them into a life of service? *One limb at a time*, she told herself. But the thought rang hollow.

This wasn't a summer's afternoon on Crabapple Hill, a contest to see if she could coax Gray higher up an oak tree.

She spun in a slow circle, taking in the swarm of people, a contingent of British soldiers sweltering in their red uniforms, the volcanic stone buildings of Charlestown, the marketplace, the slavers, the twelve ships anchored in the harbor, the ketches and rowboats moving in and out on a bright blue-green sea. Higher up on the hill, she spied the fort and her big thirty-pounder cannons, ready to ward off the French or any other foe daring to invade.

But it was Ket who already felt invaded by this place. Nearly eviscerated, as if her lungs had been pierced.

And they had yet to reach the plantation.

Four words rang through her mind as she glanced back to her sisters, as solemn as church bells tolling.

*What have I done?*

# CHAPTER ELEVEN

*The plantation*, Ket thought. *If only we can reach the plantation, I shall be surrounded by the familiar again. Find my footing. It will feel like home there. At the very least, somewhere we can rest this night, eat, wash.*

That was the hope, anyway. She remembered well the ledgers and how dismal it had appeared. And that was before the last harvest. She found she was breathing fast and shallow, growing light-headed.

Selah seemed to notice and gripped her hand. "Ket, are you going to be sick again?"

"What? No, no," she said, but her protests seemed weak, even to her own ears.

Angus Shubert, the overseer of Red Rock Plantation, ambled near and took in Selah's bewilderment and Ket's wan complexion, considering them. "Now, I must insist," he said to Selah, taking her hand and tucking it into the crook of his beefy arm. "Lord Reynolds, the owner of Red Rock and your new neighbor, would take me to task if he knew I'd come across the orphaned daughters of Richard Banning and let you find your own way to Tabletop. Come along now. I shall see you safely there."

"No. I mean, I truly thank you," Ket tried, looking about for Primus but finding it hard to keep her vision from twisting in the heat. But Shubert was already pulling Selah along, who looked helplessly over her shoulder at her sisters.

"Come, Lady Tomlinson," Mr. Shubert said, giving her a frown. He turned to a slave at his side and hissed to him to fetch fresh water for the ladies. The boy set off running. "Take a seat, here in the shade of this tree," Mr. Shubert said, his tone soothing. Placating. Like she'd heard Verity speak to agitated horses in the corral. But as much as it irked Ket, she could not find the will to resist. Obediently, she sat next to where he deposited Selah, and Verity followed behind, breathing fast as if to try to avoid another round of vomiting.

Primus arrived at last. "The new slaves are in the wagon, Lady Ket," he said, looking at the three sisters with some consternation.

"Good work, boy," Shubert said, setting a massive hand on the older man's shoulder. "Where are they?"

Primus hesitated, looking from him to Ket.

Shubert grabbed Primus's chin and forced the man to look back at him. "I said, where are they?"

"Mr. Shubert!" Ket cried, rising. She reached for his arm, even as he still clenched Primus's face in his hand. "Release him at once!"

He did so, but continued to glare at Primus. "I don't know how it was for you in England, boy, but here in the West Indies, when a white man asks you a question, you answer it. When a white man directs you to do something here, you do it. *Without hesitation.* Do you *understand* me?"

"Yes, Mr. Shubert," Primus said. "I beg your pardon if I offended you."

Shubert stared at the man, with his impeccable English and trembling hands, and laughed. Laughed and looked to his two companions who had rejoined him, as if they were watching a dancing bear rather than a man.

"We can find our own way to Tabletop, Mr. Shubert," Ket said firmly, finding her anger had steadied her vision and her stomach. All she knew was that she wanted to get as far away from this man as possible. "We do not wish to trouble you." With that, she gestured for Primus to lead the way to their carriages.

But Shubert fell into step beside Selah, who followed behind Ket and Verity. "As I said, it is no trouble at all, ma'am," he said to Keturah with a tip of his tricorn hat when she glanced back at him in irritation. "After all, you are neighbors! And since you ladies are unaccompanied and the proud owners of these two green slaves," he said and narrowed his eyes at the couple in the back of the wagon, "I feel I'd be remiss if I didn't attend you."

There was no dissuading him. He resolutely waited with them until the rest of their cargo was loaded and their people assembled.

Captain McKintrick approached them just as they were about to leave. "Lady Tomlinson!" he called, but she saw that his eyes were on Verity. Together they turned toward the captain. "Your cargo has all arrived in fine order?" he asked, his eyes running down the length of the three wagons. "Naught amiss?"

"It appears so, yes," Ket replied. "Thank you for getting it—and us—safely to Nevis, Captain. We have met some . . . neighbors," she said, gesturing toward Shubert. "They have offered to escort us to Tabletop."

"Ach, that's good." He reached out to shake Shubert's hand and introduced himself to all three before turning back to the ladies. "I shall be here for five, mayhap six days. May I come to call upon ye before I depart?"

Keturah hesitated. She'd imagined that anything begun between the sea captain and her sister would end as soon as they disembarked. She had clearly miscalculated. But what could she say? He was so earnest, Verity so eager, that she could not find it in her heart to turn him away. At least not here, with so many to observe. No, she'd have to find a way in private to dissuade him.

Grinning, McKintrick nodded and turned to Verity. "Until we meet again then, lass."

"Until then," she returned shyly.

He and Shubert assisted the ladies to the wagon seats, and they set off along the aptly named Lower Round Road, given that it encircled the island. They passed numerous shops in Charlestown—the blacksmith, the silversmith, a cooper, a leatherworks shop, and even a glassblower—until they finally cleared the last building and the first plantation came into view.

Shubert's two companions, casually introduced as Lawrence and Francis, had brought along two new slaves Shubert had purchased. The boys were about thirteen or fourteen and were forced to walk and stumble behind their horses on ten-foot leads. Keturah did her best not to look—it was too upsetting to watch them fall and narrowly rise up in time, again and again.

Even taking in the horror in the Banning servants' faces—riding in the back of the wagons—was an upset of its own. They obviously did not know quite what to do with the two new slaves in the back of the rented wagon. In fact, they had yet to speak to them. The slave girl was weeping, the long lashes on her back seeping with blood through her dirty "new" gown—apparently all that was available on short notice. The young man had his arm around her waist, face set in grim lines.

But as they moved toward the leeward side of the island where she knew Tabletop was situated, Keturah began to breathe just a wee bit easier, soothed by what she saw *outside* of the wagons.

The road was lined with flowering trees that towered above them and granted them partial shade. There were magnolia and African tulip and poui trees, all of which she recognized from studying Gray's illustrated book *Agriculture Among the Indies*, and below were West Indian ebony bushes. The jungle was alight with bright vermilion, yellow, and red blossoms. She inhaled deeply and detected a mix of jasmine and other sweet scents on the air. Among the trees that lined the road were also fruit trees—mango and guava and palms loaded with coconut. Her mouth watered at the sight of the ripe-looking mango, the ruby-red fruit making her wish she could climb *that* tree, one limb at a time, that instant.

Between the trees they caught glimpses of the ocean below with its different hues of turquoise, deep green, and royal blue. On either side of the road was nothing but acre upon acre of sugarcane— young stalks of green rustling in the trade winds—or freshly tilled soil.

They passed by lines of slaves carrying hoes and scythes across their shoulders, walking along a path while a white man on horseback followed behind. He tipped his hat, but they did not stop to make his acquaintance. He was obviously an employee, not a man of their station. There'd be time enough for that later. All Keturah wanted now was to get to her own plantation and settle into a chair for a proper dish of tea. Yes, a spot of tea would make all of what they were encountering all the more negotiable, somehow.

They drove past a windmill near the road, its huge blades of sailcloth turning at a good clip in the breeze, and more slaves with bound cane balanced on their heads. They stared at the Bannings as they passed, eyes wide and doleful. Again, Keturah noticed her own servants giving them the longest looks. It was almost as if she could hear them thinking, *That could be me.*

A half hour later, the view made all three girls gape as they stared out toward other islands in the distance, like massive turtles rising from the sea.

Noticing their awe, Mr. Shubert smiled. "That there is Saint Christopher, what we islanders call Saint Kitts, and in the distance is Saba. From the other side of the island you can see Monserrat and Guadeloupe. But we here in Cotton Ground get the finest rain on the island and the best sunsets to boot."

"Cotton Ground," Selah mused, staring off dreamily to the steep drop-offs below them and, farther off, to the turquoise sea. "Did they grow cotton here once?"

"Yes, ma'am. Until they saw the folly of their ways, of course. Cotton Ground is how the locals refer to Saint Thomas's parish."

"They tried growing ginger down in Gingerland," added Lawrence.

"They tried indigo and tobacco here too," said Francis, "but eventually they all understood that sugar was the cash crop."

Sugar. An industry that had birthed countless fortunes, her great-great-grandfather's among them, Keturah thought. The story went that, before sugar, the family was on the brink of bankruptcy, with the threat of losing Hartwick Manor very real. *And here we are again* . . .

They passed the elegant stone entrances of what Shubert told them was Red Rock Plantation—a lovely estate with a long lane of flowering trees that created a tunnel-like approach toward the main house—and twenty minutes later they had at last arrived at Tabletop.

Moving down an overgrown lane, lined on either side with more fruit trees that might someday achieve the grandeur of Red Rock, Ket found it a relief when the property opened up onto a wide grassy plain. A sprawling grand house sat at the top with several outbuildings encircling her. High above to their right, they could see a flat area that disappeared from view, and several terraced pieces of land above it, climbing their way up Mt. Nevis and disappearing among the low-lying clouds.

Mr. Shubert followed her gaze and then looked back to her. "The plantation's namesake, Tabletop," he drawled. "Your father knew that the cane grew fine up on that bluff and set to terracing other fields. He thought that erosion was the cause of our falling yields over the years and tried to make right of it. God bless his soul," he said, crossing himself, "he passed before that dream could be realized."

"Yes, well . . ." Keturah began, knowing not at all what to say to that. Father had been trying to terrace fields? Similar to how the Japanese cultivated their rice fields, as referenced in one of Gray's horticulture books? He'd mentioned no such thing in his letters. And yet Mr. Abercrombie had mentioned "land improvements" as part of the stress on the plantation over the last few years.

"Lord Reynolds," said Angus, "the owner of Red Rock, he tried to tell Mr. Banning that it was foolish, sacrificing those years of harvest to chase that idea, but Mr. Banning, well, he would hear nothing of it."

Keturah shared a glance with Verity. They could well imagine their stubborn father refusing to take advice contrary to his vision. How many harvests had he sacrificed, though, exactly? Something had been harvested every fifteen months or so . . . had that been what could be planted on the original, naturally level ground? Was this what had put their fortune in jeopardy? The plantation had been producing half of what it had at the time her grandfather owned it. But in recent years . . . .

"How was the harvest at Red Rock this last spring, Mr. Shubert?" she asked.

"Satisfactory," he said with a shrug of one shoulder. "Not as abundant as those that previous generations saw, mind you, but satisfactory."

"I see." She motioned for the driver to pull up on the reins, belatedly aware again of the boys who trailed behind Shubert's man's mount. A pang of guilt washed through her. What was the matter with her? Why had she not stopped at the entrance to Red Rock and insisted they part ways then? "Well, thank you, Mr. Shubert, for seeing us home. No doubt you need to be off to see to your own. Thank you for your trouble."

"Oh, it is no trouble a'tall," he said. "Seeing my pretty new neighbors home? No, Lady Tomlinson, I assure you, I shall be the envy of the island."

She forced a genteel smile but only kept wishing he'd leave them be and head back to Red Rock. When would he decide he'd gone far enough? When they were at their very doorstep?

To their left, the trees opened up to a worn group of twenty or more cabins, some overgrown with vines, others with porches with rotted posts and sagging roofs. Slaves' quarters, Ket surmised, grimacing at their dilapidated state. Several doors creaked open an inch or two, and Ket assumed there were people inside, curious to see who was arriving at Tabletop. *So they were not all dead.* Hope of not having to replace them all made her heart surge. *The fewer times I must face the slavers' auction platforms, the better.*

Shubert continued to ride alongside their wagon, his eyes on the big house. There was a light of both curiosity and excitement in his expression. The man was polite enough, she decided, but there was an undercurrent of some darker emotion she couldn't quite decipher. Wariness? His attention was solely on the house now.

Keturah was noting the size and condition of the structure, bracing against Shubert's silent warning, when the front door swung open and a pretty black woman in a proper English dress emerged. The dress was outdated but clean and tidy. Trailing behind her was perhaps an eight-year-old mulatto boy, also dressed in proper English attire. Hand in hand they descended two of the steps as the carriages and wagons drew to a stop in front.

"Ket," Verity whispered, moving to cover her hand with her own. Her voice was oddly low. Keturah saw she was staring at the boy. She did too for a moment.

It was as if they had already met. The boy looked startlingly familiar.

Which was impossible, of course.

Doing a poor job of hiding his smile, Angus Shubert dismounted and came over to help the ladies down from their carriage. Then he led them over to the front steps of the house. "Now, Mitilda, these here are the master's daughters, the Misses Banning and Lady Tomlinson, newly arrived from England. I think it high time you get on out of that house and let the people with *true* claim lay hold of it. Don't you?"

Keturah frowned at his contentious tone and yet bristled at its import. What was this? The woman had laid claim to the house? Is that where she'd found the fine clothes for herself and her son? Rummaging through trunks while her father lay in his cold, cruel grave? And yet . . . that did not make any sense.

The woman standing on the steps above them, with her long elegant neck and wise eyes, lifted her chin and slowly appraised each of the girls. She didn't spare Mr. Shubert more than a passing glance, moving on to the slaves in the wagon—both those in proper dress and the two new ones, who were so weary they looked ready to fall asleep where they sat.

"Welcome home, ladies," she said with a gentle, lilting Creole accent. "I am Mitilda, housekeeper to your father," she added proudly.

Mr. Shubert let out a huff of a laugh, as if tempted to say a word about that but narrowly holding back.

Primus glanced warily from Shubert to Mitilda and back again. Ket knew that Shubert had frightened him, manhandling him so, and deeply regretted it.

"Now that you are here," Mitilda said, "I will give over the care of this plantation to you and yours, Lady Tomlinson." She reached for a ring of keys, tied with a ribbon at her waist, and with trembling fingers she unlaced the knot. Gracefully, she came down the last of the front-porch steps and over to Ket, offering the keys to her. They were about the same height, and she held her gaze a moment longer than even servants in England dared. Was this what rankled Mr. Shubert, her air of . . . authority?

"These keys will give you access to the house," Mitilda said, "as well as to the storehouse and the mill."

Keturah nodded. "Thank you. But there is no need for you to go, Mitilda. If my father trusted you as housekeeper, then so shall we."

Behind her, Shubert snorted. One of his companions chuckled and lightly punched the other as if in jest. Keturah stiffened but kept her attention on Mitilda.

The thin woman with the coffee-colored skin gave her a pained smile. "I think not, Lady Tomlinson," she said, then reached out to wrap an arm around the shoulders of the boy. "Upon his death, your father set my son, Abraham, and I free. He gave us a stipend to live on—ten pounds a year. That cottage, on the edge of the clearing, and a bit of land to work. We were jus' looking after the place until proper relations could arrive."

Something about the words *proper relations* made Ket look to the boy again. She studied the line of his nose, the fullness of his lips. She noted the golden glint to his brown eyes that reminded her of her own, as well as of her father's. How odd that he would have it too.

*Proper relations.*

Those eyes, like *hers*. Like . . . *Father's*.

In that moment her heart began pounding painfully in her chest, sending a wave of vertigo through her. *A stipend to live on. Setting them free*, when he had not done the same for any of the slaves he'd held at Hartwick Manor all their lives.

There'd be only one reason he'd do that for these two.

She drew a hand to her chest, even as she heard Mr. Shubert huff another laugh under his breath. This was why he'd insisted on coming here. Why he hadn't left even after they'd arrived at the plantation. Because he wanted to witness *this*—their meeting with *that* woman and *that* child.

These two who were clearly her father's mistress . . . and his son.

# CHAPTER TWELVE

"Get out," Keturah muttered, shaking her head. Suddenly all she felt was fury, insensible fury. *How could she?* How could Mitilda have done it? Taken up with a white man? Compromised his reputation? And now she stood here before them as if she was the *very lady* of this house? "Go!" she cried, her voice cracking. "Go!"

"Ket," Verity said, grabbing her sister's wrist and turning Ket toward her. It seemed Ver hadn't put two and two together, even though she'd been startled by an uneasy recognition.

"Keturah!" Selah whispered, equally confused.

But Mitilda and her boy were already moving past the gloating Mr. Shubert, his wide mouth twisting into a sneer. "You can come keep house for *me* now, Mitilda," he called to her. It was as if he enjoyed seeing the woman being brought down a notch. As if this set an old wrong finally right.

Keturah stared at Mitilda's trim back and her swishing skirts, and at her young son, who glanced over his shoulder at them as though wondering what was happening, before she felt the first pang of regret. *What was his name?*

But it was too late for Ket to call them back. Even if she tried, what would she say? She had no idea.

*Climb this tree, Ket, one limb at a time.*

"I'm certain you must be on your way, Mr. Shubert," she said

132

curtly, dismissing him before turning to the others. "Cuffee and Edwin, please go to the slaves' cabins and report back to me what you find. How many still live and what their immediate needs are. Absalom, see to our two new arrivals. Bring them into the house and to the kitchen. Get them all the fresh water they can drink and see if there might be a bit of bread. Primus, take the keys and survey the outbuildings. I assume one is a storehouse. I expect a report on what you find too. Verity and Selah, come with me." She forced a smile, trying to encourage her shaken sisters. "Let's go see what our new home is like at last!"

She hurried up the stairs, anxious to put more distance between herself and the neighbor's overseer. "Good day, Mr. Shubert," she briskly said, once they had reached the top of the creaky stairs.

"At your service, Lady Tomlinson," he said with a nod, a bit of a smile still tugging at his lips. He'd found what he came for— some sort of comeuppance for Mitilda and surely a story to share with others. He was only a few years older than she, but Keturah felt that he knew this world as if he'd lived here decades longer. Perhaps he had. Would the Banning women spend the rest of their days providing stories for the local gossips everywhere they went?

*Most likely*, she thought with a heavy sigh. She entered the house and waited at the door until her sisters were inside, then shut out the rest. She leaned her head against the door, feeling the relief of being just their own trio for a moment.

"Ket," Verity began, putting a hand on her shoulder. "Was that child . . . was he . . . ?"

"He is our brother," Keturah whispered, nose still against the mahogany door. It held that unique tropical wood scent she had come to know aboard the *Restoration*.

Selah gasped. "What did she just say?"

"She said he's our brother," Verity answered stiffly.

"Our . . . brother?" Selah squeaked. "How is that possible?"

All sorts of unladylike thoughts came to Keturah's mind, but she kept silent, waiting for Selah to fully understand. *Father. No, Father. How could you?*

"Oh," Selah breathed. "I see. But . . . no. How could it be? How could he have done that to Mother?"

"Mother never knew," Ket said. She turned around, her back to the door but her hand on its iron latch, as if holding on to something helped her remain standing. Her knees felt wobbly beneath her skirts. "Just as Father was intent on our never knowing. He never thought we would come here. He never believed we would meet them ourselves. Many tried to warn us," she added, reaching out one hand to Verity, the other to Selah. "They told us this place would shock us to our very bones, make us quake in our shoes. They said it was no place for a lady, and if this afternoon is any indication, I would say they had ample cause."

Ket took a deep breath and let it out slowly. "But we are here, sisters. We have made it through weeks of being at sea and a threatening storm. We saved two slaves from a harsh master. We have only just endured meeting two people of . . . *relations* unlike we ever could have anticipated. And yet somehow we *managed* it," she said, squeezing their hands. "Shall we not take those steps as victories and move forward from here?"

Verity nodded slowly, and then Selah did the same, each squeezing her hand in return. Clinging to one another, they walked through the wide parlor with its large windows overlooking the steep incline of a hill and the sea far below. It was a far more marvelous view than Ket had ever imagined, with the deep green of the jungle meeting the remains of the light, bits of swaying green cane—latent stalks post-harvest—stretching all the way down to the turquoise water.

The shutters had been left open, allowing the breeze to flow in and through the room. The girls forced themselves to turn from the captivating view and take in the peeling wallpaper, a faded leaf print, and the once-impressive mahogany crown molding and millwork, stained and splintered after years of exposure to the island's humidity. The wooden floors were buckling in places, and the Turkish rugs were either rotting or nearly worn through. But it was all clean, Keturah surmised. Impeccably clean.

Shoving thoughts of Mitilda aside, Ket pushed through the swinging wooden door to the kitchen just as Absalom and the two new slaves disappeared out the back door. The kitchen was equipped with a cast-iron stove in the corner and wide marble counters. There were kettles and pans of all sizes, as well as barrels labeled FLOUR, SUGAR, and, atop the counter, a much smaller one labeled SALT. A quick peek in each told her they were empty—even the one marked SUGAR—and she sighed with disappointment. She glanced back at the stove, and her mouth began watering at the thought of bread baking or bacon frying. Silently, she prayed that the men would find some food in the storehouse, something to supplement what they had purchased in town so they might make it through until tomorrow.

Tomorrow they might find new troubles. Her only task was to find her way through today's.

They moved on to a passageway that led to her father's office—*I shall need to return here and read everything I can find*, Keturah thought—then on to a bedroom that the boy had clearly been inhabiting beside the stairs. There were toy soldiers on the floor arranged in neat lines and a leather ball in the corner. It was only then that Ket realized she'd sent the woman and child running, not even giving them time to collect their things. Where had they gone? The aforementioned cottage? She'd have to find the strength to reach out to the woman and invite her back to gather her meager belongings.

But not yet. Not yet.

Tentatively, they climbed the squeaky stairs. At the top, they found six rooms, the four in the middle small and sparse, and those on each end of grand size. "This should be yours," Verity said to Ket. "My, look at the view from here," she went on, moving closer to one of the windows.

But Keturah was shaking her head. Because as much as this had been her father's room, it was also the one he'd most likely shared with *her*. Mitilda. Bile rose in her throat. "No," she said. "Come. Let us find other quarters."

Once her sisters were out in the hallway again, she firmly shut the door to his room, as if she could shut out the very thought of her father's mistress. They each decided to take one of the smaller rooms that ushered in the leeward breezes from broad windows. Given the heat of high summer, Keturah knew it would be particularly vital to have the breeze.

"We'll get our things settled inside and soon it will feel utterly cozy," she said, thinking of their feather beds, pillows, and linens. Such finery in the midst of such a dilapidated mess! She shook her head wearily. It mattered not. She decided she could sleep just about anywhere right now, once she had a little food in her stomach. The only other items in each room were a small table, a washbasin and pitcher. There was no artwork or paper on the plaster walls. At the ceiling, there was evidence of a roof leak, the dark streaks of mold creeping their way down the plaster like a serpentine monster.

They found a larger room at the end of the hall with a receiving closet to one side. This too was empty, showing no trace of her father's mistress, and Keturah followed her sisters inside.

"Oh, Ket, then *this* should be yours," Verity said, turning in delight. "With a bit of work it shall be a quite proper room and receiving room."

"Look at all this shellwork!" Selah said, walking to one window as Keturah went to another. Each of the three windows in the room had hundreds upon hundreds of seashells in neat and tidy rows inlaid in the plaster. She'd known her father had dabbled with shell art years ago, making mirror frames for their mother and jewelry boxes for the girls after he'd visited the West Indies. As she toured it, she could not help but wonder, had he created this for Mother? Hoping that someday his wife might come here to join him?

Her mother had never displayed his mirrors. Instead, she had them moved to the attic as soon as he set sail again, considering the mirrors passé in style. But her father loved the mirrors, and Ket had spent hours in the attic, wondering over them. It was as if he had been trying to bring the Indies to her mother if she wouldn't come to see its wonders herself.

Ket had once overheard the two of them talking, on the eve of one of his departures. Ket hovered in the shadows, and the thought of her shameless spying embarrassed her even now. She recalled how she'd so wished for her father not to leave again. Even after being sent to bed, she clamored for any spare moment with him she could obtain, even if it had to be gained in secrecy. Or so she consoled herself as she stood hidden in the shadows.

"Come with me, dearest," he'd begged her mother. "We can leave the girls in the care of their governess. Simply come. See what draws me to the island, my love. Come to know what pulls me there."

"Oh, Mr. Banning," her mother had said—Mother had never called Father by his first name—"you know as well as I that a mother's place is with her children. Would you remove me from my proper place?"

"For a chance to walk with you by the sea, your pretty little toes covered in sand? To see how your golden hair curls in the heat of the tropics? To glimpse more of your beautiful skin, bared beneath the sun's rays?" He lifted her hand to his lips, and her mother ducked her head and covered her mouth with her other hand as if scandalized by the suggestion. He'd pulled her closer. "Come, dearest. I have need of you. The months there . . . they stretch on endlessly. A man . . . well, a man needs his wife by his side."

Ket's mother had pulled her hand from his. "Return to *us*, Mr. Banning," she insisted. "If you have need of your wife, then you may always find her here at Hartwick Manor, might you not?"

A flash of disappointment had frozen his face a moment, and then it sagged. He nodded. "I suppose you are right, dearest. This is the best place for you, as well as for the girls. But I confess I shall sorely miss you."

Ket turned away, the memory so vivid in her mind that it felt as though she were twelve years old again and witnessing the exchange for the first time.

*Father had missed Mother so much that he'd taken a mistress,* Keturah thought darkly.

*How could he be so weak? How could he betray Mother so? And
. . . Had Mitilda been the only one? Were there others before her?*
Keturah's own husband, Edward, had certainly felt it his right
to lie with any of the chambermaids. Had her father been the
same way?

"Ket," Verity said, and judging by her tone, she'd been waiting
on Ket again. How often had her sisters found her lost in reverie—
both good and bad—of late?

Ket turned from the seashell-lined window.

"Will you take this room as your own?" Ver asked, a hundred
other questions behind her concerned gaze.

"I shall," Ket said. "And we shall make one of the smaller rooms
a shared closet for you both. After all," she said, lifting her chin
and forcing a grin. "We are now proper ladies of the Indies. It's
time we bring what we wish of England here to Nevis."

# CHAPTER THIRTEEN

Despite what she'd hoped they would find, there was little to eat for their supper—especially considering that Edwin and Absalom had rounded up six hungry slaves. The other fifty had reportedly either died of the fever that took her father's life or been taken by creditors claiming Banning debts. A few, some said, had run away to the mountain jungles above them.

Dazed, Keturah looked upward as if to see Nevis Peak beyond her ceiling. "Runaways can find a way to live up there?" Most of the mountain had been cleared for cane, but the utmost portion appeared to remain dense jungle.

"Yes, Lady Ket," Edwin said, nodding eagerly. "They say there's a whole colony, a mix of freed men and escaped slaves. It makes the white gentlemen and ladies uneasy, them being up there, but they keep to themselves mostly, other than to steal a chicken or pig to feed themselves. On occasion the militia tries to bring them to ground, but they haven't had a great deal of luck."

Keturah looked about the group again. The slaves who were left appeared old and infirm, the reasons obvious as to why they remained. They were in poor shape to escape to the jungles, and they'd be the last to be chosen by creditors seeking to settle a debt. As abhorrent as she found the slave market that afternoon, she could see no way other than to return to it. A plantation this size

. . . well, there was a reason her father had once owned more than a hundred slaves. There was simply no other way to plant, fertilize, water, weed, and harvest an estate like this without significant numbers of people.

Keturah tried to hide how the thought made her feel physically ill. She had no desire for her sisters to sense her rising panic. "Edwin, introduce me to these people, please," she said, gesturing to the remaining slaves. He did so, and Keturah, Verity, and Selah learned the names of each. Only Mimba and Bennabe, the two men, and a woman named Sansa looked like they had anything left to give her and Tabletop. Long-faced Mimba had a scar down his left cheek and was thinner than the stooped-shouldered Sansa, who was frightfully gaunt. Bennabe was middle-aged and missing an arm. But while the others stared at her blankly and uncaring—as if their very souls had been beaten to dust—these three had a spark of interest behind their eyes, as if curious about these newcomers and what it might mean for them all.

"Bennabe," she said, focusing her attention on him, "why did you not run away?"

He shrugged, and her eyes trailed down to the stump of his right arm. "This been my home for most of my life, mum," he said. "Couldn't see myself in another."

His words stirred hope in her heart. If he'd been here most of his life, he was as close to an overseer as she might find at the moment. "Would you mind showing us about the plantation tomorrow? Telling us about how the crops are faring and . . ." Her words trailed off as he slowly shook his head. Her heart thudded to a stop, then began pounding. She forced herself to ask. "The crops? Please tell me there are crops planted."

Again, Bennabe shook his head as fear replaced that spark she'd glimpsed earlier.

Keturah's mind raced. Every plantation they'd passed had young cane in the ground. From what she'd learned in reading Gray's book, it was critical to have cane planted as soon as the harvest was complete. With a fifteen-to-eighteen-month growing cycle, every week counted. Gray himself had fretted about what he might find on his plantation—had everything come to a standstill for him too?

She'd hoped that her father, or the last overseer, had replanted following the harvest, but with funds so tight and the overseer dying, then her father . . . was it any wonder the only cane on the land might be the remnants of the harvest below the house? It had been a foolish hope to think they'd arrive to new cane in the fields.

Keturah took a long, deep breath. "Very well. We shall revisit that fact tomorrow. But might you take us about and show us the millworks and all so that I might know where we stand? What is in good working order and what needs to be repaired? How many more people we'll need to work this land?"

"Yes'm, I can do that," Bennabe said. Again, she glimpsed the spark rising behind his old eyes, and she wondered if it had been her words or her kind treatment of him that told her that spark might, in time, become flame.

"For now, Bennabe, we are clearly in need of food and water. All of us. The cupboards and pantry are bare in the house. How long has it been since you and the others ate?"

The older man averted his eyes as if not wanting to upset her with the answer. "Well now, mum . . ."

"Lady Ket," she corrected gently. "Everyone calls me Lady Ket."

"Lady Ket," he repeated. "Your father was a kind master. He let us plant gardens. Those sweet potatoes and yams are what has been keeping our bellies full these past weeks. Plus the mangoes we pick."

"I see."

"Miss Mitilda, she sometimes shares some corn or a bit of bread. But she and the boy haven't had much more than we for quite some time." He hooked a thumb over his shoulder, toward a tidy-looking cottage on the far edge of the clearing.

Keturah's eyes went to the structure the woman had mentioned. *So that is where they went.* She wondered if the tall, thin woman was hovering inside at that moment, watching them from the shadows. Wouldn't she be doing the same, curious to know more about the newcomers? Begrudgingly she admitted to herself that Mitilda could be a tremendous resource to her, helping her learn how to run a household on-island, if not the entire plantation. Between Bennabe and Mitilda, they could help her a great deal.

But that was as far as she would consider it. The thought of seeing that woman and that child . . . well, it was preposterous. It was only her Christian upbringing that kept her from driving the harlot from her land. From this very island! That, she admitted, and the caveat in Father's will that Mitilda claimed left her the cottage, a spot of land to work, and a yearly stipend. *A yearly stipend . . .*

The words made her scalp tingle with rage. And yet . . . the child. *The child.* Her own half brother. He was not culpable in this. How could she even think of driving him out?

"Lady Ket?" Primus was speaking, edging into her line of vision. "Others are inquiring if they should go about picking some fruit."

"Yes, yes," she said hurriedly. "Do so, please. And some of you fetch a bucket of fresh water from the well. I assume we have drinkable water here, correct?" She thought she remembered Father extolling the sweet water that came from a spring, fed by the mountain nearby.

Bennabe nodded eagerly and she breathed a sigh of relief. At least there was clean water available, some fruit, and later a good night's rest. It was enough for now.

Tomorrow they would take on the future.

# CHAPTER FOURTEEN

"Verity, get up! *Selah!*" Keturah hissed, peeking out her window again as she hurriedly tried to run her fingers through her knotted hair.

It was the creaking of saddles and clicking of horseshoes on stone that had awakened her out of a dead sleep. Below, she glimpsed men in tricorn hats, a wagon, a flash of pink gown, and mixed voices speaking in undertones. Judging from the sun's position in the sky, it was scandalously late to still be found sleeping.

After seeing the wagons unloaded and the servants settled in their quarters, the three of them had gotten as far as making up Keturah's bed before they collapsed together atop it as they might have when they were but wee girls. Ket awoke with Verity's arm wrapped across her waist and Selah nestled against her side.

Keturah threw open her trunk and pulled a clean gown down over her shift. "Make haste!" she groused at her sisters. "I do not wish to face our guests alone." She grimaced at the folds in her skirts, so clearly just out of the trunk.

"Oh, Ket," Verity said, sitting up and shaking her head sleepily. "Your hair . . ."

"I am aware! Yours, I fear, is little better." But what was she to do? *Her father's room.* Much as she lamented the idea of entering that oddly intimate and yet curiously foreign space, she saw no way around it. Mitilda had kept the contents intact. And somewhere in there had to be a brush, a comb, *something*. "I'll return in a moment. Please be dressed when I do."

"Lady Ket!" said Grace, knocking on her door. "You have guests."

Keturah yanked open the door and paused, trying for what seemed the thousandth time since arriving on-island to gather herself. "Good morning," she said while accepting a pitcher of water and basin from the girl. "Please tell our guests we will be down to greet them shortly."

The girl's eyes widened at the sight of her, but then she nodded and turned to leave. Her sisters took hold of pitcher and basin, as eager for a morning bath as she.

"Wait," Keturah whispered. "Who are they, Grace?"

"Your neighbors, Lady Ket. From Morning Star Plantation, they said. They have come to welcome you."

Keturah rubbed her temples as she watched the girl rush down the stairs to relay the message to their guests. How was it, she wondered, that the servant could look as if she'd already had a morning bath and put on a fresh dress? Had she washed her gown the night before and hung it to dry as she slept? For Ket and her sisters, it was all they could do to climb into bed before succumbing to unconsciousness.

She tiptoed down the hall across ancient rugs that showed the abuse of either insects or rodents—or both—well aware that her guests would hear the squeaking floorboards. Pushing open the heavy door of her father's quarters, she hurried to a dressing table and lifted a horsehair brush, looking glass, and comb. She was about to depart when she paused. Was it only her imagination or did this room still smell of Father? Tentatively, she stepped over to the bed, lifted a pillow, and inhaled.

But all she smelled was lavender. *Her* scent, she knew, never Father's. With some distaste, she tossed the pillow back on the bed and rushed out of the room. She tore down the hall, went to the dressing table, raked the brush through her matted hair, then quickly stuffed the majority of it underneath her filthy cap. She looked herself up and down, aware that her sisters were just a minute behind her in their preparations. But she could not keep their guests waiting any longer. What would they think of them, asleep at this hour? What might it be, eleven o'clock? She'd spied a clock in her father's room, but it had likely not been wound in months. And the clock they'd brought with them was not yet unpacked.

She smoothed down her skirts and then scoffed at herself for the effort. There was no disguising that Keturah and her sisters had just stepped off the boat. There was little doubt in her mind that her neighbors already had a good idea of the dilapidated state of Tabletop. Her only hope was to throw herself at their mercy and see what measure she could take of them.

She strode down the stairs and into the large parlor, where two gentlemen in fine jackets and pristine white neckcloths and shirts rose at once. A young lady and older woman stood as well.

"Lady Tomlinson, I presume," said the first, a man of about thirty. He paused to draw the barest of breaths before giving her a most charming smile, taking her hand, and bowing over it.

*Pressing through*, Keturah surmised, *despite how I must appear.* It grated on her pride, being found in such a state. But just as he had, she elected to press on, pretending nothing was amiss.

"I am Jeffrey Weland, of Morning Star Plantation." He was of average looks, slender and tan, about Ket's height, with hair bleached from hours in the sun. "This is my younger sister, Miss Esmerelda Weland, my mother, Mrs. Glorietta Weland, and my younger brother, Mr. Harrison Weland."

The women curtsied, and his brother graciously took her hand too. "At your service, Lady Tomlinson," Harrison said, who wasn't as good as his brother at disguising his distaste at her unkempt appearance. Rather, his homely face revealed both shock and curiosity.

"Is it true, Lady Tomlinson?" young Esmerelda crooned in her Creole accent, pressing between her brothers to edge nearer. "Have you and your sisters come all this way with not one man to attend you?"

Ket smiled. "Well, we did bring some of our servants from England, many of them male. But yes, we came without any male relations."

"Quite courageous of you, I'd say," said Jeffrey, looking her over with renewed interest.

A glance at his finger told her he was unmarried and judging her as prime Nevisian bride material. She stiffened at the thought.

"Quite," added their mother abruptly. "I well remember arriving on-island for the first time myself. See here. We have brought you enough food to hold you for a day or two, and other gifts to soften your . . . transition. A spot of tea. A few crumpets, which my cook made just this morning."

"Oh!" Selah interjected, arriving at last with Verity at her heels. "Crumpets? Can it be true?" she asked dreamily as introductions were made. It wasn't lost on Keturah how Harrison, the younger brother, seemed to come alive once Selah entered the room. The girls met their new neighbors with all the vivacity and charm they might use at a ball in London, and Ket felt a surge of pride. What might this adventure have felt like, encountering it all without them by her side?

*Overwhelming*, she decided, and utterly so. But still, after a night's sleep, in the light of day and with the promise of a good meal, she felt a sense of hope. An urgency to dispatch these guests and get on with it. To see what their father had truly left them, then begin making plans to make the most of it.

Cuffee came in quietly and hovered at the edge of their circle in polite hesitation, but it was Brutus's screeching that made the group turn around.

"So that is true too!" Esmerelda enthused, clasping her hands and tucking them beneath her chin. "One of you is a falconer!"

"Indeed," Verity said, striding forward to take a leather glove from Cuffee, then the bird from him. The falcon was agitated and seemed to be chastising her for his overnight abandonment.

"He's been like that all morning, Miss Verity."

"'Tis all right, Cuffee. He needs only a moment with me. To

know I am here and he will be looked after. And a chance to learn about his new environs."

"Yes, Miss Verity."

Verity removed Brutus's tiny hood and tucked it into her waistband. She untied his leg strap and lifted him up, setting him free to fly. The big bird flapped his wings and rose, climbing high and circling around them until he disappeared in the bright sun. Esmerelda laughed in delight, and her brothers hooted.

Selah's arm looped through Ket's. "It feels as if he's blessing us, and the plantation, circling like that, up into the very sun itself."

"Of all the *audacious* things to say!" Mrs. Weland said, fanning herself.

But her high color only matched Verity's, who merely smiled back at her and then looked back to the sky. "Is it not?"

"Yes, well . . ." said the older woman, clearly flummoxed by her response. "Would you care to join us for supper tomorrow night? You shall have your hands full this day, heading to Charlestown for supplies and such. But tomorrow eve, come to Morning Star. We shall see that you have a proper island greeting with a small soiree to introduce you to Nevis's finest."

"That would be most kind of you," Keturah said. After all, it was incumbent on her to learn everything she could about getting Tabletop on schedule for some sort of harvest, and what better place to begin her research than among other planters?

"Very good," Mrs. Weland said, obviously pleased. Her slanted brown eyes flicked to each of her sons, then over to the Banning sisters, resting on Keturah the longest.

It wasn't until then that Keturah understood. This wasn't merely a social call; the woman was in the market for daughters-in-law. Keturah glanced at both men again and, upon her first assessment, couldn't see how either would be a match for any of the sisters. Not that her own heart would be an option. The men seemed affable enough, yet neither appeared to have much in the way of *gumption*.

And if there was one thing a Banning girl needed, it was strength and gumption in a man.

They spent the day in Charlestown as Mrs. Weland foretold, returning their rented wagons, purchasing another, locating basic dry supplies, arranging to get another wagon on the plantation repaired. Back at Tabletop, every one of the livestock listed had been either stolen or butchered and eaten. So they bought four horses and a mule from the Carolinas, a sow and three piglets, a goat, and a dozen chickens. In addition, Keturah purchased six new pails, twenty blankets, twenty straw-tick sacks, bales of hay to stuff them, cotton gowns for the slave women, and shirts and breeches for their male counterparts.

They circumvented the slaver platforms, aware that they would need to purchase additional slaves if they were to get Tabletop back on track. Today, however, Keturah and her sisters simply had no stomach for it. They stopped at the milliner for new hats with the broader brims that were understandably fashionable in the islands, and a tailor's shop to order three new gowns for each of them, as well as shifts, stays and underthings, all of them made out of the lightest cotton and silk the tailor could possibly find. One of the gowns was to be a sturdy work dress, a second a bit fancier, and the third something they could wear to parties. In time, they would need more island-appropriate clothing—much of what they'd brought from England was too formal and too warm to wear—but this was a start.

It was their good fortune that the tailor had a number of partially completed dress gowns, so he could easily finish one for each of them by the next day, promising to send them in time for the soiree at Morning Star Plantation.

Within the first hour of being in Charlestown, Keturah became aware that the Misses Banning were the talk of the island. Most of the prominent landowners expected to attend the Morning Star soiree to meet the daughters of Richard Banning, whom many had considered a good friend. One after another they expressed the same sentiment, crossing themselves and muttering "God rest his soul."

As she walked about in the sultry heat of the island town, Keturah wondered if her father's soul was truly at rest. Did God truly offer such a thing? Day by day, night by night, had she not prayed for peace between her and Edward? For rest?

And would God welcome a sinner such as her father—a man living in open relationship with a slave girl and their child—into heaven?

She was angry at her father. Furious. For so disrespecting her mother, and his daughters, that he had dared to take up with another woman. A woman he had *purchased*.

Shame washed through her. No matter where she stood with the Almighty, surely she did not truly wish for Father's soul to be in peril, did she? Keturah sighed, well aware that a part of her thought it justice as much as the other part wished for nothing but mercy for her beloved father.

*God rest his soul.*

———

Still, she was in no mood to see her father's mistress and her illegitimate son when they pulled up in the clearing before the dilapidated, grand house of Tabletop Plantation. Mitilda and Abraham were out beside the cottage, working their small plot of land as if they had every right to be there. And with one look at the will her father had left, Keturah knew they did, despite how it grated.

Mitilda paused, wiped her forehead and upper lip of sweat, glanced at them all, then resumed her work as if they were a passing flock of pelicans, only idly interesting.

Ket frowned. Why did the woman's dismissal irritate her so? What was it that she expected of Mitilda? Respect? Surely. The woman could give her that, at least. After all, it was her father who had given her a home, land to work, a future!

*But at what cost to her?* Ket wondered. Had her father forced himself on the woman or had she welcomed his attentions? What of the stature it brought her on the plantation? She hadn't missed the woman's fine dress, her boots, as well as the boy's. No other slave on Tabletop had had anything nearly as proper to wear. *But at what cost?* railed her conscience again.

She thought of Edward and what his nightly ministrations had cost her. He'd been intent on an heir, and with each passing month in which she failed to turn up pregnant, he became more bitter, more brutal. The thought of her father forcing himself on Mitilda in any similar way . . . well, it turned her stomach.

Pushing such distasteful thoughts aside, she set Primus and Gideon upon distributing the clothes to those in need in the slaves' quarters. Grace and Edwin were tasked with baking bread and some fish for their tardy afternoon meal, and Absalom was sent to spell Bennabe, who had been left to keep an eye on the two new slaves to make sure they didn't run for the mountain refuge, as some had warned. "Find out their names!" she called after him. "Or give them names, if you must," she added.

What did one do with people with whom you had not one word in common? There might be people on Nevis who spoke the African tongue, but from what she had learned, there were many different dialects. Slavers might arrive with human cargo speaking ten versions.

She shook her head. *One limb at a time.* First, something to assuage her rumbling belly. Second, a bath and a change out of their filthy gowns. Third, a rest, before they mounted their new horses and surveyed the plantation.

She had just asked the maids to heat water for a bath when Mimba, the old Tabletop slave, came into the kitchen to ask for some bread. When he heard her, he said, "You ought to go up to the waterfall pool, Lady Ket, to bathe. That's where your father always favored."

She stared at him, wondering if she had heard him correctly. "The waterfall?" She noticed then the long scar that ran down his left cheek.

"That's right," he said with a single nod, his Creole accent and tone making his words affable. "Take that trail yonder past the stables and head up, up, up. 'Bout a mile in, you see another trail to the right, there beside a twin tree. Follow it and you'll find a lovely pool of fresh water, with enough brush around it for privacy. Your father used to take a bar of soap, a towel, and a fresh shirt, and returned home a new man. Even invited some of us to join him a few times after a long, hard day in the fields."

Keturah stared at him blankly. In all her life she could not have imagined her proper, formal father bathing in the wild, let alone with servants. But then she could not have imagined him taking a mistress and making her the lady of the house either. *And he'd certainly done that.*

"Thank you, Mimba," she said crisply, dismissing the thought. "I think I shall take my bath indoors this day," she said over her shoulder, already leaving the kitchen. She could feel rather than hear his doubt over the wisdom of that, but she knew that if her mother were here, she would never condone any sort of outdoor bathing. The closest they'd come was a swimming hole near Hartwick Manor, where they'd meet other neighbor children for a romp in the water. But that was a public swimming hole, not some hidden pool . . .

*Gray,* she thought wistfully, remembering him as a boy swinging over the swimming hole on an old rope and then falling to the surface, knees tucked, his aim to splash them all. He had been so exuberant. Delirious in the freedom. Somehow she knew he wouldn't have thought twice about bathing in the pool Mimba had mentioned.

She wondered how he was faring. In what state had he found his own plantation? He wasn't far away, and yet after becoming accustomed to their closer proximity during the voyage, it felt as though he were a hundred miles away. She climbed the stairs and went to her room, then to her window, gazing across the remains of sugarcane down to the sea. Had Gray found a home in shambles or in good working order? She hoped, for his sake, that it was in better shape than hers at Tabletop. With any luck there might even be cane in the ground already, an overseer, and slaves hard at work.

Gray had glimpsed Keturah and her sisters pass through town, through the open window of the mercantile in which he and Philip were buying supplies. The plantation house was nothing grand, only two bedrooms, a small kitchen, and a parlor, but it was all they really needed. It was in relatively good condition, other than a hole in the roof that needed patching. Along with the pile of food supplies, he added a bucket of nails, a roll of tar paper, and asked for a bundle of shingles too.

He had a hard time not letting his mouth drop open when the shopkeeper totaled his bill. He'd known, of course, that everything was ten times the expense here on the island, but facing it for the first time came as an unwelcome surprise. He was just counting out the coin to pay the shop owner when two men entered, talking about women they'd seen down the street.

"Banning's youngest, the blonde—she won't be alone for long," said one. He let out a low whistle of admiration. "She's a beauty."

Gray stiffened.

"None of them will be alone for long," said the other, slapping the back of his hand against his friend's chest. "That Keturah has her late husband's fortune as well as the deed to Tabletop, and she's fair enough," he added, lowering his voice as if becoming aware that others might be listening.

Gray gathered his things and met Philip's eye. The two moved away from the counter and toward the door.

"Ahh, who do we have here?" said one of the men, sizing up Gray and Philip and the items in their arms. "More newcomers to the island?"

"Indeed," Gray said. "I am Gray Covington. I've come to take over Teller's Landing. And this is my man, Philip."

"Welcome, welcome," said the first man, perhaps five years older than Gray. He was a rotund man with a rounded nose and shadows under his eyes that spoke of a night of drinking. "I am Xavier Armstrong, and this is my cousin, Stanley Lloyd. We hail from Silver Spring, down in Gingerland."

"At your service," Gray said with a polite nod to each.

"So . . . Teller's Landing, you say. That land has been rented out in recent years, has it not?"

"It has. The Welands of Morning Star worked it. But I've come to try my hand at running the plantation now."

"I see, I see," Armstrong said, and it was clear as his brown eyes ran over Gray that he thought he wouldn't last long. "I hope you know what you are getting into. Many arrive from England with visions of cane leaves dripping with gold florins."

"And many more depart having spent their last one," Stanley said, crossing his arms.

"So I've heard," Gray said evenly. "I did my share of studying before we set sail. I believe I'm up to the challenge."

"Good man, good man." Armstrong's words were far more encouraging than his tone. It was as if he'd already judged Gray and found him wanting.

"Well, we must be off. There is much to do at the plantation."

"I can only imagine," Armstrong said. The two men parted, allowing Gray and Philip to pass.

"Say," said Lloyd, "if you arrived on the *Restoration*, then you had the chance to make the acquaintance of the Misses Banning, did you not?"

"I did," Gray said, his hand on the doorknob.

"Then do us a favor, man. Tell us, are any of them currently . . . entangled? What I mean to say is . . . are they as single as is rumored? Open to courting?"

"Ahh, no. I doubt it," he said with a slow shake of his head. Honestly, he believed Keturah wouldn't consider a man for some time. Verity seemed to take a fancy to Captain McKintrick. And it would be over his dead body that he would allow either of these pompous fools to court sweet Selah, "the blonde" they had so crassly admired upon entering the shop. He hid a smile when their faces drooped. "The Misses Banning and Lady Tomlinson are here for one reason only, gentlemen, and that is to turn Tabletop around. Not to find husbands. Good day."

He held back a grin as they departed. Outside, they waited

for the shopkeeper's slave to bring out their goods and load them into the wagon.

Philip took off his hat and wiped both forehead and face of sweat. He gave Gray a long look. "Think that was your place, Gray? To speak for the ladies?"

Gray scowled and glanced toward the open window of the shop. "I promised their cousin Cecil I would look after them. If I can keep a few wolves from their door, why should I not?"

Philip nodded, ever conciliatory, and pursed his lips. "That's a fine reason. Or is it that you hope to court Lady Keturah yourself?"

Gray scoffed. "Me?" he said with a frown, even as a hundred different exchanges aboard the *Restoration* came to mind. "No," he said emphatically. He raised a hand. "Now, I admit that we're old friends. And aboard ship, there were a few times I thought . . ." He paused, staring off toward the sparkling blue-green of the Caribbean. Had he not dreamed of her last night? He sighed and shook his head. "No, 'tis as I said inside the shop—Keturah is only here to turn Tabletop around."

Philip nodded again. "What of Verity? Or Selah?"

Gray cocked his head. "There really is no sense in continuing this conversation. I have nothing to offer a bride. No home. No fortune. Until I turn Teller's Landing around . . ."

Philip moved to slide open the back of the wagon as the slave came outside with their things. "And when you do?" he pressed.

Gray didn't answer. Instead, he waved Philip's nosy inquiry away with a laugh. But inside he thought, *It wouldn't be Verity or Selah I would go after.*

# CHAPTER FIFTEEN

After their meal and baths, Keturah and her sisters mounted their newly purchased mares—all of them young, strong-willed animals—and rode toward the fields along with Bennabe. The sun was dropping low in the sky, but Keturah knew she would not be able to sleep if she hadn't ventured to the end of her property and back or seen the terraces her father had been intent on building high above. She had to know if his plan had been born of madness or genius. After seeing it for herself, she intended to pore over his journals and determine if she could discern which it was.

They left the house clearing behind them and soon passed the group of old cottages intended for slaves. The door of the last cabin stood open, banging with a hollow thump in the breeze, and the shadows within sent a shiver down Ket's back. She knew she would have to fill every one of those cottages. And it would have to be soon if they were to get new cane plantings in. But in all her musings and dreams of coming to Nevis, she'd never truly thought about the cost of it all . . . the inhumanity involved. The price every slave paid. The lack of choice.

"Bennabe," she said, pulling alongside the man. He was struggling a bit in the saddle, yet he was managing. "May I ask how you lost your arm?"

He shot her such a wide grin, she saw that he was missing several bottom teeth. "Now, mum, I didn't right *lose* my arm."

She could feel herself color. "Of course," she said, laughing lightly.

Then his smile faded. "My first master was Lord Ellis over at the Camel Hill Plantation." His eyes narrowed. "His overseer was a cruel man named Bennett. He caught me stealing an apple from the larder, and then took my hand for it."

Keturah sucked in a breath.

"You see, mum, I was only but twelve and it was a famine year. Most of us got a bowl of porridge for the day and that was it. And *hoooeeee*, mum, that barrel of apples, well, we could smell them from our cabins. Some were rotting in the bottom. And I just couldn't resist the chance to eat one before it rotted out too. I knew what would come after I was caught. But Mr. Bennett, well, he was right drunk when he took the ax to my wrist. He didn't make a clean cut, and soon it got thick with rot. They had to take it to the elbow. Still the rot was coming for me, leaving me to the shakes and the sweats all through the days and nights, until they cut me again just beneath my shoulder."

Keturah felt ill. "Bennabe. That is . . . reprehensible."

He shrugged, and his eyes softened as they moved to her hand hovering over her stomach. "Mine is just one story on this island, mum," he said quietly. "Some be far worse. Best prepare yourself."

She took a deep breath and steeled herself. There was no way around it. She would simply have to find a decent overseer, and *he* could see to the purchase of the slaves who would work their land. Keturah took solace in knowing that the men and women who arrived would find Tabletop more welcoming a home than other plantations. She would be a gentle but firm mistress; at Tabletop they would work hard, but they would also find themselves well cared for. Much like the slaves at Hartwick had found themselves a home, becoming friends to the family through service and mutual dedication.

Somewhat mollified, she rode on ahead of her sisters and Bennabe, past the scraggly shoots of cane emerging here and there, bordered by towering bamboo and dark shadowy jungle. They climbed the steep slope, Nevis Peak high above them. Just over the ridge to her right was Red Rock Plantation, and just over the next ridge to her left lay Teller's Landing. She learned from Bennabe that Tabletop extended from the sea to halfway up the mountain and consisted of more than fifty acres of land. Their plantation was blessed with gentle trade winds, a break from the hot afternoon sun, as well as by the clouds that descended around the peak, often releasing rain showers as they dissipated.

"Still, your papa built an aqueduct," Bennabe went on, waving toward a stone-lined channel beside them, "to make sure his fields would flow with water whether there be drought or ample rain. It feeds all the way down to the slaves' quarters and main house, bringing us fresh water, then down yonder to the sea. It was right clever, that plan," he added in admiration. "Some struggle with dry rot in their cane, 'specially down south. Never here."

They paused at the millworks, with the same conical, gray volcanic-stone structure of fifty others Ket had seen on the way to Tabletop. Two of the giant windmill blades, each covered in sailcloth, were in tatters. "How difficult will those be to repair?" she asked.

"Not difficult at all, mum," he replied. "If we fetch a length of cloth in Charlestown, we could have it fixed in a day or two." As they rode and talked, Keturah thought the man seemed a bit livelier than he had yesterday, as if her attention sparked more of that interest and hope she'd glimpsed in his eyes the day before.

"Bennabe, we are weeks behind the others in planting. Are we too late?"

"No, mum. This island will bring you a bounty most any time of the year, except for hurricane season . . ." He hesitated.

"Go on," she urged.

"There are but two problems. If your harvest is done and the sugar ready too late, then you may not be able to ship for months, not until the ships begin running again."

"Ahh," she said. That was true. From what she knew, few ships sailed in the winter. "And the other problem?"

"Getting ships to carry your sugar to England. The other plantations will be there first, filling the ships with the biggest holds. You will likely have to ship fewer hogsheads on more ships. But tha' not all bad either. Your papa thought it best to break up the shipment. That way, if a ship went down or a captain stole more than his fair share, the loss wouldn't be so great."

She stared at him, amazed by the breadth of his knowledge. Beyond him, she saw Verity's brows raised in appreciation too.

"What do you mean by a captain stealing more than his 'fair share'?" Verity asked.

Bennabe gave her a shy smile. "Well, mum, the cap'ns always take a portion for themselves. Time and again we shipped, say, ten hogsheads on a ship, and the buyer in Liverpool registered seven. Now, did the captain take those three missing hogsheads? Did the crew? Or the dockhands? Or did the hogshead itself fall into the water or rot or the rats get to it? Can't right say, mum. Most wouldn't see it as a problem, not until a plantation ships ten and only five get all the way to where they're goin'."

Ket felt her mouth drop in outrage. And yet the man seemed to think it common practice. "Did my father not press to find out what transpired with our own missing hogsheads? The captains are paid for the cargo's passage, correct? They have no right to take more!"

"No right, mum," he said, then shrugged. "Just the way 'tis. We can plant the cane and press it. Put it in hogsheads and ship it. After that, it's outta our hands."

She stared at him for a long moment. "How long have you been at Tabletop, Bennabe?"

"Your gran'papa bought me from my first master when he tired of having a one-armed slave. He was right kind, as was your papa, mum, and found me things to do. He liked to explain things to me, taught me my numbers and letters even. But mostly I think he told me things because he was putting them in proper order in his own mind."

"That sounds like Father," Verity said. "He was always going on and on to Mother while she did her needlework, seeming not to mind if she was listening or not. Thinking aloud."

"But she did," Keturah said, feeling a flash of defensiveness. "Time and time again I saw her respond."

"Well, of course she did," Verity said, tucking her head and frowning at Ket. "I'm simply saying she needed not, not always. She knew that Father needed someone to listen to him think, which is exactly what Bennabe is saying."

Keturah nodded quickly, eager to be done with their awkward exchange. Why did she feel defensive of their mother? Because of Mitilda? *Had Mother suspected?* She shook her head and then scanned the first terraced field as they reached it.

Bennabe leaned forward in the saddle and pointed. "This one took the longest. After this we had a rhythm, you see. But this field here took all of a year, and the one above a good nine months."

"And the top?" Selah said, shielding her eyes from the sun as she looked high above.

"That there is what your plantation was named after, mum. A natural butte. Up there was where we always grew the finest cane and what got your papa to thinkin'." He glanced back at them, then down toward the sea. "It was a good plan, but it took longer than your papa thought. He thought we'd be out one harvest, not two. We planted cane down below, sure, but up here is where the truly fertile ground can be found. And when we could not plant it all that second season, and we came against the blight, and the overseer died . . ." Bennabe shook his head and turned sad eyes toward Ket. "There was no food, mum. None for the slaves. Not even any food for your father and . . ."

His words trailed off and he looked away, but Keturah knew what he had been about to say. *Not even any food for your father and his woman and child.*

"And then when the fever came through and up and took so many of us . . ." Bennabe shrugged and looked sorrowfully to the empty fields, with nothing but straggling sugarcane sprouts and weeds. At the edges, Keturah could see the jungle beginning to encroach, as if hungry to reclaim what had once been hers.

"By the time the last fever came, well, we'd done had enough," he continued. "Every one of us. I tell you, jus' last week I found myself wonderin' when the next fever would end our misery—then here you three come, arrivin' like rays of sunshine on the darkest day. Did you see that, mum, on your long voyage to Nevis? Was there ever a sky covered in clouds, but then it just broke loose enough to allow a ray through, lightin' up the ocean below?"

Keturah knew what he meant. "Of course."

He held her gaze as if making sure she understood. "Do you remember how it made you feel, mum, when you saw that ray?"

Her mare pranced beneath her, eager to move on. "Surprised, I suppose. Hopeful."

"Yes," Bennabe said, gesturing to her. "That's it. You girls," he said, looking at all three of them, "have surprised us. Given me—all of us left here—hope. Now, I won' say this will be easy, but I feel hope deep in these old bones. *Hope* for Tabletop again."

She smiled. "I'm glad you're here, Bennabe. I'm glad you didn't run or that anyone else claimed you."

"Me too, mum. Me too."

They began to ride back to the house, each lost in their own thoughts. Keturah looked up into the trees. There were red-breasted blackbirds and tiny green companions flitting about, chirping, as if flaunting their beautiful feathers. And *there* . . . "Is that a *monkey*?" she asked in excitement. "There's another!"

"Where?" Verity gasped, leaning forward. "There—I see one!"

"Well, sure, mum. There be more monkeys than people about Nevis."

Keturah laughed and wondered how long it would be until Verity had a pet monkey to taunt Brutus. She eyed her sister. "Do not even think of it, Ver. 'Twill never be a consideration," she said firmly.

Verity flashed her a smile. "Never say never."

Selah caught her eye, and together they both grinned and shook their heads in resignation. Had they remained in England, Keturah knew that Verity would have driven the new French veterinarian mad with all her questions. Were she a man, Ket understood her sister would have become a veterinarian or a farrier or a falconer, just as Selah would likely have become a doctor or pastor with her compassion and care for the welfare of others. Ket considered that a moment. What career might she have pursued if she'd been born male?

With a slow smile, she looked about the plantation and down the slope of the island to the brilliant blue sea. *An adventurer*, she thought. *Or an explorer. Or a master gardener.*

*Or a plantation owner.*

*Exactly what I am*, she thought with a thrill of revelation. All along, of course, she'd known that she was walking a man's path. But being here, on-island, she knew she was walking her own path of destiny too. She didn't know what was ahead, but she knew that today—knew it deep in her bones, as Bennabe would say—she was right where she was supposed to be.

# Chapter Sixteen

The next morning, Keturah, Verity, and Selah went to meet with the banker in Charlestown. At first, Mr. Jobel seemed most kind, but it did not take long to discover he looked upon them with disapproval. She understood that he had little hard currency to lend them—cash was notoriously challenging to obtain on the island—but even after reviewing her letters from her London banker and attorney, as well as their father's and Edward's wills, he still was reluctant to set up a line of credit for them. Unfortunately they needed what only he could provide. For without an endless stream of English sterling or Spanish pieces of eight, it was through a line of credit or bartering that every plantation owner on Nevis saw to his—or her—business.

Keturah remained seated and still, patiently smiling at the banker, even as her sisters kept shifting in their seats and looking at her, clearly wanting to excuse themselves. He blustered and droned on about the complexities of running a plantation and how every *man* he knew found it challenging. He spent nearly an hour talking about the history of the island, of plantations built to respectable, even enviable stature, then demolished in a hurricane or cane blight. Something that many *men* could not even bear.

Even so, Keturah stayed where she was, nodding, listening, smiling. And she dared not meet her sisters' urgent looks.

At last the aged banker realized she did not intend to leave until she received what she expected. He sighed, gave her one last look over the rim of his spectacles, and reluctantly drew out a piece of paper. He dipped his pen in the inkwell and then let it hover over the page while he gave her yet another long look, as if hoping she had thought better of her ways in the seconds in between. "Very well," he finally said. "Out of respect for your late father . . ."

*And with an eye on the sum due to me in Edward's estate*, Keturah thought. The old dog would not lose in this deal, regardless of whether the girls made the plantation a success or not. But he played his game well. She'd have to watch him at every step, because there was something about the banker that told her he wouldn't hesitate to take advantage of her or her situation, regardless of how much he "respected" her late father.

A date, a few words, a signature, a thorough sanding to dry the ink, and Keturah and her sisters had what felt like their entire future on paper, as well as a heavy sack of coin.

"'Tis late in the season, Lady Tomlinson," Mr. Jobel said as they reached the doorway. "You'd do well to plant in haste."

"So I hear, Mr. Jobel," she said, and with a quick bob of her head Keturah and her sisters left the hot, humid building and entered the marketplace again.

With her line of credit in hand, Ket was ready to purchase everything else Tabletop needed. She would need to hire an overseer, secure more field hands, and refurbish the mill and house. The girls drew close together and shared a small, hidden squeal at their success.

"Oh, Keturah, I thought he would refuse you outright," Selah said. "However did you manage to keep so calm, so stalwart?"

"It's simple," she said as they strode past carts and tents laden with luscious mangoes and bananas and pineapple, piles of bright-colored spices, and casks of hard cider. "Observe any man in negotiation and he shall do as Mr. Jobel did. If you do not like what is transpiring, wait it out. If you are in the midst of negotiation, speak last. The one with the most fortitude—"

"Fortitude," Verity interrupted, "or stubbornness?"

"The one with the most fortitude, or *patience*," she allowed, "will certainly emerge the victor. And given that I am a lady," she said in her most prim and proper way, "a man becomes most discombobulated when I exhibit such behavior. You, my dear sisters, made it all the more apparent with your fidgeting and wringing of hands."

"Can you blame us?" Selah asked as they walked arm in arm. "The man appeared as if he might never budge. He was making me as nervous as a mouse caught in a cat's corner!"

"I wondered how we might even secure enough coin for passage home, if necessary," Verity said.

"Nonsense," Keturah said. "He merely believed it beneath him to deal with such matters on the behalf of *women*, but his financial nose told him he would be foolish to turn me away. I simply made it impossible for him to choose anything but what I wanted."

Verity and Selah laughed, each squeezing one of her arms, and they made their way to the slaver to retrieve Selah's ring, and then to the tailor to pick up their gowns. Bennabe awaited them there, while Primus and Gideon followed them everywhere, serving as their silent guardians. They visibly suffered in their formal livery, sweat pouring down their cheeks as they helped the women back into the old carriage.

"Honestly, Primus," Selah said, "we shall have to see about different clothing for you. It is far too hot here for any man to have to endure full livery. Do you not agree, Keturah?"

"I do," she said, looking the sweating men over, "but I've seen other servants in similar dress. Let us see what we discover tonight at the soiree, shall we?" As they drove off, she noted many gentlemen in full waistcoats and powdered wigs, despite the heat.

An hour later, they were home and hurriedly began the task of dressing for the Welands' soiree that night. For it was there, Keturah thought, that she might find a reference for an overseer as well as other vital information she needed to proceed with what she must. But she admitted to herself that one other thought excited her.

Seeing Gray.

No, she told herself, even as a shiver ran down her spine. It was merely friendship, a spirit of camaraderie that made her so eagerly anticipate crossing paths with him. Nothing more.

*Nothing more*, she sternly repeated to her reflection in the speckled mirror. Because she was here for her sisters. For herself. Not for a man.

They came through the grand gates of Morning Star Plantation about six in the evening, just as the sun was beginning to sink on the horizon. Golden light streamed through the flowering trees and their entwined limbs that formed a natural roof over their heads.

"Oh, is it not glorious?" Selah enthused, clasping her hands and looking round.

*Indeed, it is*, Keturah thought. The Welands—or their predecessors—had obviously been planting along the road for generations. The aroma of the flowers was an intoxicating mix of sweet and spice. "Such a heavenly smell," Ket said. She closed her eyes, lifted her chin, and breathed it in deeply.

"It is, truly," Verity agreed, doing the same.

Their eyes met, and for the first time Keturah didn't feel guilt for wrenching her sisters away from English society, for exposing them to the dangers found aboard a ship or in the midst of such a far place. Instead, she felt pure glee in sharing this moment, this moment they would never have experienced anywhere else but here.

Verity took her hand, squeezed it, and then looked upward again, as did Keturah and Selah. There were vast banks of yellow bells, reminding Ket of daffodils, and yet they grew in fat clumps forming a riot of gold. There were the curious primal red and yellow blooms of the claw crab and the teeny numerous white stars of butterfly jasmine, lending the air a heady scent. Purple- and rose-colored bougainvillea vines wound their way around tree trunks and across lava-black rocks.

"Do you think we might plant some things like this along the entrance of Tabletop?" Selah asked.

"I think it would be a grand idea," Keturah said. "But perhaps we should first replace the rotting floorboards in the big house."

Selah nodded. "And the slaves' cabins too. Many of them need much repair."

"And the mill," added Verity. "But someday, Ket, someday I know you shall make Tabletop look even better than this!"

They pulled through the end of the flowery tunnel, and their view shifted dramatically—encompassing miles of sugarcane fields, young and yet sprouting already, and stretching from mountain peak to sea. Everything about Morning Star Plantation was neat and tidy, evidence that they were entering one of the premier estates on-island. It hadn't taken long for Keturah to find that many plantations along Lower Round Road were struggling, with buildings that showed signs of financial setbacks.

Morning Star was not one of them. The Welands' home had been freshly whitewashed, and there were billowing curtains along the porch to shield guests from the bright setting sun. The porch was much bigger than their own, wrapping around what looked like the entire house, offering a grand view of the hill that sloped gently down to the seashore. Rocking chairs and swings lined the porch, allowing for guests to take in the cooler evening air as well as the vistas. At this time of day, the water appeared sapphire blue, contrasting beautifully with the green of the cane all about them. *'Tis all so idyllic,* Ket thought. What Tabletop might become too. *Perhaps what Father experienced, once . . .*

While his mother was not in view—presumably off mingling with other guests—Jeffrey was smiling cordially and patiently awaiting their driver to pull to a stop. Like others she glimpsed beyond him, he wore a perfectly powdered, curled wig, a pristine navy coat, white shirt and matching neckcloth. Tan breeches met stockings and finely polished leather shoes. A slave in livery opened the carriage door, and another stood by to assist them as they took their skirts in one hand and made their way down the two steps to stand upon the gravel courtyard. It was only then that Mr. Weland stepped forward to greet them.

"Welcome to Morning Star," he said, taking Keturah's hand in his and bending low to kiss it. She did not miss that he did not immediately drop it; in fact, he seemed reluctant to move on to Verity and Selah to do the same. And as soon as he had completed that task, he turned back to her and took her hand again, surprising her. He stretched out her arm and looked her up and down. "You look well, Lady Tomlinson. Clearly, you've had your first decent slumber on-island."

She smiled, embarrassed at his subtle reference as to the state he'd found her in yesterday. "Yes, a bit more rest, a bath, and a new gown *can* do wonders for a woman."

"Indeed," he said, his small mouth knotting up in a most peculiar grin. Still he held her hand and appraised her once more. "Indeed," he repeated with some enthusiasm.

Irritated at his impropriety, she pulled her hand free and turned to her sisters, both of whom were wide-eyed at the man's manners. "I fear we find ourselves quite parched after our ride," she said, lifting fingers to her throat.

"Oh yes, of course," he said and offered his arm. "Let me introduce you about and we shall find you ladies some punch." That last word was said with some emphasis to a nearby servant, and the man was immediately off. Mr. Weland had introduced the girls to the Takaitus family—an older man, his wife, and their three awkward sons—and seemed reluctant to introduce them to a handsome young widower named Mr. Fredrickson before abruptly moving on to a family by the name of Jones. Soon the servant returned with a silver tray with crystal cups full of a red-orange fruit juice.

Keturah and her sisters each gratefully took a cup, as did Mr. Weland. He raised his cup in a toast. "To fine new neighbors."

"To fine new neighbors," the girls intoned and then eagerly sipped from their cups. Keturah paused . . . and almost spit it out. Although she'd had rum punch before—the drink was a favorite at parties in London—what was in her cup seemed to be more rum than punch.

Selah briefly met her gaze with alarm, swallowing hard as her pretty cheeks flushed pink. Keturah did not dare look to Verity, afraid she might begin laughing in a most unladylike manner. Carefully, she held her cup in her hands, and as they followed Mr. Weland as he introduced them to more of the guests, she whispered to her youngest sister, "Drink that ever so slowly, Selah. And see if you might get a servant to fetch us tea instead, would you?"

Selah nodded, understanding her meaning. While the islanders might be accustomed to strong drink, they were not, and the last thing Keturah needed was to be intoxicated on her very first evening among her peers.

The tea was slower to arrive than the punch, and with sips here and there, Keturah began to feel the warming effects of the drink in both her belly and her countenance. The awkwardness of meeting new neighbors and fellow islanders was eased considerably, she mused. The soiree was primarily men, who either greeted the sisters with outright joy, as if starved for female companionship, or with some contempt, as if thinking what so many others had—that Nevis was the last place three unaccompanied women should be.

In time, the girls were separated, each swept away into conversation in various groups, each surrounded by men. It felt a little like being the belles of the ball, which Keturah had never been. As a young lady of society, she was one of the last to have her dance card filled. She was far too tall and not beautiful enough to draw the young men's attentions. The memory of Gray fairly ignoring her after her debutante ball came to mind. She recalled how he'd asked nearly all the other girls but her to dance, and how much that had stung. Yet here on Nevis, she felt as attractive as Verity, or even Selah, given the swarm of attention. She thought even Gray might look her way this evening were he to see her.

*Not that I want that. 'Tis perfectly suitable, our friendship. A godsend, really.* Did she not need a friend tonight more than another man on the hunt for a bride?

And yet she caught herself looking about for him again. Surely he had been invited?

Resolutely, she refused a second cup of punch when her own was empty, and finally a cup of tea arrived, strong and steamy. She smelled the welcome brew and sipped at it as she moved through the throngs of people she'd yet to meet, courteously excusing herself from the company of those who seemed to disapprove of her presence and lingering in the company of others who seemed to think her intriguing, if not perfectly acceptable. Keturah knew she would need every friend she could find on-island, men from whom she could solicit counsel and direction, if necessary. She remembered the card her father's friend had given her before they embarked on the *Restoration*—Wilson, Green, Barnes—none of whom she'd run across yet this evening. It was unfortunate, for there were myriad subjects with which she was utterly unfamiliar, countless things she had yet to learn about running a plantation, despite Philip's efforts to prepare her when aboard the ship.

*Gray.* She found herself momentarily alone on the porch, looking out toward St. Kitts and wondering again why he was not here tonight. She had been so certain he would be attending this soiree. Indeed, it seemed that most of the planters from Cotton Ground were here. *Odd*, she thought. *Surrounded by men and you so wish for your old friend?* It was *only* that, she reassured herself. All of these men and women were new to her, strangers. It was bound to make a girl homesick for the familiar.

She heard someone tuning a violin . . . *Could it be?* A few more notes and she could tell the musician was on the far side of the group below, hidden from view. Taking her skirt in hand, she hurried down the steps, grinning as more notes filled the air. She nodded graciously as she made her way through the crowd, most men turning to watch her come through. Honestly, she'd never experienced so much admiration and intense interest since her debut into society.

But when she reached the far side of the crowd, her smile faded. It wasn't Gray. It was another violinist, with two others beside him. The man gave her a curious glance, a hopeful smile, and then after tapping his foot three times the trio began to play a lively tune.

Jeffrey Weland was by her side again, and now she found his constant attentions vaguely irritating. "Do you care to dance, Lady Tomlinson?"

"Of course," she forced herself to graciously say. As he escorted her to the center of the courtyard, now cleared of people to make way for dancing, she saw that both of her sisters were also escorted.

The sun was setting beyond Mr. Weland as he bowed and she curtsied, and they began to dance. She told herself to concentrate on the things that pleased her now so as not to offend her new neighbor.

Only once had she been at a dance held out of doors. But then Lady Fairchild had always had a penchant for the *avant-garde*. Every other ball she'd attended had been in a proper ballroom. Back home, the Bannings had held an annual ball of their own and attended two or three others a week, especially those years they went to spend a season in London.

She moved from one dance partner to another. Her teacup disappeared, and feeling parched she was forced to sip more rum punch between dances. Mr. Weland appeared frequently, and she knew it might cause a stir that they had danced together so much, but what was she to do? He was her host. It was also a relief to have a dance partner who was an inch or two taller than she was, for it was ever so uncomfortable whenever she towered over her escort.

A roast pig, various fruits, and fresh bread were brought out to a long table, and Mr. Weland led her over to it. Her sisters rejoined her side, each looking dewy and happy.

Mr. Weland lifted a crystal cup—which seemed always to be magically full, as was hers—and waited for the rest to do the same. "To a fine year and a change of fortune for all Nevisians. May this be the grandest harvest on record."

"Hear, hear!" cried everyone in unison.

But Keturah fought to keep from squirming. Because as he said *the grandest harvest*, Mr. Weland had given her the oddest look. As if he half anticipated harvesting *her*. She thought it quite strange. But then the succulent smell of the roast pork distracted her, her stomach rumbling as if on cue.

They took their seats at small tables arranged about the gardens rather than at one long table. *Is this how Nevisians entertain?* Keturah wondered. It was a far cry from the paneled dining rooms of the mansions of London, and yet the breeze felt deliciously welcome, especially after eight turns on the dance floor. To go inside at that moment would have felt like a travesty—the last thing she wanted to do. And to dine here, surrounded by swaying palms and the scents of jasmine and sea salt on the air, the jungle coming alive with the sounds of crickets and chattering monkeys . . . well, it was like a heavenly picnic, she thought. Blessedly, it was only the three Banning sisters and an ancient deaf woman named Widow Foster at their table, giving her a temporary reprieve from the constant male attention.

The girls were abuzz about one handsome neighbor or another and questioned Ket about Mr. Weland's obvious interest in her.

"I believe he is only being cordial," Keturah said, trying to settle them. "Friendly just as any proper neighbor would be."

Verity lifted one brow and eyed her thoughtfully as she chewed and swallowed. "*Any* proper neighbor, Ket?"

Keturah looked past her sister to the many people gathered around fifty other tiny tables about the grounds and saw that many of them stole glances in their direction. She leaned forward. "They are merely curious. We are the newest arrivals, after all, and it appears that females are in fearfully short supply."

"True," Verity said. She paused to take a few sips of punch. "But I've also heard whispers. You, dear sister, are the talk of the party. I believe you shall have a constant stream of suitors, whether you're ready to entertain them or not."

"No," Keturah said, frowning and shaking her head. She despised how her heart began pounding, as though she were a girl of fifteen rather than a mature woman.

"*Yes*," Ver countered, her lips hovering above the rim of her cup.

"Because you are a widow and an heiress, and if there is one thing all these men want, 'tis a woman with sterling behind her name."

Keturah's breath caught, and her stomach sank. Of course. How could she be so foolish? It wasn't that Mr. Weland and all these other men thought she was beautiful. She'd not somehow become more beguiling, more alluring than even her pretty sisters merely by crossing the Atlantic.

She set down her cup of rum punch firmly and drew a deep breath. Her inheritance from Edward would be barely enough to give Tabletop a chance at recovery. Enough for two, perhaps three, harvests. And that was if they were careful. Not nearly enough to save another's failing plantation—and she would never wish it to pour into the already-full coffers of one such as Morning Star.

Why did it always boil down to wealth? When might she find someone who regarded her for who she was rather than what she could provide? Was love, true love, an utter myth?

She leaned back in her chair and surveyed the party with eyes cooled by new understanding. These men wanted to use her, to take advantage of her. Perhaps some fancied marrying her simply so they could eke every bit from her that they could, just as Edward had tried to do.

It was a game, really, as was all of life. But she would no longer be a pawn in that game. She had learned the rules the hard way.

And no one would be taking advantage of her or hers ever again.

# Chapter Seventeen

"Keturah, forgive me," Verity said with a frown as Ket rose and told them to prepare to leave. "I have managed to ruin your festive mood."

"No, no," Ket said, forcing a smile. "It is good to be reminded of the truth, no matter the setting. Come. Let us thank the Welands and summon Primus to fetch the carriage. It is best to leave them all wishing for more of our company than less, is it not?"

Her sisters nodded, but she could tell that her swiftly evolving perspective was affecting them too. That was all right, for if men here sought Keturah out for her wealth, so might they attempt the same with her sisters. While neither Verity nor Selah had to their names what Keturah had, few here knew it. Certainly, they could see Tabletop had fallen on difficult times, yet they also knew the Bannings still held Hartwick Manor and quite a large tract of land back home. None would know of the debts on the ledgers there; they'd only see what so many saw. The outside. How things appeared. The grand, pristine lines of a mansion. The manicured gardens. The fine gowns the girls wore and the many servants.

All while the foundation crumbled from beneath their feet.

Keturah swallowed hard, said farewell to her new acquaintances, artfully dodging one flirtatious comment after another, keen now to the game that was afoot. It was with some relief that she sank into the back of the carriage, surrounded by her sisters' stiff silences, displeased that they'd been pulled from what they considered a delightful party.

As they rode along in the quiet of the carriage, it was Verity who tried again. "Ket," she whispered so that Primus wouldn't overhear, "forgive me, but did it bring up memories of Edward?"

"It brought up memories of being used as a woman, in every sense of the word," Keturah bit out. Instantly, she regretted her words. She should have framed them more delicately. She let out a groan and took Verity's hand, then Selah's. "It made me remember that I will not allow a man to take advantage of any of us. Ever again."

They both paused. Then Selah said, "You can try. But our lives are in God's hands, Ket. Not our own."

This time, Keturah managed to hold her tongue a moment. Then, "But does not God himself expect us to use our minds? Our sound judgment?"

"Of course," Selah said. "But this is a harsh world, full of harsh realities. We cannot expect to shield ourselves from all harm, forever. You cannot assume you can do that for us. We shall, as you say, use our good minds. Look for God's lead and do our best to follow. But we cannot live in fear of hurt. It will keep us from venturing into new things, welcoming new people."

"And we need to welcome new people into our lives," Verity put in. "If we are to make it here, Ket, we cannot do it alone."

Ket shook her head slowly. She was thankful for the dark, so her sisters couldn't see her roll her eyes. They were so naïve. And she was glad for it, in some ways. Glad they hadn't yet experienced the hurts that had left her so guarded. And yet she was determined to protect them as well as she could, for as long as she could. Despite their wishes.

She sighed. "True, we must welcome others into our lives. Make friends. People we can trust. But that soiree was full of men not seeking friends, but rather people who might help them to get ahead. I cannot abide such a thing, not for long anyway." She knew she would need to negotiate future gatherings on occasion, but she did not wish to encourage suitors.

"Speaking of friends, I had expected Gray would be there," Verity said carefully. By her tone, she was clearly fishing for a response from Ket.

"Did you?" she returned dryly. "He's likely lit a lamp to work his fields even now alongside Philip." What was she doing at a soiree when there was so much to do at Tabletop?

They had a full day ahead on the morrow, with more work than any of them could imagine. They had to begin to remake Tabletop into a success, and quickly.

Could she manage it? she wondered as the carriage bounced along Lower Round Road and her sisters gave in to her desired silence. Could they truly turn Tabletop into what her father had imagined—one of the finest, most fruitful plantations on Nevis? She'd learned much over the course of the evening, surrounded by men. In between flirtatious comments and social niceties, the men had shared vital knowledge amongst themselves, some of which Keturah overheard. And as the rum punch did its soothing work, more and more shared what they might have kept close to the vest in the sober light of day.

Once, the island had produced more sugar per acre than any other in the Leeward or Windward Isles. Today Nevis had fallen behind Jamaica, Antigua, and even—and this produced much consternation among the Nevisians—*St. Kitts*. Clearly, there was a good measure of competition between the sister islands. But many believed the Nevisian soil to be exhausted, with erosion half the battle, constant planting and harvest the other half. The planters were importing barges full of manure—*manure*, of all things—and they constantly needed more to feed the tender plantings. Cane stalks had once survived for three seasons. Now the cane had to be replanted every year.

And Keturah was not the only planter in search of a new overseer. The best were in high demand and frequently wooed away by the promise of higher pay. The worst . . . well, from what she could gather, there were more of them than she cared to think about. She thought of Angus Shubert, the ruthless man with square jaw and wide-set eyes. Even though he had treated her and her sisters politely, she saw the way Mitilda glanced back at him when they'd first arrived, her expression marked by wariness.

Keturah looked up to see the intertwined flowering branches as black silhouettes, stars twinkling in the sky above. She thought about the straggling remnants of cane in her fields, like the last soldiers standing among a fallen army, and her father's madcap idea to terrace acres of land. Perhaps . . . just perhaps it hadn't been as mad as it first seemed. Now that those acres were finally flat and the soil had rested for a couple of years, could she not plant her crop late and still bring in a harvest?

She hoped so. The thought strengthened her. Because she did not intend to marry in order to make Tabletop a success, nor give over any portion that rightfully belonged to her to another man. Ever. Even if her sisters married. Even if she spent her life as a lonely spinster.

Because Ket knew from experience that it was vastly better to choose to be alone than to utter vows and yet feel more lonely than ever before.

# CHAPTER EIGHTEEN

She went to sleep that night feeling resolved, her sisters on either side of her once again. While they now each had established bedrooms, they chose to do this each night their first week on-island, finding comfort in silent proximity. Verity was the first to move to her own room, and Selah left her alone a couple of nights later. By that time, Keturah was so mindlessly weary she only briefly recognized the fact before she fell fast asleep.

Mornings came too early most days, the roosters cackling their welcome to the dawn. Each day, Keturah had three of the men saddle horses and set off with her for Charlestown, intent on greeting each ship that had docked, seeking an overseer. A burly man was what she had in mind, as broad-shouldered as Mr. Shubert, one with keen intelligence as well as an abiding kindness. Ket knew that managing a hundred slaves would require an overseer with a firm hand, but she had little tolerance for the sort of abuse she'd witnessed on the auction platforms every time she passed through town.

Nevis was fortunate to get some of the first picks among slaves. Many slaver ships stopped here first for water and supplies, and while the island was falling behind in production compared to others, it was still admired for its plantations. And every Nevisian planter remained hungry for more slaves to work their fields.

Planting continued, even this late in the season, which comforted Ket. But with each passing day that she did not find the right man to hire, she grew more anxious about Tabletop's delays.

Most prospective overseers dismissed her as soon as she approached them, seeming to believe it beneath them to work for a woman—that or doubting her odds at lasting for long on-island. Worse were those who looked her up and down as if she herself might be a part of their weekly pay. Facing such outrage, she simply turned and walked away each time it occurred.

She followed each disappointing visit to Charlestown with a trip to see one of the men Lord Shantall had recommended—Lord Wilson, Mr. Green, and Mr. Barnes—hopeful that they might assist her, since they'd been friends of her father.

Lord Wilson had sailed for the Carolinas and wasn't due back for a year. Mr. Green had taken ill with the ague and was unable to receive visitors. And Mr. Barnes's plantation had suffered a devastating fire, so the family returned to England.

Each discovery was disappointing, and the evaporating promise of aid left Keturah feeling abandoned, desolate. On the fourth morning, she rose and dressed, but found herself dreading another trip to town. What if she never found an overseer? The thought of it made her breath come in shallow pants, and she hurriedly slipped from the big house and took the path down to the beach, knowing she needed some air, a fresh view, in order to regain her perspective.

*What can you accomplish by wallowing here all day?* she silently chided herself as she took to the trail. *You must go to town. You must try again.* Her sisters, their servants, the remaining slaves— *even Mitilda and Abraham*, she added darkly—were all relying on her to bring this plantation back.

*But how on earth can I do that if I cannot even begin?* she argued with herself, wiping away tears.

She walked, faster and faster, until she was almost running. Finally, she broke through the last of the coco plum shrubs, sending a pair of birds feasting on the fruit to the sky in alarm, and her feet sank into golden sand. The sound of the gentle waves washing along the shore, combined with the heat of the sun on her head and face as she lifted it, helped her take her first full breath all morning. She removed her slippers and set them beneath the dense branches of a nearby bush.

Lifting her skirts, she moved to wet sand and let the warm tropical waters dance around her feet. It made her smile, the sensation. How much colder was the Irish Sea as compared to this! This, why, *this* felt like tepid bathwater. Ket began walking through the waves, letting them douse her feet and ankles and even the bottoms of her skirts, admiring the swaying palms that lined the beach. Up ahead there even appeared to be a mango grove. She decided she must bring her sisters down here for a swim—it would do them all a world of good. And there was no one about the beach in either direction, so it would likely be relatively private. *No need for a bathing machine here*, she thought with delight.

Every year, the girls had traveled to the English coast to take their annual restorative summer dip in the ocean. Their favorite resort had ten machines—huts on wagons that were lowered by horse and driver into the water, shielding bathers from viewers on the beach—and it was so delightful they had always been reluctant to leave, despite the fierce chill of the water. They'd followed it by a visit to a hot springs, and all agreed that it was a most sensible health regimen. In fact, many in their set had taken to following them to both locations, making it a rather festive weekend.

*Before Edward*, she thought as she began walking southward down the beach. *After* marrying Edward, he'd refused her request to join her sisters for the annual excursion to the coast. "Allow my wife to be ogled in her bathing smock on some godforsaken beach?" he'd huffed. "I think not."

It mattered not to him that the bathers were always shielded by wagons and awnings, nor that they were attended only by female dippers, nor that the smocks were made of a stiff fabric with weights to prevent them from rising in the waves. He heard none of that—nor did he consider allowing her to do something else together. He only wanted her home. "Here, as the lady of the house. Doing as you ought. Cease your girlish daydreaming, Keturah, and do what your lord and husband require."

*Require*, she thought, musing again over his word as she continued her walk. How he'd said it. She'd never been able to do *all* that he required. Never hit every mark he wished her to hit. She'd never even come close, because every time she improved, hoping for his approval—and peace in their union—he would move the target. She'd arrange for his favorite meal, with every course just as he'd liked it the last time, and then he mused over a neighbor's new soup or dessert he favored more, wishing she would stay ahead of the culinary passions of the day. She'd completed a needlepoint picture—a pastime she loathed—because he'd gone on and on about how he found women with needle and thread in their hands most genteel and comely. Once it was finished, he'd taken but one cursory look at her project and asked her if she might seek out Lady Wimble's advice on detailed shading techniques.

No, she thought gleefully, she was glad to be free of her husband and all he *required*. And she would bring her sisters down to bathe in the ocean this very night, without fretting if anyone saw them in their stiff fabric bathing smocks. Why, they were as modest, if not more, than many of the gowns they wore to soirees. No, here on Nevis she would claim her independence in more ways than one. Deciding when and where they would swim would be but one.

Heartened by the idea, she was about to turn back when she heard a child laughing and a man joining in.

She knew that laugh.

*Gray*, she thought, her heart beginning to pound. *Could it be?*

Looking around, she saw that she'd nearly reached the southern border of her property. Up ahead loomed that massive grove of mango trees, which extended over the ridge toward Gray's plantation.

Again she heard a child shout and the man laugh. Curious, she began picking her way up a path toward the grove, wincing as sticks and rocks poked her feet.

It was Gray.

She smiled and was about to call out to him when she spotted Mitilda. On her arm hung a basketful of mangoes, another basket by her feet. Then Ket saw Gray backing up to catch a piece of fruit that fell from the tree. "Well done!" he called up. "This would have been a monkey's dinner for certain had you not harvested it yourself! Look at the rosy hue!" he said admiringly, lifting the fruit. "Are there others like that?"

One more step and she could see the boy—Abraham—twenty feet up on a large mango branch, reaching precariously for another.

*Another piece of my fruit*, Keturah thought angrily. *Fruit that could feed us all!* What were they doing here? Worse, what were they doing *together*?

Rage began to make her heart pound. And even as she told herself she was overreacting, that they weren't doing anything that warranted such a response, it made her feel like she was spinning into an even darker realm. "What right have you?" she cried. Loudly. Accusingly. Her tone more shriek than question.

Mitilda, who was facing away from Ket, looked back over her shoulder, obviously startled.

"And what are *you* doing here with *them?*" Ket said to Gray, stepping forward. Her rage twined with hurt, betrayal. How could he? How *could* he? He'd not found the time to come and call upon her, but—

"Keturah!" he said, stepping forward, looking half pleased to see her, half alarmed and baffled by her greeting. His dark blue eyes darted down to Ket's trembling hands, which she'd set to wringing, then over to Mitilda—clearly wondering why she was acting in such a manner, which only served to fuel her rage.

"Abraham!" Mitilda called. "C'mon down, child. This instant."

"Yes, mum," said the boy, obediently setting to scramble down the tree.

Keturah stepped past Gray as he reached her side, intent only on the woman. "You may take a few mangoes, but I expect you to leave the rest behind. *I* shall distribute them among the hungry people of Tabletop, not see you selling Tabletop bounty at market on the morrow."

"Keturah!" Gray exclaimed, aghast.

Ket ignored him, still focused on Mitilda. "You may not take what is not yours!" she shouted, stepping toward her. "Do you hear me? Nothing! Have you not already taken more than you deserve?"

Even as she said it, she felt a pang of regret. But she could do little but give way to the bubbling, swirling anger inside her.

Gray tried to intervene, subtly shifting between them, raising a hand partially up in both directions as if he expected this to dissolve into a common brawl. Truth be told, there was a part of Ket that itched to do just that.

Had not this woman been here at Tabletop . . . and lain with her father, might he have come home? Might he be alive today? Even as she thought it, she knew it to be partial madness. Misguided hope. Mislaid blame.

Mitilda's wide steady eyes remained on hers. Slowly, chin still high, she slipped the basket from her arm and handed it over to Ket. "'Tis yours, Lady Ket. As it was your father's." She nodded, lifting her light-palmed, elegant hands in a way that reminded Keturah of Verity with an alarmed Brutus. "Just as when your father was here," she went on, "we were harvesting for the good of *all* on Tabletop. Not to use the fruit for our own gain."

Abraham had reached her side and looked from his mother to Ket and back again, concern and confusion etching lines in his handsome young face.

Keturah faltered. Was it true? Was this something the woman and her child did every week? Part of what had sustained the slaves left at Tabletop when there was no one else to see to them?

"I—uh," she began, a far more sensible mood beginning to settle her racing heart.

But then the woman raised her chin higher, looking down her nose at Ket, and the anger quickly returned. Keturah squared her shoulders and took a firmer hold of the basket. "Be on your way,

Mitilda. Abraham. I shall see this fruit back to the big house and properly distributed."

The woman left then, all elegance and grace, the boy silently glancing over his shoulder at Ket again, eyebrows knit.

Keturah hurriedly looked back to the massive tree, the sprawling limbs—one of twenty or more in this grove but clearly one of the better producers. Belatedly she remembered she was not alone.

"What are you doing here, Gray?" she asked wearily, lifting a hand to massage her forehead.

"Pay *me* no heed!" he said in a growl. "What has come over you, Ket?" he asked. "I've never seen you behave so rudely before. Ever! Even as children."

She let out a humorless laugh. "You think I am rude? I?" She leaned toward him, feeling the blush color her cheeks. "*That* woman," she said, gesturing over her shoulder to where Mitilda and the boy had disappeared, "was my father's mistress! His *mistress*! Can you imagine? And that boy? Why, Abraham is my half brother." She felt an odd victory in seeing Gray pull back in consternation and shock. *So, he hadn't known.*

"They were living here in the big house when I arrived, she pretending to be mistress of Tabletop! Can you believe it?"

Gray took a deep breath and studied her. "Keturah, you are positively ashen," he said, taking the basket and setting it aside, then grabbing hold of her waist. "Come."

As she felt his firm, familiar strong hand take hold of her, Ket finally understood that her vision was swirling, her stomach turning. *Oh, I do not wish to faint . . . Please, God, I know I have no right to ask it of you . . .*

He led her over to a rock, eased her down and, once seated, took hold of her shoulders. "Lean forward, Ket. Breathe. Nice and slowly."

With her head down between her knees, she breathed deeply in and out, fighting not to faint or vomit. He left her as she did so, then returned a moment later and knelt beside her. "When you do not think you shall be sick or faint, sit up again," he said. "Slowly."

Keturah took a few more breaths, thought she had a hold of herself, and then straightened and blinked.

He uncorked a hollowed-out gourd that had a shoulder strap attached and extended it toward her. "Here. Drink."

She did so, finding her mouth surprisingly dry. Then she dripped more into her hand and washed it over her hot forehead and cheeks, the back of her neck. Feeling a bit more restored, even as remorse washed through her, she leveled a gaze at him. "Oh, Gray. Was I . . . was I quite ghastly?"

"Quite," he said lightly.

She heaved a long, heavy sigh.

He reached out as if to touch her shoulder, then pulled his hand back and took a few steps away, crossed his arms and looked at her. "So . . . I had been coming to call on you. Tell me here, Ket. Tell me of Tabletop. I take it that meeting Mitilda and Abraham is not the sole reason for your apparent . . . exhaustion."

Keturah let out a scoffing laugh, even as she inwardly recognized how good it felt to be understood. To be seen. Then she told him of her utter failure in town to find an overseer. That no one would give her the time of day as a woman, and how anxious it made her that they were not yet planting. On and on she went, about her ragged group of slaves, of how she couldn't see herself finding the courage to purchase more . . . even of how she was dismayed by how her fine furnishings brought from England looked so out of place inside the dilapidated house.

"But where am I to spend money first?" she asked, rising and beginning to pace. "The house? The fields? The millworks?" She shook her head and blinked rapidly. "'Tis too much. Is it not the same for you at Teller's Landing?"

He nodded once and put a booted foot up on a rock beside him. "Fairly similar. Other than the furnishings aspect," he said with a wry grin. Keturah leaned back on the rock, needing something of substance to bolster her in the welcome face of that handsome grin—all the while striving to appear relaxed. "Our house is modest, nothing but two rooms and a parlor," he continued, "and the kitchen is outside. 'Tis clear that no Covington has lived here for generations, absentee planters leaving it to sharecropping. However, I find it suits me quite well. And Philip and I have a good group of slaves, good workers all. Ten, so far. We had to repair a few cabins, but now we're on to planting our northern field."

Keturah heaved another sigh and shook her head, feeling his relative success as if it somehow shined light on her own failures. What had she been thinking? Paying so much attention to how she might set up a proper West Indian home, but so little to how she would run it? "I do not know how I am to do this, Gray," she whispered, more to herself than to him. With some horror, she realized tears welled in her eyes, and her chin trembled.

She startled when she heard the crack of a branch beneath his foot and knew he was right before her. Gently he opened his arms. "Come, Ket," he said. "Come."

Hesitating but a moment, she tentatively rose and slid into them, gratefully resting her cheek against his chest. He wrapped his arms around her and, after a moment's pause, rubbed her back.

How long had it been since she'd been held so? Since she was a little girl? They stood there for several long moments. Was it her imagination or had the crickets and monkeys gone silent? Or was it only the rush of blood in her own ears?

"Oh, Ket," he murmured, "I'm sorry it has been so trying. But can you see the beauty here too? Can you keep a sense of the potential? The hope? I believe that's the key as we encounter trials."

Embarrassed by more tears, she turned from him and wiped her face.

He stepped toward her again. "Perhaps I could—"

"No, no," she said, lifting a hand. She knew he was feeling responsible somehow, feeling an urge to intervene, to assist her. But she had to do this on her own. She had to! There was only one thing he could do to really help. She glanced over her shoulder. "Have you . . . have you perhaps heard of any overseers in search of new placement?"

Sorrowfully, he shook his head, and she quickly looked back

to the beach, feeling fresh tears of disappointment burn her eyes. She fished a handkerchief from her waistband and dried her eyes and cheeks. "I must get back. My sisters shall be quite worried."

"May I escort you?"

"No," she said, flashing him a grin. "I quite know the way."

"But you are in a rare state."

"A state I shall endeavor to recover from by the time I reach home." She strode toward the basket of mangoes and lifted it to her elbow. Then she took hold of the second and handed it to him. "For you and Philip and your people," she said. "Now, I must go and make amends with my father's mistress."

His smile held a measure of sorrow, but also understanding and approval. "Perhaps," he said, daring to reach out to push a strand of hair from her damp forehead and tuck it behind her ear, "'twould be best not to think of her as your father's *mistress*, but instead simply *Mitilda*—a woman with a lifetime of Tabletop knowledge in her head. Even perhaps, in time . . . a friend?"

Keturah swallowed hard, feeling the inch or two of her temple and ear he'd touched as if he'd set it aflame. "You're right, of course. That's quite sensible."

"I'm a quite sensible fellow when I put my mind to it." He quirked a smile and Ket blinked, realizing anew just how handsome he was.

"You've been quite sensible ever since you turned your head toward Nevis, haven't you?" she asked.

"Done my best."

"Far better than I."

"Keturah," he said, his smile fading, "give yourself some measure . . . some grace. Along with everyone around you. You have been working so hard, for so long . . . Take it from me, I am well aware of what it means to need to prove oneself. But I've come to believe . . . to think . . . well, all God asks of us is to do our best, from morning until night. He does not expect us to do things that only He can accomplish, only what we've been given to do, and to trust Him with the rest."

186

"Indeed," she said with some surprise. *This*, from Gray? Clearly, he had become more devout in the years they'd spent apart, even as she and God had settled at an uneasy distance. And yet his words resonated with her as truth. "Well." She lifted her chin and squared her shoulders. "Good day, Gray. Do come and call on my sisters and me soon, would you?"

"Count on it," he promised.

# CHAPTER NINETEEN

That night, Keturah agonized over how to make amends with Mitilda. Belatedly, she recalled Bennabe mentioning how Mitilda had helped everyone remaining on Tabletop survive . . . which only made Ket feel worse. Mangoes were a large part of that. Weekly harvests from her garden plot were the rest. Ket was deeply ashamed of how she'd acted. Needing to be away from her sisters in order to think, she paced her father's room, pausing to trace the seashell-lined window wells with her fingers.

She thought once more of the frames he had made for Mother and how she had stowed them away as soon as he'd set sail. He had loved Mother, and when she refused to come to the West Indies, he'd tried to bring a piece of the islands to her. He must have been very lonely here . . . but did that excuse his taking up with another woman?

Keturah sighed. There was no innocent. The blame could be shifted in either direction. And what choice had Mitilda had? Ket thought back. Abraham was about eight years old. Nine years ago, the woman had been, what . . . seventeen, eighteen? What had Ket been like at that age? Could she have withstood the advances of a man, without protection, especially as a slave?

*No, likely not.* Had she herself not gone along with the plan to marry Edward, despite her trepidation? Why, she'd never uttered one question, one complaint.

Keturah leaned over the windowsill and looked out at the glory of Tabletop's view. Sloping landscape, in shades of green, down to a turquoise sea lapping at creamy sand. She brought her eyes back up and fingered the finely crafted shutters, folding so easily—even in the island's humidity—allowing in the gentle welcome breeze. Her fingers traced her father's carefully laid lines of shell. She knew each one, because he had sent them samples as part of his monthly letter, and the girls had committed each to memory.

The multicolored and conical Triton's trumpet. The bespeckled lines of the hawk-wing conch. The crenellated spiky curls of the Latirus shell, appearing like a tiny fairy fortress. The creamy-tea stripes of the measled cowrie. The pristine white shape of the Atlantic cone. The freckled Atlantic cowrie that always made Ket think of an old woman's toothless grin. The milky white of the Caribbean vase shell. The oddly obscure and smooth flamingo tongue, its ridges worn smooth by sea and sand. And her favorite, the West Indian crown conch, which was essentially every color one might expect from the earth.

*Oh, Father,* she thought. *If only I had known you as well as I know these shells. I . . . I behaved despicably today. To someone you likely . . . loved. But 'tis all such a mess, Father. How could you have left us in such a state? How could you have up and died, abandoning us all?*

She paused as her trembling clarified something. She was *angry* at Father. Angry at him for the trouble he had left behind. For not providing for her and her sisters. For leading them into danger and chaos rather than saving them.

Just as she was angry at God.

Neither her earthly father nor her heavenly Father had prevented her from marrying Edward. Neither of them had rescued her as she suffered, day after day. Neither had given her a way out.

Or had they?

Was this not her opportunity? Her rescue? A chance to make a life here on Nevis with her sisters? To determine her own future? For the first time in a very long time she felt the brush of her heavenly Father's presence. She closed her eyes to the breeze coming off the ocean and into the room.

She could no longer reach her earthly father. But could she not reach out to her Lord and God? Take comfort in Him once again? *Oh, Lord, how far I am from you.* Her breath caught as she realized the vast divide that had occurred, and how her anger had driven Him farther away. *How far?*

And then a breeze rose outside, wafting the brush and palms to and fro, then upward, inward, across her. Ket closed her eyes again, letting it wash over her.

"How far . . ." she whispered sorrowfully.

But He was not far at all. For the first time in forever, her Lord felt *near*. Positively near. On her skin, covering her, filling her ears, washing over her . . .

"God. Lord," she whispered, sinking to her knees.

*Child, daughter, beloved* were what she heard in response.

"Father. *Savior*," she returned, swallowing hard.

Then, at last, *Protector. Comforter.*

"Oh, Lord, I've fallen short," she whispered. "In so many ways. I've been so angry," she rasped as tears ran down her face. "So angry for so long. I blamed you for letting me marry Edward. But it was my choice. My parents' choice. A terrible choice. Forgive me for blaming you, for becoming angry at you for a trial of our own making. For not turning to you . . . you who could have brought me healing. Comfort. Even in the midst of the trial."

She braced her hands on the sill and felt the shells against her forehead as she wept. But she welcomed the bite, the pain of them, as if they echoed the memory of her pain. She cried for her departed father and mother. She cried for the death of her own innocence through the years of marriage with Edward. She cried that she could not bear children. She cried for her sisters and their own losses. She cried for Mitilda, a slave girl put in a terrible position, and Abraham, a boy who would never know his father.

On and on she cried, until she believed she had no more tears to weep. She was empty, but for the first time in a long while, she felt cleansed.

As she rose to her feet, she felt the shadows of Edward's dark memories splinter and shard and fall from her shoulders.

The damage. The hurt. The injustices.

The discouragement. The shame.

Like thin shells drying for years in the sun, she broke through them, casting them to the sea—thrusting them out to the Atlantic and Caribbean like spikes meant for the depths, never to return.

Because Keturah was new.

Reborn.

And with God beside her, there wasn't anything or anyone who could defeat her again.

# CHAPTER TWENTY

The next morning, Keturah set Verity and Selah to leading the others in cutting in a garden. While she didn't feel equipped or ready to begin planting cane, she could certainly start a garden and make headway on feeding those of Tabletop. There had to be a better way than buying the exorbitantly expensive hogsheads of corn and flour and salted fish imported to the islands. Even taking this small step had buoyed her spirits.

When she, Primus, and Gideon reached town, she felt hope fill her heart. And sure enough, right off she ran into the banker, Mr. Jobel, who told her that two new men from Jamaica had only just arrived, both with good experience on other sugar plantations. One had already been secured as an overseer for South Winds, but the other was reportedly available for hire. Hastening forward, pressing between groups of men on the docks, ignoring Primus's whispered warning, she boldly approached the two gentlemen Mr. Jobel had pointed her toward.

They turned toward her and looked her up and down as if she were a common prostitute. It brought her up short, but she stood straighter and still, waiting for them to understand that she was nothing if not a lady. After this long on Nevis, she had learned this trick, at the very least.

The two sobered, somewhat.

"I am Lady Tomlinson of Tabletop Plantation," she began. "Which of you is Mr. Eason?"

The long-faced, tall one cocked his head and looked her over again—this time only so far as her chest. "I am," he allowed.

She took a deep breath, reminding herself of Tabletop's desperate need for an overseer. "Mr. Eason, I am the owner of a plantation of fifty acres, one of the finest on Nevis."

His eyes widened a bit at that.

"We are in need of a new overseer, our last having succumbed to the ague, and are in the position to pay quite a handsome salary."

"Oh?" he said, lifting a brow.

Again his eyes flicked down to her chest, and Ket fought the urge to lift her hand to cover any cleavage that might be showing. She felt Primus and Gideon both inch forward, each on her flanks. Silent sentinels, not true guardians, she reminded herself. Because if they fought, it might very well mean their lives. Still, their presence gave her courage.

Mr. Eason glanced at each of them, dismissed them, and returned his attention to her. "I'm to entertain offers from Mr. Lawson of Fern Gulch and a Mr. Hamilton this evening, my *lady*," he said, fairly smirking over the last word. "I doubt that Tabletop could compete, unless there might be some unspoken bonuses found on your plantation . . ." With that he again let his eyes drift down her body.

The man laughed at her—not even having the decency to hide his merriment—as she spun on her heel and walked away. Stiff-backed, she'd turned the corner of the tiny bank building and strode down the alleyway, aware that Primus and Gideon hovered at the entrance standing guard. Giving in to her trembling knees at last, she collapsed on a small crate.

She'd been wrong. She still had tears to weep, even after last night. But she couldn't help it—she was so utterly disappointed. She had been so certain. So certain that after last night, after her relinquishment, after she had come to understand . . . she'd thought that perhaps today God would smile, would help her. That He had used Mr. Jobel to send her to one of the two men who would at last become her overseer.

Instead, she'd run up against a man who treated her with all the disdain that Edward had.

Keturah shuddered as she remembered the man's leering gaze. *What do you think you are doing?* she asked herself. There was no way for her to make it here, as a woman, without experience. And in the face of her abject failure at hiring the right man—let alone obtaining the hundred slaves they needed—now they were behind yet another week.

She wept bitter tears, soaking through one handkerchief and then another. She was just fishing through her purse for another when a shadow brought her head up.

She blinked once, twice, at the blurry figures.

It was Mitilda, and beside her the boy. Abraham.

It was the child who handed her a clean handkerchief, drawn from his pocket. She stared at it a moment, as if she did not recognize what it was. In truth, she wasn't certain what she should do.

"For you, miss," said the boy in English laced with the island-ers' Creole accent as he extended the handkerchief to her. The child wore an impeccably clean little suit jacket and short pants, stockings and shoes, not a speck of dirt on him.

"*Lady Tomlinson*," corrected his mother, squeezing the boy's shoulder.

"Lady Tom—" he began.

"No, no," Keturah said, gratefully taking the handkerchief to wipe her eyes and nose. "Please. You may call me Lady Ket. All the . . ." Her words failed her. She'd been about to say *all the servants do*. But these two were not servants, not slaves. This child—she forced herself to look at him steadily—*this* child was . . . *kin*.

Then she made herself look up at his mother, wondering what the woman wanted of her, why she had intruded upon her private moment. It made her feel vulnerable, when she wanted to feel anything but weak. But before she found the words to ask, the woman drawled, "We received the mangoes this morning. That was right kind of you, Lady Ket."

The small basket of mangoes. Keturah had left it on their porch last night. "Oh. Good, good," she said, a rush of embarrassment bringing heat to her cheeks at the memory of how she'd treated them in the grove. She knew she should apologize and was searching for the right words.

But Mitilda only gave her a frown of concern. "Why all the tears, Lady Ket?"

In that small kindness, someone acknowledging distress, Ket felt a tenuous bridge rise between them. Taking a deep breath, she rose and looked the woman in the eye. Mitilda was plainly a beauty, with her oval face and soft doe eyes.

Ket put aside thoughts of what her father might have seen in the woman, what obviously drew him. Necessity demanded her to wonder if perhaps this islander might have a solution to her problem. Gray had even suggested that Mitilda might be a *friend* in time. Which was preposterous, she told herself. What would a black woman, the mistress of a dead planter, have to offer her, a white woman of means? Even as she thought it, shame washed through her.

"I . . . We need an overseer at Tabletop, someone to manage the fields. Someone to purchase and train the . . . slaves." Ket tried to swallow but found her mouth was dry. It was so infernally hot. . . .

But Mitilda did not flinch. "You will not find the overseer you want, Lady Ket. All the best are taken by others."

Keturah bit her cheek, holding back a hot reply. "I am well aware of that difficulty," she said.

"There is more," Mitilda said, big eyes furtively glancing about to make sure they remained the alley's only occupants. "The men of this island do not wish for you to succeed."

Keturah frowned. She knew they suspected her, maybe even resented her. But . . .

"They move together as one to keep you from hiring an overseer," Mitilda went on, placing one hand atop her other and looking at

Ket sadly. "They want you to marry one of them. Put you in your proper place, I heard one man say. I fear that only in marrying into another family here, Lady Ket, shall you find hope for Tabletop."

Keturah stared at her a moment. She blew her nose again. "But . . . I do not intend to marry ever again."

Mitilda studied her, hands coming to her hips. "'Ever again' is a long time," she mused. Keturah only stared back at her. With a sigh, she said, "Come with me." And with that she turned and walked down the alley. The boy hung back, waiting for Ket to follow. She hesitated, and then after a moment decided, why not find out what the woman had in mind? After all, her only other option was to return to Tabletop in defeat.

But when she reached the town road, she paused, mouth agape. The woman had had the audacity to climb into her very own carriage. Gideon clambered up into the driver's seat and held the reins, glancing nervously between Mitilda and Ket, then back again. Sweat ran down his black cheeks, and Ket decided it was as likely from the heat between the women as from the heat of town. Primus was still behind her.

Keturah willed herself to move forward and took Primus's hand to climb into the carriage. Perhaps Mitilda truly did have some sort of solution for her. If the woman was right and the planters of Nevis had somehow conspired against her, then she might spend weeks in Charlestown, encountering men of the sort she had just met. Did she really wish to do that? She shoved back the anger that had set her hands to trembling, carefully interlacing them in her lap. Anger, after all, was not ladylike. And she was done being angry. At God. At anyone at all. *Right?*

She cocked her head in Mitilda's direction. "To where would you suggest we go?" she asked, every word carefully enunciated.

Mitilda didn't give her the courtesy of a reply. Instead, she leaned forward and said to Gideon, "Head south out of town. About a mile yon."

The servant looked back at Keturah, awaiting her approval, and Keturah pointed forward with two fingers, silently giving her assent. The boy climbed onto the back of the carriage, Primus onto the front bench, and then they were off. While Ket could feel the intense gaze of many as they passed, and could see in her peripheral vision several leaning close to gossip, she did not give them the satisfaction of meeting their gaze. After all, it was they who had proven to be of no aid to her. Clearly there was not a gentleman among them.

Lower Round Road proceeded uphill at a fairly steep grade. Keturah glanced over the edge. She hadn't had occasion to travel the road on this side of the island—always heading the other direction en route to Tabletop—and she looked with interest at the smaller plantations found here. The hillside, with fewer fruit and flower trees, spread wide and open with only windmills to break up the miles and miles of knee-high green cane. Slaves worked in groups, and it encouraged Ket's heart to see they still planted cane on the outer edges of the fields, digging holes, sliding in a seedling, and surrounding it with manure and soil. Another slave followed right behind the first, carrying a skin heavy with water to douse it when they were done. *If they can still be planting now*, she thought, *so can we.*

They passed grand estates, some with front gates in pristine order, others with stone pillars leaning or in some disrepair. And they passed tiny plots of land with no more than shacks for shelter. There were also no millworks on those pieces of property, and Keturah wondered if they took their cane to their neighbors to process. But at what cost? She thought about her own mill and the progress that had been made at fixing the blades. According to Bennabe, it was set to test on the morrow. If she could offer it, what might others pay? Might she undercut what others offered to mill cane in order to generate funds? After all, a penny earned was better than no pennies at all.

She glanced toward Mitilda, considering asking the woman, but pride kept her silent. She chastised herself, that pride held her back. But Keturah stubbornly held on to it. *Is it not progress enough, Lord, that I am willing to sit in this carriage with her?*

Ket glanced past the woman and out toward sea. There were three schooners closing in on Charlestown, all about an hour apart from the next. So it went on the isle, all day long. New arrivals—slaves from Africa, importers from the colonies, traders from all over the world. Here they laid hold of sugar, molasses and rum, but primarily sugar. The most valuable crop Nevis could produce. Every speck of wheat and corn were imported. Everything was imported, really. Livestock was kept from slaughter because the manure they produced was more valuable than the meat. Tiny crops of vegetables—sweet potatoes and cava, mostly—were planted by slaves, testimony to the planters' grudging admission that they had to keep their field hands fed in order to produce more sugar.

King Sugar still reigned here on Nevis, the Queen of the Caribbees.

*Queen of the Caribbees*, she thought with an internal scoff, looking about with jaundiced eyes. The Queen had certainly entered her elder years; she was aged, weak, and in places clearly infirm. Was there room to bring her back to what she once was? Keturah thought it a possible farce, a dream that grew more and more distant each day. *Especially if I cannot even find an overseer.*

Mitilda leaned forward as they rounded the bend and told Gideon to take the next right. The driver did as she asked, and they moved off the road at such a steep angle that it made Ket's stomach turn a somersault. She reached out to grab hold of the edge of the carriage and braced her legs against the floorboards so as not be tossed to the side. Primus looked back, stricken, ready to grasp her hand. But through it all, Mitilda endured the jostling as if it were nothing but a stiff breeze off the water. It took everything in Ket not to turn around and see if little Abraham had been shaken off the back. It was only his mother's lack of concern that kept her from doing so. Surely, the child was still there.

*Abraham. My father's child. My half brother.*

The thought still galled more than moved her, and Ket found herself grateful for the distraction of the impossibly steep road. She was wondering if they would have to walk back up rather than

ride when the cane on either side caught her attention. *The cane.*
She blinked quickly as if she might be seeing some mad vision.

Here, in a wide *gaut*—what the islanders called a ravine—with a
creek running down the edge of the road, the cane was a foot taller
than anything else she'd seen. At last the road eased in grade and
the little valley widened just before it met the sea. To their right,
three slaves worked in a tidy trio. Weeding, it appeared.

Hearing the whinny of one of their horses, the man in the lead
looked up, straightened, and rubbed his forehead of sweat. Mitilda
lifted her arm, calling out, and told Gideon to pull up. As soon as
he'd done so, she hurried out of the carriage and ran over to the
man, her son right behind her, and threw herself into his arms.
The man grinned and picked her up a moment, giving her such a
freely loving hug that it made Keturah blush and look away.

*Honestly! Who might this be? Some other illicit lover?*

But a moment later, she knew she could do nothing but look
back their way. The man had his arm around Mitilda's shoulder,
a broad grin still splitting across his brown cheeks. She was gesturing toward the carriage, and for the first time the man looked
in Keturah's direction. He leaned closer to Mitilda, listening to
what she said, and his smile began to fade. Stalwartly, Keturah
continued to look in his direction. Whatever was being said, she
had nothing over which *she* might feel ashamed.

The man shook his head and took a step away from Mitilda.
Then he shook his head more vehemently and gestured about,
from the road to the sea. They were talking about this cane. Was
Mitilda trying to get him to introduce Keturah to his master? Or
the overseer here?

Mitilda gestured to Keturah and then tapped her finger on his
chest, pointed to the sky and then out to sea. She lifted her hands,
and the boy took a few steps away, as if he didn't want to be anywhere near if his mother decided to redirect her anger to him. The
man stood there for several long moments, hands on his hips, while
the other two slaves looked on. Then he swung his head toward
Keturah. And in that movement, Ket saw it at last. Mitilda and

this man were *related* somehow. He was darker-skinned, broader of face, but there was the same elegance in their necks, similar movements and nuances between them.

Keturah shifted uneasily. "Primus," she said quietly, "who is that?"

"Forgive me, Lady Ket, but I do not know. I have not been to this side of the island, nor to this . . . estate. Rest assured if I had, I would never have assumed I could safely bring you down that road."

She sat back, waiting. Mitilda still stood with her hands on hips. The watching slaves and Abraham also waited quietly.

After what seemed an eternity, the man heaved a sigh and turned toward the carriage. Mitilda hurried behind, looking as though she was trying to swallow a victorious smile.

Keturah braced herself. *What is this?*

The man approached the carriage and halted three steps away, a customary distance of respect. He took off his soiled hat and held it in his hands before him. "You are Lady Tomlinson, I hear," he said.

"I am," she replied.

"I am Matthew." He gestured to his sweat-soaked, dirty shirt with his hat. "Mitilda told me you needin' an overseer for Tabletop."

"Yes. Do you know of someone?"

They locked eyes for a moment, and she could feel his assessment, his inclination to look her over—and then catching himself, knowing that was a punishable offense. Instead, he glanced to the ground, then to the tree to his right, then over to Primus and back again. "My sister here is thinkin' that I might be the man for the job."

He dared to hold her gaze then, and it was her turn to fight the desire to look anywhere but into his dark eyes. She tried to swallow and failed, finding her mouth dry. "You . . ." she began. "But is . . . ?"

And then it came to her. The man had to be a free man, with land of his own. Impossibly *challenging* land that another planter might have thrown away as unsuitable, but he was making it *thrive*.

"This," she said, her voice strengthening as she gestured about, "is yours? Those . . . people," she said carefully, narrowly avoiding the term *slaves*, "are yours?"

"Yes'm," he said. He lifted his chin, prepared now for her dismissal. Even glanced over at his sister with a sly look as if to say he'd seen it coming, and she was a fool to even suggest it.

Keturah considered that. Freed slaves owned slaves? "How long have you been working this land, Mr. . . . ?"

"Mr. Rollins," he said, a touch of bravado in his tone now that she hadn't used his given name, offering him the respect due a free man. "And 'tis been two years, Lady Tomlinson."

"And how was your last harvest, Mr. Rollins?" she asked, her heart beginning to thud in excitement, even as her mind raced.

"One of the best on Nevis," he said, this time not bothering to try to disguise his pride.

She nodded, looking around in admiration. "But it is a small property, is it not, Mr. Rollins?"

"The smallest. Only a few acres."

She leaned slightly forward, hands on her knees, and paused a moment. "So, Mr. Rollins, if you had the acreage of Tabletop at your disposal, do you believe you would be able to replicate what you have done here?"

He paused, took a breath, and looked at her. Sorrow filled his round eyes. "That not likely, ma'am."

"Lady Ket," she corrected him. "Please call me Lady Ket." But she liked him, liked that he dared to tell her the truth. "Why is it that you believe that you could not do on Tabletop what you are doing here?"

He looked around, then back to her. "Because this land is virgin, Lady Ket. I'm workin' land like the planters did backin' a hundred years ago. Backin' when Nevis *was* the Queen. And this side of the island . . . well, she gets different rainfall and sunshine thanna you do over at Tabletop. This ravine, for sure."

She thought about the planters talking, the thinly disguised jealousy and competition that sometimes rose between them. "How long ago were you freed, Mr. Rollins?"

"Three years ago. Yes'm." He said that with some pride.

"And are your neighbors taking notice of your success, Mr. Rollins, here in your gully plantation?"

He hesitated, and she sensed him falter for but a moment. "Here an' there," he said. "But most lettin' me be."

"They prefer not to consider your success," she surmised.

"Could be."

"And where do you take your cane to be processed?"

A muscle at his jaw tensed. "Over at Summer's Ridge."

She recognized the plantation name, had met the owner, an unseemly man. A drunkard, she assumed, judging from his actions at Morning Star. "And does he charge you a fair amount to crush your cane?"

He glanced down, then dared to look her in the eye again. "No, Lady Ket. No, he does not."

"What is a fair price?"

"Ten percent of market value."

She nodded and sat back against the seat of the carriage, wondering if she truly had the courage to do what she was thinking. And yet what other option did she have? Would Mitilda have brought her here if she thought she had another? Ket's eyes flicked over to the woman, thinking of how she'd said the other planters were conspiring against her.

"Mr. Rollins, I am in need of an overseer. I am weeks behind in planting. I have no slaves of note to work the fields. If you come and assist me in my endeavors at Tabletop, you can process your cane in my millworks—which should be up and running again on the morrow—for *five* percent. In addition, I will pay you what any white overseer of a plantation of Tabletop's size would earn. And above that," she added, "if you help me bring in a crop that brings Tabletop back into the black on our ledgers, I shall reward you with five percent of *those* profits as well."

He stared at her, utterly still. Mitilda, beside him, had frozen too. Both looked dazed, as if they hadn't heard her right.

She nodded slowly, knowing she had made an offer that no man in his place could refuse. Ket expected that his own bit of land was but a twentieth in size compared to hers. Moreover, she knew she was proposing something that no white man would support. Why, when it got out that she had hired a black man, freed or not, to run her plantation, there would be no shortage of neighbors coming over to counsel her on her folly.

"But I think, Mr. Rollins, that it would be wise if we kept the details of our arrangement quiet," she said. "My neighbors already wonder if they would not be better served sending me to an asylum for coming here, a woman alone with her sisters, without aid of a man. Once they hear I have hired a Negro to run my plantation . . ."

"Lady Ket," he said, tucking his head to one side in warning, "if your neighbors hear I am your overseer, they might see fit to run me off, or worse."

"Not while I am there," she pledged, lifting her chin. "I have my father's pistols. I have clear ownership of the land. And I have my sisters to back me."

He looked at her, a wry smile quirking at the edges of his mouth.

"And you are a freeman, with papers," she added, assuming. "Do I have that correct?"

"You do, Lady Ket."

"Then you have every right to accept my offer. What do you say?"

Again, that tuck of his head, chin in hand for a moment. "I say you don' know how things are done here."

She sobered, abandoning her playful stance. She'd heard stories, knew this was no game. "Mr. Rollins, I am in desperate need. And in desperate times, desperate gambles are made. At times those gambles pay off, and at times they do not." She glanced at Mitilda. "But if your sister thought it a poor wager, would she have brought me here?"

He paused, although a hint of his broad smile was tugging again at his lips. His eyes shifted back and forth across hers, as if trying to accept that this was really occurring and not a dream.

"What say you, Mr. Rollins?" she asked. "May I count on your arrival come the morrow?"

He slapped his hat against his thigh, openly smiling now and daring to envelop his sister and nephew with his grin too. "*Before* that," he promised. "Because, Lady Ket, best I understand it, we have quite a bit of work to do."

# CHAPTER TWENTY-ONE

Gray was at the tavern in Charlestown taking his supper, as had been their tradition since they'd arrived. Each day he and Philip would work from sunup until midafternoon in the fields, bathe, change into a fresh shirt and breeches, reluctantly pull on jackets— a gentleman had to preserve certain traditions in spite of the heat— and went to town. To learn what they could, to form relationships with those in power—and those who weren't—and begin to secure Teller's Landing's foothold again. He'd come alone this evening, however. Philip had twisted his ankle that afternoon and decided to stay back to rest it. "You go on without me," he told Gray. "Unless you'd rather sit here tending me," he teased.

"Never have been much of a nurse," Gray said. "But I will ask Martha to bring you some soup and a bit of feverfew."

"And you say you're not much of a nurse," Philip quipped with a half grin.

Heaven knew Gray wasn't fooling many about his being a gentleman, despite his upbringing. No other plantation owner he had met would have been caught in the mud and manure of the trenches. But Gray had no choice. Fifty acres was too much ground to cover for ten slaves, especially when time was of the essence. If he was to make a go of it, he had to get cane in the ground as soon as he could, even if he had to plant each stalk himself.

He eagerly slathered a piece of bread with freshly churned butter, but then paused mid-bite when he heard the men behind him talking.

"I hear tell Widow Tomlinson is still desperate for an overseer."

Gray glanced casually over his shoulder. Two merchants were drinking ale from pewter mugs and sharing a plate of cheese and bread. He turned back around and took a bite and then another as if he weren't listening. But he leaned back in his chair and crossed one booted ankle over his knee in order to hear them better. The tavern was crowded this time of day, full of men from the harbor.

"Won't be long now until she learns that a woman can only make it on-island when she has a decent man by her side. The planters have seen to that. Drawn together to make certain she never finds an overseer."

"Ach, 'tis a mercy, really. No woman can run a plantation. The sooner she learns that, the sooner she can choose her husband. Hopefully he can make Tabletop a success again. To old Banning's memory."

"To old Banning," said the other, and the two clinked their mugs in toast. "Who do you think it will be? Young Weland?"

"His mother did honor them with that welcoming party. She's been on the hunt for a bride for him for years. Widow Tomlinson, with her fat purse and the deed to Tabletop to boot, must have seemed a godsend to her."

Gray dug the fingernails of one hand into his thigh beneath the table and remained quiet. He lifted his mug and sipped, staring out the window, showing no interest in the men's conversation.

"Well, if she remains in need of a man," jested one lewdly, "perhaps I'll go over and sow her fields. I fancy the thought, leaving the trades and becoming a gentleman planter." He leaned back in his squeaky chair, as if he was honestly considering it. "I hear tell she's ungainly but not bad to look at."

"I've seen her. Pay no heed to the talk. She's a fine strapping woman. Good planter stock. But 'tis a bit of truth to it—her sisters are the beauties, especially the young one. Regardless, were I a younger man, I'd be angling for an invitation to Tabletop."

Gray started as a maid came by with his plate, a steaming fish stew, full of potatoes, onions, and cod. As he took a spoonful, he thought about the man's words. It was true, in measure. Keturah wasn't the obvious beauty of the trio, but it was that which was *within* her that had always drawn him. Her strength, her loyalty, her tenacity, and a courageousness that made her climb every tree ahead of him—the same courage that told her she should come here to the islands and bring her father's plantation back to its former glory.

He chewed and swallowed angrily as he thought of her reported troubles, then took another bite. Maybe this was why she had been so despicable to the Negress yesterday—why, he'd never seen her act in such an uncharitable manner, regardless of who Mitilda had once been. He shook his head. Had she not been warned, lectured by Cecil and others? Had he not tried to offer himself as a helpmate, a friend, and yet been firmly put down? What kind of woman did such a thing? Left behind the comforts of home, all that was good and proper, to come to the islands?

Gray let out a hollow laugh through his nose, around a mouthful of food, admitting it to himself. *My kind of woman.*

Besides, he knew there had to be other reasons. It was something beyond the financial peril of Tabletop; it had to be the idea of men saying no to her—and finding a way to succeed in spite of them—that drove her.

*Because Edward Tomlinson had made her believe she could do far less.*

Which was why he had stayed so far away. Not sought her out. Declined the Welands' invitation to Morning Star. Stubbornly refused to call, until yesterday, when curiosity drove him to do it. And that had ended in such a frustrating manner, he wasn't anxious to return.

He lifted his hand and turned it over in the meager light from the window, considering the hundred cuts the cane had wrought on his skin. Was this what was ahead of Keturah too? He shook his head in dismay, his stomach turning at the thought. If it was poor form for a gentleman of the islands to be so obviously involved with the day-to-day labors of running a plantation, how would her neighbors look upon a lady doing the same?

The merchants at the neighboring table had shifted to conversations of supplying a planter for his party in a few weeks, which was sure to draw Widow Tomlinson and every other planter on the island. "Perhaps she'll find a beau there. Among the pools of rum punch and Madeira, even the old fools begin to look appealing to the ladies."

"Then perhaps we should attend!" said the one, hitting the other man's shoulder. The two burst out in merriment, and it was clear to Gray then that their mugs were not their first round of rum they'd had that day.

He went on eating, grimly wondering how Ket would manage without an overseer soon. Might he find one for her? It was true that a decent man for hire was a rare thing indeed. Many were imported from other islands, wooed away for frightful sums that Gray could only dream of paying—which was why he had decided to manage his own crop and slaves, along with Philip's steady assistance. But Ket had an inheritance . . . could she not spend a portion of that? Move beyond the Nevisians' perimeter of defense to find a decent fellow to work for her?

*If she is even aware of their plans*, he thought bitterly. Could they truly be doing such a thing? Did they not have bigger concerns to captivate their attention?

Hurriedly, he finished the last of the stew, gulped down his mead, and dropped a coin on the table. He'd been waiting for her to send word to him, to ask for his counsel. But if the planters were circling round to tie her hands before she'd even begun, then he had no choice but to intervene. Friendship, if not honor, demanded it.

*Yes, at my earliest opportunity*, he thought, snugging his tricorn hat firmly on his head, strengthened by his decision.

Twenty times, Ket started to say something to Mitilda on the way back to Tabletop. But over and over she was torn between chastising the woman for cornering her into hiring her brother—which was sure to infuriate the neighboring planters—and clasping her hands in sincere gratitude for helping her find a solution.

But there never seemed to be the right moment for either.

It mattered little; Mitilda looked not in Ket's direction, which would have been the final catalyst. Primus and Gideon were silent too, leaving only the crunch and squeak of the metal-covered carriage wheels against gravel as they moved down the road and around the island, heading home. Perhaps they were all thinking what Ket was thinking. *What have we done?*

*The only thing I could have*, she corrected herself. *This is my plantation, my responsibility.* Yes, her sisters had a partial interest. But it was her name listed first on the will as the heiress in line. Her sisters had shares, she knew, to provide for their dowries. And yet if she did not generate enough funds to keep their London and Nevisian creditors at bay, she'd soon find herself funding those dowries herself, out of Edward's remaining fortune.

*Is this of you, Lord?* She prayed silently, passing another plantation with a small group of slaves' cabins set among a grove of fruit and flowering trees to provide shade. *Have you given me a way to succeed here, at last, no matter what my neighbors might think?*

But as she prayed about it, exploring that habit as if greasing a long-rusty wheel—and gazed across one plantation after another as they passed by—she recognized the spark of hope in her heart. She knew she'd had little choice, hiring Matthew Rollins. While cane was planted year-round on the island, the main crop for most planters had been in for a good three months to take advantage of the prime growing season—June through September. She'd learned from Gray that it was important for plants to reach a decent maturity before autumn's hurricane season, so they had a better chance of surviving wind and flood. Yet she'd read enough in her father's journals that said sometimes mature cane had a greater propensity to fall or get uprooted in strong winds. Sometimes young plants fared better.

To her, it all seemed as if the process of planting cane was more a gamble than a science. And today she'd gambled that Mr. Rollins would help her make Tabletop a success.

Her sisters received the news fairly well. In truth, neither had had a suggestion for her each afternoon when she returned from Charlestown without the company of a newly hired overseer. She thought Selah was relieved to know it wouldn't be a man on the order of Angus Shubert, who seemed to wheedle his way closer to her at every neighborly function he could. Verity had given her a hard look when she told them both that Matthew Rollins was Mitilda's brother, as if she wondered if it was wise to bring him here. "Might he not hold some ill will toward us?" she whispered, eying Selah warily, who was working on her embroidery. Together, the elder sisters tried to shield her from the worst of things.

Keturah thought about that. "I sensed no ill will," she whispered back. "Perhaps fear. Doubt. But that would be natural for anyone in his shoes to feel. And yet, Verity, think of it. If we are not able to make a go of this plantation, if our fortune dissolves, there shall be no annual stipend for Mitilda and Abraham. She has a vested interest in our success."

Verity nodded thoughtfully.

"In any case, could the man truly blame us?" Ket went on, rising to stride over to the window to watch the sun sink into the ocean, leaving broad skirts of orange and red trailing in the sky behind her. She leaned down on the wide sill, feeling the weariness of the day seep from her neck muscles down to her feet. "Would they not," she said, turning to cross her arms and lowering her voice so only her sister could hear, "be somewhat grateful to us? After all, did Mitilda not gain stature as Father's . . . *housekeeper*, as well as her freedom."

"Keturah," Verity said with a gasp, glancing toward Selah in protective alarm, "we must not speak of such things."

"We must, Ver," she said, lifting a hand toward the window. "This place is . . . wild. Barely tame, despite how it might seem, from her people to the land itself. Can you feel it? It is as if Nevis has reluctantly allowed us to stay, but is doing her best to send us back on the next ship to England. This finding an overseer was but our first battle. She'll bring more, undoubtedly. And we must be prepared to face those battles together."

Verity frowned. "Are you suffering a fever? What an odd thing to say, Ket."

"Is it?" she asked in response, knowing she should be doing something to assuage her sister's fears. After all, ladies of London never spoke in such a manner, introducing such fanciful thoughts. She could hear them now, in their salons and closets twittering on about Lady Tomlinson and the outrageous things that came out of her mouth. *As if the land had a mind of her own!* Such things were the domain of poets, not respectable society. Everyone knew that.

*Everyone but me*, she thought, turning back to the window and staring at the lingering sunset. Maybe one had to learn to treat Nevis as a welcome friend instead of a potential enemy. Perhaps addressing each day as a battle to be fought rather than a welcome invitation was the wrong approach.

*What are some of the things I like about this new friend so far?* Her thoughts turned immediately to the beach and the welcome feel of the water around her ankles. "Girls, go and fetch your bathing smocks," she said. "I want to take you to the beach for a swim."

"Alone?" Selah asked, letting her embroidery hoop sag in her hands.

"Without . . . without a bathing machine?" Verity asked. "Attendants?"

Keturah grinned. "Attendants and bathing machines are the English way. Let us go and swim as the Nevisians do."

# CHAPTER TWENTY-TWO

That evening, on his way back to Teller's Landing, Gray caught up to Captain McKintrick on Lower Round Road. The man looked far more ungainly astride the mare than he ever did on the deck of his ship, but he was whistling a merry tune.

"Ho there, Captain!" Gray greeted when he turned to see who was coming.

"Why, Mr. Covington," the man said with his warm brogue. "'Tis good to see you. I take it that I head in the right direction, to reach Tabletop?"

"Indeed," Gray said, pulling alongside the man. "I'm going there myself. I learned something in town I feel I must discuss with Lady Keturah."

"Ah, so I see. We've re-provisioned and our hold is full. We sail for the Carolinas on the morrow."

"And so you wish to say farewell to the Banning women?"

"Indeed," he said, sliding a look Gray's way that seemed to say, *At least to one woman in particular.* "I awaited an invitation to come and call, but ach, do ye ken I received naught but silence?" The man seemed a bit miffed, confused.

Gray gave him a rueful smile. "If it helps, they have not reached out to me either. And yet I can tell you that there is a great deal to accomplish, on both plantations. I know the Bannings have had much to negotiate."

"Aye, well I can imagine. This thing you caught wind of in town—I take it gave you fair alarm."

"Yes," Gray said, hesitating. "I figure I may as well offer my counsel, even if she does not wish for me to share it."

"These women are a rather stubborn sort, are they not, man?"

"Indeed." *Especially Keturah.*

"Uncommon in many ways. Quick of wit. Fair of countenance. Ever since they left my ship, I confess I've missed their company. And I'm right curious about their plantation. It will do me good to know where she—*they*," he hurriedly amended, "have found themselves settled."

"You mean, Captain, that you would like to envision her new home as you pen letters to Verity," Gray teased, cocking a brow.

The captain laughed under his breath and shook his head as if in wonderment. "Why is it that the minx now seems to occupy my every free thought? I dinna think when she first crossed my deck that she'd fair cross into my heart by the time our voyage came to an end."

Gray smiled with him, even as the captain's words rotated in his mind. He wished he had an answer for him. But was it not the same for him? Day in and day out, he had sought a reason to come and call upon Ket, to share discoveries and trials and solutions. To visit with her to see if she was learning what she must to survive. And now he hungered for a way to help her through this challenge in finding an overseer.

"Ah, there it is," he said, gesturing to the old stone pillar that marked the front entrance of Tabletop.

Captain McKintrick turned his mare's nose down the lane and whistled lowly. "Quite a view," he said. "If I wasn't one who favored the waves, this would not be a bad second option. Where does your plantation sit?"

"Just to the south," Gray answered. "My view is nearly as grand, but here, with Saint Christopher and Saba there on the horizon . . . well, 'tis something, isn't it?"

"Aye. 'Tis indeed."

They rode through the deepening shadows of the trees, past the slave cabins with newly patched roofs and freshly hewn boards. He could sense their eyes—wondering who came to call at this hour—but it wasn't until they reached the house that he actually saw someone.

Primus came out the door and onto the front porch steps. "Good evening," he said, wiping his hands on a towel that was slung over his shoulder.

"Good evening, Primus," Gray said. "Are the Misses Banning and Lady Ket at home this evening?"

"Well, they are and yet they are not. They said they were off for a stroll to the beach and perhaps a swim."

"A swim, ye say," Captain McKintrick said, eyes alight with interest.

"Perhaps we ought to wait here for them to return," Gray said.

But then they heard a shriek in the distance, followed by a fainter scream on the wind. The men shared a quick glance of alarm, then turned their horses down the path that led to the beach, racing downward. In seconds they were on a knoll above a line of coco plum bushes along the sand and pulled up, eyes searching for the women.

Captain McKintrick laughed first. The three women were playing—shrieking and shouting as they dunked and chased and splashed one another. Above them, Brutus took lazy turns in the air as if keeping silent watch. "Saints in heaven," McKintrick said. "Have you ever seen anything as bonny as that, man? Why, they're veritable sirens. I have half a mind to join them."

Gray nodded and grinned. They did look lovely, with their hair slicked back from their faces, bobbing among the waves. He felt a sudden pang in his chest, remembering what it had been like to swim with Keturah at the swimming hole as children, but knowing it was hardly his place—or Captain McKintrick's—to do so now.

It was Keturah who caught sight of them first, and she stilled and lowered herself to her jawline in the water before whispering something to her sisters. The other two hurriedly faced them.

"Ho, there!" called the captain merrily. "Forgive our intrusion, ladies. We heard your shrieks and hastened here to make sure all was well. I see that it is *more* than well."

"Quite!" Keturah called back primly. "Is there something the matter, gentlemen, or is this purely a social visit?"

"Purely social," said the captain, even as Gray said, "Perhaps both." They looked at each other and shared a smile tinged with regret.

"We shall await you at the house," Gray called, taking off his hat and putting it to his chest, then bowing his head. "Come at your leisure, ladies. We do not wish to curtail your fun."

"We will attend you shortly," Ket said.

The two reluctantly turned their mounts back up the hill just as Gideon and Primus reached the beach, chests heaving after the run. Clearly, they had been as alarmed as Gray and McKintrick had. "All is well here," Gray said. "The women are only having a bit of sport. They intend to join us at the house but need a bit of privacy as they dry off and dress."

"Oh yes," Primus said, leaning down to put hands on his knees, his back to the sea. "Very good," he panted. "I'll return shortly and see that you gentlemen receive refreshments."

"That will be grand, Primus."

Slowly the two men took to the path, not rushing their mounts now, aware that the climb was steep for the slaves. It heartened him, however, to see how they had risen to what seemed like their mistresses' call of distress. Clearly, the men felt some responsibility for the ladies' care.

They reached the house, dismounted, and Cuffee was there to take their reins. Grace was at the door, eyes wide with alarm.

"All is well," Gray said to her. "They were merely . . . cavorting."

"Oh, good. Come in, gentlemen," she said shyly, "and I shall fetch a pot of tea. Or would you prefer something stronger? A bit of wine perhaps?"

"Tea will do well," Gray said, even as he saw that Captain Mc-Kintrick was considering her "something stronger" offer.

They sat down together on a new settee that had likely come with them on the ship, and each set their hat to the side. McKintrick carried a shallow, elaborately inlaid wooden box, which he placed on the table, but he made no explanation for it.

Looking around, Gray noticed that the small parlor was stuffed. An old harpsichord sat in the corner, but the island's humidity had done some damage; here and there the wood was cracked and buckling. Most of the furnishings were new, including a tall standing clock, which seemed to fill the room with its steady ticking. Some floorboards had been replaced, the new wood fairly gleaming next to the old burnished planks. And it was clear that the girls had set to stripping wallpaper on one wall. The untouched portion of faded ivy print was bubbling and peeling. He knew that Ket had spent most of her days in town on the hunt for an overseer, so it had to be Verity and Selah's task in evidence.

"This was once a grand room," Gray said admiringly.

"With the lasses at work," the captain said, gesturing to the paper, "'twill soon be set to rights. To my mind 'tis already verra comfortable."

"Indeed." Two big windows were open wide, their shutters neatly folded on the sides. It allowed a pleasant breeze to waft in from the ocean. What would Keturah think of his small cottage? Philip and he had concentrated on the fields, on obtaining new slaves, on planting, with little thought to the house other than new straw ticks to welcome their aching bodies home at the end of each day.

But being here, in a home, filled with so many things that were so English, Gray felt another pang of longing. As if he wanted to linger here a long while. But was it the things, or the mistress to whom they belonged?

Grace arrived with a tea tray, and shortly thereafter, so did the women.

"If it isn't the three wee water sprites," Captain McKintrick teased, rising beside Gray as they entered, each with their hair neatly combed back, their bodies covered in light, airy gowns he'd never seen before.

"And if it isn't our would-be guardians," Verity said with a shy grin, pulling her wet hair over her shoulder and idly beginning to braid it.

"If only I had my chance to beat back some rogue and carry you to safety this evening, Miss Verity," he said with a slight bow, "well ye'd ken my mettle."

"And is it not a rogue, Captain," Keturah intervened, "who would imagine such a thing?"

McKintrick flashed her a wide grin and nodded once in acquiescence. Selah went to the table and began pouring them all tea.

Keturah turned to Gray. "You intimated that something was wrong. Is all well?"

"Please," he said, gesturing to the window. "Might I have a word?"

She nodded and took her dish of tea from Selah, following him there. "What is it, Gray?"

"Ket, I was in town this evening and I overheard something most distressing."

"Oh?"

"It sounds as if the planters have conspired against you to keep you from ever hiring an overseer. It is their collective thought that it is in your best interest to force you into a union with an established planter—a man who can aid you in running Tabletop."

She stilled. "A man who can take over me and mine, you mean."

He frowned and rubbed the back of his neck. "'Tis not my view, Keturah," he said with a shake of his head. "But the men here . . . well, they're a bit of an old guard, I take it. Used to doing things as their fathers and grandfathers and great-grandfathers did before them. The notion of a woman coming in . . . what you're trying to do, well, Ket, I fear they're against it."

She huffed a laugh. "That confirms what I suspected." She sipped from her cup and looked up at him, lifting one brow. "But pay it no heed, Gray. I already knew of their devious plan. And I found my overseer this day," she said with a smile, leaning toward him.

"You did? Where? Who?"

"A man from the other side of the island," she said, turning toward the window. His breath caught at the sight of her profile, rimmed in the golden light of the setting sun. "He has but a tiny bit of a plantation there. But, Gray, he's doing a fine job with it. You should see his cane! It's already as high as my shoulders!"

"And he's agreed to come and work for you?"

"Indeed. He starts on the morrow. So do not worry yourself further, my friend." She laid a hand on his forearm, and warmth seemed to spread from her hand across his skin. "No matter what the men of this island intended, I have found the solution to my troubles."

She looked up to him then, golden eyes warm and hopeful.

Gray smiled and sipped his tea, pretending he didn't mind when her long fingers slipped from his arm, but her words agitated him. Did she not know that this island would likely make them face one trouble after another? Was she truly prepared?

And yet there was something different in her tonight, a peace he hadn't seen in her for years. Was it merely the fact that she'd finally managed to find an overseer? Or something more? She was more willing to smile, more willing to meet his gaze . . .

"Keturah," he said, "I do believe this island is doing you some good. You are positively glowing." The last word left his mouth feeling dry. Had he overstepped?

"Am I?" she asked, lifting a hand to her cheek. "Perhaps." She leaned forward, studied him a moment, and whispered, "I decided to treat this island as my friend, Gray, rather than my enemy."

He blinked, a bit swayed at the feel of her breath on his cheek. "Oh?"

"Yes. It finally came to me that no fruitful alliance can form between uneasy partners. One must be open, welcoming, trusting if there is fruit to be born."

He paused, considering her words. Briefly, he wondered if she truly spoke of more . . . "And before that, you were treating Nevis as your enemy?"

"More as a *potential* enemy. And I decided that was no way to begin relations." She sobered and studied him again. "I think I must deal with Mitilda in the same manner. I am . . . I am finding my way with her. It was she who helped me find my overseer, Matthew Rollins."

"Mitilda," he said with a nod, remembering the woman in the mango grove and her son and how Ket had treated them. The awkward exchange . . . and the revelation.

"Mitilda," Ket repeated.

"That is good, Ket," he said, nodding slowly. "Better for you both, over the course of time, to find your way forward together."

She gave him a rueful smile and then looked out toward the sea again. "That was my thought exactly."

Captain McKintrick's warm laugh brought their heads around. He had been regaling Verity and Selah with a story of a pirate along the Barbary Coast who had nearly slit his throat. Both girls were enthralled.

"That is why I have brought ye ladies this gift," he said, leaning toward the wooden box. He pulled it into his lap and lifted its lid. "Ye have embarked on a journey that is rife with dangers. And whilst I wish I might remain nearby in order to save you from any trials"—his eyes slid to Verity and then back to the box—"I fear I must be off. I shall return in a matter of months, but I knew I could not leave ye defenseless, not in good conscience."

Inside the box were six small sharp blades, each set in an ornately carved ivory handle. "These are a set of *sgian dhu*, carried by Highland warriors." He looked at all three of them, Verity longest of all. "I pray ye shall be treated with utmost respect. But as my *seanahm-hair* would have said, even the lasses must be ready for battle. I beg you to arm yourselves. Truth be told, nine times out of ten, ye shall not need either knife or man to protect ye. But on that tenth day, would it not be wise to have the knife at the ready? I leave it to ye to ponder, and pray ye shall carry one in either sheath or stocking."

Verity stared at him, while Keturah found herself startled by his care and concern. It felt . . . genuine to her. Familial in some measure. Helpful rather than possessive.

"Thank you, Captain McKintrick," Ket said, moving toward him. "That is most thoughtful of you. We shall look forward to the day you return to Charlestown."

"As shall I," he said, rising and looking Verity's way again. "As shall I."

Gray felt now was the time. He should aid Keturah in separating the captain from Verity. Cecil would wish it as much as Ket. "Yes, well. We bid you ladies good night. Thank you for allowing us to come and call upon you."

He half expected an eager reply. Something that indicated Ket's agitation over their interruption of their dip in the sea, their intrusion upon their household, or his meddling in her affairs. Instead, she said softly, "Thank you for coming, Gray. And Captain McKintrick, blessings on your voyage."

"Captain McKintrick!" said the Scotsman. "So formal, lass. So formal. Might ye not all call me Duncan, since I've gone as far as to aid ye in arming yourselves?"

"Thank you for coming, Duncan," Verity said first, stepping forward. "I, for one, shall look forward to your return." She lay hold of one of the shining blades and lifted it with a smile.

The captain paused and stared at the girl intently.

Inwardly, Gray groaned. *So much for aiding Ket in their separation.* Clearly the two were avidly drawn to the other. In fact, since they had left the *Restoration*, their attraction seemed to have grown tenfold. Was this because of the impending separation?

Captain McKintrick took Verity's hand and bowed so lowly over it, they might have been in a formal English drawing room. "Miss Verity," he said, "trust me when I say that my sole goal is to get to the Carolinas, and then back to ye, before winter."

"Trust me when I say, Captain," she returned, looking full upon his face, "that I pray the winds are in your favor."

He grinned so widely that Gray took a steep breath. Why could he not be so audacious with Ket? Press her in similar manner? *Why not?* he asked himself.

*Because she would not welcome it.*

*She is not ready.*

*And even if she was, I have not the means to court her.*

# CHAPTER TWENTY-THREE

Keturah awakened before sunrise to the smell of baking bread and fire in the kitchen, which they all knew by now tended to smoke a great deal. It was something else on her endless list of things needing done—she must either find a chimney sweep or a mason to address the hundred-year-old stone structure's ailments. From what she had been told, the grand old volcanic chimney stood in what was now the third house built around her.

"They always said it be a good luck charm," said Sansa, currently serving as a kitchen maid, running her hand over the black rock when Keturah entered the room, candle in hand. "I thought she jus' needed to be warmed up again, Lady Ket, since there been no cook fire in here for months." She waved her hand through the smoke and pinched her nose, squinting her eyes.

"Yes, well, I think we might need to tear down this good luck charm and begin anew," Ket said, picking up a wooden paddle to encourage the smoke to waft out the window.

"Oh, Lady Ket, we cannot do that," Grace said. "Surviving three houses over a hundred years? 'Tis a bit of your family's history, it is."

"But look at it," Ket said, gesturing in frustration toward the fireplace. "'Tis liable to ignite and bring down the third with it!"

"Just a sweep is what she needs," Grace said, peering up and into the chimney, as if she could see through the billowing smoke. "Surely they have chimney sweeps, even here on Nevis."

"I would not be so certain," Keturah said with a weary sigh. "They have porcelain from the Orient and cattle from the colonies, but they might not have a body dedicated to preserving something like a chimney. No," she said with a second sigh, hand on hip surveying the stone structure, "this island seems more bent on treating all as they might a new harvest."

*Would that I had the funds to begin anew.* Again it haunted her thoughts. There was much in the house that would be more costly to repair than she liked to think about. The stairs had begun to separate a bit from the wall and seemed to shift with each step one took on them. Selah refused to take to the stairs at the same time as either of her sisters or Grace. The rugs were threadbare, and they needed to peel the rest of the wallpaper. In fact, there was not a room in the house that didn't need considerable work.

Truth be told, Keturah had spent hours daydreaming about razing the house and beginning again. But running her hand over the fireplace mantel, thinking of her father before her, her grandfather before him, and other planters too . . . well, it gave her a sense of permanence, hope in its longevity. She knew that if she had to take down this house and rebuild, she too would do so with this fireplace as the cornerstone, just as her ancestors had before her.

*Yet I would give it a thorough cleaning,* she thought.

"What did my father do?" she asked Bennabe, who had wandered into the kitchen in search of something to break his fast. The two new slaves—named by the others as Hope and Tolmus—timidly peeked in the door behind him. She was glad he had taken them under his wing. Day by day they seemed a bit more settled, a bit more brave in meeting her welcoming smile with one of their own. "Surely Father did not live with such smoke, billowing out each day."

"No, mum. They cooked outside," Bennabe said, "to avoid the smoke and heat. They built up a fire every day in that pit in the far corner. Mitilda could show you. She outside even now, settin' to fire more pots."

Keturah took that in. Mitilda made pots? Perhaps pottery was part of what she used for income, on top of the annual stipend her father had promised her. Ket had seen slaves on Sunday at the market in Charlestown, selling their wares, from pottery to parrot fish to yams. Few of the slaves were Christian, she'd learned, but the plantation owners felt it gave them time to rest and work their own ground, which in turn helped feed them and their families.

It was through the billowing smoke of the kitchen that Matthew Rollins arrived, coughing into a fist. "Good morning, Lady Ket," he said, making her and Bennabe jump in surprise. *It was as if he'd arrived down the chimney itself!*

She put a hand to her chest. "Ahh, Mr. Rollins. When you said before sunrise, you clearly meant it."

He cocked his head to one side. "One thing you may count on, Lady Ket, is me telling you like it is. If I say it so, it so."

She nodded. She liked that. She wished everyone was more apt to do so.

Mr. Rollins reached out to shake Bennabe's hand. Gideon, Absalom, and Edwin arrived, introductions made. "Where are the rest?" he asked. "Mimba and Sansa? The old slaves are still about, are they not?"

"I'm here," Sansa said, emerging again from the smoke, this time armed with a rattan fan.

"Well, yes," Ket said, "but I am not quite sure what earthly good they will do us, Mr. Rollins. Mimba has had a cough that seems to stick with him, day and night. Sansa is just regaining her strength—she was terribly thin when we arrived. The others, well, I'd thought we could head to Charlestown today and see about purchasing some new help for Tabletop rather than try to rally the rest. They are in rather poor condition. Perhaps in time . . ."

He considered her a moment, twisting his hat in a slow circle between his hands. "That your right, Lady Ket," he drawled in his relaxed Creole accent, much more pronounced than Mitilda's, "to do what you think wise. But you see, I brought my own slaves with me today. I can hire them out to you by the day, and since time is of the essence, why don' we see what we can do with your remaining slaves, plus mine, in the fields? After a day's work, then we can decide if a trip to Charlestown is the wisest road."

It was her turn to consider him. She'd never had a Negro dare to attempt to change her mind. But then this was a man with his manumission papers, a planter in his own right. *My new overseer*, she reminded herself.

He was not only demanding her respect, he deserved it. Just as she sought the same as a planter, did she not?

"Very well, Mr. Rollins," she said. "Raise the old slaves from their beds if you can, but please, do not resort to cruelty in order to do so." It seemed strange to have to warn a former slave of being a harsh master, but she wanted no doubts as to her wishes. "After a bit of a meal," she rushed on, "I shall join you in the upper field. I presume that is where you wish to begin?"

He frowned at that, clearly surprised that she knew it was tradition to begin high and work their way down. Or was it that he did not think a white woman's place was anywhere near the fields?

As much as she had to learn about Mr. Rollins and his ways, she knew he had an equal amount to learn of her. She remained where she stood, not looking away.

"Very well, Lady Ket. This is your plantation," he said.

"That it is, Mr. Rollins," she said steadily, willing him to remember that. "I shall follow you all in an hour's time."

———

Verity and Selah rose and insisted they accompany her to the upper field. They passed by the trail to the waterfall—which they had yet to explore—and on to the top of the plantation, the butte that had given the place her name.

Mr. Rollins had roused three of the six other slaves, men named Antony, July, and Meriday, and did indeed have his own already hard at work as well. Keturah drew up on her horse's reins when she caught sight of Mitilda and the boy Abraham working alongside them. "Well, why would they be here?" she muttered, watching as the line of workers hoed a steady line in the dark soil, the second neat, tidy furrow in the field.

Following her gaze, Selah said, "Perhaps they merely wish to help," she tried. "After all, Tabletop is their home too."

On the edge, in the far corner, her new overseer was shirtless, his broad black chest already glistening with sweat as he used a machete to chop into an old stand of cane. He bent over to cut each eight-foot stalk into two-foot sections, tossing them in a pile. His nephew, also shirtless, gathered the fragments and carried them over to the furrow, placing them lengthwise in the shallow gulley. It was the child who glimpsed the ladies first. He looked dolefully over at them even as they returned his long look.

"Honestly, the way that child looks at us! 'Tis as if we were not English ladies but Guinevere and her maids, emerging from the fog," Verity said.

"And perhaps we are," Keturah murmured. "For to his young mind, if Father ever spoke of us, we were but folklore, really. A made-up story of young ladies across the great sea. And now . . . here we are." *His half sisters.* Did the child understand such things? Had his mother even told him who his father was?

Both of her sisters were silent a moment. Keturah moved her horse across the field, aware that her sisters followed behind and Matthew waited her arrival. "How does it appear?" she asked when he was within earshot.

"It appears well, Lady Ket," he said, looking approvingly over the level plain of her father's field. "If you can send us a meal and water come noontime, I think we can plant a good ten to twelve rows in this field today."

She nodded and scanned the field, finding heart in his words. It was perhaps fifteen acres in dimension. If they planted even twelve rows, that'd leave another two hundred to go. *A month then to plant the whole thing, to say nothing of the two terraces below.* "So," she said, leaning over to stroke her mare's neck, "we shall go to Charlestown tomorrow to purchase more slaves?"

226

"We shall see, Lady Ket. We shall see. Slaves cost their owner a pretty penny, you see. The old ones—"

"The old ones are our family's responsibility," Selah interrupted, pulling up alongside Keturah.

"Yes, yes," he said slowly, thoughtfully. "That's right, Miss . . . ?"

"Miss Selah," Keturah supplied.

"Miss Selah," he said. "But new slaves add to the cost. I'm urging your sister here to be careful of the cost. We want to be wise in what we spend on labor in order to bring Tabletop the biggest profits."

"And your sister? Your nephew?" Ket asked tightly. "What do they cost us per day? And what of your own slaves?"

"Less than labor you own, tha's for certain, Lady Ket," he replied. "Labor you own has its own expenses." His dark eyes moved over to the three people he'd brought with him. "There are days that they pay for themselves; others when you must care for them, and they do not earn a ha'penny for their owner."

Keturah decided she liked his forthright manner, his gentle authority. "All right then, Mr. Rollins, let us see how things progress over the next few days."

"Very good, Lady Ket. Very good." He put a hand to his lower back to stretch a mite. "And on the morrow, Sansa, Primus, Grace, and Cuffee could join us?"

She stilled, shocked at his insinuation. "I think not, Mr. Rollins. We need a few to attend us. And Primus has been a house slave since he was little. He'd be of no use out here."

"Beggin' your pardon, Lady Ket, but I can make use of most anyone out here. And given that time is short and the need for a profitable crop is great, would it not be wise to put everyone with two hands to work?"

Ket's eyes moved to Mitilda, who had paused, wrists crossed over the end of her hoe, and stared her way. How much did she know of her father's financial woes? Had her father shared everything with the woman? And had she shared it with her brother? Or did he simply assume correctly about her needs?

"Is there a soul on Tabletop land who isn't counting on this crop?" Mr. Rollins asked gently.

She bit her cheek and glanced at her sisters. "Very well, Mr. Rollins. I will speak to the remaining servants tonight. Given our circumstances, perhaps even we ladies must take regular turns in our fields."

That made his eyes go wide, and he hooted a laugh. "Oh, I did not mean you, Lady Ket. Or your sisters," he said with a respectful nod to each. "But wouldn' that set your neighbors' tongues to waggin'? Hoo, boy!"

But even as his laughter faded, Keturah began to ponder. Why should she *not* join them in the fields? Her fingers itched to do something useful, to dig into the soil, to compare it to England's. She would not make her sisters do so, but would it not set a good example for Primus and Grace, who might feel themselves above such work? Was it not as Matthew said—vital for them all to be working for their common good, their future?

Memories of the dismal ledgers back home in London, as well as the few gloomy journal entries from her father here that she'd forced herself to read, cascaded through her mind. Mr. Rollins had promised to tell her things as they truly were; he'd once been a slave and now owned slaves to work his own land. She had no choice but to trust him to give her wise counsel on that front. She'd been planning to spend a fair amount of her fortune on slaves, as an investment of Tabletop and her future profits. But might there be a wiser route? She'd seen enough to know that most other planters on the island with an estate her size—more than fifty acres—had two slaves per acre. Conventional wisdom told her she'd need a hundred.

But was there a wiser way? Her father had nearly lost Tabletop over the two decades he ran this land. Yes, his endeavors to level out the two other fields had nearly bankrupted him. It had meant three years of but a portion of their normal harvest. But was there more to his financial woes than that? She'd seen the ramshackle buildings in Charlestown. The once-fine plantations, here and there, now falling into disrepair. Had those planters also made poor decisions—such as purchasing too many slaves—which would contribute to their own demise?

---

That evening, as Grace and Sansa cooked and packed baskets for the field crew's lunch the next day, Keturah found the courage to again enter her father's study—so redolent with echoes of him all about her—and go to the leather-bound journal on his desk. She sat down and went back ten years, to before he had the madcap idea to terrace the fields. She wanted to know what he'd experienced then. His trials. His triumphs.

There were long pages full of line items unique to the plantation but foreign to her English upbringing. Yet as her eyes ran over the numbers—captured in the meticulous double-entry method of bookkeeping—she slowly came to terms with the exorbitant expense of working this land. Her stomach clenched. She'd spent three years presiding over the household ledgers of Clymore Castle, but even running that old estate paled in comparison to running one here on Nevis. Importing almost every chicken, cow, hog, as well as every cask of flour, sugar, and salt from America added up to a staggering expense.

She understood the pressures that prevailed. Sugar reigned. It was a far more valuable crop than corn or wheat. The returns on each sugar shipment were handsome indeed. But because they had to import all provisions in from the colonies, the Nevisians spent twenty times the amount that Londoners did for the same supplies. And what would happen if something kept Nevis from the imports of America? What would happen if they could not regularly receive livestock, flour, salt, and more?

*Worse, what if we could not receive tea from the Orient?*

She smiled at her own internal jest. But at last she understood it, staring at the ledgers that so clearly showed both profits and expenses. The draw that had kept her father here. It was a mad gamble, this island life. The idea that she could pay these sorts of expenses and yet make this land pay for itself in spades . . . Or be utterly decimated by the forces of either nature or market. But if she could somehow reduce expenses and bring in a new sugar crop—the best ever—would that not have made her father proud? It made her heart quicken as she strode to the window, the same window her father had stood near, and looked out.

Keturah wondered what he had thought and felt while standing here. She ran her fingers over the sill, knowing his hands had rested there too once. She longed for the opportunity to sit and talk with him. Indeed, the last time she'd seen him, she'd been all of nineteen, her mother dead and buried a good year by then. Father had spoken of love, of duty, and she'd absorbed that fully. *"And your mother always thought Lord Tomlinson a charming man,"* he'd said. *"She'd be proud of you, becoming a lady. As am I, Ket."*

It was those words she focused on most as she walked down the aisle at St. John's that fateful morn and moved from her father's arm to Edward's.

Passed along like chattel. Controlled as if she had not a mind nor will of her own. *Until now*, she thought, looking out over Tabletop. *Now it is all up to me.*

And in that moment she did not know if that was the worst or greatest thing to ever occur to her.

Gray's words came back to her. *"All God asks of us is to do our best, from morning until night. He doesn't expect us to do things that only He can accomplish—only what we've been given to do and to trust Him with the rest."*

It'd been enough, this day. She'd done what God asked of her. And now she would rest.

<hr />

By the time her sisters found her the next morning, Keturah had emptied half of her father's chests of clothes on the floor.

"What," Verity said, moving between the piles, "are you doing?"

"Finding proper clothing," Keturah said, straightening and tightening the sash around her breeches to hold them up. It was fortunate that her father had been a slender man, but they still were big on her.

Verity's eyebrows rose as she looked her over. "Are you completely mad?"

Ket smiled. "I do not think so. But I can well imagine that you think it true." She stepped forward, lifted a pile of shirts from yet another trunk, and sifted through them. Finding a good option, she pulled it from the stack and set the others aside. "We need to offer these to the house servants or field slaves. They're not doing Father any good."

Both of her sisters gaped at her. "Ket," Selah began quietly, "are you aware that you are in nothing but breeches and stays?"

"And stockings," Ket said, turning this way and that before the tall mirror she'd brought with her on the *Restoration*, never imagining she'd see herself dressed in this manner. "I believe I need a shirt, do you not agree?" She turned left and right to examine her imperfect wavy image. "Although the stays alone would be ever so much cooler."

Her sisters continued to gape, only pausing to glance at each other. Keturah edged past Verity and dug through another trunk of Father's that appeared to hold older shirts. She lifted one up and hesitated, wondering if she remembered it on him when she was but a child. She pulled it close, inhaling deeply, hoping she could still smell him somewhere within the folds, but it was no use. All that remained was dust and mold. Blinking rapidly, before her sisters could detect her tears, she pulled it around her body, laced up the front, then rummaged around for a belt. Finding one, she wound it around her waist and fastened it. Hands on hips, she faced her sisters.

"And . . . you are dressing for a costume ball?" Verity asked, arms crossed.

"I am going to work," Keturah said.

Both of them stared at her, not comprehending.

"I want this plantation to succeed," she went on. "A vital part of it succeeding is getting cane in the ground as soon as possible.

I have wasted precious days waiting for an overseer, waiting for help. Now we have him." She shrugged. "And I can be a *part* of the solution by digging in that soil myself. Cutting cane. Fertilizing, watering it. Do you not see?"

She moved to her sisters, her excitement brimming over, making her hands tremble. "I am done waiting on others. Becoming a victim of another's choice. This is *mine*."

Verity continued to stare, her mossy-green gaze hard and concerned.

Selah only looked wan and frightened, rubbing her small hands together in agitation.

"Do you not see?" Keturah repeated with a grin. "I am finished waiting. For the right man. For the right help. I want to do what I can with the two hands God gave me," she said, furiously rolling up one of her father's sleeves and then the other. "I want to dig in the soil we call ours by *making* it ours. By working it, planting it, growing our crop. I do not wish for this to be Mr. Rollins's crop. I wish for it to be *ours*."

She looked from one to the other, desperate for them to make the leap that she had. To understand the import of this. But with each passing breath, she knew she wanted more of them than they were capable of giving her. She knew what she did because of what she had experienced, because of what Edward had been, and what he had not.

"It is all right, dear ones. Do not be alarmed. Stay here and continue with your efforts with the house. I shall return come sunset."

She practically fled the room and hurried down the stairs. Primus and Grace, obedient as ever, had changed into their least fine and stood in the front hall, looking upon her just as her sisters had.

As if she were three steps shy of the madhouse.

Or—and this shook her to the core—as if she were *herself*, truly who she was meant to be . . . as Keturah Elizabeth Banning Tomlinson, for the first time in her entire life.

Not posturing for society.

Or her husband.

Or her family.

Only *Keturah* . . . all she was and could be in the moment. Utterly *herself*.

For a moment, she hovered there, halfway down the rickety stairwell, and she was glad for every bit of it. No matter if she succeeded or failed at Tabletop, she would praise the Almighty for bringing her here to this place. To remember—or discover at last—just who she was, deep within. To think for the first time, *I am enough. Just as I am. Because God has made me so.*

# CHAPTER TWENTY-FOUR

Philip had been working with the Teller's Landing slaves on the far side of the fields, closest to Tabletop, while Gray worked on a stubbornly rusted-shut irrigation sluice. He'd been at it all day and was about to give up and create an entirely new channel when he saw Philip riding hard toward him.

Warily he rose, then glanced around for his own new horse, a chestnut mare named Mariah, happily munching away on the greenery of the jungle. Philip pulled up and looked down at Gray. "'Tis Lady Ket," he panted, brows furrowed in concern. "Angus Shubert and his men are there, and they appear to be arguing with her."

Gray's eyes narrowed. Hidden among the narrow strip of jungle that separated their two properties on the ridge, he'd taken to looking over each evening to see how she fared. For weeks now he'd been fretting, covertly observing them make progress on refurbishing the mill and repairs about the house, but no planting in the fields. Then yesterday his heart had leapt, seeing them below, planting at last. At long last . . .

Until he noted whom Ket had finally found as an overseer.

A Negro.

And if Angus Shubert was taking issue . . .

He ran to his mare, swung up into the saddle, and gestured for Philip to follow him. The overseer of Red Rock was a brawler.

He'd seen him pick a fight in a Charlestown tavern, and he'd seen how he eyed Selah that first day in town like he might a tavern wench rather than a gentlewoman. While he'd patiently done his best to wait for Keturah to call on *him* for aid, he would not wait through *this*.

He had a pistol in the saddlebag, as well as a sword, taking stock as he rode. And he'd taken to tucking a dagger in his boot, ever since Captain McKintrick urged the Banning women to do the same. Still, he managed to rein himself—and his horse—in a bit as he reached the ridge. The best way to intervene was through the art of subtlety, resorting to physical force only if required. It was the way of gentlemen. The way he'd been bred from boyhood.

But as he eased over the ridge and rode down toward Tabletop and her highest field, where Keturah gathered with the slaves to face Shubert and two others from Red Rock Plantation, he knew how little he resembled a gentleman. He ran a hand through his hair to try to slick it into some sort of proper order. Not that Shubert was a gentleman himself. Why did he bother? For Shubert, or for Ket?

As he neared them, he discovered that Keturah was not in a brown day dress as he had expected. Nor were Selah and Verity, whom he had not recognized as present at all given their field hats and . . . men's clothes? His stomach twisted. Of all things . . .

All three of the Banning sisters were in breeches, stockings, and shirts, covered with mud to their elbows and knees! He did his best to swallow his surprise as he came near, hearing Keturah's voice rising in anger and seeing her hand rise, index finger pointing Angus Shubert away.

"Go home, Mr. Shubert," he heard her say. "This is no concern of yours."

"Well now, *Lady* Tomlinson," the man sneered, ignoring Gray's arrival, "I believe it *is* my concern, with you here hiring a Negro to run your land, land that borders our own."

"A Negro, sir, with *manumission papers*," the tall, bare-chested man at her side quietly corrected him.

Shubert caught sight of Gray then, with Philip right behind

him. "Go on home, Mr. Covington," he said in his Carolina drawl. "This here conversation is between my neighbor and me. It doesn't involve you."

Keturah turned, her pretty mouth gaping open in surprise. He saw her run her hands down her shirt and then glance down, as if she'd forgotten what she wore. She blushed—out of embarrassment? Or was it anger that he was here uninvited? Mouth clamping shut, she turned back to Shubert.

Gray bit his cheek, forcing himself to stay in the saddle and appear relaxed. He looped the reins around the saddle horn and crossed his wrists atop it, listening, ignoring Shubert's demand that he leave. He wasn't going anywhere, not unless Keturah asked him to do so.

"This . . . *man*," Shubert said, looking at Keturah's companion with distaste, "is not allowed to work for you."

"Why not? He is a freed man with papers. He has every right to work for whomever he pleases."

"Listen to me," Shubert went on in rising agitation, as if speaking to a wayward child rather than his superior, "we simply do not *do* such things here."

She drew herself upward. "Well, it is the way it shall be done *here* on Tabletop. Because *I* choose to do it this way, and I am mistress of these fifty acres, not you."

He lifted his square stubble-covered chin and considered her. When he let his eyes drift down her body, slowly, then flick over toward Selah, Gray had had enough. He swung down from his saddle and strode over to Keturah, intent on demanding Shubert face him like a man. But as he reached her, Keturah raised a hand, stopping his progress. "No, Gray. Allow me to do this," she whispered. She turned back to her neighbor. "Be on your way, Mr. Shubert. You have said your piece."

Angus Shubert snorted and gave each of them a derisive glance. "You'd best know that the way you are going about this is not natural, woman. Your daddy would be—"

"*Lady* Tomlinson," Gray said, stepping forward. "You shall

address Lady Tomlinson in the manner to which she is due. Never again as 'woman.'"

"Have you ever seen any *lady* in a man's breeches and shirt, Covington?" Shubert scoffed. "The only birds I've seen in such things are whores in the tavern." He cocked an eyebrow at Selah, as if imagining her there.

It infuriated Gray, the utter disrespect. "Get down off that horse, Shubert," he hissed, hands clenching. "Come down here and I shall remind you what it means to treat a lady as she ought to be treated, whether she be in breeches or a gown."

"No! *Gray*," Keturah said, grabbing hold of his arm. "Be gone, Mr. Shubert!" she shouted. "You and your men are not welcome here. You leave me to my own business as I leave you to yours. *Now*."

Instead, Angus lifted a leg over his mount, as if preparing to answer Gray's demand.

The sound of a pistol cocking drew all of their heads around to Philip. The man stood beside Gray's mare, pistol trained on Shubert. "When the lady said *now*," he said politely, "I believe she meant immediately, Mr. Shubert."

"Well, I'll be," Angus said, smiling in wonder. "Can this day get any more strange, boys? Women masquerading as men. A freed man masquerading as an overseer. And some *butler*," he sneered at Philip, "fancying himself a soldier."

"I am no butler," Philip returned steadily. "But I was once a valet."

Shubert snorted again, then settled back into his saddle. "We'll be on our way, Lady Tomlinson. But rest assured, my boss is not going to like this any more than I do. None of the planters will abide by this."

"Then send them to me to discuss it," she said.

He lifted his reins and swept them to the side, urging his mount to turn and casually trot homeward. His two companions followed suit after giving the women one final lingering look.

"Those men are more dangerous than any of McKintrick's

sailors, and with half their honor," Gray spat once they were out of earshot.

"That may well be, but why are *you* here, Gray?" Keturah said, turning to face him.

"Is it not good that we were?" he asked in surprise, gesturing to Philip, who was putting the pistol back into his saddlebag, then across to the three interlopers, now casually climbing the northern hills as if out for a restful afternoon ride. "What do you girls think you are doing, dressed like that?"

"We are working our land," Keturah answered. She stepped closer, inches away from his face, as angry as he. "We have the right to do as we wish here. Because it is *our* land. Regardless of what any man thinks!"

Gray shook his head, feeling a headache growing behind his temples. He put his hands on his hips and leaned back from her. "Do you not know that you being here at *all* flies in the face of how they think things should be done?"

He glanced over at the black man behind her, who stood with his arms crossed, listening while Mitilda neared him. She resembled him. Was she his sister? It was then that understanding dawned.

"You hired *her* brother as your *overseer*?" he asked in a high, surprised tone. He blinked rapidly, trying to catch up, even as he knew his words might be offensive.

"What would you have me do, Gray?" Ket asked. "I couldn't find an overseer. They blocked me at every turn. And Mr. Rollins . . ." She paused to look over her shoulder at him. "As I told you, he's doing right with his own crop, Gray. Already harvesting well in a gaut that everyone else had ignored. I figured if he could make land others considered worthless *fruitful*, he might well be able to do the same here at Tabletop."

Gray sighed heavily, staring at her.

"What would you have me do?" she repeated.

Before he could stop himself, he reached out and cupped her shoulders. "I would have had you come to me. Ask for my assistance. I would have eagerly agreed. Do you not know that?"

She shifted from his grasp and stepped backward, as if his touch had burned her. "I did not need it," she said quickly. "I found my own way."

"I see that," he said, crossing his arms. "Don't you always?"

Keturah shifted uneasily. "I have made my way forward, Gray, the only way I could." She kept her eyes on his for a long, silent moment.

"Lady Ket, if you want me to go . . ." Mr. Rollins said, stepping forward.

"No, Matthew," Keturah said tiredly. "I want you here, serving as my overseer. And Mr. Covington here, well, he must not tarry. Surely he has his own trials to face over at Teller's Landing."

Gray turned back toward his mare. He mounted and looked down at Keturah. "Tell me this. If you are in need, will you please send for me? I am your neighbor, Ket. Your friend. As I've always been."

They were all silent, holding their breath.

But Gray kept his eyes only on her as she considered him. He could plainly see that half of her wanted to say no, but the other half wanted to say yes.

*Please, Lord. Let this be the beginning of a bridge between us.*

"All right, Gray," she finally said. Her eyes softened then. "Thank you for coming to our aid today. But please . . . if we need further assistance, wait for us to send word, all right? The men of this island plainly do not wish to respect our rights as landowners. Rest assured that in the days to come, I shall carry a pistol myself. Until you hear it go off, or someone comes to fetch you, do not come riding to our aid from Teller's Landing. Agreed?"

Gray nodded slowly. He paused, hoping there might be another plank in their tenuous bridge laid before he parted. A dinner invitation. A question about planting. But she said nothing more.

He put a hand to the rim of his tricorn and nodded at her, then each of her sisters, and, with one long look at Matthew Rollins, rode away.

# CHAPTER TWENTY-FIVE

A week later, a messenger arrived with an invitation.

"It's a party at Nisbet Plantation!" Selah said excitedly as she read it over. "A Harvest Moon party, in two months' time," she added dreamily. "The island girls say they have the finest parties."

Keturah inwardly groaned. While she knew her youngest sister longed for a bit of their old life, it felt less appealing to her than ever. After a week in the fields, she didn't remember ever being so exhausted. She glanced down at her hands. Though clean, the black of the island's volcanic soil had a way of staining the cuticles and sinking so deep beneath her nails, there was no way to scrape it all away. While they might don fine gowns—now that the tailor had delivered the rest of them—one look at their hands would confirm any of the hundred rumors that likely had spread across the island. She assumed they had been invited more as a novelty than any true overture of friendship.

Still, with the aid of three new slaves Mr. Rollins had finally agreed to purchase on her behalf a few days prior, and every able body on the premises working beside them, the upper field was at last planted. That helped Keturah breathe a little more easily. She would spend the next two days with her sisters here at the house, allowing her battered hands to heal, her sunburned skin to fade, before she dressed for town and prepared to pretend she was every inch the lady her title insinuated, no matter what her neighbors might think. Meanwhile, Mr. Rollins and the others could begin work on the middle field.

---

The next day, Sansa came tearing down the road to the main house. "Lady Ket!" she screamed. "*Lady Ket!*"

Hearing the young woman through the library window, Keturah shoved her father's heavy chair back from the desk and raced down the stairs and out to the front. She took the girl's hands in hers, trying to decipher what she was saying through tears and heaving breaths and thick Creole accent. "It's Mas' Rollins, Lady Ket. They got 'im. They got 'im good."

"Who, Sansa?" Keturah urged. "Who did what?"

"That Mas' Shubert from Red Rock," the girl panted. "He came o'er and tol' Mas' Rollins . . . tol' him he had to teach him to remember his place, freed man or not."

Ket could practically feel the blood draining from her face. "Are they gone now, Sansa?"

"Yes'm. Took off when Mas' Rollins finally quit risin'."

Keturah lifted a hand to her throat, horrified and furious at once. She looked over her shoulder—Cuffee, bless him, was already bringing her mare around at a trot. He swung down and waited to help her mount. Keturah hurriedly did so, ignoring her skirts rising to her knees. She had bigger concerns. Like Matthew Rollins. Had they killed him? Or beaten him so severely he might soon die?

Verity and Selah arrived on the porch. "What is it?" Selah asked.

"'Tis Mr. Rollins," Keturah said. "Get water boiling. Clean rags. Father's medicine chest." She looked down at Cuffee. "Bring another horse and the wagon up to the field. We shall need to get him down here to the house."

"Yes, Lady Ket," he said and took off running back toward the stables.

With that, she dug her heels into the mare's flanks and rode as fast as she could, praying her new overseer would not die. It was her fault he was here. Her fault. She'd put him in this danger. Guilt and rage swirled in her mind, uneasy dance partners.

When she saw him on the ground, with his sister on her knees beside him and holding his hand, the other slaves standing dazed in a circle around him as if in a death vigil . . . she wanted to cry herself. She pushed her way between them and sank to her knees at his side. She took his other hand in hers. "Help is coming," she said softly. "Hang on, my friend." She tried to sound strong and assuring, but his battered mouth and bloody lips, his bruised cheek and swelling eye made her break down and weep. "Oh, Mr. Rollins," she whispered through her tears. "I'm so sorry. How horrible . . . It seems I've brought you a terrible turn."

"This isn' on account of you, Lady Ket," he grunted, blinking up toward the sun, his teeth gruesomely stained with blood. "This all on account of me and my freedom. Those men—" he paused to take several breaths, wincing against the pain—"they don' like it that I am free. But don' fret, Lady Ket." Again he paused, and his hand slid to his belly. "I'm used to it. Just the way of it here on Nevis."

"It might be the way it is *elsewhere* on Nevis," she said, pulling apart his shirt to inspect the man's belly where the louts had clearly pummeled him, "but it shall not be the way on Tabletop Plantation."

The man looked at her sadly, clearly not believing her, but in too much pain to argue. His eyes rolled back in his head and he choked.

"Matthew!" Mitilda cried, shaking his shoulder with her long, slender hand. "Matt!"

But then his breathing eased. He didn't open his eyes, but he breathed. "He's unconscious," Keturah said, "but lives yet," she added, reaching out to touch Mitilda's thin arm. "Cuffee will be here in a moment with a wagon to get him down to the main house. We shall see to him there."

"No," Mitilda said sharply. "Bring him to my house. I shall see to him myself."

"As you wish," Ket said slowly. She did not want to argue with the woman. It seemed as if it were a point of pride, even though Keturah felt responsible for him. But he was the woman's brother, after all.

The wagon came up over the rise, Cuffee whipping the mule into a gallop. He brought it as close to them as he could, without getting stuck in the mud, and together four men carried Matthew to the wagon bed. Mitilda climbed in beside him, Sansa at his other side, and Keturah mounted her mare. "Get back to your quarters," she told the other slaves, warily eyeing the northern ridge. "I do not want any of you out here if I am not around to defend you."

They nodded, eyes wide with fear, and huddled closer together. Her stomach clenched at the sight. *Her* people, fearing for *their* safety, on *her* land. The new slaves having witnessed such a horror when she so wanted them to understand that they were safe at Tabletop. She had pledged to herself that the horrific things slaves feared most were not things that would transpire here, under her guardianship. She looked after the wagon, knowing Verity and Selah would help Mitilda see to her brother.

But right now she had words for Mr. Shubert . . . and his master.

## CHAPTER TWENTY-SIX

Keturah rode hard for Red Rock Plantation, tearing down their pretty tree-covered lane at a gallop. She discovered the men halfway down the lane, not quite yet home, laughing and at ease. *While a man lies wounded, perhaps dying, at Tabletop!*

Shubert was the first to see her. Slowly, he drew his horse sideways, blocking her path. His two men flanked him. She drew up at the last second, her mare prancing nervously beneath her, awaiting her mistress's next command.

"Lady Tomlinson," Shubert drawled, letting his eyes linger on her bare calves. "In a proper dress today, I see. Much more suitable, I'd say."

"You," she seethed. "Make way. I intend to have a word with your master."

"Ahh, 'tis a pity Lord Reynolds is away at the moment. I serve as the master of Red Rock in his absence."

Keturah clamped her mouth shut. She had planned on appealing to Lord Reynolds's nobility, his sense of honor. Even if men behaved differently here on Nevis, there was a certain measure a body could count on in a proper Englishman. But he was not here. Shubert's two companions moved past either side of her and came to a stop behind her. The hair on her damp neck rose in warning as she realized they now surrounded her.

She clung to her anger to drive away her rising fear. "You *dared*," she spat at Shubert, "to come on *my* land and beat *my* man."

He lifted his brows in surprise. "What? I think someone's been filling your head with lies. The boys and I were simply out for an afternoon's ride. Weren't we, boys?"

"That's the way of it," said one behind her.

"Lies!" she cried. "You stole onto my land and beat Mr. Rollins senseless!"

"'Twasn't me," Shubert said, frowning and shrugging his bulky shoulders.

"There is blood splattered all over your shirt, Mr. Shubert," she ground out.

He glanced down, then up, peering in concern at her. "Are you seeing visions now, Lady Tomlinson?"

Keturah let out a cry of rage. "It was you! They said it was so!"

"Who?" he asked, idly lifting a brow again.

"My field hands! Every one of them would attest to it!"

"Field hands? You mean *Negroes*?"

She stared at him. "Of course!"

In her anger, she had missed the fact that one of the men behind her had slipped from his horse. He appeared by her mare's head and swiftly yanked the reins out of her hands.

"What—what is the meaning of this?" she demanded, looking to the man in outrage. "How dare you!" She reached for the reins, vainly trying to wrestle them free.

"Seems to me," Shubert said, now on the ground, "*Lady* Tomlinson, that you need to be reminded of your place, just as your *overseer* needed a reminder." He grabbed hold of her arm and yanked her from the saddle.

She came down messily—her left foot still lodged in the stirrup, her skirts rising as high as her thighs. But Shubert hauled her to her feet, her back against his wide chest, his meaty arms around her belly, pinning her arms beside her.

"Cease this at once!" she sputtered. "I shall report you to the authorities! The audacity of this manhandling. If—"

"Hush now, Lady Tomlinson," he said in her ear. "Hush. It seems you came to the island with all manner of misconceptions. Negroes have their place, you see. Women have their place too. And men—whether they be noble or like us—lord over both. If you continue to try my patience," he said, lifting one hand to run it down her neck and toward her heaving chest, "I shall have to find another way to help you understand the way of things. Who truly holds the power here."

"You would *not*," she sputtered, hating that his actions had set her to trembling.

"Would I not?" he asked, leaning so close his lips brushed the edge of her ear. "Things are different here than in England, my lady. Shall I teach you how they are, here on-island? Right now?"

"Let . . . me . . . go," she fumed, almost managing to break free. But the lout was impossibly strong.

"Not until you tell me we understand each other now." His hand spread wide across her belly, pulling her even more firmly against him, stilling her as he whispered in her ear. "White men rule here. Then women. The Negroes come last. And like it or not, only what a white man has to say matters in the end."

"That is a lie," she gritted out.

"That's the truth. At least here on Nevis. Right, boys?"

"That's right," said the skinnier one. The other looked uneasy, as if unsure whether what they were doing was wise.

She appealed to him. "I shall go to the authorities. Report your manhandling of me, and your abuse of my overseer!"

"You shall do no such thing," Shubert said, "because it shall do you no good. No judge will listen to your testimony—especially confirmed only by slaves. Negroes aren't allowed to testify. And there are three of us, all with the same story—that we were merely out for a ride on this fine day. And three men's testimony will always trump one woman's."

"Let me go this instant," she seethed. Desperately she reached down, trying to slip her fingers to the strap at her calf that held the small knife Captain McKintrick had given her.

But he held on to her with an iron grip. "Ask your old slaves, those who've been here a while. They know who rules this island. And if that won't convince you, perhaps your pretty little sister might find herself surrounded one day just as you have."

Keturah's skin crawled. *Is he intimating . . . ? How dare he!*

Then she realized the truth of the matter. He held the power. Just like Edward had.

Here on Nevis he had the ability to do exactly what he threatened to do. How could she fight it? How had she fought Edward?

She had not.

She never found a way.

Only the means to seal herself away. Make her heart as stone. Just as she began to do now.

Feeling her acquiesce, Shubert released her, abruptly dropping his arms. She stumbled, narrowly keeping herself from falling, and looked at him in a daze.

"Go home, Lady Tomlinson," he sneered. "And consider how you best fit in here. Find a man to marry and look over your plantation. If push comes to shove, come to me, and I'll marry you and look after you all myself."

"Never," she managed to say. But she no longer sounded strong, defiant. She sounded beaten. Like she had after particularly hard nights with Edward.

"So you say now," he said with a half smile. "We shall see how long it takes this island to make you say otherwise. You can give in easy. Or you can give in hard. But either way, you shall give in, Lady Ket." He tipped his head and added, "Best get home now and see to that Negro who needed a reminder of his proper place. We'll keep an ear to the ground to try and figure out who did it." He laughed under his breath, as did his companion.

Numbly, Keturah watched them ride away.

She did not know how she managed to get back to Tabletop.
She did not remember the ride.
The road.
Anyone she saw.
Just a terrible darkening tunnel from which she could not escape . . .

# CHAPTER TWENTY-SEVEN

Keturah woke in the deep watches of the night, starting when she thought she felt Mr. Shubert's hand on her belly again. Or was it . . . Edward's?

She cried out and pulled away, stumbling across the wide, smooth wooden planks of her bedroom floor.

*My bedroom. Here in Nevis*, she told herself, willing herself to cease this madness. *Not at Clymore Castle, Ket. Not for a long time.*

Still, she stood there, trembling, staring at the dark form in her bed, hand to her mouth, wondering. But then that person rose up, and no, it wasn't big enough for Mr. Shubert. Not even Edward . . . *Who? What?* She lifted a hand to her mouth, narrowly stifling a scream.

"Ket?" the girl asked.

Dimly, Keturah recognized the voice.

*Selah*. It was *Selah* in her bed. Another body stirred in the armchair by the window, and Ket whirled. *Verity*, she decided quickly—who was more visible in the half-moon's light streaming through her open window. *My sisters . . . only my sisters!*

"Ket, are you quite all right?" Selah asked.

Verity was beside her then too, placing a gentle hand on her

249

shoulder. At her touch, Keturah flinched, gasped and then choked on a sob.

"Oh, Keturah," Verity said, grabbing her more firmly and pulling her around to face her as Selah turned up the lamplight. "What is it? What happened to you? You came home in such a state. Sobbing . . ."

Ket searched her sisters' eyes and could plainly see she'd given them a terrible fright. She wanted to deny anything had happened—that there was nothing to fear. But she knew that was senseless. Her sisters had plainly seen to her in her hysteria—in whatever dark fugue that had engulfed her—and undressed her and put her to bed. Ket's eyes moved to the bedside table and saw the bottle of laudanum. Perhaps that was why she could remember so little.

But she knew it was more. There had been many nights at Clymore that she could not remember come morn. Nights when she remembered Edward raging, herself running, hiding, and little more. Only darkness. Like a blank slate.

"Keturah," Verity said, taking her hands in hers, "you are trembling again! What is it? What has happened?"

Tears welled in Ket's eyes. She had to tell them, her dear sisters. Tell what she had told no one.

"Come, sit," Selah said, pulling her to the edge of the bed.

Obediently, she went. Selah wrapped a blanket around her shoulders while Verity sank to her knees beside Ket's legs, waiting expectantly.

"After I found Mr. Rollins beaten in the field . . ." she began, hot tears drifting down her cheeks. She started, remembering. "Mr. Rollins. How is he?" she asked, heart beating in fear.

Verity squeezed her legs. "He fares decently enough, Ket. He says himself he'll be up and about in a few days."

Keturah breathed a prayer of thanks. "I . . . I went to speak to Lord Reynolds. To gain his assistance in confronting Mr. Shubert about his unspeakable act. But . . ." She paused and swallowed hard. "Lord Reynolds is away. And I met Mr. Shubert and his men on the road."

Selah sucked in the tiniest of breaths. So she had recognized him as a menace too. That was good, since the man had taken such notice of her . . . Keturah paused. How much did she dare say? Verity was a woman grown. Selah too, but only barely. To speak of such things would strip away precious innocence. And she didn't want that for her little sister. She wanted to protect both of them . . . wished that they may never know anything in life but peace and prosperity.

*But few enjoy only peace and prosperity in this world,* she thought. They lived in a fallen world, with depraved men and women alike. Sin was bound to impact them, just as it had Ket. And it was best that they be prepared to battle it, alongside her. There was no protecting them. Not in total. Not here. Perhaps not anywhere.

Again, she swallowed hard and wiped her cheeks. "My sisters, I must tell you something quite difficult."

Both were silent, waiting. She looked from one to the other. So beautiful. So caring.

"My marriage to Edward was not as we all wished it would be."

"So you have said," Verity said gently, taking her hand. "Was he a . . . brute?"

A brute. Keturah had never stopped to think of calling him that. She'd dismissed his behavior as frustration for some time. Blamed herself for not doing things exactly as he'd asked. And for her waist never growing thick with the promise of a child . . .

*A brute.*

*Brutal.*

*Brutalized.*

"Yes," she said. "*Yes,*" she said again, claiming the word more thoroughly the second time. "Edward was a brute," she whispered, looking to the open window, then back to her sisters. "And so when I returned to Hartwick, I knew I never wished to marry again. Then when Father died, I knew I wanted each of you to marry, only when and to whom you wished. I knew I would never ever force you into a union or even encourage it. I wished for you both to make your own choice."

"Which made saving Hartwick, and making Tabletop a success, all the more important," Verity said, taking her hand. "You wanted us not to choose a man purely because of financial need, social or stature."

"Never," Keturah said with a slow shake of her head. "For judging from my own experience, that led to nothing but heartache."

"Oh, Ket," Selah said, wrapping her arms around Keturah. "I am so sorry that happened to you."

"Me too," Verity said.

It was their loving, soothing words and presence that undid Ket. She wept then for several long moments.

When she had gathered herself, Verity asked carefully, "So what exactly transpired at Red Rock?"

"Lord Reynolds was away, as I said." Ket sniffed. "I encountered Mr. Shubert and his men." She paused to consider her words. "They . . . made it quite clear that no judge would agree to hear our slaves' testimony of Mr. Rollins's abuse in court. They made up a story that they were merely out for an afternoon ride and had never been at Tabletop."

Verity's eyes narrowed. "That is infuriating. But there must be more. To bring you home in such a state . . ."

"They pulled me from my saddle. Threatened me." She couldn't bear to tell them they threatened Selah too.

Both girls gasped. Verity leaned back, fingers covering her lips. "How did they *dare*? We must go to the authorities!"

Keturah shook her head. "Perhaps if we were in England, we could do so. But here on Nevis . . . No, sisters, we must find a way to beat the horrors at their own game."

Both girls were silent. Then Selah said, "Not all men are horrors, Ket."

"All men have some dark, hidden sin within, Selah," she said, her righteous anger rising, feeling more welcome than her sorrow and fear. "'Tis best for you to know this now."

"It is as you say," Selah returned carefully, turning to sit beside her on the bed. "But Ket, do not women have the same dark, hidden sins too? Does not Verity, or I, or you?"

"Look at Father," Verity said with a sigh. "We adored him. He was good to us. He loved Mother. And yet . . ." Her eyes went to the window. "Here we find Mitilda. And Abraham."

"And yet there are good men out there," Selah said, taking her hand in both of hers. "Consider Mr. Covington!"

"And Mr. Philip," Verity added quickly, seeing her bristle. "And Captain McKintrick!"

"Oh, and dear cousin Cecil," Selah said.

"Mr. Kruger," Verity said triumphantly, naming Keturah's favorite gardener, who had been with the family since before they were born.

"Mr. Yates!" Selah added, recalling a kindly neighbor. "And Mr. Eckley!" The local fishmonger, who had always made them laugh.

Keturah gave them both a small smile. "All right, dear ones. All right. Clearly *all* men are not monsters."

"No," Verity said darkly. "Only *one* of our neighbors."

"While another is a saint," Selah said dreamily.

Keturah scoffed at her little sister's overly romantic view of Gray Covington. But then could she truly see Gray doing anything as despicable as Mr. Shubert had done yesterday? No, if she was honest, she knew the worst Gray had likely ever done was steal kisses from every girl he could.

Except her.

She rose from the bed and went to the window. Dawn was close now, the eastern horizon growing warm with the approaching sun. With it came warmth for Keturah, comfort, even though she did not yet feel its rays.

If she were to beat those who rose against her at their own game, she would need a strategic partner in order to do so. This chessboard—here on Nevis—was unlike any she had encountered. Things were different here, as Mr. Shubert had so clearly laid out.

So she would adapt. Utilize the mind and heart her Lord had given her. And dare to trust one of the *good* men again.

"Send Cuffee to Teller's Landing," she said to Selah over her shoulder. "Tell him to tell Mr. Covington . . ." She paused, wondering if she really dared do what she thought she must. *Yes. Yes, I must.*

"Tell Mr. Covington I have need of his aid."

# CHAPTER TWENTY-EIGHT

Gray stepped out of Mitilda's home, where Mr. Rollins was convalescing in his sister's small bedroom. He began pacing the front porch. Philip stood on the ground, one foot perched atop the aging, rotting wood of the porch. Keturah stood to one side, arms crossed, looking alarmed at his obvious fury. He immediately willed himself to calm.

Taking a long, deep breath, he looked to Mitilda on the other side. "Tell me what happened to your brother, please. From start to finish."

The woman's pretty brown eyes shifted over him, as if trying to decide if she trusted him or not. After she sent a questioning look to Keturah, and Ket nodded, she told him. They'd been working in the field. The three men from Red Rock had come riding in—right through their freshly planted cane, the woman added indignantly—and insisted Matthew be on his way "to his side of the island." They'd said that no black man would ever be overseer, not while they lived on Nevis, and with him gone, maybe Lady Tomlinson would see the "error of her ways too."

Keturah blanched at that, then flushed with anger, as did Gray. He found his hands balled into fists and carefully flexed them, even as he longed to go over and do to Shubert what the men had done to poor Rollins.

"But your brother stood up to them."

"Ye'sir," she said. "Told them that as a freed man, he should be able to work where he wanted. Told them he wasn't going anywhere until Lady Ket sent him on his way. And then . . ." She broke off, shook her head, and looked to the waves in the distance.

Gray shook his head. "I am sorry you had to watch such brutality," he said gently.

"Not the first time I've seen it. Likely not the last," Mitilda said.

"It shall be the last if I have anything to say about it," Keturah said.

But now Gray could see why Keturah had summoned him. By the look on her face, she had no idea as to *how* she would prevent it from happening again . . . or worse. He furiously wished he were in the financial position to offer more to Ket, to bring her and her sisters under the shelter of his wing. And yet as soon as he had that thought, he knew she would not welcome it anyway.

*Not yet* came the thought from deep within.

For the first time, he counted it a blessing—that he was not yet prepared to ask Keturah to marry him. No, she had finally asked for help, and he counted that as no small victory. Now he had to respond in such a manner that preserved her pride and independence. Things he so appreciated in her.

"I propose that we become partners," he said to her, eyes shifting over the swaying deep-green palms that lined the ridge between their land. "I am in need of additional field hands, as are you. You are in need of a man to back your overseer so he endures no further harm. I wouldn't mind if that overseer watched over *both* our plantations." He dared to look Keturah in the eye.

She and her sisters stared at him as if they had not heard him right. "Think of it," he pressed on. "We shall alternate our planting work—first a portion of your fields, then mine, then yours again. Both of our crops will be planted as quickly as they would be on our own, because we'll have twice the number of field hands. We

LISA T. BERGREN

shall use my furrow plough on as much of your land as you wish. Then we shall share a certain percentage of our own profits with our partner."

Keturah's eyes shifted back and forth over his, contemplating his offer. It was a good one, he knew. Fair. Advantageous to them both.

Keturah blinked slowly, obviously thinking it over. He became distracted with how her golden-brown lashes seemed to glow in the reflected sun. A hint of a mischievous smile tugged at her beautiful lips, even as she tried to look at him with warning. "The other planters might frown upon this plan. A Negro overseer in charge of not one plantation but two."

"Then they shall have to take it up with me," he said.

"Their overseers shall like it even less," Mitilda put in, joining Ket with the first smile he'd ever seen from her.

"Undoubtedly," he said, smiling with them.

"We shall each retain our own properties," Ket said, quickly sobering. "We shall not mingle our profits, as you suggested. Only our methods of getting to said profits."

*Drawing back to her defense lines again*, he thought. With a would-be enemy threatening to encroach . . . But he was no enemy. How could he convince her? "Whatever you wish," he said easily.

"Then we are partners," she said, extending her hand to him.

After a moment's hesitation, Gray took it and, with a grin, shook it. Because any sort of partnership he could form with Keturah Tomlinson was a partnership he would celebrate.

———

Within a week they had Tabletop's second field planted. Mr. Rollins was back on his feet, and although one eye remained terribly bruised, the swelling reluctant to recede, his cuts had healed. After some consideration, with Gray's backing, he assumed his role as overseer of both plantations, now giving his advice to both Gray and Keturah as to how he would modify their fields and place-ment of the tender cane. At first, he was terribly skeptical about Gray's plough and furrows, rather than the traditional mounds planters had used for centuries on-island. But after the first solid rain, and seeing how the furrows held the water for just the right length of time rather than letting it slide away, he suggested they use the plough for the remainder of Tabletop's fields.

Keturah and her sisters insisted on continuing to help with the planting—even on Teller's Landing—but in turn he insisted on sending them home during the hottest part of the day. Gray noticed they did not don their father's old clothing at his plantation as they had at first at Tabletop, perhaps reluctant to be too audacious in the company of a gentleman. Truth be told, he thought Keturah fetching in any clothing, even perspiring and red-faced in the late-morning heat as she was.

Or was her choice to wear the sensible day dress due to how Shubert had taken to peering down at them from each of their plantation's borders? Gray had spotted the man and his cohorts at Red Rock, when they were at Tabletop, and from Gray's southern neighbor's plantation, Chandler's Point. Out of habit, he glanced over his shoulder. He despised the man, watching them as he did—like a hungry vulture simply waiting for his prey to drop in the oppressive summer heat. As soon as Gray brought in his first harvest and had the money in hand—as soon as Lord Reynolds could look at him with some respect—he would speak to him about his loathsome overseer, and see Shubert driven from Nevis's shores.

That afternoon, though, Shubert did not hover. Gray's eyes moved to Keturah, tipping back her wide-brimmed hat to wipe her forehead of sweat. Then over to Verity, keeping pace with Absalom in dropping cane pieces and covering them—exchanging sly smiles as they raced down neighboring furrows. Selah was with the wary girl named Hope and her brooding man, Tolmus, teaching them one English word after another as they worked together to fertilize each cane stalk. What would the sugar baron have thought of his daughters, working here in the fields of Nevis like common indentured servants, rather than living as noblewomen? He'd already heard many tongues agog in Charlestown—everyone, it seemed, anxious to speak about the unspeakable ways of the

Banning sisters—until he came around. Then they would abruptly hush, recognizing Gray as *him—the Bannings' neighbor.*

Yesterday in the market, he'd heard two women at a mango stand yammering on about calling upon Mr. Thompson, thinking that the priest might be able to speak some sense into the women. Remind them of their place and their station. He knew others surmised that the Bannings were nearly destitute, unable to buy enough slaves to do what they ought, and working themselves to the bone to try to save what surely would be lost. Clearly, none of them knew Keturah. Or her sisters. And he rather liked that. Because it was as if out of all ten thousand souls on Nevis, Gray was the only one in on their secret.

*Will they not be surprised in time?* he wondered, sneaking another glance at Ket. *Why, yes*, he thought with a grin. *Yes, they would.*

She caught him, just as he was turning away, and straightened, casting him a curious, sly look. "What is it?"

"Ah, nothing," he lied, allowing his grin to widen. He turned back to his mule and tightened a strap.

"Gray Covington, you tell me this instant," she demanded.

"No," he said, still smiling as she trudged through the deep furrows to come closer.

"You stand there smiling at me like a fat tabby cat who has just swallowed a mouse, and you will not tell me why?"

"Do you truly think me fat?" He frowned and rubbed a hand over his flat belly.

She reached out to swat his arm. "You know what I mean. Tell me."

He laughed under his breath and gave her a little bow. "Respectfully, no. Despite the fact that we are now partners, Keturah, I *am* still allowed to keep my own counsel at times."

"Even if 'tis considered rude to do so?" she asked, hands on her hips. A blush hovered on her cheeks, as if she had some idea that he remained quiet because he had been caught admiring her.

"Even if," he said, with another brief bow. "Now, I must beg your pardon. I aim to be done with this quarter of the field before sundown."

Reluctantly, she allowed him to part. He didn't look back, but he hoped that he felt the heat of her gaze on his broad, shirtless back. That she was noting the muscles that had hardened after weeks of work, even if the island sun had left his skin far darker than was fashionable. He hoped she saw how the slaves and even Mr. Rollins looked to him with respect and admiration.

Was that pride, vanity, that made him think such unscrupulous thoughts?

No, he told himself with another smile. *'Tis merely strategy.*

In another week's time, they had planted an additional portion of his land. Mr. Rollins had to depart then, agreeing to return the following week, after he saw to his own crop of cane. Gray knew he had to be concerned that other planters had done damage to his little plot of land as angry retribution; Shubert was not the only overseer or planter up in arms over their decision to employ him. He hoped they had not taken such rash action. Thankfully, between what he and Keturah promised to pay him, once their crops came in, would surely make him the richest black man on the island, regardless of what his own crop yielded.

They had just begun planting Tabletop's lowest field one sultry Saturday morning when Mr. Shubert boldly crossed the property line and rode directly toward Keturah, his men slightly behind him on their own horses. Gray saw him first and immediately strolled toward his mare, lolling in the shade of a banyan tree, and withdrew his sword. The sound of the blade against the metal sheath brought Philip's head around. Gray went back to Keturah, who had edged near Selah, just as Shubert pulled up.

"You are not welcome here," Keturah said, fists clenching at her side.

Mr. Shubert's eyes shifted lazily from one to the next of them. "Now that is impolite, Lady Tomlinson," he said. "Hardly genteel, if I do say so myself."

260

He reached beneath his jacket, and Gray raised his sword. "Mind yourself, man."

"'Tis you who must mind himself," Mr. Shubert said, pulling out a note. "We are here solely to present you with an invitation from Red Rock's mistress. The lord and lady returned the night before last, and there is to be a soiree Saturday next. The mistress seems intent upon your acceptance to her invitation, Lady Tomlinson." He reached down, offering the invitation, but Keturah didn't move.

He was testing her, taunting her. Telling her that the Reynoldses had returned. Would she attempt to reach them again with her account of Matthew's beating? Would she risk retribution from him?

Gray glanced at her, narrowing his gaze when he saw the woman appeared wan. Was it the heat? Or this man's presence? He knew she despised the man, but . . . He stepped forward and took the card from the man's meaty fist himself. "Be on your way, Shubert," he said tightly.

"For now," Mr. Shubert said, his face dissolving into lines of satisfaction. He laughed lightly and tipped his hat, then wheeled his horse around. "See to it that you send word as to your plans of attendance," he called over his shoulder. "The mistress requires such niceties."

Gray ignored him. His eyes returned to Keturah, who held Selah's hand as if the girl were helping her make it across a tightrope. Her breaths came in shallow pants. "Keturah?" he asked softly, stepping closer. When neither woman looked at him, he said, "Ket, *what is it?*"

She didn't answer. But Selah looked at him, then to the three men now on the far side of the field, then back at her sister. Alarm swept through Gray.

"What has happened?" he asked, willing himself not to allow his fear and fury to seep into his tone, but only doing so with modest success.

Keturah mumbled something about heading to the house to

see to their noon meal and started walking away, Selah at her side.

"Keturah!" he called, more sharply than he intended. But she did not stop. He stood there, stymied, aware that the field hands all stared at them. Then he went after her, knowing he could not sleep this night if he didn't discover what had upset her so.

He caught up to them just as they cleared the field and reached the road. "*Keturah*," he repeated.

She reluctantly stopped, but only partially turned toward him. She could not look him in the eye. "Let it be, Gray," she said.

"I cannot. You must tell me. Those men have been hovering over our shoulder for weeks. I thought your agitation was only because you feared for Rollins. But has he threatened you too?"

"'Tis none of your concern," she said, turning to go again.

He caught her wrist, gently, then eased her back around. "Please, Ket," he said, "tell me."

Selah took a few steps away, turning to look to the sea and give them a bit of privacy.

"I . . . cannot," she said, glancing nervously behind his shoulder at the field hands, all pretending to work again.

"Elsewhere then. Later?"

"No," she said, her voice hardening. "As I said, it is not your concern." She strode swiftly away, down the road toward the house, not seeming to even remember that she'd left her sister behind.

Selah edged closer. Once Ket was out of earshot, she said, "After they attacked Mr. Rollins, Keturah went after them."

Gray felt the blood drain from his face. What was this?

"She meant to speak to Lord Reynolds, you see," Selah rushed on, wringing her hands and glancing back to make sure Keturah would not overhear. "To inform him of his overseer's foul behavior."

"But Lord Reynolds was away," he finished for her.

She nodded eagerly, her big, brown eyes round with worry.

"And then?" he forced himself to ask, wishing he need not know, as Keturah insisted.

"They dragged her from her horse, Gray," she said softly. "Manhandled and threatened her. Made it clear that she had no voice, no authority on-island."

He studied her but could only see Shubert's jeering face. *The pig. The big lout.* He would strangle him with his bare hands. . . .

"That was when they told Ket that things were different here," Selah went on. "They said white men rule. Women were clearly to be subservient. And Negroes . . ." She paused and looked again toward the sea. "They made it clear that any assurances we had as gentlewomen in England did not apply here. That was when she decided she couldn't do this alone. Not if she was to protect Matthew and the slaves. And so she sent for you."

Gray nodded, forcing himself to remember to breathe, to find something reassuring to say to the girl. "'Tis good that she did," he finally replied. "So that I might be the friend to you all I've always longed to be."

"You're more than a friend," Selah said tenderly, putting her small hand on his forearm. "You're a brother to Ver and me." She glanced back at her sister, now growing small in the distance.

"What of her?" he dared in a whisper. "What does Ket think of me, Selah?"

He felt terrible in that moment, for prying, pressing the younger woman. She was guileless and he knew it. But just as he had needed to know what happened with Angus Shubert, now he needed to know the truth of what Keturah thought of him.

"Oh!" Selah said, lifting filthy hands to her pink cheeks. "You mustn't ask me to betray such intimacies, Gray!"

"I see," he said slowly, surmising what that meant. He tried to hold back a smile. *For there could not be intimacies if no intimacy was felt in the first place.* "So your sister might . . . favor me?" he dared.

"She has granted you more favor than any other man in her life since Edward passed."

"Because of necessity? Or is it something more?" he pressed.

"I have already disclosed far too much," Selah said, moving away from him now.

"Forgive me," he managed to say. But in his heart he knew he desired no such forgiveness. Selah's odd reaction, her wording . . . it told him that Keturah *did* feel something for him.

Whether she recognized it yet or not.

# Chapter Twenty-Nine

At Gray's insistence, he came to collect the Banning women at seven o'clock for the party at Red Rock. Keturah had wanted to decline the invitation, but Selah insisted they go. "Will it not further prove to them that they cannot cow you," she said, "if you enter that drawing room in your fine bronze gown, with your head held high?"

"And with hands that resemble our field hands'?" Ket said, wiggling her palms at her sister.

"We shall wear gloves," Selah had said, "and then we shall face Angus Shubert together."

The thought of it made Ket's stomach turn. But she had to find a way to separate Shubert's brutality from the memory of her husband's. Edward was not here. He could no longer reach her. Touch her. And next time Angus tried, she'd be certain her small Scottish dagger was in hand.

In fact, she'd insisted both her sisters wear theirs too. "If that man dares to come near any of us, I want you to have your knife ready. And if he dares to manhandle you, you have my permission to stab him!"

"Oh, Ket!" Selah had said, eyes round. "He wouldn't dare such a thing, would he?"

"Not at his master's party," Verity soothed, putting an arm

around the girl's shoulder. "But Ket's right. If he tries, he shall not find a Banning girl without a sharp little surprise for him. I'm putting mine in my sleeve!"

Gray arrived, resembling what she remembered of him in England, given his clean coat, white shirt, fancy cravat, and breeches above new stockings and freshly shined buckled shoes. He also wore a powdered wig, which she hadn't seen on him since they'd embarked upon the *Restoration*. Aboard ship and working in the fields, it wasn't practical. But after several social gatherings, Keturah knew that society here still preferred their gentlemen in wigs. Given her fight for respect and her quiet partnership with Gray, she was glad to see he intended to try to fit in with the others. Perhaps if he could gain a foothold, it would assist them both were future troubles to arise.

Yet, as he helped Selah into the double-seated wagon, then Verity, Ket knew it was to her that his eyes strayed, again and again. She hadn't worn this gown since that very first dinner aboard the ship when he had so obviously wished to rise to her defense with Mr. Burr. And now here he was again, rising to her aid. Insisting he escort them to the party, a party where Angus Shubert might appear. Shepherding them, she told herself. Yet the way he looked at her was not purely as a shepherd, she mused. His blue eyes lingered on her bare shoulders, the pearls at her neck . . . and the warmth of his gaze sent shivers down her back. She accepted his gloved hand, glad for the task and distraction of lifting her skirt and climbing in beside Verity.

Primus helped tuck the end of her skirt in beside her feet, then joined Philip on the bench seat in front of them. It was not as fancy as the old carriage they'd found on Tabletop, but it would do, Ket thought. There was something especially apropos about it, something representative of them here, straddling two worlds. All dressed up in their finery and yet utilizing Gray's very sensible wagon. She knew that others would be arriving in fine carriages, imported from England and America, and she shoved away a twinge of embarrassment. What falderal was that?

As if reading her mind, Selah said, "What do you suppose our compatriots say of us, traveling in such a fashion? I wish Father's carriage did not have a broken wheel."

"They shall think us sensible and stalwart," Verity said firmly, "because they are English too."

"Well, some are," Keturah said. "Some are Danes or Scotsmen."

"Scotsmen," Selah mused, giving her sister a playful nudge. "Hmm."

"All I know," Gray said from the front seat, "is that I thank God every day for a *certain* Scotsman getting us safely to this island."

"Do you believe he will truly return?" Verity asked tentatively. "Some say that men such as him have a girl in every port."

"But not every girl is Verity Banning," Ket said. "Do you wish for him to return, Ver?" As much as she did not like the idea of a sailor courting her sister, if it was what Verity wanted . . .

"I . . . know not. Leave it be now. All of you."

Keturah's heart began to pound as they came down the lane of Red Rock Plantation. Ver reached out and covered her hands with hers, holding her as if willing her to remain strong. Selah cuddled closer to her. Ket fought to concentrate on all the blessings in her life rather than her old fears. She whispered a prayer of thanksgiving for her sisters, enough people to work their plantations, her three fields now nearly planted, and the Lord's protection so far. It helped to see Lord and Lady Reynolds waiting to greet them as they pulled up before the grand house—with no Mr. Shubert in sight.

Ket had not decided how she might approach Lord Reynolds about Mr. Shubert's attack on Matthew, nor his manhandling of her. She would have to pick her time carefully, but first the man needed to know she was a woman of consequence. She must gain his respect. So she summoned her finest manners, wrought at Hartwick Manor and honed at Clymore Castle, to greet both Lord and Lady Reynolds, then introduce them to Gray and her sisters.

The Reynoldses were polite, but Keturah could sense their cold assessment. She caught a meaningful glance from lady to lord as Selah's silk gloves slipped down to her wrists and they saw her tanned skin. But she ignored it, all with the hope of forging a friend-ship with these people who would have once known her father.

Her father. Was that part of their suspicious reception of the Bannings? Because he had taken up with Mitilda and fathered a child? By now Keturah had learned that he was one of many who had dalliances with a slave. A number of plantations had a fair number of mixed offspring. Not that it made it right. Yet why were she and her sisters to bear the stain of her father's sin if they did not hold other planters' feet to the fire?

*Stop it, Ket.* Assuming another's thoughts was something her mother always took her to task over. She accepted Gray's proffered arm and busied herself with trying to name every person she'd previously met in the room before they were directly encountered. It was with some relief that she saw nearly every gentleman wore a wig, and none of those without had the blond hair of Mr. Shubert. It was silly, really, fearing that he would be present. It wasn't the place for an overseer to be at his master's soiree.

Gray, picking up on her agitation, pulled her hand higher on his arm and covered it with his own. He seemed to forget it was there—his warm hand on her icy fingers—and she knew she would be wise to shift her grip to subtly remind him. But she couldn't help it. She liked the feel of his hand on hers—the quiet reassurance, the steady pulse. How the intimacy of it sent delicious shivers up her arm to her shoulder and neck.

Ket noticed several ladies giving him lingering glances, undoubt-edly taken with his visage, as she herself had always been. There was something about him that was so frightfully handsome that she felt somewhat like the ostrich beside the peacock. And yet there was nothing about Gray—particularly in these last months—that spoke of a peacock's ways. Not like he'd been as a younger man . . . no, there was something changed about him now. More settled. More directed.

Not that he'd become an ostrich like her. Perhaps more like a solid . . . turkey, with a grand array of tail feathers. *That was it*, she thought with a giggle. *A handsome turkey.*

He eyed her and smiled too. "What amuses you?"

"Oh!" she said, coloring at being caught in her reverie. "I fear I cannot share," she said, giving into another giggle.

"Well," he said, laughing under his breath. "I welcome it, regardless of what it might be. Because you, Ket," he whispered, leaning closer, "are quite captivating. Especially when you smile."

It was her turn to blush, not from embarrassment but from pleasure. He seemed true in his speech, not giving in to flirtation. No, what was in his eyes was genuine.

*He thinks me captivating,* she thought, trying to pretend as if her heart had not begun to race wildly. But surely he was simply trying to reinforce her confidence, here where she felt ill at ease. That was it, she decided. He was merely continuing to be a good *friend* to her, encouraging her every which way he might.

Jeffrey Weland appeared before them, escorting his sister, Esmerelda. "Lady Tomlinson," he said, bowing before her. "I am glad to see you again. You have been frightfully absent of late from our gatherings."

She considered him. His tone held a measure of both chastisement and hurt. "I fear I have been most taxed of late, Mr. Weland, with the running of my estate. Have you been introduced to my friend and partner, Mr. Gray Covington?"

The two men greeted each other, and by their paltry exchange, she quickly saw that they had met before—and both thought the other somehow lacking. Or was it a measure of competition she sensed between them?

Her scalp tingled. She chastised herself for feeling some pleasure over it. *You need not men to be vying for you, Ket. You need no man!*

And yet her eyes moved to Gray as he turned to speak to Esmerelda Weland. The thoughtful question he asked her, the teasing quirk of his lips. Clearly the girl was flirting, but he seamlessly drew Selah into conversation with her and smoothly turned back to Ket and Jeffrey Weland, as if she were his first priority.

"I hear tell you purchased a fair number of new slaves," Jeffrey said. "How are you finding it, keeping them all fed? 'Tis a challenge for most new planters." There was something smug in the way he said it. Did he assume she would fail in her endeavor?

"Actually, Mr. Covington and I are sharing our field hands," she said. "So together we have found our way through. That said—to assist with our needs—I am considering planting an acre of corn, each stalk with a fish and squash seed too. I've heard tell that is how the Indians of the Americas do it. Considering the cost of corn and grain, I have a difficult time believing it would not pay off well, in time."

Jeffrey scoffed at this, but Gray turned toward her. "Why, Ket, that's brilliant!" Clearly he had learned of the method too—a stalk of corn, surrounded by a squash vine, and the whole mound fertilized with a big, fat fish.

"Don't you agree?" she asked, flashing him a grin. "What might it cost us? Seed corn, squash seed . . . we have plenty of fish on-island."

"Cost you?" Jeffrey guffawed. "It would cost you the bounty that acre of land would produce in sugar! Perhaps you don't have a head for numbers."

Ket stiffened. "I do have a head for numbers."

"And far more," Gray put in approvingly. "I believe that Teller's Landing shall do as Tabletop does and try this method of planting food crops. Surely it cannot hurt. Now if you will excuse us, Mr. Weland," he said smoothly, taking her arm again with some gentle sense of claim, a claim to which Keturah found she did not wish to object, "it appears Lady Reynolds would like for us to take our seats now."

The guests were led to long tables that extended from the dining room through the Reynolds' front parlor, covered in white linen and lined with fifty finely crafted chairs. Ket shared a glance with Verity and Selah, having not seen such a finely set table since they had left Rivenshire. There was silver cutlery beside china plates, crystal goblets, candles and flower arrangements placed between every four settings. The room was filled with the heavenly fragrance of orange blossoms and hyacinth, magnolia and jasmine, all carried on a heady scent of beeswax.

*Beeswax candles*, Keturah thought, instantly transported by a different scent that was purely home. The far more common oily tallow candle was what most Nevisian homes used—certainly at Tabletop where every penny was counted. But as they were seated and the wine began to flow and platter after platter of food was served, she could see that pennies were not counted in this house, only social cachet.

*Do they know how their overseer is undermining them? Or is Shubert just what they want?* she wondered, glancing over to where Lord and Lady Reynolds were seated. Was he a carefully selected part of their orchestra, directed by them? Left to guard how things were done on Nevis and make certain it remained the same in their absence? Or were they blissfully unaware of his brutish ways? Was it more his cause than theirs to keep things as they had always been on-island?

Conversation came faster as the evening wore on, laughter more boisterous. Through it all, Ket became more and more aware of Gray, observing it all as he was, as if cataloguing it for future reference. He made polite conversation with the lady at his right—an older widow who giggled like a schoolgirl whenever he made a clever comment—and engaged Mr. and Mrs. Malone, a planter and his wife from the southern part of the island, with conversation about their crops. They had dared to plant a portion of indigo this year, rather than all sugar, as the majority of planters favored. Even with declining profits, sugar was still the best bet, and yet fortunately demand for indigo was high with a blight rampant in India causing a shortage, which gave Malone hopes of a fine return.

Gray grew animated with such talk as they moved on to the island's history with cotton, ginger, and tobacco, none of which had ever been particularly successful, at least as compared with the Carolinas and elsewhere. There were some who had tried wheat, given the expense of importing it from America. But again, acre for acre, sugar ruled. Ket thought this reassuring, especially as she remembered her work-roughened hands hidden beneath her gloves. After all their work planting, she prayed it would pay, and pay well. But she knew they had months now to wait and see.

They were halfway through their dessert—something called a "Lemon Cloud"—when the first gusts of wind began blowing through the open dining room. Most of the candles were snuffed out, immediately plunging the room into relative darkness. The guests seemed to collectively hold their breath, hoping as one that it was an anomaly, a memory of some distant storm finally making its way to shore. But another gust blew through then that extinguished the remaining candles. Servants rushed in with lamps, covered by glass, but everyone was on their feet at once. Keturah felt their alarm, but why? What was it? Surely storms were common on Nevis. It rained practically every night as they slept.

But women were calling to servants to fetch wraps and their husbands' coats. Everyone seemed to be in motion at once, hurriedly exchanging their farewells. Keturah blinked, surprised that the Reynolds did not seem offended by their guests' hasty preparations to abandon what had been one of the most elaborate dinner parties of her life. Yet men were laughing and talking about the "storm of sixty-four," others grumbling that it "best not be a hurricane."

*A hurricane?* Memories of her father's journal, his reports of all but half the house destroyed, sent a chill down her spine. *Oh no. Not now, Lord. Not ever. Please . . .*

Gray ushered her out to the front of the manor, where servants had already lined up carriages and wagons and horses, clearly noting the storm before the guests inside recognized one was brewing. The first carriage was quickly loaded and moving, flicking whips over horses' backs, urging them to pick up their pace. Some of the guests were staying over, Ket realized, perhaps too far from home—like the Malones—to safely return without the light of the moon to guide them.

Their own wagon was in the middle of the pack, and the first heavy drops of rain had begun to fall when the girls climbed in with Ket. Philip threw a canvas tarp across their shoulders, and the sisters pulled it over their heads, vainly hoping to save their best dresses from the downpour to come. Gray turned as the wagon lurched forward and handed his powdered wig to her. "Here," he said with a grin, "keep that under wraps too, would you?"

"Yes," she said, placing the perfect white mound of curls on her lap while sneaking a look at his slicked-back dark waves. As dashing as he appeared in his wig, she preferred him this way—the way she saw him in the field or lounging on her front porch after a long day. It was more Gray, somehow. More of *her* Gray, rather than some version of the quintessential British gentleman she'd seen this night. She wanted to see more of who Gray was now, not more of who her countrymen wanted him to be or what she remembered. It made her feel closer to him.

She caught herself with the embarrassing thought and was glad for the cover of the canvas and darkness and rain that might have betrayed her blush. She needed to stop her silly infatuation, once and for all, because where could it possibly lead? Her arrangement with Gray—their steadfast friendship, their partnership as neighboring planters—why, it was as ideal and chaste as she could hope for. To consider anything else was to invite trouble.

Still . . . she reluctantly admitted to herself that she had been disappointed the party had come to such an abrupt end before the promised dancing had begun. Because she had wondered what it would be like to dance with Gray.

Not as a new debutante, anxiously awaiting her old friend to look her way. Not as another's bride, anxious her husband would see. But here. After all they had been through together, from the moment they had embarked upon the *Restoration* to becoming neighbors and fellow planters on Nevis. She'd like to experience Gray bowing, taking her hand, leading her to the dance floor and then into his arms . . . What would it have been like to have him look down at her in all her finery for once, rather than in her sweat-soaked day dress?

Memory of him calling her *captivating* warmed her cheeks.

*Stop, Keturah. Stop.* He was a friend, nothing more. He could not be anything more. Even if he did have different intentions, it wasn't seemly, proper to be imagining such things.

Still, her thoughts strayed to Gray's finances. Was he even in a position to offer for a wife? She thought not. He'd poured his all into Teller's Landing. His past. His future.

*Such idle imaginings!* she reprimanded herself. *Haven't you declared that you shall be no one's wife ever again? Haven't you sworn that no man shall ever lord over you?*

The rain was pounding down now, but she peeked out to see Philip say something to Gray, and Gray laugh heartily. Primus lifted a rod with a covered lantern high and far ahead of them, doing his best to give Philip light for the road. They had slowed down to a lazy walk, fearing a hole in the road that might cost them a wheel.

Rivulets of water formed along the road, which soon created gullies. Another gust of wind came through—so mighty that it ripped the girls' tarp from their hands. Selah screamed, and Keturah groaned as it went sailing into the dark sheets of rain, knowing her beautiful bronze dress would be ruined in moments.

But she could not help herself. She laughed and looked up to the sky, feeling the rain drench her face and hair and shoulders. There was something exhilarating about it all, wild, as if beckoning her. Despite the wind and water, it was still *warm*.

Her sisters continued to try to vainly cover themselves with their hands—a patently hopeless endeavor—and Gray gallantly shrugged out of his soaked coat and offered it to them. He looked at Keturah, and even though his face was in too-deep a shadow to make out, she could feel his warm gaze on her. Again, she could not help it—she grinned as she remembered him admiring her smile and wanting to encourage that admiration further.

*Perhaps I am going mad*, she thought.

But she didn't feel like she was going mad. She felt curious, more hopeful, more *alive* than ever. And as long as this was merely a tropical storm and not a hurricane, she believed all would be well enough come morn.

That was her thought, right before lightning cracked, thunder rolled, and then a most terrible, foreign, mucky sound filled her ears.

"What is that?" she cried, glancing up the mountain. As lightning flashed again, a horrible sight filled her vision. The trees and rocks were . . . *moving*.

"Mudslide!" Gray called. "Hold on!"

# Chapter Thirty

Gray seized the whip and reins from Philip. He'd read of mudslides in the tropics, which could bury houses and fields and carry bodies miles to the sea. If he was to save them all, as well as the horses, they had no choice but to ignore caution and hasten up the road as fast as they could. What did he have? A minute? Seconds?

They bounced and whipped back and forth, Selah and Verity yelping and crying out. Keturah remained so silent he feared she'd fallen off, but he dared not look. She was there. She had to be! He fought to see anything he could in the torrent of rain but with little success. They struggled to climb the hill in time, nearly reaching its apex before the mud swept past and caught them, sucking in their rear wheels, pulling them backward.

"Jump!" he cried to those behind him. "Get off the wagon! Past the flow of the mud!" He hoped they all could hear him over the buffeting wind.

He dived forward, astride one of the horses, reaching to release buckles and ties that kept them secured to the wagon. He'd spent hundreds of pounds to buy four for the estate—he couldn't see two taken from him this night. The team tried to hold the wagon in place, digging in when they felt it slipping. But then the mud was gathering around their legs. Theo, the stallion beneath him, faltered, nearly lost his footing, but then Gray finally had him free.

Palms rustled and rattled in the fierce wind, and rain splattered against their broad leaves. But louder was the terrifying sound of earth moving and sliding and sloshing past. Never had he heard anything so ghastly.

Gray turned to the mare Gussy, panicked now, as she fought the awkward twisting of the wagon behind her—the slow, terrible slide. He climbed astride her and forced himself to do what he had done with the first, reaching for straps and belts he could feel but not see. In another few seconds, the mare was free, and he rode her to safety. A flash of lightning allowed him to see the wagon rise five feet on a mound of mud, then ten, before disappearing in the darkness. Gussy heaved, stumbled, regained her feet, then heaved again, struggling to make her way through the swiftly moving muddy water.

Then the earth abruptly came to a slurping, slow stop. All around him the storm still raged, but with each lightning strike he became more convinced the worst was over.

If his companions had made it to safety . . .

He urged the mare higher, back to the road, hoping he would find the girls where he'd shouted at them to jump. But no one awaited him. "Keturah!" he yelled. "Verity! Selah! Philip! Primus!"

But the only response was the keening cry of the wind.

Gray tried to remain calm as he set about searching the hill at the edge of the slide in a methodical manner. Not wanting to risk Gussy breaking a leg, he left her tethered to a tree and walked it himself. A few minutes later, the storm finally passed, and the moon illuminated the soaked forest about him. He called for one after another of his companions, his heart in his throat. Was he the only survivor? *Please, God, no.* Over and over he shouted their names.

"Over here!" Philip called out at last, sounding weak. Gray slogged his way toward the man—frustratingly slow through calf-deep slippery mud—and found him stuck against the base of a banyan tree.

"Are you all right, man?" Gray said, digging madly at the mud to try to free his friend. One of Philip's arms was completely buried, as were his legs.

"Better in a moment when you get me loose of this muck," he said.

Gray frowned as he dug and flung the mud away, realizing how perilously close it came to completely drowning Philip. "Keturah!" he shouted. "Verity! Selah!"

But the forest remained eerily silent. Even the crickets seemed to have taken cover.

Gray's heart thundered—half from physical effort, half from fear. If the mud had so nearly swallowed Philip, what of the women? And where was Primus? The stallion? As if he'd sensed his thoughts, the stallion whinnied. He was somewhat near.

He got Philip mostly uncovered and grabbed hold of his hand. "Ready?" he asked.

"Ready," he responded, understanding that he aimed to pry him the rest of the way out. Over the weeks of working together at Teller's Landing, they'd become accustomed to communicating in shorthand.

Gray rose, settled his boots against the roots of the banyan, took a firmer grip on his friend's hands and pulled. The mud held, as if jealously guarding its prize, but then seconds later relinquished him. He slid to the surface, panting. If he alone was in danger, Gray would have laughed. But the mud seemed to become more compact, more dense with every moment that passed. What if the others were similarly trapped?

"Keturah!" bellowed Gray. "Verity! Primus! Selah!"

"Over here!" called a feminine voice. Selah, he thought.

"I'll go to her," Philip said. "You keep looking for the others."

He knew whose voice Gray most wanted to hear. He shoved away a sense of guilt at the thought. But he called for the others first. "Verity! Primus! Keturah!"

A man yelled from what seemed an impossible distance. Could they have possibly been carried that far?

"Primus?"

"Over here! I am all right!" the man called, his voice seeming to grow stronger.

Gray said a brief prayer of thanks. He slipped, found new footing among a pair of boulders, and climbed atop them. "Verity! Keturah!"

"Gray!" called a voice, again from a good distance toward the sea. "Gray, I'm here!"

*Verity.*

"Verity! Is Keturah with you?" he yelled.

"No! Gray!" Terror now laced her tone too. "I do not know where she is! What of Selah?"

"We found her! Can you make your way back to us?"

"I . . . I think not!"

"Stay where you are. I'm coming!" he called. It was just as well; if he found Ver, perhaps Keturah was somewhere nearby. But why was she not responding? Panic made his mouth dry even as sweat ran down his face. He pulled off his torn and mud-caked jacket and tossed it aside. It would not matter if even a skilled washerwoman took it repeatedly between board and paddle, there would be no way to make it suitable again.

The monkeys, birds, and cicadas were beginning to find their voices. High above and in the trees that divided Red Rock from Tabletop, chirps and whistles began to sound. "Keturah!" he shouted, still making his way toward Verity. He feared that if the jungle's chorus reached its nightly zenith, he might not hear her if she was injured or faint. *"Keturah!"*

In response, the jungle seemed to quiet. But still there was no answer. *Please, Lord. Please let her be all right. Please . . .* "I am coming, Verity!" he cried, wanting to reassure the girl. "Shout to me again!"

"Here! I am here!" she yelled back, a bit closer now. He shoved through a patch of coco plum to his left, the mud having lifted several boulders in his direct path. He had a brief, horrible thought of Keturah under the deep mud against the rocks—caught beneath—and shoved it hurriedly away.

*Surely not. Please, Lord, no . . .*

He called Verity's name again on the other side of the brush, and finding that free of the mud, he made better time down the hill. In minutes he had found her, climbing toward him. She fell into his arms. "Oh, Gray," she sobbed, trembling. "Where is Keturah?"

"I do not know. Were you not together at first?"

"Yes," she said, sniffing. "She had my hand for a bit. Then she pushed me toward a tree and we lost each other. There was so much water, Gray. So much mud. It sent us tumbling."

*Tumbling. Was she unconscious, then? Knocked against a tree or rock?*

"Are you hurt?" he asked.

"No. At least nothing that won't heal in a few days . . . Never mind that. Let us find Ket."

They agreed to each take a side of the mud, moving their way downward. "Surely she cannot be much farther than where you came to rest," Gray said, already making his way across the twenty feet of sludge.

"I don't know," Verity said. "We were moving so fast . . . she might have gone another fifty paces in the time I was able to hold to that tree limb. Or a hundred. My memory of it is a bit dim."

"For good reason," Gray muttered. The poor girl had been tossed about by a mudslide that had carried her hundreds of feet downhill! Perhaps she too had suffered a bump or two on the head. And given the dark and rain . . .

"Keturah!" he called, this time controlling his voice. He didn't want his own panic to ignite Verity's.

"Ket!" she echoed.

By the sound of it, it didn't matter what he did or how he called to Keturah. Her sister was feeling every bit of the terror he was. It was so terribly dark. Even with the moonlight, now clear of the storm clouds, it was difficult to see much more than the outline of trees and brush. How were they to find her? If she was partially covered by mud? Unconscious?

*"Prayer before panic,"* a vicar once told him. *"Always the best choice, my boy."*

*Lord*, he groaned inwardly, *settle my heart. Help me to think. To see. Help me to find her, Father.*

The sense of urgency and alarm continued to waft through him. Was that from God, not just his own desire to have Ket back in his arms? Or rather the *ability* to pull her into his arms? How he'd longed for it. Tonight as he watched her speak to one person after another, he'd jealously wished that they were alone, just them on her front porch.

Truly he'd never met any woman like her in all his life. There was not another white woman on even Nevis who would work as hard as she had on Tabletop, and in turn on Teller's Landing. Together, planting their fields . . . the thought of watching the cane grow in the coming months, the harvest . . . and now? Was it over?

Was Keturah gone?

Gray stopped and bent partially over, wondering if he was going to be sick. But no. She could not be dead. She could not. There was too much life ahead of them. Too much for them to share. Beyond the plantations. Between them.

*Please, God. Please, please . . .* "Keturah!" he bellowed.

Again all was silent.

The mud diverged here, divided by a huge mango tree. He paused, panting, hand on a tree limb, and looked down the far side. It was steeper and moved into a gaut—one of the island's many ravines carved by centuries of runoff.

He leaned over and shouted again. Waited, holding his breath.

*Please, Keturah. Please, darling. Call out. Let me hear you.*

But there was nothing.

*Lord? Lord! Help me!*

Verity called to her too, sounding choked by sobs. He stepped toward her, thinking he might cross the river of mud again to give her some comfort, to search together, then stopped.

Gray looked back and forth, carefully studying each line of rock, of earth—anything that might be a body. He could hear

Verity crying. Again he turned to go to her, but then stopped, as if feeling a visceral pull in the other direction.

"Hold on, Verity," he called. "Stay right there and I'll be with you in a moment. Just let me search this small area over here."

Keturah had been holding Verity's hand, the two of them trying to make it to higher ground together when a wave of water and mud pushed her from her feet. They had slid together for some distance when she was able to shove Ver toward a tree. Ket somersaulted and twisted, hit the base of what she thought was a palm and fairly bounced off it, carried by a virtual slide of water and slick mud. She hit another tree and this time managed to grasp a palm branch, swinging enough out of the forceful gush of water to claw her way to safety.

But then the mud came from the other side of the tree and rammed her against a rock, she thought. The memory was dim. All she knew now was that she had awakened, and she was pinned. Barely able to breathe. One of her legs was caught beneath a large rock and in an awkward, painful position. Worse was the bigger rock lodged against her chest.

She concentrated on breathing as shallowly as she could—anything to get some oxygen into her lungs. She was growing dizzy, but she thought she could hear someone calling.

"Here!" she cried. "Here!"

But each one was little more than a whisper, her throat raspy and weak.

"Keturah!" called a man.

*Gray.* He was close.

"Gray!" she tried. But again it was painfully quiet. "Help me!"

She thought she could hear him, grunting, growling in frustration as he shoved aside a branch. Then closer.

"Keturah!" he shouted, so close that it startled her.

"Gray," she tried again, praying he would know she was here.

That she was so near. "Gray," she whispered. Then she needed to concentrate on the next breath. And the next . . .

When he next called, he was beside her. Her eyes drifted to the right, and she could see him then, his fine features a silhouette in the moonlight. He lifted his hands and rubbed his face, plainly in anguish.

"Please, God," he whispered. "Please. Help me find her." He let out a sound of agony. "Oh, my love. My love. Where are you?"

Keturah willed herself to keep concentrating on the next breath, and the next, when her heart made her want to hold it. Gray Covington . . . loved her?

He turned slowly, and she thought, in that moment, that she had never seen a more magnificent man in her life. And it was not only that God had made him handsome. He moved her because she could see how much he cared for her. He wouldn't have to say another word at all. She could see it as he turned in the moonlight . . . in the biting of his cheek, the agonized arch of his brows, the clawing of his hand at the neck of his shirt. He wanted nothing more than to find her. Because he loved her.

She tried to swallow, but her mouth was painfully dry. "Gray," she whispered. She moved her left hand. It was nearer to him, but was the only thing she could move. Perhaps if she could squeeze it through that opening there . . .

"Gray," she whispered again.

She didn't know if it was her movement or her final attempt at calling to him, or the Lord Almighty himself, but he turned and seemed to see her at last.

"Keturah?" he breathed, rushing to her. "Ket!"

She smiled as tears formed in her eyes, but again all she could concentrate on was the next breath, and the next . . .

"Oh, my Ket, there you are!" he said, kneeling next to her, his fingers running over the curve of the cursed rock that pinned her. "I see," he said to her silent plea. "I will get you out. Hold on, Ket. Hold on."

He pivoted, put a foot against the rock at her back, and pushed at the one atop her, but the rock would not budge. Grunting, he shifted and repositioned himself. Then with another tremendous shove, he sent the stone rolling away.

She tentatively took her first free breath, and then another as he shoved the other rock from her leg. She could breathe. She could breathe!

"She's here!" he called. "Verity! She's over here!" He sank down to his knees beside her. "Keturah, darling," he said, taking her hand in his, "where are you hurt? Can you breathe well now? What of your leg?"

His broad hands moved from her shoulders to her neck to her face, as if he intended to decide for himself.

"I am all right," she said in wonder, gingerly testing arms, hands, neck, back. "Except . . ." With the barest of movements, she knew. "Oh no. I think my leg is broken."

"I'll get you home, Ket. Don't worry."

"I'm . . . not. Not now. With you. Gray, you said . . . you called me . . ."

He stilled, paused a moment. Then, "You heard. You heard me call you my love."

Verity called out, getting closer. "Over here!" Gray called back. "She's all right, Ver!" But his eyes remained on Ket. His hands gently cradled her face, then tightened in intensity. And she felt none of Edward's threat in his touch, only . . . devotion. Fervor.

"Yes, Keturah Banning Tomlinson. I love you. I think I have always loved you, though I was dreadfully slow in recognizing it. Do you . . . do you think you could ever come to love me? In time?"

Ket paused. Did she love him? She'd never permitted herself to think of it. Not in truth. But she knew that she had loved these last weeks of working beside him. Of seeing how he treated others— from her sisters to his slaves—with kindness. And how through it all, he cared for her, in both big and small ways. How he had respected her, even when she didn't deserve it. Did she love him?

She laughed under her breath. "Yes," she said to him, nodding. "Yes."

"Yes?" he said, as if he hardly dared to believe it. *"Yes?"*

"Yes," she said with another breathy laugh.

"Oh, Ket. My Ket. May I kiss you?"

"Yes," she said again, this time in a whisper.

"Your leg . . . I do not wish to hurt you."

"Come to this side of me," she said.

He crossed over her and bent closer. Tenderly, reverently, he kissed her lips, then slowly drew back a bit. "I fear, Lady Ket, you taste like mud."

She laughed lightly and pulled his head closer. "As do you," she whispered, inviting him to kiss her again. Together they ignored their filth, their bruises, the blood. And in that moment Keturah thought it a thousand times more moving, more beautiful, more lovely than any kiss she'd ever shared with Edward.

"Keturah! Gray!" Verity cried, still searching and at last finding them. "Oh!" she said, shocked at seeing them so close. "Keturah! *And Gray* . . ."

Verity said his name with a tilt of a smile to her tone, and Ket grinned too. She lifted a hand to his chest and turned to her sister. "He found me," she said. "Saved me, really."

But Verity just crossed her arms and smiled back. "So I see."

❧

By the time Gray carried her up the hill to place her on his horse's back, both of them were panting and sweating—Gray from the effort, Ket from the pain. Her leg hadn't hurt that badly when she stayed still, encased as it was in mud. But as soon as Gray pulled her free and lifted her, tears began streaming down her cheeks. Every step sent a shudder of agony through her. She concentrated on two things to get her through. How glad she was the bone hadn't broken through the skin—it would be far easier to set—and the wonder of what just had transpired between her and Gray.

He loved her.

And she loved him.

The men put Verity and Selah astride the other horse, and together they gingerly moved down the road toward Tabletop. They would have to wait until morning to negotiate the mud and fetch a doctor from town.

"Or we could set it," said Philip. "'Tis a clean break, you think?"

"I do. But still, I might need a fair dose of laudanum," Keturah said. She knew that there were few doctors on-island. One, maybe two. She'd heard a woman say at the party say that the fevers kept claiming every decent doctor who arrived. "That or the drink," said the other. Was it not better to have her friends set her leg than to entrust herself to an intoxicated physician?

They reached the house, and Gray led Keturah's mount close to the steps and then carefully pulled her off the mare's back and into his arms. "Please forgive me, my lady. I'm about to track some mud into your house."

She grinned through her weary tears. "You and everyone else."

"Where would you like me to take you?" he asked, trudging up the steps and across the porch.

Grace opened the door for them, lifting a lamp, and gasped. "Mr. Covington! Lady Ket! What has happened?"

"Hot water, Grace," he returned over his shoulder as he passed her. "We'll need lots of hot water. I just fished your mistress out of a mudslide."

# Chapter Thirty-One

Her sisters had stripped her out of her ruined gown and did their best to bathe her and get her into a clean gown before the men joined them. They placed a light board beneath her broken leg, with strips of cloth stretched out to either side. Verity then took one hand, Selah the other, while Grace stood beside her, wringing her hands. "I may need more laudanum," Keturah said fearfully.

"Dear lady," Philip said, sliding a gentle hand beneath her calf and turning a bit so her leg was not in shadow as he studied it. "I doubt there'd be enough for this. It will most certainly hurt, but then your recovery shall begin in earnest."

"You have set bones before, Philip?"

"Ten or more, back in England. I'm rather good at it." He flashed her a grin, and she tried to smile back but knew she was failing.

She supposed her mother would be scandalized, what with these two men at her feet, seeing her leg bared to the knee. But at that moment, she had a difficult time caring who was in the room with her. She only wanted it done. Anticipating what was to come had to be worse than it actually—

With a swift nod to Gray—who grabbed hold of her ankle to

keep her from lurching—Philip set his other hand directly atop the break and pressed down.

Keturah screamed and then was left panting, sweat pouring off her brow and down into her hair as one wave of pain after another wracked her body.

"Forgive me, Lady Ket," Philip said, gently placing a layer of cloth over her leg and then a board on top, quickly tying front and back boards together with neat efficiency. "I find it best not to warn my patients before I do that."

"I . . . can . . . see . . . why . . ." Ket panted, crying now too. There was no relief in having the bones back in alignment, only a whole new level of agonizing pain. Her vision was swimming. She fought to stay conscious.

And then lost.

It was Matthew who shook Gray's shoulder at sunup. "Mr. Gray," he said. "You best come."

His black brows were knit, and the lines of his face told him it wasn't good.

"Keturah . . ." he said, sitting up fast.

"No, no. Lady Ket is still asleep. It is the fields, Mr. Gray. Red Rock had their mudslide. But so did Tabletop."

*Oh no . . .*

He rose on shaking legs and followed the man out of Keturah's parlor and to the front porch. Cuffee had washed and brushed Theo sometime last night or this morning, and the boy stood waiting with him.

"Thank you, Cuffee," Gray said, taking the horse's reins from his hand. Matthew was already mounted.

"Yes, Mr. Gray." From the somber look in the boy's eyes, news had already traveled among the slaves about whatever difficulty lay before them.

They trotted up the hill as the sun rose, filling the sky with peach-colored clouds above an azure sea. It was so tranquil, so inviting, that Gray had a hard time believing this was the same island that had nearly killed them all the night before. But he smelled it before they reached the lowest field. That unique deep-earth odor that he hadn't quite known before last night. Even after all these weeks of planting, of tilling the soil and covering each stretch of cane, it was different. Somehow more primal.

They paused beside the field, now covered in mud. Just yesterday the cane had begun to sprout, tiny light-green shoots that dotted the field. Now not a single sprout was visible.

Gray dragged a hand over his mouth and stared. "How deep do you think it is?"

"Two, maybe three feet, I expect," Matthew said.

*Too deep for the cane to work through.*

"And the other fields?" he ground out. "What of those up top?"

"The middle looks like this," the overseer said. "The top field is all right."

Gray's hand moved to his eyes. He rubbed them, wishing that when he opened them he'd see something different. But it remained the same.

"It will take us weeks to replant these two fields."

"Yes, sir. I expec' so. There's something else."

Wearily, Gray looked to him.

"Some of the slaves came down with fever last night. Eight, maybe nine will not be able to work today."

Gray's brow furrowed in alarm. They'd been blessed, so far, that no yellow fever or malaria had visited their plantations. But of all days . . .

"Best we get to town and buy some more, sir," Matthew said. "We cannot get Lady Ket's fields replanted with so few. Truth be told, we've been running too lean for a while now. And the way these fevers go . . ."

"You expect some shall not survive," he finished for him.

"Yes, sir. That's the way of it, most days."

Gray rubbed the back of his neck and sighed heavily. "All right.

Let's head to market in an hour or so. First I need to look in on Lady Ket and find a way to tell her."

"There is some good in this," Matthew said. "Tabletop just got served a whole lot of virgin earth. She might produce better than ever."

Gray nodded thoughtfully, grateful for that measure of hope. "So long as we can get the cane planted and mature enough to survive storm season."

"Yes, sir."

Gray took a long, deep breath. How would Keturah take the news? Another month behind everyone else's crops on-island . . . she had so counted on this crop. So believed it was going to be a part of her family's rescue, provision for the future.

And now he would have to tell her that it was at risk.

The two were nearly back to the house when Lord Reynolds and Angus Shubert met them on the road. Their horses' legs were caked with mud, plain testimony that the men had made it through the slide area that now cut off Tabletop from Charlestown.

"Lord Reynolds!" Gray called, moving alongside the man's mount and reaching over to shake his hand. "Is all well at Red Rock?" he asked, giving Shubert nothing more than a cursory nod.

"We are well," the older man said, but his face was as wan as his gray wig. "And you and yours? What of the Ladies Banning?"

"Well enough," he said. "I lost a wagon, but the women, Philip, Primus, and I all escaped with our lives."

"Glad I am to hear of it." But the man remained somber. "Mr. and Mrs. Malone perished in that slide."

Gray's eyebrows shot upward. The indigo planters? From the southern side? "I thought . . . were they not going to spend the night at Red Rock?"

Lord Reynolds winced and shook his head. "That was their intent." His chin dropped to his chest. "But in the haste of preparation, the servants mistakenly set their wagon in the lineup. It was holding others from moving, so Malone must have decided to try to make it home. We found the remains of their wagon this morning . . . and Leo's body. But not Jane's yet."

His light eyes traced Gray's, assessing him as if he wondered how they had escaped. "We feared some of you might have died too." He sniffed. "How delightful to find that you were spared."

Gray nodded, but he was confused. *How delightful?* Were those the best words? *Poor Mr. and Mrs. Malone . . .*

"We saw the remains of your wagon," Shubert said, his mount prancing beneath him. "Halfway down the hill. But when we saw your tracks, we figured you'd made it out."

"Yes. The slide . . . it very nearly overtook us. We raced for the ridge, and nearly made it, when the mudslide struck."

"And no one was harmed?" Reynolds asked.

"Most of us have a fair number of bruises, I expect, this morning," Gray allowed. "And Lady Keturah has a broken leg."

"How ghastly!" Lord Reynolds exclaimed. "We shall send for the doctor right away."

"No need. We set it last night. She's resting now."

"And your fields?" Shubert pressed, letting his eyes slide to Matthew as if he already knew. Was it Gray's imagination or did the man look as if he held back a grin? Surely he wouldn't dare. Not right in front of Lord Reynolds.

To his credit, Matthew didn't look away. "The fields have some damage," he said calmly, as if it were just another trifling issue. "We'll be setting that to rights, beginning today."

Shubert let out a scoffing breath, and Lord Reynolds frowned. "You mean to say you need to plant again? Is it not too late?" he inquired of Shubert, ignoring Matt and Gray.

"Most would say so," Shubert answered.

"But it is not up to *most*," Gray said. "Only *us*. Now we must bid you good day, Lord Reynolds, Mr. Shubert. We are grateful you came to check on our welfare, but we have much to see to."

"Quite," Reynolds said. "Good day."

As they rode away and Gray started with Matthew back toward the house, he thought again of the finery at Red Rock. The crystal.

The china. The chairs. The candles. Clearly, Reynolds was a wealthy man. And few wealthy men became so without being fairly ruthless.

While he seemed genuinely caring this morning, had he truly come to check on their welfare? Or to see if Tabletop and Teller's Landing had suddenly become land without living owners?

# CHAPTER THIRTY-TWO

Despite the fact that Keturah's body ached from neck to ankle and her leg throbbed, she couldn't stop smiling when Gray visited her the next morning. It was as if with the knowledge of his love, and the memory of his kiss, she felt she could conquer anything. But his dark blue eyes—almost a reflection of the late-morning sky out her window—seemed to search every inch of her face as he soberly neared her bed.

She frowned. "That is not the face of a man who faced a terrible storm and beat it," she said. *Nor the face of a man in love . . .*

"No," he agreed, sinking to one knee and taking her hand. "'Tis the face of a man who has more hard news for you."

Her heart stuttered, twisted, then found its pace again. "What is it, Gray? Tell me quickly. As Philip did with setting my leg to rights."

"There was a slide on Tabletop last night too. Your middle and lower fields are buried."

She blinked slowly, wondering if she'd heard him right. "B-buried?"

"Covered. Every last seedling is gone, Ket. The fields will have to be replanted."

She took a deep breath and then let it out. "I see."

293

"There's more. Last night . . . well, last night the Malones were behind us in their wagon. They died, Ket."

Salty tears sprang to her eyes. The Malones, the young couple from the southern end of the island . . . gone?

"How? I thought . . ."

"I did too. They decided to try to make it home. And now they never will." He let his chin fall to his chest a moment before looking at her again. "That could have easily been us, Ket. So while this is terribly hard news for you—about your fields— remember that, will you? That we were blessed to live through last night?"

He reached out and cradled her cheek. She closed her eyes and leaned into it. He was right, of course. She fought to hold on to what he'd said . . . but two out of three fields gone? Needing replanting? It was late, so late in the season.

"It will be all right," Gray said, letting his thumb slide across her cheekbone as she looked to him again. "Somehow. We'll find a way. Your sisters, you, me. We'll find a way together."

She nodded slowly, not believing him but finding no more strength to discuss it further. If they lost this next crop, if it was torn out come storm season, if they harvested too late to make the last ships . . .

"Today, Keturah. Think about what you must today," he said gently. "Not beyond it. You are not alone. You have me," he said, bringing her hand to his chest. "You have your sisters, Matthew and Mitilda, and many more."

She nodded again, although she still felt the weight of the burden squarely on her own shoulders. But he was right. She must remain focused on what was good, what was true, not the fears that threatened to overtake her. "Gray, thank you. For finding me last night. For . . ." The intimacy of the moment struck her, and she began to blush, glancing to the window a moment. "For saving all of us. If you had not been with us . . . if you had not driven so hard for the ridge . . ."

She tried to pull her hand away but he gently held on, waiting for her to look him in the eye. "We have much to be thankful for," he said solemnly. "Perhaps most of all, our new understanding."

Ket smiled, forcing herself not to look away. She knew she was blushing furiously now. But the way Gray looked upon her made her feel . . . enticing, rather than an invalid in bed.

"I do love you, Keturah Banning Tomlinson. I want you to hear that from me now, in the light of day. Last night . . ." It was his turn to look away to the window and rub the back of his neck before turning back to her. "Well, I wondered if in the moment, and being in the throes of so much pain . . . might it have left you rather overwrought? Predisposed to say things you regret today?"

Ket's smile grew. Here was this man, her beautiful, wonderful friend, fretting that she was having second thoughts today? His doubt, his fear, his clear need of reassurance moved her. "No, Gray. Morning light has not changed my mind . . . nor my heart. I love you too."

His brows lifted at the center, naked hope and joy mingling in his blue eyes. "Truly?" he breathed.

"Truly," she said.

He looked as if he might burst, and then he became very intent. "Do you know how much I wish you were well? So that I could kiss you again? Not that it kept me from doing so last night."

Now she knew that her blush had overtaken her. "Gray . . ." she said with a nervous look toward the door. But his intensity made her realize he meant every word, and it set her skin to tingling.

"We have much to discuss," he said, sobering. "Clearly, I am not in a position to offer for your hand. But, Keturah, know that everything I do on Teller's Landing—everything I have done and will do—is to pursue my heart's desire. And what began as a desire to prove myself, to emerge from my brother's shadow, has now solely become a desire to provide for a wife. You, Keturah. You."

She pulled her hand from his at last. His . . . wife?

Hearing the word on his lips, faced with it now . . . set her heart to pounding. And not for good reasons.

"Can we not . . . can we not simply enjoy this? A time of court-ship without discussing that?" she asked, even as her own vows came back to her. *I shall never marry again. No man shall ever lord over me.*

Gray's brows knitted, and he lifted his chin and stared down his nose at her. "I know you fear it. Marriage. Your first was—"

"Was something I do not wish to ponder."

He paused. "Right. But," he said slowly, carefully, "*our* marriage would be something altogether different, Ket."

"Would it?" she asked tightly. Deep down, she knew she was being rash, unfair. "Let us not discuss it further now."

"As you say," he said in reluctant agreement.

"Tell me. Was there damage at Teller's Landing?"

"I know not. I assume Philip is there now. I must go to them as well." He looked to the window again. "I wonder if all plantations suffered so? And how often it happens."

Ket shook her head, relieved to be back to a conversation that both could agree upon. "I've read through all of Father's journals. He mentioned mudslides only once or twice."

"'Tis not surprising, really," Gray said. "The planters have unearthed every bit of jungle they could to plant in cane. And sugarcane does not delve nearly as deep as the trees and brush the Almighty set here upon Nevis."

"Can you imagine it, Gray?" she mused. "As it once was? Beset with nothing but palm and banyan and coco plum, from beach to peak?"

"It must have been a sight." He placed his tricorn atop his head. "It still is." Then he bent to kiss her hand and stood. "I've always heard that being a planter requires one to learn to make coconut pudding out of cracked coconuts. What do you say, Lady Partner? Shall we begin to replant your fields on the morrow?"

She smiled. "What of today?"

"Today, Matthew and I must get to Charlestown. Some of the slaves have come down with fever. And with this new, pressing need in your fields, we have no choice but to purchase more hands."

"Fever? Who?"

"I know not. But I saw your sisters carrying baskets of food to the cabins. I am certain they will return to you with news of who it is. While they will likely make a recovery, time is of the essence—we must see to your fields."

"Oh dear. Might you locate a doctor in town while you're there to see to them?"

"We'll do our best." He turned to go but then paused, gesturing back toward her. "We shall table our conversation of marriage for a time, Keturah Banning," he pledged solemnly.

"Keturah Banning?" she asked. "Not Lady Tomlinson?"

"No," he said, shaking his head slowly. "I refuse to acknowledge that man's claim on you any longer, even in uttering his name. You should never have been his, Keturah." His jaw clenched. "Never. For it was he who set your mind against marriage, was it not?"

"Perhaps," she whispered back.

A breath passed between them in the acknowledgment. An impish spark lit his blue eyes. "Then I shall endeavor to change your mind again, over time. Fair warning," he said, lifting a finger, "as we court, and you heal, and I wait for you to decide a union such as ours could be an entirely different experience from what you shared with . . . *him*, I do mean to claim more kisses." He bent to take her hand in his again and lifted it to his lips, staring at her all the while. "Might you agree to that? Even if we are not yet betrothed?"

She laughed under her breath and shook her head. "We shall see, Gray. We shall see."

But as he turned to leave, she hoped he knew that she might be readily persuaded.

*Oh, how I hope he knows.*

Keturah caught Selah's wrist that afternoon as the girl placed a fresh pitcher of water by her bed. "Selah, what is it?" When her sister turned back to her, her suspicions were confirmed. She'd been weeping. "Selah . . ."

The girl sank to the edge of the bed beside her, new tears sliding down her face as she stared at the wall. "It is all . . . so much, Ket. Nearly losing you. Having to plant again. Seeing new slaves arrive—so frightened, so malnourished. And the sick slaves . . . Oh, Ket, what if one of them dies?"

Keturah should have expected this. Selah had taken to watching over the slaves of Tabletop, intent on making their lives as comfortable as possible. She and Primus were the ones who told Ket what must be done to fix their cottages or what they needed to buy in clothing, bedding, and the like. She was the one who worked to teach the new ones English. And likely the one who had taken lead in tending the sick today.

"Who is sick, Selah?"

"Grace and Gideon are among them. And Bennabe and . . ." She dissolved into tears.

*Grace.* That was why the girl wasn't about. It had been her sisters who had taken care of her all day, and she'd only assumed they had sent the maid to do something else. *And Gideon, usually so strong.* She had heard that newcomers to the island were most susceptible to the fevers. She'd taken to thanking God over these last weeks when she heard of plantations battling a fever while Tabletop remained blessedly free of it. And Bennabe, the earnest one-armed slave, had he not enough to deal with without this too?

"Gray promised to seek out a doctor," Ket said.

Selah nodded and wiped away her tears. "He did as he promised. The doctor should arrive tomorrow. And Gray did bring some cinchona bark to brew into a tea for those who are sick, which we pray will ease their symptoms. 'Tis so awful, Ket. They shiver so hard that their teeth chatter!"

"You are a dear," Ket said, stroking the girl's back, "tending to them and me. I know Mother would be proud of you." She sighed. "Today is a hard day. But we are alive, Selah. We will make it through, and tomorrow will be better."

*Unless the slaves begin to die,* she thought with a shiver of fear. But she kept the thought to herself.

Selah nodded, pulled a handkerchief from her pocket, and noisily blew her nose. "I'll go and find something for us to eat for supper."

"Thank you, dearest." Ket turned, wincing at the movement, feeling both exhausted from the constant pain and agitated after an entire day abed. She fretted over every one of her slaves, even if she didn't spend the time with them that Selah did. The cost of replacing any of them—emotionally and financially—made her fret more. Every time new slaves came to Tabletop or Teller's Landing, it was like a physical blow. The infernal practice tore at her. Wearied her. Angered and frustrated her. Yet time and again, she and Gray could come up with no other solution. Few indentured servants voyaged to the Indies, not over the last hundred years anyway. Rumors of the death rates on-island had made the practice unfavorable in Europe. Africans, by comparison, were more resistant to the tropical diseases.

Resistant . . . enough? And Gideon, Grace . . . why, they were as British as she.

*One limb at a time,* she told herself. She would not grieve potential losses of the morrow. Not when she had enough to cope with in facing the realized losses of today. And when it became too much, when tears threatened her own eyes, she returned to praising God for all that was well.

That not *all* of the slaves were sick.

That they all had been spared from the mudslide last night.

And that she was not alone. She had Selah. And Verity. And Gray . . .

Was it really true? Was Gray . . . hers?

She thought back to his declaration at her bedside, in her doorway. Of love. Of anger toward Edward. Of hope for a future . . . of marriage. Could he truly make her believe in marriage again? Want it? Would she really be able to utter vows ever again?

*Do not worry over the morrow, Ket,* she reminded herself. *Only revel in the good you can find in today.*

And then she smiled. Because her first thought was of Gray again.

She sank back against her pillow and stared at the empty doorway, remembering his smile and his pledge to claim more kisses. And that pledge, she decided, might keep her smiling, even through her dreams.

# Chapter Thirty-Three

Over the next few days, Gray watched as more of Keturah's thirty slaves took to their beds. The fever, nausea, and dizziness were the same as malaria. But people complained of severe headaches, and the sun itself seemed to bring them pain.

In groups they succumbed to what Dr. McMillian—who had finally arrived—described as the "acute" phase of yellow fever until now eighteen were abed.

"Bloodletting is a must," Dr. McMillian slurred, and Gray wondered how he had ever made it between the tavern and Tabletop. Clearly, the short, gray-haired, red-faced man with ample jowls had had his share of rum. Or did he have a flask in his bag? "Best to do them all this evening," he said, abstractly waving over the group of cabins before them as they conferred.

"Even those who are in good health?" Selah cried, wringing her hands.

"Aye," said the doctor. "Only a matter of time 'fore the rest are down with it too, miss. 'Tis the way of it."

Gray moved to block the doctor's way toward his bag, sitting on the nearest porch, and the lancet he knew was likely inside. While he seemed coherent enough to diagnose the fever, he was not at all sure the doctor was steady enough to lance one arm after another.

"Pardon me," Gray said. "You said this was the acute phase. So it will not become any worse?" Surely they could manage the symptoms for now, given that the doctor was not in any shape to do the bloodletting.

"Heavens no, good sir. 'Twill get much worse for some. Have ye never seen this fever before? If we do not manage to nip this in the bud, a good number of Tabletop's slaves shall see the toxic phase," he finished, wobbling a bit on his feet.

"And that means . . . ?" Gray asked, moving more solidly between the doctor and his bag. Somewhere, somehow, he had indeed been imbibing over the last hour. The man reeked of rum.

The doctor squinted up at him as if trying to remember the question. "In the acute stage," he said with a brush of his hand, "there is blood everywhere. From the nose, mouth, and eyes. Seizures. Failure of both liver and kidneys. No," he said, pushing past him. "Best get to my lancet and get on with it."

"No, Doctor." Gray reached out to stay him. "I do not wish you to do any bloodletting this day. Perhaps after you sit for a spell on the porch and take a cup of tea. But not now when you've been imbibing."

"Imbibing!" he grumbled, lifting himself up to his full height, a good six inches shorter than Gray. He glowered up at him. "I assure you," he slurred, pulling his waistcoat straight with some effort, "I have not had any spirits since the customary dose in my morning tea."

Gray glanced at Selah behind the doctor, and she rolled her eyes. Clearly that had not been the only rum Dr. McMillian had had today. He swerved as if he struggled to remain standing.

"Still, I must insist you take your ease, either at the house or back in town," Selah soothed, looping his arm through hers and guiding him toward the door. "You must be exhausted, poor man. After caring for so many. What is it like to be one of only two doctors on-island? You must be constantly in demand! Here, let me see you on your way."

Charmed and a bit overwhelmed by the pretty young blonde,

the doctor allowed himself to be led as far as the door before he seemed to remember himself.

"No, no, lass," he said, pulling his arm free of hers in agitation. "I shall see to your slaves and then be on my way. I have other patients to see in Charlestown before sundown."

"Then I ask you to go immediately to them," she said resolutely, moving to lift his bag and offering it to him. "Because you shall not be wielding a blade today among our own."

"Pshaw," he said, frowning and tucking his head. "Do not be foolish, woman." He turned to Gray. "Speak some sense into her, man! You'd best utilize my services while I am present!"

"We'd best utilize your services when you are not inebriated," he said firmly, crossing his arms.

"What a perfectly outrageous claim! I am quite offended," he said, yanking the bag from Selah. "Do not call upon my services when this fever spreads among the others and becomes worse," he added, shaking his finger at Selah.

She blinked, glanced at Gray for encouragement, then said, "I understand, Dr. McMillian. Good day to you."

"Good day," he ground out, turning to stride toward his smart, black carriage and patient horse. Gray could only pray that he managed to get himself safely back to Charlestown. He knew he would not countenance any other suggestion.

Selah and he watched as the small man rode up their lane . . . and saw that Angus Shubert and his two men observed his passing too. Selah drew closer to him, taking his arm. Gray frowned as the men rode lazily down the lane and pulled up outside the cabin. Had not the week proven sufficiently trying without a visit from these three?

"Good afternoon, Covington, Miss Banning," Angus said, touching the brim of his tricorn, letting his eyes linger over Selah. "We heard a rumor over at Red Rock that Lord Reynolds wished us to dispel."

"And that was?" Gray asked.

"That you had yellow fever among your slaves."

"That's no rumor," he said, wondering what business it was of his.

Angus looked over his shoulder at the now-empty lane. "And you sent the good doctor away?"

"He was rather . . . incapacitated. I feared if he took a lancet to the sick, the blood loss might be more a danger than the fever."

"I see," Angus said, crossing his hands on his pommel and eying the nearest cabin. Even from here they could hear several people crying, overwrought by the pain. "So he didn't see to the bloodletting before he left?"

"No, he did not," Gray said. "Now, if you'll excuse us—"

Shubert shook his head. "You're still green to this island, I know. But bloodletting is our chief defense, Covington. And you just sent away the only available doctor on-island. Dr. Simmons was called over to Saint Kitts."

Simmons was away? For the first time, Gray wondered if he had made the right decision.

"Are there not well and able slaves available to serve those who are sick, Miss Banning?" Shubert asked. "Yellow fever is a messy business. The cabins are no place for a lady."

"I actually favor nursing, Mr. Shubert," she said. "It does my heart good to see to my friends here."

"Your *friends*," he said with a huff of a laugh. "Don't be telling me that a woman as fine as you has become a Negro-lover."

She recoiled at the way he said it. "I aim to care for our servants as I would any of my white friends."

Shubert took off his hat and beat it across his leg, shaking his head in disgust. "Slaves tend to get uppity when you coddle them. Best to maintain a distance, I say. Because do you know what happens when a slave gets uppity? *Uprisings*," he hissed. "Give a black man the chance to believe he deserves what the whites have and he begins to *want* what the whites have. And when he isn't given it, he tries to *take* it." He looked Selah up and down. "There's been more than one white woman raped on this island by her slaves. Others carried off. More—"

"That's quite enough, Shubert," Gray interrupted, stepping forward. "Be on your way."

"I don't think so," he said, dismounting. "Because slaves talk, Mr. Covington. And if my slaves hear your slaves talk about what goes on here, then, well, my slaves are going to be gettin' foolish ideas in *their* heads."

Gray strode toward him at equal pace. "You are on Banning land," Gray said. "You have no say here on how these women run their plantation." The man was about his height but outweighed him by a good thirty pounds. But there was nothing to do but face him down. And truth be told, he'd been itching for a reason to pummel him ever since he heard how he'd manhandled Ket. His fists clenched at his side.

"Do not tell me you're a Negro-lover too," spat Shubert. "Maybe you have something unnatural going on with your new overseer," he said with a sly smile. "That why you signed him on too?"

Gray needed no further invitation. He feinted left and then pounded Shubert's right cheek when the man dodged. The big oaf went sprawling to his left hip. He let out a snarl and was scrambling to his feet when he paused, eyes widening. Shubert slowly straightened, his jaw clenching, the veins at his temple bulging. But he did not advance on Gray.

Gray saw what he had, then—the sick slaves of Tabletop. Everyone had come out of their cabins and surrounded them. They were trembling with fever, sweat pouring from their brows, but all sixteen of the ill had left their sickbeds to stand behind him, beside him, surrounding Selah protectively as well.

Shubert swore and sneered as he glanced around at them, then finally back at Gray. "You're a fool, Covington. Mark me, this will come back to haunt you." He let out a humorless laugh and looked at all the slaves again, shaking his head in disgust. "You'd be better off letting this lot die out of the fever and start again. Come by Red Rock. I'll show you how a plantation should be run." He pointed a finger at him and waggled it. "I shoulda known. From the day Lady Keturah hired that Negro as overseer, I shoulda known what was coming."

He mounted up and stared hard at Gray as he dabbed at a bit of blood at the corner of his mouth. "Lord Reynolds, the other planters, they will not hold with this. Not a one of them."

"And I will tell them what I've told you. We have a right to run our plantations as we see fit."

Shubert scoffed. "Until the day you all are murdered in your beds."

Selah edged nearer to Gray as they watched the men ride away, wrapping her small hand around his arm. "Thank you, Gray, for standing up to them," she whispered.

Gray nodded, finally able to take a full breath as the riders disappeared from sight. Then he broke away from her and rushed over to Gideon, who was wobbling on his feet, his eyes rolling. He caught the large man and, with grunting effort, eased him over to the porch. "Everyone, back to your sickbeds," he said. "Thank you for coming to our aid."

They left then, stumbling, dragging themselves back to one cabin after another. "Come with me, Selah. We need to fetch fresh water, rags, broth. We need to feed the ailing, give them strength to fight this fever."

"And pray they all survive," she said quietly as they walked.

# CHAPTER THIRTY-FOUR

Keturah watched as the circles under Selah's eyes grew darker over the coming days. "Tell Primus I need him to carry me out there," Ket said to her. "I can sit between Gideon and Grace. Or by Bennabe. Give me a pail and some rags and I can put cool cloths on their heads or feed them some soup."

"No, Ket. You must remain here. Regain your strength."

"My strength is fine. And I must do *something* or I shall go mad. Anything is better than another day of convalescing while you all run ragged."

"It . . . Keturah, well, 'tis rather awful," Selah said, rubbing her face. "Are you quite certain you are up to it?"

She was already easing her leg over the side of the bed, trying not to wince but quite failing. Still she insisted, "I am this plantation's mistress. And I must go to my people."

Selah shook her head. "Gideon . . . Ket, I think we might be losing him. This morning he was convulsing. And their eyes. Ket, the whites of their *eyes*. They're all turning a ghastly yellow."

"Thus the name," Keturah returned grimly. "'Tis all right, sister. You need not try and protect me any longer. Let us face this together."

Truth be told, her words were brave. But when she first saw the sick, she faltered. Gideon opened his eyes—and they were indeed

307

an eerie yellow—but he didn't seem to see or hear her. How had the fever taken such a strapping, strong man down to this?

Gray arrived with the other doctor from town, this one named Simmons, who thankfully had returned from St. Kitts and appeared quite sober. Both men looked surprised when they entered Gideon's cabin and found her there on a chair between his bed and Meriday's.

"Ket!" Gray barked in surprise. "I mean, Lady Keturah, this is Dr. Simmons."

"At your service," the doctor said with a short nod. "It appears you met with a calamity of your own, m'lady," he said, gesturing to her splinted leg.

"It was broken the night of the mudslide," she said.

"Oh? And who set it?"

"Gray's man, Philip. I was fortunate he had experience."

"Yes, well, let us hope he did not leave you a cripple," he sniffed. He obviously did not approve of people taking medical matters into their own hands.

"Quite," she said with a raised brow, not wishing to argue. "Thank you for coming to see to my people."

"But of course," he said, opening a wooden box to extract a lancet and cups, then a large jar full of leeches.

She blanched. She never liked the business of bloodletting. But she supposed it was necessary, and for some perhaps their only hope.

---

Despite the doctor's best efforts, they began dying that night. Old Meriday died first, then a thin newcomer named Mack, followed by a shy girl named Ruth. Bennabe, dear Bennabe.

But the hardest to see go was Grace.

Keturah remained in the cabins all night and through the next day, weeping as each one died. But it was her servant from Hartwick for whom she felt the most keenly. Grace, dear Grace, who had so faithfully served as their maid for years, who had helped dress her, brushed her hair, seen to her every need . . . and yet, in the end, Ket could not return the favor. She leaned against the wall of the cabin and gave into her tears once again.

That was where Gray found her.

"Oh, Gray," she said, falling into his arms. "It is so awful. I feel so responsible," she cried. "If it weren't for me, for us, they'd be back at Hartwick now, whole and hale. And these others . . ." she choked out.

"The others would have been on some other plantation," he said gently, "likely facing a fever there too at some point. Shhh, love," he said, stroking her back. "It is awful, but 'tis not your doing. You must not take that upon your shoulders."

"But Grace . . . oh, Gray, how I shall miss her!"

He said nothing to that, only held her while she wept. "Come," he said, bending down to lift her into his arms. "I'm taking you back to the house. You need some sleep."

She wanted to protest, but she knew the truth in his words. "Do not bury them without me, Gray," she whispered into his neck as he carried her down the hill. "I want to be there. I need to be there."

"As well you should. Rest assured we will wait." He paused. "Perhaps you can use a bit of good news."

"Please," she said.

"Matthew, Verity, and the slaves almost have your middle field planted again."

"Oh, Gray, that *is* good news. What . . . what would we do without you?"

He smiled down at her. "You'd find your way. Somehow. You always have. But I'm glad for it, Ket. Glad to be here for you. With you."

It frightened her, how much she liked hearing that from him. How she felt when she was around him. He gave her hope. Strength. And he cared for her—for them all, really—in such a sacrificial way. Every time she was with him she felt walls around her heart—walls that had been her protection during her years at Clymore Castle— begin to crumble. And that made her feel like she both wanted to shout in victory and cower in the face of such vulnerability.

So when he set her to her feet in the house, she limped away a bit, needing some space. He squinted at her, plainly seeing how it pained her to hobble about and wondering why she had scrambled away. But he didn't press her.

The smell of something cooking in the kitchen brought both their noses up. They could hear someone working in there. The clank of an iron pot. A ceramic dish set down on stone. "Well, that would be an answer to prayer," Gray mused. "Supper?" He left her to peek in the kitchen, and Keturah sank to the settee.

In a few minutes he returned, handing her a hunk of bread and a slice of cheese. "'Tis Mitilda," he said.

"Mitilda?" she exclaimed. Ket didn't like what immediately leapt to her heart—a resentment that the woman had assumed she could come inside the big house and treat the kitchen as her own. But wasn't she grateful? That someone—anyone—was cooking? The field hands, her sisters, everyone needed food this night.

Gray gave her another long, steady look, as if giving her the chance to collect herself.

"'Tis kind of her," Ket said carefully. "To think ahead and set to supper."

"Indeed," he said. "And it looks like a fine lamb stew. I'll need to hasten home to Teller's Landing, though, as soon as we've eaten. I must look in on Philip, see how they're faring on weeding the fields, and make sure none of my own has taken sick."

"Oh yes, of course," Ket said. Belatedly, guilt swept through her. The poor man had spent many nights on this very settee—why, she doubted he'd gone home more than once since she'd broken her leg and the fever had come to Tabletop. And yet the idea of his leaving, of his spending the night away, left her feeling unaccountably sorrowful.

*Make up your mind, Ket,* she tiredly told herself. *Do you want him to maintain some distance or never leave your side again?*

# CHAPTER THIRTY-FIVE

Everyone agreed that Mitilda was the finest cook among them. Ket grudgingly admitted that the stew had been perfectly seasoned, the lamb tender, and she sent the woman back to her cottage with an extra portion for Abraham.

"It was most kind of you, Mitilda," she said, hating that she sounded so stiff, so formal. "For you to help us as you did today. How you have helped us in the fields . . ."

"Ahh, that's all right, Lady Ket," Mitilda said. "You ladies have been pouring yourself into those sick ones. I wanted to do something more for you in turn. Something without pay."

"Thank you."

The woman hesitated by the door. "Could I be of service, Lady Ket? Do you need a woman to cook for you and your sisters every day?"

She was asking for a job. Again, Ket shoved down a flash of resentment. Was it not enough, her annual stipend from her father? Another of suspicion. Had she made them supper just so they would know how fine a cook she was?

Around the table, Verity and Selah and Gray were waiting, wide-eyed, on her response.

At last the word *forgive* sprang to her mind.

*Is it not time to find a new way forward with Mitilda?* Keturah

311

wondered. To treat her with the grace that she herself would wish for were their positions reversed? And honestly, would it not be good to have meals as fine as this every night?

"It'd be a great service to us, Mitilda," she said, "if you would become our new cook. And, please, invite Abraham up to the kitchen each evening. He should eat his supper while 'tis still warm."

"That's right kind of you, Lady Ket." She gave her a single, graceful nod, her eyes meeting Ket's in gentle understanding.

Ket nodded in return, and the woman left, quietly closing the door behind her. Ket sighed. "We've just given the neighbors a whole new reason to talk about us and our ways."

"Once they're your guests and have tasted Mitilda's cooking," Gray said, lifting a glass in toast, "they shall curse themselves for not hiring her first."

This last decision had seemed to sap what little strength she had regained as the stew hit her belly. She reached up and rubbed her forehead.

"Shall I carry you up to your room?" Gray asked, reaching over to cover her hand with his.

"No. I shall get Primus to do so. You must be on your way. You can return, on the morrow?"

"I shall return at sunup," he promised. Then he rose, bent to kiss her hand, gave an encouraging smile to both the girls, and left.

The fever reached its apex the next day and then began to recede. In the end, they lost seven slaves and saw them buried together on a small rocky plot near the road that had served such purpose for generations.

Seeing each of their burial mounds made Ket cry anew, as did Verity and Selah. Meriday. Mack. Ruth. Two she had not even met—Jonathan and Delia. And then Bennabe and Grace. *Dear, dear Grace,* she thought as tears streamed down her face, remembering her in England and here. Bennabe, helping her so much

312

during those first days on-island. *So faithful. So true. I am sorry, dear ones. I am sorry I could not save you.*

When the others from Tabletop and Teller's Landing had gathered around, Selah prayed sweetly for each of them, and Matthew spoke of their long journey now done and how they were across the great river now. Hope and Sansa had collected buckets of white seashells. Together they spread a line of them down the length of each mound of dirt. Mimba began singing a haunting, mournful song in an African tongue while Antony kept time, striking a stick against a rock. Ket didn't know if any of the others knew what the words of that song meant, but it was clear enough to all of them. They were saying a sad farewell.

July and Sansa and Mitilda brought forth pots and utensils that each of the dead had used, now broken, and laid a few on each grave. Looking around the cemetery, Ket could see it was another custom, for the entire plot was scattered with shards of pottery. Two even had broken chairs atop theirs.

"What is this?" she whispered to Matthew. "Why do they do this?"

"It is a symbol," he said, blinking slowly as if trying to remember the reason for a custom he'd seen all his life. "The spirit, now free from its earthly vessel."

"Ahh," Ket said. She liked that. And for the first time she knew she was ready to go to her father's gravesite over at the parish cemetery. Before now, she had not been. Now she wanted to find something of her father's, break it, and lay it upon his grave, whispering prayers of hope that he was free and at rest after a lifetime of toil.

He had done his best. Failed, in obvious ways, but he had loved her and her sisters, loved her mother. Deep down she knew that to be true. And life was so short . . . did she not wish peace for everyone in her path? Everyone who had crossed it? Everyone who would? Was that not the way of Christ?

Was it not far less wearisome than carrying resentment and hate and anger and frustration? To wish peace upon them all?

*"He that is without sin among you, let him cast the first stone. . . ."*

Ket's eyes moved to Mitilda. *Peace, I wish you peace*, she thought. As the words moved through her mind, she felt her heart lift, lighten.

And then she thought of Edward. *You never gave me peace. Not a day of it. But I wish you peace, Edward.*

Then of Angus Shubert. *You seem intent on disturbing our peace. But I wish you peace, Mr. Shubert.*

Lastly of her father. *Rest, Father. Rest in peace. And please . . . would you greet sweet Grace for us?*

# CHAPTER THIRTY-SIX

"You are practically giddy," Philip chided Gray as they drove over to Tabletop to escort the women to Nisbet Plantation for their grand island-wide party.

"I am not," Gray said. "If there is anything to describe a gentleman, it is never *giddy*."

Philip laughed beneath his breath.

"Well, all right," Gray admitted. "Perhaps I am a tad giddy. But can you blame me, man? Our crops are coming along well, and we get to escort the three most beautiful women on-island to this party, one of whom appears to be rather fond of me."

"I think they're all fond of you," Philip said with a grin. "But yes, one in particular."

They rode on in silence for a while, bumping and bouncing over the road.

"Let this party not end like the one two months ago," Gray said. Thoughts of that night—how close he had been to losing Ket—still made him shudder.

"No, no," Philip said. "That is behind us. Tonight there isn't a whisper of a storm, only the promise of a big, fat moon reflecting in the sea. It may prove the perfect setting to steal a kiss," he said, nudging Gray.

"Why, Philip, I'd never allow you such an intimacy," Gray said with mock outrage. Philip let out a guffaw and shook his head.

They'd reached Tabletop and turned down the lane. The slaves came to their cabin doors, eager to see the men in their finery, and Gray nodded or waved to each. He knew they'd come out again when they drove out with the women.

But when they drove past again, he couldn't remember seeing them. All he could concentrate on was the thought of Keturah, directly behind him, in a deep-green gown that had the barest hold of each shoulder before plunging in a U-shaped neckline. The skirts of each of their dresses were so wide they could barely fit on the bench side by side. Even so, they had made do, giggling together.

He was in a new jacket and wig himself, the last one lost in the mudslide. And he'd splurged on new stockings and buckled shoes when in Charlestown, intent on cutting a fine figure if he was to meet all those who held any measure of power on Nevis. The memory of Ket's expression of admiration when she came to the door battled to win sway over the look of her from head to foot . . . every inch a lady. And since she was at last free of her splint, he hoped he could convince her to try at least one dance.

*Yes, indeed, I have reason to be giddy this night.*

Keturah was introduced to Lord and Lady Nisbet, who both greeted her with looks of honest welcome and curiosity. They had been away in England until now. "But we always return in time for the Harvest Moon feast," Lady Nisbet said. "'Tis a tradition."

"A tradition in which we are blessed to take part," Keturah said, curtsying.

"Please," Lord Nisbet said, "the dancing shall begin shortly. Will you be so kind as to escort these ladies down to the beach?" he asked Gray and Philip.

"Of course," Gray said.

"What would the man think if he knew Philip was your servant in England?" Ket whispered to him.

"It matters not what we were in England," Gray said. "Any of us. All that matters is what we are here."

His words resonated with her. It mattered little that she had once been Edward's wife, mistress of Clymore Castle. It was true—most were curious about who she was as mistress of Tabletop, and who she intended to be. Other than those who suspected she had a fat inheritance after Edward's death. *If only it had been fatter . . .*

Ket shoved away her financial worries. She would have been better served not going through the ledgers that morning before preparing for the party. If there was anything that killed a festive spirit, it was thoughts of money and the clarity on how quickly it was being spent.

Before they reached the sand, they were stopped by a servant who was taking every person's boots or slippers.

"How perfectly scandalous," Verity said.

"Indeed it is, lass," said a voice behind them. "But I rather like it."

They all turned to greet Captain Duncan McKintrick.

"Why, Captain!" Verity said, bringing a hand to her heart. "You have returned!"

"Indeed I have," he said, bowing low over her other hand. "For a precious few nights before I set sail again for England. What good fortune for me to find I was in time for the Nisbet party, knowing you would be in attendance."

"Oh," she said, mouth rounding prettily. "Me?"

"You and your beautiful sisters," he added smoothly, finally looking to Ket and Selah. "Do tell me," he said, settling Verity's hand through the crook of his arm, "of how things have transpired at Tabletop since we parted company."

Keturah and Gray shared a knowing look, and Philip offered Selah a brotherly arm. The men—aside from Captain McKintrick— elected to keep their boots, but as appeared customary, every woman shed her slippers. Perhaps it was because they knew they would soon be full of sand, or perhaps it was that each longed to feel as though a barefoot girl again, carefree. Ket herself relished the cool, damp sand seeping between her toes. It was far better this way. And she had to smile when she glimpsed Captain McKintrick's bare white feet and calves, skin that had not seen the sun in some time. But the man was smiling too much at Ver to notice how the men—and some of the women—stared and hid grins behind fans.

Down at the beach, thirty tents had been erected to provide shelter should it rain. It was a rare evening, however, as there wasn't a cloud in the sky. Servants in livery rotated among the small gatherings clustered together, offering glasses of champagne and hors d'oeuvres. Oysters on the shell, sliced beef tongue, bits of cheese, a square of roasted veal wrapped in pastry . . .

"Heavens," Keturah said, a hand to her belly, "if they keep up with such offerings I shall be quite sated before supper!"

"Never fear," Gray said with a smile. "Now with your leg at last healed, I mean to escort you through many dances. I shall do my best to make certain you recover your appetite."

She smiled back at him. "Why, thank you, Gray. That is most kind, looking after *my* needs."

"This night my sole hope in the world, m'lady," he said with a gallant bow and sweep of his hand, "is to dance with you."

"I do hope that does not preclude me from a few dances myself," said a voice behind them.

Ket turned. It was Jeffrey Weland and his brother, each eyeing her expectantly.

"Oh, good evening, Mr. Weland," she said and slipped a hand through the crook of Gray's arm. "I wish I could accept such a fine invitation, but you see, I have been recently convalescing with a broken leg, so I fear that any of the few dances I can accept this night have been claimed by Mr. Covington alone. I am certain you understand." She then gave a curtsy and bow of her head.

"Oh. Of course," he said with obvious disappointment. "'Tis true, then? Are you two . . . engaged?"

Ket glanced at Gray, a hand flying to her cheek. "Oh no, we are not engaged."

"I have not yet claimed the lady's hand," Gray added swiftly, "but I believe I have done a somewhat admirable job in winning her heart." He looked to Ket, one brow raised.

"Somewhat," she repeated with a teasing grin.

Gray turned back to the Welands. "It appears I must endeavor to change the lady's 'somewhat' into a fervent 'completely.' Good eve, gentlemen," he finished, leading her away. They angled down the beach to where a platform had been erected, which held an ensemble of musicians. A few couples were already dancing.

"Is that what you've been doing since we departed for Nevis, Gray?" she whispered. "Winning my heart?"

"I suppose that is a question best answered by you," he said.

But as he took her in his arms and they entered the lines of men and women for a *folie à huit*, as they separated, turned, and came together again and again, the look in her eyes told him what he most needed to know.

He was not simply in the process of winning her heart. Perhaps, *perhaps*, he had already won it.

# CHAPTER THIRTY-SEVEN

Gray found her a seat when her leg began aching. "Forgive me," she said. "Standing on tiptoe and hopping is perhaps not the best choice for me. Yet it did feel so grand to dance with you, Gray."

"Thank you." He handed her a glass of champagne. "But I am certain that I am the honored partner. In fact," he said, leaning closer to her ear, "I believe I am the most admired man here."

"Because of your new coat?" she asked, laughing lightly.

He shook his head. "Because of whom I am honored to escort."

They partook of more food—bits of cheese imported from France—and chatted with neighbors from around the island. Apparently many had heard of them, with more than one daring to ask probing questions.

"I hear tell you created a partnership, sharing labor between your plantations?" asked a gentleman.

"Some say you decided to plant again, after the mudslide?" asked an imperious Mr. Noland, peering down his long nose at them. "Why not wait until next spring?"

"Because every month counts," Keturah replied. "Best to risk it and potentially win than to hold back and count the entire year as a loss, no?"

"Yes, well, we shall see," the man sniffed, dismissing her as if she was already bankrupt and on her way back to England.

"I for one applaud you," said the handsome Mr. Fredrickson, raising a goblet in her honor. "'Tis always best to gamble on potential rather than bet on failure."

Ket smiled at him, and he gave her a sad smile in return. He was the widower she'd met at the Welands' soiree when she first arrived. Was it her imagination or did their warm exchange agitate Gray? Was he . . . could he be . . . jealous?

"The servants are inviting us to the fires," Gray said, offering his hand.

She took it, and together they strode down the beach to a huge bonfire, crackling and sending sparks dancing into the night sky. Servants were roasting filleted fish on long iron stakes. Others soon removed them, cut them into portions, and slid the fish onto the guests' plates that included small dishes of melted butter. They ate the luscious chunks with their hands and shared looks of delight as they licked their fingers.

"It is an utterly unorthodox means of eating," she said.

"Well, I could become well accustomed to this particular unorthodox method," he laughed.

"As could I."

Before long, they continued their stroll along the beach, arm in arm. Others were gathering on the far end, away from the fire, awaiting the rising moon. They could see it illuminating Nevis Peak, a warm glow behind its conical silhouette. Servants circulated, pouring champagne. And when the moon finally emerged, the guests cheered. Raucous toasts to the moon, to the island, and to the Nisbets were offered. But as the crowd continued to imbibe, Gray and Keturah set down their goblets and headed back toward the house. It was time to find her sisters and Philip and return home.

Because tomorrow was a new day, and whilst many of these planters had few cares that had to be addressed before noon, that was not the case for Gray and Keturah.

They found Verity in earnest conversation with Captain McKintrick and two other men, debating the future of the American

321

colonies' favor with Britain. "They'd be foolish to stand against the mother country," Verity was saying. "To whom would they look if France moved against them? Or Spain?"

"The Americans are gaining strength and numbers year by year," argued a middle-aged planter. "Who is to say they need the mother country? Perhaps they could defend themselves."

"Pshaw," Verity said. "They are far too young to stand on their own two feet."

"Some would say, Miss Verity," the captain said, "that you and your sisters were too young to do the same. And look at how you have all flourished here!"

She half scowled, half smiled at him.

"Speaking of standing on our own two feet," Ket interjected smoothly, looping her arm through Verity's, "I think mine are about worn out. Shall we?"

Captain McKintrick stood slowly as if reluctant to let her go. "May I come and call on ye, lass, on the morrow? Perhaps we can take a stroll, even if your infernal falcon need keep us company?"

"I would welcome that, Captain."

"Good," he said, bending to kiss her hand. He rose, still holding it, and covered it with his other hand. "I shall look most forward to it."

"Until the morrow, then, Captain," Ket said, taking her sister's hand from his and leading her away. "I'll be certain to have a suitable *human* companion, as well as Brutus, available to chaperone you and my sister."

He nodded, giving her a sly smile.

Now where was Selah? They had not seen her since before they took to the dance floor. Nor Philip. Keturah felt a pang of guilt. What sort of guardian was she? Allowing her youngest sister to flit about a party of this size? She scanned the figures about her, then those in deeper shadow beyond them.

"Gray, do you see Selah?"

"No. But do not worry. I asked Philip to keep watch over her."

She breathed a sigh of relief. The girl was probably down at the platform, dancing. Or on the beach and eating fish. They had merely missed her in the crowd.

But that was before Philip staggered into view, his eye swollen and his nose bleeding.

"Philip!" Gray cried, rushing to him.

"They have her, Gray," the man gasped. "Out by the stables."

He didn't need to say more. She knew whom he meant. So did Gray.

Angus Shubert had Selah.

# CHAPTER THIRTY-EIGHT

They set off at a run. Fredrickson and McKintrick with Gray. Ket and Verity right behind them.

They could hear her screaming, crying, before they got close, and the sound of it made Keturah want to scream too. If he had dared to harm Selah, her precious, perfect Selah . . . well, she would kill the man herself. The girl's cry was muffled. Men laughed. Then she cried out again.

Finally, they were there.

Shubert had Selah pressed up against the back wall of the stables, her skirts lifted to her thighs. His meaty hand was across her mouth, and he swore as she bit down, then took a half step away from her. He looked down at his hand as if he could not quite believe she had done it. He raised a hand to strike her.

But Gray caught it. He yanked on his wrist, turning the drunken overseer around, and struck him hard in the belly. As the man bent over, Gray swiftly lifted his knee into the man's nose.

Ket hoped he had broken it.

Shubert stumbled away and held a hand to his belly, scowling. "She's all right," he slurred. "We were only having a word with the girl. Settin' her straight."

Selah rushed into Ket's arms, weeping.

"Reminding her that she needn't spend so much time with the Negroes," put in his companion, Lawrence. "What her proper place is. And if she's needin' a man's attention, she need only come to us."

"You," said McKintrick, grabbing hold of the man's shirt in a fist, "will regret that." He then punched the man's cheek, sending him sprawling. He spun around and, with Gray at his side, closed in on Shubert again.

They all stilled when they heard a distinct *click*—the hammer of a pistol being cocked. Slowly, all turned to Shubert's other man, who had the pistol trained on Gray.

Keturah gasped, lifting a hand to her mouth. *No, please, no . . .*

A slow smile spread across Shubert's face. "I told you," he said, stepping forward to tap Gray on the chest. "I told you we would not tolerate you leading the island's slaves into rebellion. It seems you did not take that warning to heart, so we decided to take a different course of action."

"And you shall pay dearly for that," Gray bit out.

"Yes, you shall," Verity said, rushing forward and lifting her dagger beneath Shubert's chin. "Tell your man to set aside his weapon."

Feeling the blade at his throat, Shubert's eyes narrowed and he slowly raised his hands. "You wouldn't have the courage to cut me, girl," he sneered.

"Oh no?" she said. "I had the courage to follow my sister half-way around the world. What would make you doubt I could kill the would-be rapist of another?"

She pressed upward, and Ket saw a line of red form under the folds of the man's neck, then begin dripping downward. No matter how horrid the man was, she did not want to see Verity kill him! "Verity . . ." she began.

"Let me see this through, Ket," she said over her shoulder. Again she pressed the knife upward.

"Set it aside," Shubert choked out to his companion with the pistol, waving over his shoulder.

Reluctantly, the man did as his boss directed, even as others gathered behind them. Ket glanced around. There were more than fifty about them now.

But it was a staid aristocratic voice that brought order.

"You there!" Lord Reynolds barked out. "What has transpired here?"

"Your man Shubert," Keturah said, "has been found manhandling my sister."

Lord Reynolds blinked rapidly. "The one with the knife at his throat?"

"No. Selah, here. We all saw him. He must be held accountable."

Lord Reynolds hesitated. Keturah well knew that he was loath to give up his overseer, one who had served him for years. And in that moment she felt a measure of justice too. Would he have half the challenge she'd had in finding a replacement? Surely he was one of the planters who had gathered together with others to try to stop her.

She turned toward him and took a step. "Shall I call for the constable? For this man," she gestured back to Shubert, "beat my overseer so badly he only narrowly retained his eye. And now my sister . . . mistreated so. We *shall* see justice done here, Lord Reynolds."

He blanched a bit at that. "Eh? What's this?"

"You heard me plain enough, Lord Reynolds. He beat my man and manhandled my sister. There shall be immediate reparations or I shall seek justice elsewhere. Shall I summon the constable from Charlestown? Make a report among the British soldiers?"

"No, no, woman. I shall take care of this. No need to make it a larger ordeal than it already is." He looked back to Shubert. "Go home. Pack your things. You as well, Lawrence and Francis. I want you off Red Rock land this very night."

Verity lowered her knife and moved away as Shubert blustered and glowered at them all. He took a few steps back, spit and swore. Finally, he turned toward Keturah with a long, cold gaze. Gray moved slightly in front of her, on guard. "You think this is over, woman?" Shubert spat. "No, it has only just *begun*. You shall pay for this, and pay for it dearly."

# CHAPTER THIRTY-NINE

It grated on Ket that Shubert was somewhere on-island and free. And over the following weeks and months, she learned that support was slowly growing for the overseer, who had done little but "try and set the Bannings straight." Now that Shubert kept to the other side of the island—he'd accepted the position of overseer of Camel Hill, owned by absentee-owner Lord Ellis—most thought the Bannings should allow everything that had happened to be forgotten.

It should not have surprised her, she thought. After all, the majority of whites on Nevis seemed to fear what Shubert preached—the potential rebellion of slaves, who outnumbered the whites nine to one. And there was little she could do. The judge was still not due back until spring, and most thought that Shubert—and Reynolds—had paid a steep price.

Gray and Philip had been approached to join the militia, something required of every white man on-island. They met monthly, and each planter was required to make certain that each of their white family members or employees were armed and ready to answer a call for help at any time. It was their intent to put down any slave rebellion that arose.

It was the dark side of this island life, Keturah thought. A sickness born out of fear, and in order to survive she simply could not dwell on it for too long. So they concentrated on their growing cane, on weeding and fertilizing, on producing a good portion of their food—which was drawing attention from other planters—and making the needed repairs to their mill and home. They watched each storm that arrived with fear, and greeted each morn they found their crops intact with relief.

The people of Tabletop and Teller's Landing settled into a rhythm of work and rest, spending five of seven days each week in company. Most Saturdays, Keturah and Gray found a way to be together—riding high above their plantations, deep into the jungle, or attending a neighbor's party, or simply swinging in hammocks down by the beach. And the women took to what they called a weekly "Sabbath double-dip," first swimming in the sea, then heading up to the waterfall their father had favored for a true bath, with lavender soap and clear spring water.

When they'd first arrived at the waterfall pool two months prior, they chastised themselves for taking so long to explore. In the beginning, daily life had demanded everything in them simply to survive. But this place . . . the beauty of it made her wish she could go back to those first weeks and do as Bennabe had directed—visit the waterfall pool from the start.

Keturah leaned back against the mossy bank and looked up to Nevis Peak. To her right, a gentle, wide waterfall spilled three feet down over a ledge, into the pool that was lined with lava rock, lending it an inky color. The various shades of lush jungle green surrounded them, and the heady scent of blooming jasmine filled their nostrils, even though none was visible . . . it must be nearby. She looked for it but could not see the telltale blooms, but spied a family of monkeys chattering and jumping from branch to branch in a tree. Selah and Verity took turns, sudsing up their hair with lavender soap, then rinsing beneath the falls. Later, they played a game, seeing who could hold their breath the longest under the constant pounding stream of cold water, emerging red-faced and laughing.

Goose bumps covered Keturah's flesh. It was not nearly as warm as the ocean. But it felt so good to be here, so good to get thoroughly clean and relax in this hidden paradise. She and her sisters were always reluctant to leave.

"Can you imagine Father here?" Verity asked, swimming across the onyx pool to her.

"Not at first," Keturah said, "but more and more. With each passing month, 'tis as if I feel I know him better. By knowing the island, what it is to be Nevisian, I believe I understand him in a whole new way."

"Yes," she said, turning to lean against the bank beside Ket. "I think I'm coming to love it here. Brutus is quite content." She glanced up to see the circling bird.

"I *know* I love it here," Selah said, making her way toward them. "I cannot imagine returning to Hartwick now. It would feel most . . . staid."

"Truly?" Ket frowned in surprise. "Ever?"

"Well, I'd like to return home someday, but this . . . well, this is feeling like home now too." She rested against the bank on Ket's other side.

For a time, the three of them just remained like that, staring up at the green peak while Brutus circled and listening to the waterfall's gentle thrum like a welcome drumbeat.

"Ket, if it comes down to saving Hartwick or Tabletop," Verity said, "we want you to save Tabletop."

Keturah moved away from the bank and turned to face them both. "What's this?"

"We know you're trying to save Hartwick for us," Selah said.

"For all of us," Keturah corrected.

"But mostly for us," Selah said. "As if you feel responsible for holding on to our childhood home."

"But we've been studying the ledgers," Verity said with a glance in Selah's direction.

"You have?" Keturah said in surprise.

Selah nodded earnestly. "Yes." Already her curls were beginning

330

to recoil as her hair dried. They bobbed with her nod. "We do not wish for you to carry that burden alone any longer, Keturah."

"We know you've invested a fair amount of your inheritance from Edward," Verity added, "and that your funds are likely not stretching as far as you'd hoped. It's quite expensive to run Tabletop."

"Well, it appears you two have become quite the financiers," Keturah said, crossing her arms.

"We want you to be reimbursed, once the harvest is in," Selah said. "That is your money. Yours, Ket."

"Any money I have invested was hard-won," Keturah allowed. "But it does my heart good to think that anything I gained from *him* could be used to build something like this for *us*. 'Tis a way of redeeming it, really."

Both were silent for a bit. Then Verity climbed out of the pool, moved over to her towel, dried off and pulled on a clean shift. She set to combing out her hair as Selah and Ket did the same. "I simply cannot envision it, Ket. Even if Tabletop manages to bring in a bountiful harvest, it shan't be until next year. And the expenses of Hartwick . . ."

"What are you saying?" Ket asked, tugging her own shift down over sticky-wet skin.

"We want you to be free to sell it," they said together.

"If we cannot save both Tabletop and Hartwick, Hartwick must go," Verity said.

Keturah sat down hard. "S-sell it?"

Both were nodding.

"'Tis a tether to our old life," Verity said. She gave a little shrug. "We find we like who we are here. Who knows where God will lead us next?"

"Not that I can ever imagine leaving," Selah put in. "Whatever would the slaves do without us? And we certainly cannot sell them to another. I could not . . . bear it."

"For me," Verity said, "it feels like a stepping-stone. I may return to England. I may go elsewhere."

Ket's eyes narrowed. "Is this because of a certain sea captain?"

"No!" Verity replied. But they both knew it was too vociferous of a response.

"What? Do you see yourself taking to the sea with him?" Ket asked carefully. As much as the thought terrified her, Ket knew she wanted it to be Verity's decision alone. Whom she loved. Where she went. But, oh, how she hoped her sister would not go far . . .

"I do not know. Perhaps. If he is the right man for me." She reached out and grabbed her sister's hand. "But watching you and Gray, Ket . . . you've made me realize that I want to be open to how God leads. To whomever He might guide my heart, whether it be Duncan or some other man. Because watching you . . . heal? *Blossom* in the shelter of Gray's love?" She shook her head, her eyes filling with tears. "That has been the best blessing of all since arriving here."

Selah took Ket's other hand again and nodded, silently agreeing with everything Verity said.

Keturah felt her defenses soften a bit in light of their tenderness. "You called Hartwick a tether. And I understand the negative connotations of that. But 'tis also a tether to Mother and Father. To our childhood. Our friends. Our kin . . ." She paused and drew a deep breath. "For me, it was a lifeline. I wanted it to be the same for you two. No matter where life takes you, what you suffer, you know you have a shelter in that storm."

"Oh, Ket," Selah said, "you and Verity are my lifelines. God is my shelter. I need no place when I have the three of you."

"Agreed," Verity said. "If it came down to Tabletop or Hartwick, Ket, which would you choose?"

She was reluctant to answer. Was it true? Had this place, this island, so thoroughly stolen her heart? All of their hearts? After all she had put them through?

"Hartwick is less costly to run but generates far less income, especially since Father sold off that piece of land to the Covingtons," Verity said. "The opportunity is here. The opportunity is still in sugar. Just look at how our cane is growing! 'Tis the talk of the island! Why, 'tis nearly reached Red Rock's height, and theirs was planted three months prior."

"And a hurricane could still sweep through and take it all. Or blight. Or rot," Ket said.

"Or it shan't and this shall be the finest harvest in some time," Selah said reprovingly. "Perhaps with the first harvest we could enter a different, more *consistent* business. Use the proceeds to invest in a mercantile. Or an inn. Those in such businesses seem to do nearly as well as some planters."

"We could sell Hartwick and buy a tidy apartment in London," Verity said. "Someplace we all knew would be there."

"For a tenth of the cost to run it," added Selah.

Keturah let out a breathy laugh of wonder. "How long have you been scheming together?" she asked in wonder. It was a surprise, these revelations, but also a welcome relief. She did not have to figure out a way to forge ahead alone. They were together in it. All in all, it made her feel less . . . trapped. Less like it was all her responsibility. Less likely to end in disaster.

She reached out and took each of their hands. "I am so grateful, sisters, that you came with me. That this was not my journey alone."

"As are we, Ket," Verity said softly. "But we want you to be free to journey where you wish—with us or without—and not let *our* future tie you down. You have taught us well. You have shown us how to let go of the past and embrace the present . . . and trust our future to God's hands."

Keturah smiled as they began walking home, each of them lost in her own thoughts.

"You could not return to England anyway," Selah said after they passed the cut-off. "Not while Gray is here."

"'Tis true," she admitted.

"We wanted to speak to you about Gray as well," Verity said. "Beyond teasing."

Keturah warily glanced back at her sisters. What was *this* now?

"He loves you, Ket," Selah said.

"I know," she said, nodding.

"He wants to marry you," Verity said.

"I . . . I think I know that too."

"Then why not make a way for him?" Selah began.

And then, the rest of the way home, they told Ket what she should do.

# CHAPTER FORTY

Gray bade her farewell on her doorstep after an evening near Charlestown. He kissed her deeply, slowly, cradling her head in his hands. Reluctantly, he pulled away, closing his eyes as if it pained him. "Oh, Keturah, how I wish I did not have to part from you each night," he whispered in her ear, pulling her close again. "How I wish we were already married. That you were mine," he growled, "in every sense of the word."

"Why imagine being married when we could actually do so?" she asked. The words made her breath catch. Had she actually had the courage to say what her sisters had convinced her to?

He pulled back from her, blinking once, twice. "What did you say?"

"I want to be your wife, Gray," she said, taking his hand and forcing herself to look him in the eye. "Not someday, but soon."

His mouth dropped open. "Keturah . . ."

"I am saying that this last year has been one of the most difficult and yet also one of the best of my life. And that is largely because of you, Gray. I am saying I cannot be without you. That I do not *want* to be without you. Because I *love* you. I love you, Gray." She lifted his hand to her lips and kissed it, tears burning her eyes. "I love you," she added a third time, in a whisper.

He smiled, and she could see a bit of spark in his blue eyes. But then he frowned a little, as if he had dreamed it all. "You love me enough to marry me? When you did not wish to marry ever again?"

"I only wish to marry once more. And only one man could have made me reconsider. You, Gray. You."

His tentative smile grew wider. He reached up to trace the curve of her cheek, from her temple to her lips. "How I've longed to hear such words from you, Keturah." He wrapped his hands more firmly around her back. "After the harvest, love. We shall marry as soon as those ships reach England with our sugar and the money is in the bank."

"Why wait?" she asked.

Again he paused, as if not quite understanding her. "We must wait so that I have more than two pence to rub together in my pocket. So that I have the means to go to your cousin Cecil and ask for your hand. So that I can build a new house at Teller's Landing and offer you the sort of home you deserve."

"Do you not see?" Ket asked. "I have all the home I want. At Tabletop. Or your little cottage at Teller's Landing. What matters is you, Gray. *You* would make any sort of house my home."

"Keturah," he said, pulling away in agitation, "can you imagine how others would talk of us?"

"Do they not already talk of us?" she asked with a laugh. Ket shook her head. "Truly, it seems the Misses Banning will forever make people talk. But Gray . . . our days are not promised to us. Fever or mudslide or hurricane might take either one of us before we ever get the chance to exchange our vows. We must make the most of the days we have *whilst* we have them. I care not for what society demands. I do not care if you ask Cecil for my hand. The only people you must convince are my sisters, and they are the ones who have compelled me to say this to you today. And I do not care if you are rich or poor, Gray Covington. Whether we live in a hut or a castle, I only know that I want to be with you."

He stared at her for a long moment. "Am I dreaming?"

"No," she said with a shake of her head.

He huffed a laugh and ran a hand through his messy, matted

curls. "Keturah Banning . . . we always did climb the tree you chose or went swimming when *you* wished to do so."

She smiled with him. "There you have it."

It was his turn to pull her hand to his lips, kissing one knuckle after another as he stared into her eyes. "Could it be true? Shall you truly be mine, Keturah? Forever?"

"Oh, Gray," she breathed, pulling him closer for a true kiss. "I believe I have always been yours."

A month later, Verity grinned as she placed an ivory seashell circlet around Keturah's head. She had worked on it for a week, carefully drilling holes in each of the shells and sewing them to the crown.

"Oh, it's perfect, Ver," Ket said, staring at her reflection in the mirror. "It reminds me of Father, on this day that I'm missing him again." She wished he were here to witness this day. He'd led her down the aisle to marry Edward, and somehow it would have redeemed that day if he'd been here for this too. *Did you know, Father? Did you have any inkling that the man I was marrying was a wretch of a man? Or did you always choose to believe the best in everyone you met?*

She thought that was it. Father had been an optimist. But if he'd had hopes for Edward, how much more might he have had for Gray?

*Gray.* Just the thought of him made her smile. *I am marrying Gray today. Becoming his wife.* The thought did not make her pale in fear. Instead, she blushed with excitement. She pressed a hand to her cheek.

"What is it?" Selah asked, peeking over her shoulder at Ket's reflection, even as she continued to use a hook to button the back of her gown.

"I am . . . I am simply . . . happy. So happy," she said with a grin.

"As well you should be," Selah said, grinning back and then resuming her work on the forty buttons.

As soon as Ket and Gray were engaged, the girls had insisted she purchase the beautiful ivory silk gown in a shop on St. Kitts, despite its steep cost, and Selah had carefully embroidered flowers down the center of the bodice and along the three-quarter sleeves that bunched in luxurious folds at her elbow, then embellished each with seed pearls to catch the light. The U-shaped neckline plunged deeply and was edged with fine lace. The bodice was tight, and at the hip the skirts flared outward.

Studying herself in the mirror, she noted the deep tan of her arms and neck and face. Her first reaction was condemnation—after all, no lady allowed her skin to become so dark. *Edward would have been aghast!* But her second quickly followed—that it was perfect for who she was now. And Gray, she knew, reveled in the fact that their skin reflected the work they had put into their land. "I find your skin's color to be," he'd said once, looking slowly down her tanned arm as he lifted her hand to kiss it, "most beguiling. Exotic." Just the thought of that intimacy set her cheeks aflame once more.

"Ahh, Ket. You're so beautiful," Verity said as Selah finished her work.

"Thank you. I *feel* beautiful." Beautiful enough to meet Gray in that church. Beautiful enough to stand by his side. "His love, sisters. His love . . . and God's have made me whole again. Whole enough to feel beautiful."

They grinned at her for a moment. Then Verity glanced at the hourglass. "Come, 'tis time," she said. "You cannot leave your groom waiting."

Cuffee had hitched up a team to their father's fine black carriage, now repaired. Gideon and Primus were in the front seat, each dressed in full livery in honor of the day. A wagon behind it carried the rest of their servants from Hartwick, plus Matthew, Mitilda, Abraham, and Sansa. These would be their only wedding guests, as well as Philip. No others had been invited. And they hoped that spying Keturah and her sisters in their finery would be the first hint any islander might have that something like this was about to take place.

Because she didn't want any others present. This was her wedding, and Gray's, and she only wanted those close to her heart there. So far, none but these had found their way closer, which was fine by Ket.

They made the trip to the edge of Charlestown and pulled down the drive that led to St. Philip's, a tidy gray-stone Anglican church with teardrop-shaped windows and a white cupola. She stood high on a hill, the sprawling Caribbean Sea beyond her. Outside was parked one lone carriage.

*Gray is already here.*

The others poured out of the wagon behind them and hurried inside. Primus assisted Ket down, and then her sisters. Gideon held the door for them. They walked inside, and the girls turned toward her as Gideon moved to the inner door that opened to the sanctuary.

"Are you ready, Sissy?" Selah asked, taking her hand.

Keturah nodded, not trusting herself to speak.

"He's a good man," Verity said. "The finest. We would not allow this to be transpiring if we did not believe it."

Again, Keturah nodded.

"We shall await you," Verity said. "Have Gideon open the door when you're ready to approach."

Keturah stepped over to the side so that Gray would not catch a glimpse of her, and her sisters moved inside, Gideon closing the door behind them. She glanced up at her dear friend and servant. He'd made a good recovery from the fever, though he was still a good twenty pounds lighter than he had once been. Still, his presence steadied her. Gideon was home, a part of Hartwick and a part of Tabletop too—her past and her present.

"Time to embrace my future, Gideon," she whispered, nodding toward the door.

"Go with God, Lady Ket," he said as she swept past him into the sanctuary.

And as she paused at the end of the aisle, taking in Gray in his fine new clothing, his hair pulled back at the nape of his neck, she thought, *God has brought me here. I am with God again. And He is with me. No matter what comes, He is with me.*

No man led her down the aisle, because she no longer belonged to any man. And when she placed her hand into Gray's, she knew it was fully her choice, her will, her hope . . . and felt God's pleasure in it.

"Shall we do this, darling?" he whispered. "Are you truly ready?"

"One limb at a time?" she whispered back.

"One limb at a time," he returned with a grin, settling her hand in the crook of his elbow as they turned to face the priest.

# HISTORICAL NOTES

I did quite a bit of research to prepare to write this series and did my best to represent the people of this time well. However, I have made the language a bit more contemporary, because if one reads letters, dialogue, or direct quotes from this era, it feels quite stilted. So for the sake of clarity and flow, I changed it.

Readers might be surprised at the amount of alcohol my characters drank. Actually grog, mead, hard cider, and the like were often watered down, and it was common practice to drink it instead of water because the alcohol killed the bacteria that often lived in their water sources. Pretty ingenious, really. As to the copious amounts that many sugar plantation owners drank—well, that's straight out of my research. It was a hard place, in a hard time, to live. People were just trying to cope, in both good and bad ways.

To my knowledge, Nevis did not have a mudslide or runaway slave colony on the mountain. I borrowed those elements from St. Kitts's history. But the threat of a slave revolt was constant throughout the West Indies, which only led to further horrid mistreatment of slaves. Enslaving others was an act of war—it only makes sense that many slaves planned retribution and craved freedom at any cost.

One source noted that Nevis Peak was practically denuded to

the top at one point in history, every acre used for sugar. But if one visits the island today, it's hard to imagine the very top and between plantations being utilized. I elected to keep a healthy amount of green up top and between plantations because I liked the idea of the jungle, ever-ready to reclaim what was hers.

Historically, women really did entertain men in their "closets" while in dressing robes, as well as hide away behind bathing machines to swim. The Georgian era was a rather confusing one, mixing both social liberties and conservative ways, especially looking back on it from the vantage point of our modern times. After a lot of reading, I've done my best to depict life as I imagined it. A full bibliography for this series can be viewed on my website, www.lisatawnbergren.com.

# Author's Note

I know that for some, Keturah's story might have been challenging to read, especially for those who have suffered abuse. If it proved triggering to you, I'm sorry. I have loved ones who suffered in abusive relationships and made it out, and I thought it an important element to explore in this story to offer others hope too. If you are in an abusive relationship, know that there is hope. God wants you to be loved, and loved well. He does not want to see you hurt. He has good intentions for your future and longs to give you renewed vision and direction. He is your refuge.

If you need a place to start, check out *The Emotionally Destructive Marriage* by Leslie Vernick, or visit these websites: thehotline .org; domesticshelters.org; womenagainstabuse.org.

# ACKNOWLEDGMENTS

A big thank you to the research librarians at the Nevis Historical Society; to my editors, Raela Schoenherr, Luke Hinrichs, and Kate Hauge; to four beta readers who gave me feedback about sensitive subject matters in the book—Mahalia Hilts, Jamie Lapeyrolerie, Gianna Greer, and Toni Shiloh; to my family who dealt with me in a fugue state for weeks as I finished this tale; and to all my readers who continue to read my books, wherever I roam in my imagination. I appreciate you all!

Lisa T. Bergren has published more than fifty books with combined sales exceeding three million copies. She's the author of the Christy Award-winning *Waterfall*, RITA-finalist *Firestorm*, bestselling *God Gave Us You*, and several historical series such as HOMEWARD and GRAND TOUR. She's also a recipient of the RT Lifetime Achievement Award. Lisa lives in Colorado with her husband and three teen-and-older children. To learn more, visit www.lisatawnbergren.com.

# Sign Up for Lisa's Newsletter!

Keep up to date with Lisa's news on upcoming book releases, signings, and other events by signing up for her email list at lisatbergren.com

## You May Also Like

Vivienne Rivard fled revolutionary France and now seeks a new life for herself and a boy in her care, who some say is the Dauphin. But America is far from safe, as militiaman Liam Delaney knows. He proudly served in the American Revolution but is less sure of his role in the Whiskey Rebellion. Drawn together, will Liam and Vivienne find the peace they long for?

*A Refuge Assured* by Jocelyn Green
jocelyngreen.com

# You May Also Like

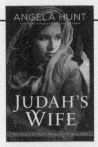

The miraculous story of the Maccabees told through the eyes of a woman who learns that love requires both courage and sacrifice. Seeking safety after a hard childhood, Leah marries a strong and gentle man of the nation of Judah. But when the ruler of the land issues a life-altering decree, her newfound peace—and the entire Jewish heritage—is put in jeopardy.

*Judah's Wife* by Angela Hunt
THE SILENT Years
angelahuntbooks.com

At the outset of WWI, high-end thief Willa Forsythe is hired to steal a cypher from famous violinist Lukas De Wilde. Given the value of his father's work as a cryptologist, Lukas fears for his family and doesn't know who to trust. He likes Willa—and the feeling is mutual. But if Willa doesn't betray him as ordered, her own family will pay the price.

*A Song Unheard* by Roseanna M. White
SHADOWS OVER ENGLAND #2
roseannawhite.com

After being branded during the battle of Jericho, Moriyah has had no prospects for marriage—until now. She hopes to please the man, but things go horribly wrong and she is forced to flee for her life. Seeking safety at one of the Levitical cities of refuge, she is unprepared for the dangers she faces, and the enemies—and allies—she encounters on her way.

*A Light on the Hill* by Connilyn Cossette
CITIES OF REFUGE #1
connilyncossette.com

◆ BETHANYHOUSE